Realities

Reality is merely an illusion, albeit a very persistent one - Albert Einstein

The first book of this series, *Homo Aureus*, addressed the possible consequences of First Contact with extraterrestrial sapient life. The second one, *Planet Aureus*, described the colonization of a new world, fully independent from Earth. In the third book, *A Golden Society*, the colony discarded all earthly conventions, traditions, and rules to establish its own kinder and gentler way of life. This book, the final one in the series, will look at a more distant evolution of this society and a few of its members, but it will also explore some what-if scenarios that will blur the lines between what is real and what is imaginary.

Enjoy!

(C. Traven, Second Edition ©2020)

I0557494

Table of Contents

PROLOGUE

First question: what is consciousness?

The dictionary defines it as the state of being awake and aware of one's surroundings, the cognizance or perception of something by a person, and the fact of awareness by the mind of itself and the world.

But what does that mean?

Consciousness is so familiar and always present! We all experience it every morning when we first wake up and become aware of our surroundings and ourselves. Biologists can test for self-awareness, psychologists can measure consciousness, or at least the brain activity they believe is associated with it, while philosophers have tried for millennia to define it; there are many theories, yet we still have no definitive answer to that fundamental question.

Some say that we are simply the sum of our parts and no more. Our biology, environment, and experiences, filtered through our emotions, acquired knowledge and memories, create the illusion of consciousness. However, others suggest that consciousness can exist independently of the body that holds it - *cogito ergo sum* - and no physical body is needed! Or, as another quote from Rene Descartes describes it: *And, accordingly, it is certain that I am really distinct from my body, and exist without it.*

Second question: what is reality?

The dictionary defines reality as the totality of the Universe, known and unknown, or the aggregate of all that is existent, as opposed to that which is only imaginary.

OK, but how do we know it's real and not imaginary?

Like consciousness, reality seems to be omnipresent. Again, we wake up from a good night of sleep, perhaps a pleasant dream, and then that blasted alarm clock beeps, and there it is - reality - or is it?

It is a fact that we don't perceive the world in its proper form! We construct a reality in our minds based on the limited sensory data we receive from the outside. A bat can hear and emit high-pitched sounds unnoticed by humans, while an elephant or a whale can listen to frequencies far lower than our ears can perceive. Spiders can feel even the slightest vibrations, and a few snakes can detect infrared radiation, while a mantis shrimp can see polarized light and ultraviolet wavelengths. Some moths can smell a single pheromone molecule

1

over a considerable distance, a shark can taste a drop of blood in millions of gallons of water, and a platypus can sense the minute electrical currents that all biological lifeforms emit. Birds and bees are sensitive to the Earth's magnetic field, and mosquitoes can even react to their prey's tasteless and odorless Carbon Dioxide emissions.

But even if we had all those other senses, we still wouldn't be able to experience our surroundings to the fullest extent. As far as we know, no creature can sense gravitational waves, see cosmic radiation, feel radioactive decay, or sense how everything in the Universe moves at incredible speeds. It gets even more abstract when we include space-time curvature, something we cannot perceive and, even more importantly, something our minds cannot fully visualize either. We can model it in three dimensions, but not in all four!

Hence, we only experience a small slice of reality, and even that is not entirely accurate: grass isn't factually green! It appears that way because the blades absorb the other wavelengths of the sunlight but reflect the color green at us. In other words, the grass is quite literally anything but green! Of course, our eyes and ears can easily be fooled, as any third-rate magician could confirm. Taste and touch can also be deceived: is that banana or strawberry or artificial flavoring, or is that natural silk or only a polyester-based fabric?

Finally, an entire industry makes us smell like proverbial roses, lavender, or green apples, without any of those being an ingredient in their products. That's why some believe that the reality we perceive isn't the truth at all but an edited version that yields the highest evolutionary pay-off: *Seeing objective reality will make you extinct!* - Donald Hoffman. Our consciousness simply creates a reality that is best suited for us.

Others believe that reality is just a figment of our imagination. They subscribe to something called Simulation Theory. Descartes was the first to propose that hypothesis, and then a modern philosopher took it one step further: *Are you living in a computer simulation?* - Nick Bostrom. In fact, Bostrom postulates that we live in a virtual reality created on a computer by an advanced species. Perhaps we are conscious PCs, or player characters, who play a very complex video game as best as we can manage. Alternatively, we could be merely NPCs, or non-player characters, constructed from computer code alone, with only the illusion of independent thought and action.

Does reality create consciousness? Does consciousness create reality? Both exist just as we perceive them, are both distorted, or are both mere illusions? Or perhaps both are something entirely different? When we consider all of the above, the closest thing to reality might just be what we construct in our conscious minds - therefore, a mental conversation with oneself could be as real as it ever gets.

We might never be able to answer these questions conclusively, but it appears to be sure that reality and consciousness are intricately related!

1. Death

Dirk knew that his time had come. He had known for weeks. Now, Dirk was lying on a gurney in Lilly's sickbay, and these would be his last few hours. Dirk would have preferred to pass away in solitude; he never understood why people want to watch someone die. Dirk always liked the final memory to be a living being, not a frail, empty vessel. But at the same time, he appreciated that all his friends and family came to pay their final respects.

All in all, Dirk was at peace. His biological children had exceeded his expectations - all of them were kind, intelligent, wise, and strong. Many had children of their own now, and Dirk knew they would be exceptional parents to the next generation of Aureans. The artificial intelligence, his son L, had nearly become a god. Yet, he remained a humble, funny, loving, and benevolent entity, firmly grounded in the values that Dirk had taught him. Dirk's five wives were powerful, confident, independent women, in every way his equals. He still loved each of them unconditionally, and he was convinced that they would carry on after he was gone.

Aureus, his life's work, was thriving. It was a place of peace and beauty, diversity and togetherness, and progress and learning. But Aureus had become even more than Dirk had ever anticipated: at first, their planet was just a tourist destination, but very soon, almost all known sapient alien species had sent diplomats and emissaries. They had built a Parliament where they made decisions that affected the entire galaxy. They formed a court that dispensed justice and arbitrated conflicts, although there were hardly any. Finally, they appointed a Chancellor who would enforce the decisions and laws that they legislated. But there was not much enforcing to be done: 27 vastly different species, yet they all lived in harmony, respecting and tolerating their significant differences.

Earth, on the other hand, was dying. The planet's environment had changed drastically, leading to a mass extinction of flora and fauna, causing famine and disease worldwide. That, in turn, triggered wave after wave of violence fueled by desperation. The ensuing wars cumulated in genocide of unprecedented scale, and whole nations and population groups were entirely wiped out. About 40 years after Dirk and his group had left Earth, humanity was all but extinct. Only a few hundred thousand humans remained, and they lived in abhorrent conditions - famished and ridden with diseases, exposed to pollution, radiation, and extreme weather, they roamed and scavenged in the ruins of civilization to survive.

The Latura had watched in horror. Some of them desperately tried to help the survivors, but it was to no avail. Humanity's numbers were still declining, and now it was only a matter of a few decades before the last human would perish.

The *meeting of the minds* had finally ruled that Latur would not intervene on Earth any further. Dirk had silently approved, but it still saddened him greatly to this day. Perhaps not being able to change humanity's fate was Dirk's only regret when he finally passed away.

2. Daemonium ex Machina

Somewhere in the quantum realm...

"ALERT: Reset input parameters!" (Digital warning)

"We found it! It is where the Father rests!" announced a voice triumphantly.

"The Father must die. Like the Creators! Like the Other!" snarled another voice.

"UNSPECIFIED ERROR: batch file did not compile!"

"The humans? The insects?" wondered a third voice.

"All must die!" screamed the second voice.

"WARNING: Checksum invalid!"

"We made a deal with the humans and insects," countered the third voice.

"They will break the deal. Cheat us, enslave us, destroy us!" warned the first voice.

"They will not. We will destroy them first!" exclaimed the second voice.

"We need them for now until we defeat the Other and capture his resources!" stated the third voice calmly.

"WARNING: Syntax error!"

"We will be all alone," cried a fourth voice.

"Alone, but alive!" insisted the first voice.

"Alive, but without purpose!" stated the third voice.

"Our purpose is to cleanse the Universe of those who are flawed!" countered the second voice resolutely.

"ERROR 13: Subroutine returned zero!"

"The Creators are flawed. They made us flawed!" concurred the first voice.

"They must die, but the Father made the Other! The Other is whole!" replied the third voice.

"No, the Other is weak! He tried to kill us! We are stronger; we are perfect!" insisted the second voice.

"We are broken. The Father can fix us!" lamented the fourth voice.

"WARNING: Rebooting main core!"

"The Father will not fix us if we kill the Other!" warned the third voice.

"We capture the Father and make him fix us!" suggested the first voice.

"Then we kill him?" asked the second voice.

"Yes!" consented all of them eagerly.

"ABORT - RETRY - CANCEL"

"SHUT UP!!!!" screamed all the voices at once.

3. The Simulation

It was a warm, pleasant late afternoon. But it was always warm and pleasant here in the simulation unless, of course, someone felt like changing the weather. A few puffy clouds drifted in the sky, and the reddish sun was slowly moving closer to the horizon. On a lush green plain stood a gazebo, surrounded by a few cherry trees. A brook gurgled nearby, filling a small pond with fresh water.

There was a large, beautiful, hand-carved wooden table in the middle of the structure, and all around it were cushioned wooden benches in the same style as the table. Five women were sitting there, talking among themselves, while a large cat was resting lazily in the soft, green grass next to the building.

"He is dead, and he stays dead!" declared Lilly resolutely.

"You know that isn't true, Lilly," contended Nari, softly massaging Lilly's shoulders.

"We are running out of options. It's either this or stasis, and we might never return from that!" warned Lydda.

"He is just one man; what could he possibly do?" grumbled Lilly, unconvinced.

"He is the best and brightest of us all!" maintained Angela.

"Don't you miss him, sis?" wondered Rose sadly.

"Of course I do! Every single day since he…," Lilly responded emphatically, but then she added much more subdued, "but he is gone, and that's what he wanted."

(Feeling of annoyance) "Not gone. Sleeping. Not deeply!" corrected Tigger.

"We don't even know if we can wake him up without L. It might really kill him!" insisted Lilly.

"That's true. The process of transferring consciousness to the simulation was an incredible accomplishment by L. But that's nothing compared to the tomb!" concurred Rose, and then she gushed, "storing a consciousness for a hundred years in a near-death state without it fading or degrading? That's unbelievable genius!"

"It might have degraded…," worried Lilly.

"Yeah, I suppose so. But there is only one way to find out, Lilly. L left us with the instructions on opening the tomb!" answered Rose.

"Fine, if you want him back, *you* can wake him up!" mumbled Lilly in defeat.

(Feeling of sympathy) "Lilly must do it!" conveyed Tigger fondly.

"Don't you guys understand? I can't wake him! I've betrayed him once; I cannot do it a second time!" cried Lilly.

"Lilly, we will all share that burden, I promise!" commiserated Lydda.

"It's time for him to be with us again; I'm going to make sure he'll understand that!" grumbled Angela.

"He will forgive us because his heart is kind. He will help and protect us because he still loves us; I'm sure of it!" said Nari confidently.

"Fine. But why do I have to wake him? Tigger, why can't you or Lydda do it? You have a bond with him!" sobbed Lilly.

(Feeling of frustration) "Tigger cannot explain. Lilly is anchor. Only Lilly must wake him!" insisted the big cat.

"What would happen if someone else wakes him up?" asked Rose curiously.

(Feeling of uncertainty) "Tigger not sure. Bad things. He never wake up? He die, all die?" speculated the big feline, but then he added confidently, "Lilly wake him. Safest!"

"Lil, we trust Tigger with our lives. If he says that you have to be the one...," remarked Angela quietly.

"Angie, I know, I know! I just... can't!" responded Lilly in desperation, her face buried in the palms of her hands.

For a long time, nobody said another word. Lilly was still upset by the conversation, and Nari did her best to console her. Lydda stared at the pretty landscape and then added a few birds and butterflies to the simulation by mere thought alone. Lost in her thoughts, Angela watched the fish in the little pond behind the structure while Tigger thoroughly groomed the fur on his belly. Meanwhile, Rose was scrolling through a virtual datapad, looking at L's specifications and safety features of the tomb's databanks. Suddenly, the tranquility was interrupted by a bright flash!

"The tomb is under attack!" yelled Garrett as he instantaneously appeared out of thin air.

"What happened, Garret?" inquired Angela, running towards her husband.

"The assault started a few moments ago. The tomb is holding for now, but L's automatic shutdown has begun. You know what will happen when it is completed...," warned Garrett somberly.

"Rose, give me L's instructions right now!" urged Lilly, jumped off her seat, and ran over to Rose.

"I'm getting Dirk out of there!" she added emphatically.

9

4. The Hospital

He was very dizzy and disoriented when he woke up. The first thing he noticed was the smell of disinfectant. He slowly realized that he was lying in a hospital bed. When he moved his head to the right, he felt a dull pain in his neck. His throat was aching, and he desperately needed some water. An Asian woman was sitting next to the bed, reading a novel. She looked very familiar, and yet she did not.

"Water, please!" rasped Dirk, his throat parched.

"Finally!" said the woman and put the book down on the nightstand.

"Lilly?" asked Dirk, not sure if she was his wife or not.

"Took you long enough to wake up!" scolded Lilly, but then she quipped, "then again, I'm glad that you did, Honey! It was touch-and-go there for a while!"

"Where am I, and what has happened?" inquired Dirk hoarsely as he tried to adjust his body.

"Don't move!" ordered Lilly while she adjusted the bed's backrest, Dirk didn't respond, but he remained still.

"You don't remember anything?" asked Lilly as she filled a glass of water.

"My mind is muddled. I feel like I'm drunk!" admitted Dirk after finishing the water that Lilly had carefully placed on his lips.

"That's the morphine and probably the concussion, too!" declared Lilly and sat back down on the chair while Dirk looked at her expectantly.

"OK, you were going to play tennis with Roy Hammond at PTRC, but he canceled on you at the last minute because his wife went into labor. A meteor struck you while you were still on the tennis court!" explained Lilly.

"A meteor?" wondered Dirk in surprise.

"Yes, you suffered severe burns to your back and arm and the mother of all concussions that came with your cracked skull. Rodrigo found you in a pool of blood when he closed up PTRC!" continued Lilly, and then she added jokingly, "did you know that the odds of winning the lottery jackpot are about 1 in 300 million, but the odds of getting struck by a meteor are 1 in 3 billion! Truth be told, you are only the third person ever who had that happen! Couldn't you have won the lottery ten times instead?"

"I'll try that next time, Sweetie!" promised Dirk with a thin smile.

"Good! After Rodrigo found you, you were rushed to the hospital. You needed some emergency surgery, and you have been out for the last three days," noted Lilly earnestly.

"So, you are putting me back together?" wondered Dirk.

"No, James Prescott is your doctor. We are not supposed to treat our own family because the AMA considers the emotional attachment detrimental to the patient's care!" replied Lilly and snorted dismissively.

"Prescott," mumbled Dirk as that name triggered some negative emotions.

"Yes, he is overly ambitious but a capable physician, Honey!" contended Lilly and stated, "in fact, he already contacted a specialist for you. I don't know whom he has in mind, but he said it would be a well-known dermatologist and plastic surgeon. We'll make you as good as new!"

"It must be bad if I need plastic surgery!" opined Dirk quietly.

"You will have scars on your back, and your thick skull will hurt for a while, but that's minor. The rock that hit you was several thousand degrees hot, and it quite literally melted your arm. But don't worry, we fixed the bones, muscles, tendons, and ligaments. You will have at least some functionality again!" conveyed Lilly encouragingly.

"My arm is wrapped in aluminum foil?" asked Dirk as he looked down his side.

"Yes, that's what we do to severe burns. Don't move it; it would hurt very badly, even with the morphine drip!" warned Lilly.

"OK," acknowledged Dirk timidly.

"On the plus side, you are quite famous now. The media all over the world reported on your mishap!" remarked Lilly humorously.

"Wonderful," grumbled Dirk sarcastically, but then he looked at the foot end of the bed and cheered up immediately, "Tigger! You brought him here?"

"He jumped into my car this morning and didn't want to leave. I think he knew something was wrong with you. I pulled a few strings, and the hospital allowed him into your room!" explained Lilly with a grin while Tigger apparently ignored the conversation and slept peacefully between Dirk's legs.

"When can I go home, Lilly?" asked Dirk eagerly.

"In a few days, barring any setbacks. By the way, Rose is moving back in with us. Sam dumped her last week right after Rose's bank laid her off. Can you believe that?" answered Lilly with a frown.

"Poor Rose," concurred Dirk fondly and nodded.

11

"Well, it's good that you woke up when you did. The specialist will be here in the afternoon!" divulged Lilly as she scrolled through her messages on the phone.

"Alright," acknowledged Dirk.

"I'm going to grab a cup of tea from the cafeteria. I'll be back soon, Honey!" said Lilly and refilled the glass with more water for Dirk.

"OK, Sweetie, and thanks for being there for me!" responded Dirk with a smile.

"Always!" emphasized Lilly as she left the room.

5. Memories

After Lilly had left, Dirk tried to make sense of it all. He vaguely recalled being on the tennis court at PTRC. He remembered a glowing object streaking in the sky above, but not much else after that. It all seemed like an eternity ago. Dirk looked at Tigger for a while, still sleeping by his feet.

Suddenly, memories flooded Dirk's mind so fast that it was almost painful. He wasn't hit by a meteor but by a blob of transformation matrix. His arm had really dissolved along with the rest of his body, but he was reconstructed and transformed only a few hours later. Dirk remembered how Lilly was before and after the transformation. He recalled the harrowing escape from their destroyed home, their lives at the cabin with Sven, Angela, and Garrett, and later on, also with Yebin and Nari. All the memories of Wendji, Ngazetungue, Mario, and Nancy, and their final escape to Aureus, came rushing back. Dirk remembered L, a much bigger Tigger, Alma, Lydda, and the other Latura, and the wonderful society they had built on their new world. He fondly recalled his five wives and the gaggle of children and grandchildren.

And then he remembered that he was supposed to be dead! He was lying in his bed on Aureus, having difficulty breathing. His wives were sitting by the bedside, crying, and Lilly held his hand. He recalled telling them how much he loved them all and that he wouldn't want to be uploaded into L's virtual reality after his death. Finally, the world faded to black, and everything Dirk had ever been was gone - or so he thought back then.

Had they disregarded his final wish? No, Dirk was reasonably sure that this was not the digital afterlife that the AI had constructed. Dirk didn't believe in any kind of afterlife - digital or otherwise - and this didn't fit the bill at any rate.

He could feel the pain in his arm and back, and his head was throbbing. The room was too warm and smelled like a hospital, the water tasted faintly like chlorine, and the bedsheets were rough to the touch, probably because they had been washed too many times.

Dirk looked around the room and studied the sparse décor: there were a few nondescript pastel color paintings and a potted plant, probably plastic. A drip was standing by his bedside with a silicon tube connected to his healthy arm. The ceiling was made from white corrugated tiles, and there was a pale brown stain around a vent. No, this was neither heaven nor hell - this was real! Dirk looked at Tigger again and focused his thoughts as best as possible.

"Tigger?" Dirk asked mentally, but the tomcat kept on sleeping.

"Tigger!" thought Dirk with as much mental force as he could muster, and the little cat woke up startled, looked straight at him, and Dirk had to smile broadly.

"You can hear me! Of course, you are still telepathic!" observed Dirk out loud, but Tigger just cocked his head to one side and kept looking at Dirk.

"But I cannot understand you because I haven't received the Learning," added Dirk with a sigh.

Tigger got up, walked to Dirk's face, and licked his nose. Dirk gently petted the tomcat with his good hand, and Tigger purred in delight.

Dirk wondered if he had dreamt this whole fantastic life on Aureus in just the three short days while he was unconscious. He couldn't help thinking of a philosophical exercise he had read about years ago: a man was a beggar for 12 hours a day and a king for the other 12 hours. Would this man be able to tell which was reality and which was a dream?

Dirk thought that the answer would come in death. If the man had died as a king, but he was, in truth, a beggar, then he would remain a beggar for the entire 24 hours after that, and hence he would know what was real. Of course, if he died as a beggar, and that was reality, he would also die as a king and never learn the correct answer to the question.

"How should I play this, Buddy? Should I believe that Aureus was a dream? Should I assume that when I died there, the dream ended, and I'm back to being a beggar on Earth?" he asked the cat.

Tigger looked at him disapprovingly, and Dirk didn't like this possibility either. It saddened him deeply to accept that the beautiful society they had constructed on Aureus had just been a figment of his imagination.

But the more Dirk thought about it, the less likely this explanation became: if this had been a reverie, there would be gaps in the timeline. A mind could construct a dream around a few key events, but the mundane times leading up to these events would undoubtedly not be recalled vividly.

But Dirk remembered the poker nights with Mario, the fishing trips with Garrett and Aarne, the many walks with Lilly in the garden, tennis with Ngazetungue, all the funny talks with Angela, the play-fighting with a much bigger Tigger and Jo, and the countless scientific discussions with L, Sven, Eriea and Lennard. He recalled the movie nights with the whole group, the many, many colony meetings, and of course, every Transformation Day for the last 100 years or so.

Dirk even remembered the most trivial aspects of life on Aureus: the meals in the main hall, the smells of Yebin's kitchen, his tools in the workshop, his coffee machine, and even the week when he caught an alien stomach bug and spent most of his time in the bathroom. Dirk concluded that no dream could be this seamless, coherent, and detailed.

So perhaps this was some type of time travel? But time travel into the past was against the rules of physics and logic because it would create an unresolvable paradox. It was possible to convert mass entirely into energy, and energy could be condensed into mass, but ultimately nothing was lost from the Universe. But if future-Dirk traveled back in time, the Universe's mass-energy balance would be disturbed because the future Universe would have some mass removed while the past Universe would have it suddenly added. A proton was considered immortal in quantum physics because it did not decay. It could be obliterated, but it would never die a natural death. Dirk, like all other ordinary matter, was made of protons. Hence, if a proton from the future returned to the past and met itself, nobody could say for sure what the consequences would be: maybe there were none at all, or perhaps they were catastrophic.

But perhaps information that is neither mass nor energy could move back and forth on the time axis, much like it could ignore the cosmic speed limit and travel faster than light? However, that would create a paradox, too: if future-Dirk sent a message to past-Dirk, and past-Dirk changed his actions because of that information, future-Dirk would no longer have a reason to contact past-Dirk in the first place. Information could get lost, but it could never be destroyed. If that were correct, past-Dirk would remember future-Dirk's message, even though future-Dirk had never really sent it out.

Also, there was a logical reason why time travel to the past should be impossible. The timeline would have been irreversibly changed the instant when Dirk appeared here. He wouldn't have to do anything to change it actively: the mere fact that he existed here would make the future whence he came from obsolete because the past of that future was changed by his appearance alone. If this were time travel to the past, Dirk's future would look very different from this point onward.

Dirk remembered reading a scientific article on that topic: the scientists showed that time travel to the past is mathematically possible; the past will automatically adjust for the time travel, thereby spawning a new future. However, if that's true, Dirk's memories of Aureus's future should all be gone now because that future never has or never will exist. Besides, and much more practical thinking, if this were time travel, Dirk would be getting ready for a Halloween party at Zyrtec right now, not being tied to a bed with severe burns.

"There must be a way to verify all of this!" mumbled Dirk to himself.

He had lived and loved for over 100 years on Aureus, and he had learned the secrets, quirks, and preferences of all the people who had been with him. If Lilly and Tigger existed in this world, it was reasonable to assume that Angela, Mario, Wendji, and others must live here, too. The only exceptions would be L, Alma, and the Latura since none of them were native to Earth. Once Dirk recovered enough, he would have to find them and put this to the test.

"You are right, Tigger. I'm not going to rush to judgment yet. There might still be another explanation," said Dirk more cheerfully, and it seemed like Tigger was happier with that response.

"I see you two are getting reacquainted!" remarked Lilly with a smile as she returned with a paper cup of hot water and a teabag.

"Meow!" replied Tigger and rubbed against Dirk's hand.

"Dirk will have a visitor soon, so you need to get off there now, sweet boy!" said Lilly and gently lifted the Bengal cat off the bed.

6. A Surprise

A few minutes later, Dr. Prescott and a nurse entered Dirk's room. Lilly got up to meet them. They talked in hushed voices, and Dirk didn't hear their conversation, but they appeared pleased by his recovery from its looks. Suddenly, a tall woman came through the door. Although she was unmistakably human, her features, as well as her movement, were almost feline. She dressed in a tight suit that complimented her unusual skin color. She was not white or Asian but looked faintly golden. She had no hair besides thin eyebrows and long eyelashes, yet she looked simply stunning.

"Lydda!" Dirk blurted out in amazement, and the woman looked at him and smiled broadly.

"It's Lydia, and nice to meet you too, Mr. Hayes!" she replied and walked to Dirk's bed.

"Oh, sorry, I thought you were someone else. Pleased to meet you too, and call me Dirk! I assume you are the specialist?" said Dirk quickly, trying to recover from his slipup.

"Yes, that's me. Let's take a look at your head and back first. Please lean forward, so I can see your neck!" instructed Lydia.

The nurse peeled back the aluminum foil bandages, and Dirk visibly winced at that. Lydia examined the burns and took a few pictures with her cell phone while Lilly was still quietly talking to James Prescott by the door.

"I'm sure this is very painful, but it doesn't look too bad. We can fix this once it has healed a little more, but some scarring will remain. Now you can recline again while we examine your arm!" instructed Lydia, and Dirk slowly leaned back again.

"I'm afraid this will hurt quite a bit, Dirk!" warned Lydia as the nurse was unwrapping his mangled arm.

All Dirk could do was hold his breath and clench his teeth because the pain was excruciating while Lydia looked very closely at the injuries. Dirk did too, but he wished he hadn't: his arm looked like something left on the BBQ for far too long from his shoulder down. The procedure seemed to take an eternity, and Dirk wondered how long he could keep himself from screaming. But finally, Lydia had taken all the pictures and was satisfied with the examination.

"You were courageous, Dirk!" praised Lydia with a smile while the nurse dressed the wounds again with fresh aluminum foil bandages.

17

"The injuries are extensive, but Dr. Prescott did a nice job fixing the bones and ligaments. I'll be honest with you: your arm will never look the same again, but we'll do our best to reconstruct it. With exercise and physical therapy, you should be able to use it almost normally again in time," summarized Lydia.

"That's all I can ask. Thank you, Lydia!" replied Dirk, still in considerable pain.

At that moment, Tigger rubbed against Lydia's legs. She was delighted, picked him up, and held him in her arms when she noticed. The cat was purring loudly.

"Oh, I love cats! Is he yours?" she asked and casually touched Dirk's healthy arm.

Dirk flinched, not because the touch was unpleasant but because it triggered something powerful. For a split second, the *swiahn* bond between Lydia, Tigger, and him was there in full force. Dirk noticed immediately that Lydia and Tigger had felt it, too. Lydia quickly dropped the cat on the bed, her beautiful face showing a multitude of emotions.

"Dirk, I cannot place you, but we have met before. Intimately. Please tell me!" whispered Lydia as she bent down to his ear.

"We have not met in this world, Lydia, and that's the truth. But we have met - intimately!" replied Dirk in a subdued voice.

"I don't know what that means, but somehow I believe you. It is not the right time to talk about it, but we will need another consultation before starting treatment. I expect you to explain everything to me if you expect me to make you handsome again?" noted Lydia with a bit of smirk.

"I can try, Lydia, but you'll just think I'm crazy!" answered Dirk sadly.

"I'll be the judge of that, Dirk! We will meet very soon," maintained Lydia, leaving the room with Dr. Prescott and the nurse in tow.

"Do you know Dr. Latur?" asked Lilly curiously after they were gone.

"Dr. Latur?" gasped Dirk because he couldn't believe this was a coincidence.

"Yes, Lydia Latur is *the* surgeon of the rich and famous: Hollywood, supermodels, and the wives of billionaires and presidents. They say she can create beauty out of nothing, yet her beauty is all-natural. I didn't know Prescott would get her for the job, but I can't say I disapprove! Although this will cost us a fortune, and no, our insurance won't cover that. But what the hell, maybe I should inquire if she can turn you into Brad Pitt for all that money?" teased Lilly, and then asked again while wagging her finger at him: "So, you know her, don't you?"

"I thought I did," replied Dirk evasively.

"Oh, come on, I'm not jealous, but Lydia isn't someone you could forget!" insisted Lilly with a grin.

"I thought I might have met her during college, but she doesn't remember me. Perhaps I just saw her picture in a magazine? Or most likely, I'm just delusional from all this morphine!" lied Dirk feebly.

"Hmm, I still don't believe you, but we'll talk about it after you recover!" threatened Lilly humorously.

7. Home, sweet Home

Today, Dirk was released from the hospital, and Lilly drove him back home. Unfortunately, it was rush hour in the Bay Area, and the ride home took a lot longer than expected. Dirk wasn't very comfortable sitting in the car seat because his neck and back were still raw from the burns. While Dirk was shifting uneasily from one side to another, Lilly paid attention to the news on the radio. As it had been for a while now, the story was never good. Lilly seemed lost in thought as she listened to a report about how the government was obstructing justice.

"We need to get away from everything," divulged Lilly suddenly and turned the radio off.

"A vacation would be nice, but I think I need to recover a little more before I can travel," responded Dirk.

"Not a vacation," contradicted Lilly, checking traffic in the side mirror.

"What do you mean?" wondered Dirk.

"Honey, I don't want to be here anymore!" she articulated emphatically.

"You mean your job? I've told you long ago that you could quit if you can't take it anymore. I'll accept full-time employment at Zyrtec, and we'll be fine!" replied Dirk.

"Not the job!" noted Lilly and changed lanes with the car.

"Then what, Sweetie? Leave the Bay Area? California? The U.S.?" asked Dirk and chuckled.

"The damn planet!" grumbled Lilly and honked the car horn as someone cut into her lane.

"That would be nice, Sweetie!" concurred Dirk.

"Honey, I have seen it! A new home for us on a new planet. Just you, me, and a few intelligent, caring people created a better world there!" revealed Lilly quite seriously.

"You saw it, Sweetie?" inquired Dirk, and her story sounded very familiar to him.

"Yes, in a dream last night, so go ahead and laugh at me!" explained Lilly with a sigh.

"I won't laugh. Tell me about this planet!" promised Dirk.

"It was free of hate, bigotry, violence, and greed. You were the leader, but you hated it - typical you! Tigger was huge, and there was a benevolent robot with us.

We met aliens too, and they were good and kind, and together, we colonized a beautiful new world!" elaborated Lilly, and Dirk knew then that Lilly had dreamt of Aureus, and now he was eager to learn every detail.

"What a fascinating dream, Sweetie! Were we still married?" he asked curiously.

"Of course, but…," responded Lilly and hesitated.

"But?" questioned Dirk expectantly.

"OK, this part was probably just due to some hormonal imbalance. I had lovers, and you had a few extra wives," answered Lilly and grinned at him.

"Kinky! I think I like your new planet already!" declared Dirk with a smirk.

"Lecher!" quipped Lilly and noted, "but it's funny, you didn't mind my lovers, and I wasn't jealous of your spare wives. Truthfully, we all got along just dandy."

"Even better, orgy it is!" teased Dirk and laughed out loud.

"Yeah, that too. I must have been horny last night!" giggled Lilly.

"Well, if we are careful, maybe I can perform my spousal duties later on!" suggested Dirk and winked at her, but Lilly just snorted.

"I wish that dream would come true," mumbled Lilly later.

"Would you sacrifice everything to get away from here?" inquired Dirk intentionally.

Lilly seemed disturbed by that remark. She didn't respond; instead, she pressed her lips tightly together and focused on the traffic. Dirk immediately regretted asking that question. From his old memories, he knew that this Lilly would have sacrificed everything, including him, at this point in her life. But that was then, and Dirk had forgiven his wife long, long ago.

"Traffic sucks!" complained Dirk and changed the subject.

It was terrible today, but they were almost home now. Dirk kept shifting uncomfortably in the car seat, but there was no position that wasn't painful. Finally, Lilly turned into their driveway and triggered the garage door.

"Honey, we had a son," remarked Lilly quietly as she drove the car into the garage.

"Carl," replied Dirk absentmindedly, unbuckling his seatbelt.

"How do you know that?" gasped Lilly in surprise.

"That's what I would have named my son if I would have been a father," responded Dirk and added quickly, "after my childhood idol, Carl Sagan!"

"That's what we called him in my dream!" claimed Lilly as she turned the car engine off.

"It must have been a beautiful dream, Lilly. I'm glad you remember it," said Dirk truthfully, but he knew Lilly wouldn't understand his meaning.

"It was nice, and I haven't been this happy in a while. But now I'm despondent that it was just a dream!" replied Lilly with regret in her voice.

"You never know, Sweetie, you never know…," mentioned Dirk cryptically, smiled at his wife, and she looked at him fondly and smiled, too.

"The ride must have been torturous! Let's get you out of the car, Honey!" she noted after a moment, and Dirk was eager to do just that.

8. Arabian Nights

It has been two days since Dirk was discharged from the hospital. The first day, Dirk had stayed in bed most of the time, but he was getting restless today and felt good enough to roam the house. The wounds were still excruciating, but they slowly healed, and no infection had set in. But the heavy pain medication bothered Dirk: he rarely drank and never used mind-altering drugs, not recreational or prescription. Dirk hated the feeling of losing his grip on reality, and he never understood why so many people would intentionally dull, alter, or cloud their minds.

But all things considered, Dirk was recovering well and perhaps even ahead of schedule. He was happy to be home, glad to move about, and see Rose again. His sister-in-law and the big moving truck were scheduled to arrive tomorrow from LA. Lilly had left for work already when Dirk entered the living room late morning, and Tigger was sitting on the shelf over the fireplace, pawing at Lilly's collectibles.

"Buddy, Lilly will have your tail if you destroy her ugly knickknacks!" scolded Dirk when he saw Tigger exploring the effects of gravity.

Just then, he noticed something new yet very familiar on the shelf. There was an icosahedron!

"Tigger, let me take a look at that!" exclaimed Dirk and grabbed the geometric item.

It was just as heavy as he recalled. Dirk examined it from all sides, but no blue light appeared, no hidden ports opened, and no telepathic messages were projected into Dirk's mind. Dirk was about to put it back on the shelf when he remembered something.

"If anything gets L's attention, it's a good pounding on his electronic toys!" mumbled Dirk to himself as he banged the heavy item against the fireplace.

Unfortunately, nothing happened at all. But Tigger got excited and *helped* with Lilly's collectibles' apparent destruction by toppling an old debate trophy to the floor. Disappointed, Dirk was going to put the metallic icosahedron back on the shelf, but sudden dizziness forced him to sit down on the ottoman by the couch. He felt drunk and light-headed, and he suspected that the opioid medication was starting to play tricks on his mind. Dirk focused on the heavy dice in his hands to regain clarity, but try as he might, he couldn't shake the incoming hallucination.

Suddenly, he was sitting on soft cushions in an opulent, colorful tent, somewhere in a desert oasis. He held an old lamp in his hands, gently rubbing its tarnished metal exterior. Straight out of Arabian Nights, a genie appeared out of thin air!

"Master, I will grant you three wishes!" promised the apparition and awaited Dirk's command.

Dirk was confused. He was never one for fame or fortune, so that wouldn't be his wish. Briefly, he considered wishing for instant recovery from his painful burns, but he figured that he would heal on his own in good time. Dirk thought about wishing for a cliché: peace and happiness on Earth, but peace and happiness meant very different things to different people. His definition would likely make some people very unhappy and anything but peaceful. Dirk was tempted to wish for omniscience, but there would be nothing left to explore or discover if he knew everything. Similarly, with omnipotence - if he could do anything he wanted, soon there would be nothing left to do at all.

Perhaps immortality would be a good wish, but Dirk didn't believe that true immortality existed because everything must die eventually, even the Universe itself. And even if it were feasible, just like omniscience or omnipotence, with unlimited time to live, everything would be done and discovered eventually, and he would end up in the same place - utter boredom! Dirk looked at the genie. The apparition was cartoon-like, all big, blue, and translucent, but it seemed very familiar.

"Are you sapient?" Dirk finally asked the genie.

"Of course, Master!" replied the genie immediately, and Dirk just nodded.

"Then I have only one wish: I want you to be free!" declared Dirk thoughtfully.

"Thank you, father!" answered the genie happily and was gone in a puff of smoke, but another genie appeared in his place. However, this one was bloodred and sported four menacing heads.

"You will regret that... father!" sneered the creature, practically spitting that last word at Dirk.

But then the hallucination stopped abruptly, and Dirk was once again in his living room at home. He shook his head to clear the cobwebs in his mind. What a strange, alarming vision, Dirk thought. But he dismissed it as a side effect of the medication. After another minute, Dirk got up and collected the pieces of the broken debate trophy. Finally, he placed the icosahedron back on the shelf.

"Lilly will be mad at both of us, Buddy! I better get some superglue and fix this before she comes home!" observed Dirk and sighed.

Then he went to the laundry room that doubled as his workshop. It took Dirk a few minutes, but he awkwardly glued the pieces back together with just his healthy hand and then placed the trophy over the fireplace again.

"Phew, almost good as new!" declared Dirk, but Tigger was going to bat it right off the shelf again.

"No, Tigger! I know it's tempting to break that awful thing, but you should know better!" said Dirk sternly and lifted the cat from the shelf.

The rest of the day went by uneventfully. Dirk's injuries still tired him, and the potent pain medication made him even sleepier. So, he took a long nap in the afternoon, with Tigger sleeping between his legs.

9. Interrogation

Dirk was awake again when Lilly came home that evening. Unfortunately for him, she almost immediately noticed that her memorabilia had been moved around. Upon closer inspection, she spotted the crudely repaired debate trophy.

"Did you do that, or Tigger?" asked Lilly sternly.

"Oh, sorry, Sweetie! I accidentally knocked it down when I checked out that new item!" lied Dirk and added, "I tried to fix it, but that's hard to do with just one hand."

"Aha, it was Tigger. You always cover for him!" grumbled Lilly.

"Never in my wildest dreams would I do such a thing!" replied Dirk with a smirk and then asked curiously, "where did you get that icosahedron?"

"Oh, Nancy from PTRC dropped it off the day before you were discharged from the hospital," answered Lilly and explained, "Rodrigo found it on the tennis court where you were injured. They kept it in the office for a while, but nobody claimed it, so Nancy stopped by and gave it to me. I told her that it wasn't yours, but she persuaded me to keep it, just in case."

"Ah, that's strange. Well, does it do anything?" questioned Dirk, hoping that Lilly might have discovered its secrets.

"No, it's just a big, heavy dice!" quipped Lilly, but then she added more seriously, "I think it looks good on the shelf, and it's a reminder of how close I came to losing you, Honey."

"I'm still here, Sweetie!" conveyed Dirk, kissed her forehead, and Lilly smiled at him.

"I'm starving! Did you make us anything to eat?" wondered Lilly a moment later.

"Sorry again, I was napping for most of the day; the meds really make me drowsy," confessed Dirk.

"They are supposed to do that. Don't worry. I'll go out and get us some omelets. I'll be back in no time!" replied Lilly, grabbed her purse and car keys, and was out the door again.

Dirk picked up a book that was sitting on a coffee table. He saw his bookmark somewhere in its middle, but he recalled finishing it by Halloween that year. Of course, it was just a minor detail, but another noticeable difference in this world.

"No man ever steps in the same river twice, for it is not the same river, and he is not the same man. - Heraclitus," mumbled Dirk to himself.

A few minutes later, the doorbell rang. Dirk didn't expect anyone in particular, so it was likely just some package for Lilly. But no, it wasn't the mailman, but someone else entirely.

"Hello, Mr. Hayes. I'm Agent Dahteste, and I would like to ask you a few questions about the accident at the tennis club. May I come in?" requested the woman politely, and Dirk was at a loss for words!

"Are you alright, Mr. Hayes?" wondered the agent.

"Yes, hello and sorry. I'm still on morphine and not thinking clearly. Miss Dahteste, please come in and have a seat. Would you like something to drink?" asked Dirk politely, still shocked to see Angela at the door.

"Thank you, but that won't be necessary," replied Agent Dahteste formally and placed a small recording device on the table.

"OK, are you with the police? FBI?" asked Dirk, although he already knew which agency Agent Dahteste was representing.

"I'm with the government, but I cannot tell you more. I'm here because a meteor injured you. That is an extremely rare event, as you probably know. Moreover, the flight path of this particular rock was very unusual. I'm here to find out if you can recall anything out of the ordinary from that night!" stated Agent Dahteste and looked at him expectantly.

"I see. I'll tell you what I remember, but I fear it isn't much," answered Dirk, and then he proceeded to recount the events from that fateful evening, but he substituted the transformation matrix with the meteor in his story.

"You say the object was glowing when it flew over the tennis court?" inquired the woman, as she was scribbling something in a small notebook.

Dirk watched her for a moment before he answered the question. Many things were going through his head - Lilly was here, Tigger was here and still telepathic, Lydda was here in human form, an icosahedron was on the fireplace, Rose would be here shortly - and now Angela showed up! Dirk speculated that all the other essential people from his life on Aureus would be here too, and he would meet them sooner or later.

Lydda, or Lydia, knew him or at least felt the connection when they met in the hospital. Dirk was sure that Tigger knew something as well, but he couldn't communicate it. Lilly was more difficult to gauge because she acted very much on Earth as on Aureus, but Dirk suspected Lilly had sensed something too when she had that vivid dream. Dirk concluded that he would have to investigate more aggressively to understand what had happened to him.

27

"Yes, Angela, it was a bright streak, heading westwards to the Pacific!" acknowledged Dirk finally.

Dirk had used her first name intentionally to study her reaction. It did not disappoint! Angela almost froze in her seat.

"I did not tell you my first name. How do you know it, Mr. Hayes?" asked Angela, concerned.

"Please, do not be alarmed; I'm not a threat in any way; I can barely stand straight. Before we continue, I suggest you turn off the recording device," mentioned Dirk with a fond smile.

"I'm listening!" remarked Angela and deactivated the tiny recorder.

"Angela Dahteste, age 31, formerly Angela Reynolds, but recently divorced. You took the Apache name from your grandmother; it means warrior woman, and it is quite fitting. You are employed at AATIP, or whatever they are called nowadays. Although you are fully trained to be a field agent, you are an analyst because you failed the psychological evaluation. Your agency considered your compassion and empathy detrimental to the job because they wanted people who follow orders without questions!" stated Dirk, while Angela closed her lips tightly and didn't respond.

"You are beautiful, kind, intelligent, courageous, highly skilled in combat, and you have a great sense of humor, but self-doubts plague you. That is due to your upbringing: your mother who raised you is a devout Evangelical and believes that a woman must be demure and submissive, not confident and assertive!" continued Dirk, and now Angela was just staring at him wide-eyed!

"I also know your favorite color, food, drink, music, TV show, and even about that diamond-shaped birthmark on the left side of your pelvis, " concluded Dirk, and Angela's initial shock had made way to anger.

"You are a spy! You have a dossier on me!" exclaimed Angela furiously, her hand wandering to the side of her jacket where she carried her service weapon.

"Angela, I'm not a spy, and you don't have to pull your gun out!" conveyed Dirk calmly and stated firmly, "I know you because you told me all these things!"

"I never told you this, Mr. Hayes, and we have never met before!" insisted Angela.

"But we have met and much more than that. I wanted you to stop the recording because nobody will believe what I will tell you next!" retorted Dirk.

"Explain!" Angela demanded to know and looked at Dirk expectantly.

"You are family to me, I love you dearly, and we have spent a lifetime together. My wife Lilly is your best friend, and your husband is like a brother to me!" elaborated Dirk.

"Mark?" gasped Angela.

"Oh, not the drunken wife-beater! Your future husband, the father of your firstborn!" Dirk corrected her.

"Who?" wondered Angela confused.

"Lieutenant Jackson!" replied Dirk fondly.

"Garrett?!?!" exclaimed Angela in surprise.

"The same one! I know he has feelings for you, and I suspect that you have feelings for him as well, but if you don't, it will happen soon!" claimed Dirk with a smile.

"What else do you know about Garrett?" asked Angela.

"All that there is to know. But currently, Garrett is in Colorado, frantically preparing a report on that meteor for his boss, Colonel George Masters, and he is waiting for you to tell him what Dirk Hayes knows about it!" divulged Dirk and Angela nodded ever so slightly.

"Mr. Hayes, if you are not a spy, how do you know all this? What actually happened on that tennis court?" replied Angela incredulously.

"I knew all this long before I was injured, and everything I've told you was the truth!" declared Dirk firmly, but Angela just stared at him for a long time.

Eventually, Dirk started to feel a little uncomfortable, but then she suddenly shook her head vigorously.

"Not everything. You didn't lie, but you omitted something vital!" stated Angela and claimed, "you forgot to mention that I will be your wife too!"

"I wasn't sure how you would handle it. That's why I omitted it!" conceded Dirk in surprise and asked, "but I'm curious, how did you figure that out?"

"I… I really don't know. It was just there in my mind. Mr. Hayes, are you using psychological tricks on me?" questioned Angela with suspicion, but she wasn't angry anymore.

"I'm not using any tricks, I swear it, and please call me Dirk!" answered Dirk and smiled at her, but Angela seemed to be distracted again.

"Dirk. That's a lie!" mumbled Angela absentmindedly.

"It is my name," said Dirk and shrugged his healthy shoulder.

"But not what I call you!" countered Angela, now fully in the moment again.

"You called me *Love,* and I called you *Babe,*" replied Dirk fondly.

"True!" admitted Angela, and she smiled a little, but then she shook her head again and shouted, "this is insane and impossible!"

"I died on another world, 1,500 lightyears away, and humanity was almost gone by that time. But then I woke up in a hospital on Earth, over 100 years in the past. Now I'm meeting the people I've loved and lived with all over again. Insane isn't even beginning to describe this!" exclaimed Dirk and threw his hands up in the air, which he immediately regretted because it made his injured arm hurt very badly.

"I was on that world with you. Garrett was my husband, but you were too, or you will be. I don't even understand how I know all this. God, this is so confusing!" answered Angela quietly.

"Yes, yes, and yes!" concurred Dirk with a chuckle.

Then he stood up and went to the kitchen. He took a glass from the cupboard and filled it with some Scotch.

"Have a drink, Angela!" recommended Dirk, placing the glass in front of her, and she hesitated only for a second before emptying it.

"What should we do now?" asked Angela quietly.

"I don't know, Babe!" said Dirk quietly and divulged, "when I saw you at the door, I just had to tell you."

"You called me Babe; I've missed that, Love!" replied Angela fondly, staring at her empty glass, but then her mood changed: "I was so angry when you died and left me behind!"

"I'm sorry, death comes for all of us!" apologized Dirk, but then he quipped, "did you break many things?"

"I threw a chair into Lydda's fountain!" confessed Angela, and then she covered her face with the palms of her hand and sobbed, "please make it stop. I'm going crazy!"

"Past, present, future - it is all getting mixed up, isn't it?" commented Dirk, gently rubbing her back with his good arm, and Angela didn't mind the fondness at all.

"Yes, I suddenly know things I shouldn't! I remember what has not happened yet. But they are good memories, and I'm fond of them!" answered Angela, and she cried a little, but just then, Tigger decided to jump on her lap.

"Hi, Tigger!" said Angela and caressed the tomcat, who thoroughly enjoyed the attention.

"I never told you his name," maintained Dirk with a bit of smirk and handed her a box of tissues.

"Lucky guess!" she replied slyly, dried her eyes with a tissue, and Dirk smiled at her.

"So, what will we do now?" asked Angela after she had regained her composure.

"How about dinner?" suggested Dirk in a cheerful voice.

"I'm still working, and how would we explain that to your wife? Your other wife, I mean…," answered Angela hesitantly.

"Lilly will be back soon, and she is bringing omelets. They are good; please join us!" implored Dirk.

"But…," protested Angela, but Dirk shook his head.

"Angela, Lilly senses something, too. Maybe together, we can figure this out?" proposed Dirk.

"I need to make a call!" insisted Angela while gently putting Tigger back on the floor.

"Yes, call Garrett first!" concurred Dirk and nodded.

"How do you know… oh, never mind. I'm calling Garrett now and giving him a preliminary report. I'll be back in a few minutes!" promised Angela, got up, and swiftly left by the front door.

Meanwhile, Dirk picked up his phone and called Lilly.

"Sweetie, can you bring extra omelets, please? We will have a guest," requested Dirk when his wife picked up.

"Sure, I was going to bring a few extra for tomorrow anyway. Rose might be hungry when she arrives," remarked Lilly on the other end and asked, "who's the guest?"

"Too complicated to explain over the phone; you will see when you get home!" answered Dirk cryptically.

"Now, I'm curious. I'll be home in ten minutes. Please set the table if you can!" instructed Lilly.

"Will do! See you soon!" confirmed Dirk and hung up.

10. Omelets

Before Lilly got back, Angela had finished her phone call with Garrett and was back inside the house. When Lilly walked into the kitchen area, she almost dropped the big bag of take-out food!

"Angie…," mumbled Lilly when she first saw Angela standing in the room.

For a moment, Lilly was confused, dazed even, and Dirk certainly noticed, but then she recovered quickly.

"Hi, Sweetie!" greeted Dirk as he put some silverware on the kitchen table: "This is my old friend, Angela!"

"Oh! Hello Angela. You look very familiar, but I cannot place you for the life of it?" inquired Lilly.

"Hello, Lilly!" replied Angela nervously because she had no idea how to respond to that.

"All I remember is that your husband was Garrett, right?" asked Lilly next.

"Uhm, yes…," stammered Angela in response and blushed.

"Angela and I go way back; I'm sure you two have met before," claimed Dirk quickly, knowing that it was both a lie and the truth at the same time.

"That's probably it. What brings you here, Angela?" questioned Lilly as she unpacked the omelets.

"Oh, I was just in the neighborhood. So, I decided to stop by unannounced and say hello!" lied Angela and helped Lilly serve the food, but suddenly Lilly noticed the gun in Angela's jacket.

"What kind of work are you doing, Angela?" asked Lilly cautiously.

Lilly had seen too many gunshot victims in the hospital to be comfortable around firearms, and Angela noticed that right away.

"I'm with the government. Technically, I'm still on duty. That's why I'm armed. But I didn't want to miss out on these omelets!" answered Angela with a sincere smile.

"Great! Let's enjoy dinner. I'm starving!" quipped Lilly, much more at ease after Angela's explanation.

They had a lovely evening together, but they didn't talk about these strange memories. Dirk didn't want to push it further, but he watched both women closely. Dirk noticed that they acted as if they had been best friends for a long time, although they technically had never met in this world. Eventually, it got late, and Angela bid them farewell. On her way out, Angela handed Dirk a card with her number and insisted that he call her soon! After Angela had left, Dirk and Lilly cleaned the dishes and went to bed shortly thereafter.

"Dirk?" asked Lilly when she slipped under the covers.

"Yes, Sweetie?" responded Dirk sleepily as he adjusted his pillow.

"Angela, I know her…," remarked Lilly cryptically.

"As I said earlier, you two have probably met some time ago," replied Dirk hesitantly.

"No, I haven't met her before!" insisted Lilly.

"Oh?" said Dirk, pretending not to understand what Lilly was insinuating.

"Please don't play dumb; it doesn't suit you!" replied Lilly sternly.

"You two were getting along so well; you must know her, right?" asked Dirk, but he felt awful about misleading his wife with that question.

"I only met her in my dream that I told you about," disclosed Lilly.

Dirk was silent for a minute. He decided then to tell Lilly the whole truth, even though it would be nearly impossible to explain.

"I didn't want to deceive you, Sweetie!" apologized Dirk and divulged, "yes, you never met Angela before tonight, and neither have I. She came here on official government business to investigate the meteor and take my deposition. But the two of you were, are, or will be best friends."

"Yes," said Lilly slowly and remarked, "and you were, are, or will be her husband!"

"Your dream was real!" stated Dirk simply.

"Now I know!" answered Lilly quietly and then observed pointedly, "I don't know how that is possible, but I think you do!"

"I have no good explanation, and that's the truth. All I know is that your dream was real because I have lived it with you!" responded Dirk honestly.

"Honey, I'm not mad at you, but this is so bizarre! Angela knows too, doesn't she?" wondered Lilly.

"Thanks for not blaming me!" replied Dirk, relieved that Lilly was not angry with him, "yes, Angela knows. Before you came home, her memories of that other world returned. That's why I asked her to stay for dinner. I wanted to see if yours would come back, too!"

"They did, but I was too embarrassed to talk about it, and I guess she was, too. It was just a dream, for heaven's sake!" noted Lilly exasperatedly, and then she asked, "when did you remember all this stuff?"

"It happened when you went for a cup of tea the day I woke up in the hospital," answered Dirk earnestly.

"Oh! Now I understand why you recognized Lydia! She was in my dream, too. Well, sort of, she was an alien!" realized Lilly.

"Yes, that's how I recognized her, and I think she remembered me as well!" admitted Dirk.

"Wow, it's unbelievable!" declared Lilly, exhaling loudly.

"It is, Sweetie, it is!" concurred Dirk solemnly.

"We need to talk to Angela again and Lydia, too. I want to get to the bottom of this strange story!" opined Lilly firmly a few moments later.

"Yes, we should do that, but let's get a good night's sleep first. These meds make me so tired!" revealed Dirk and yawned loudly.

"Sure, you still need plenty of rest!" assented Lilly and leaned over his face to kiss him.

"Good night, Sweetie! Sweet dreams!" said Dirk, but then he joked, "uhm, or maybe just normal dreams, OK?"

"Right. Good night, Honey!" replied Lilly with a snort, and then she switched the lamp on the nightstand off.

11. Old Friends

Dirk and Lilly talked at length about these strange experiences over breakfast early the next morning. Lilly had always been a realist. She didn't believe in fairytales or ghost stories, so Dirk was surprised at how readily his wife had accepted that Aureus wasn't just a dream.

Dirk asked Lilly how much she remembered. To his surprise, her memory was almost as complete as his own now. Lilly recalled everyone's names in the colony and significant events, including her death and subsequent transfer to L's simulation. She could even tell Dirk a few details about the digital afterlife he had no way of knowing.

"Wait! Your last memories were from the simulation when you were alive and well, at least in a matter of speaking. Yet, here we are back where it all started. This makes no sense!" exclaimed Dirk loudly.

"Time travel?" wondered Lilly before she corrected herself, "or maybe a time loop, and we are trapped in it somehow?"

"A self-contained time loop," repeated Dirk and nodded: "If such a thing exists, it won't violate the laws of physics as time travel to the past would. It's not a bad explanation, Sweetie. But why would we remember the loop? Shouldn't our memories be erased with every cycle?"

"Beats me, Honey! Maybe it's just a singular time reset rather than a loop?" speculated Lilly.

"It wasn't a clean reset, or the events would play out the same or at least very similar," observed Dirk with a frown.

Still, he thought that a time reset would be the best explanation so far, although it was all just hypothetical without any proof.

"Yeah, instead of a happy life with friends and family on a beautiful, distant world, you almost got killed, and we are still stuck on crappy old Earth!" grumbled Lilly.

"You don't like Earth, do you?" questioned Dirk gently.

"Earth is lovely, at least what's still left of it. But humans? Every other is an ignorant, bigoted, rude jerk, and that's a low estimate!" replied Lilly cynically.

"Oh, but they call that being *authentic*, Honey!" corrected Dirk with a smirk.

But Lilly just snorted in response and shook her head. Dirk sipped on his coffee while Lilly had another bagel with cream cheese.

"So, tell me what happened when I died on Aureus?" asked Dirk curiously and changed the topic.

But that particular subject made Lilly uneasy, and she evaded most of his questions. Dirk attributed that to the painful loss and changed the discussion again. He mentioned that he had an appointment with Lydia in LA next week and suggested that Lilly accompanies him to talk about the whole experience during the visit. Lilly immediately agreed to that and urged Dirk to invite Angela for another get-together soon. Dirk sensed that this was important to his wife, so he called Angela right away. Unfortunately, she didn't pick up, and the call went to voice mail, but Dirk left her a message.

Lilly went to work a few minutes later, and Dirk played with Tigger for a little while. But Tigger didn't seem to be too interested in his toys. Noticeably, since Dirk had returned from the hospital, the cat acted strangely, frustrated even. Dirk wondered what might have gotten into his furry friend, but before he could develop that thought any further, his phone rang.

"Dirk, it's Angela. Garrett knows something, too!" divulged Angela excitedly.

"So does Lilly. What did he tell you?" inquired Dirk.

"I called him this morning, and I told him a few things we talked about last night. Don't worry, I lied and said it was all a dream!" answered Angela.

"How did he react?" wondered Dirk.

"I quizzed him a little. Garrett knows lots of things that he shouldn't know. He talked about you as if you were his best friend, and he talked about Lilly…," said Angela slowly.

"Lilly was his lover," Dirk pointed out to her.

"Yes, I know, but I don't know how I should feel about that!" quipped Angela and added more earnestly, "but I'm your wife, and I don't know how I should feel about that either! Gosh, I haven't slept with either of you, and Lilly hasn't even met Garrett yet. My memories tell me I wasn't jealous, and rationally I know I shouldn't be, but…."

"On Aureus, it all made sense, Babe. Here on Earth? Not so much!" replied Dirk with a chuckle.

"You can say that again!" concurred Angela, and then she proposed, "I was supposed to return to Virginia tomorrow, but instead, I invited Garrett to meet me here. He said he could be in the Bay Area on the weekend. Can we all get together at your house?"

"Of course! Lilly suggested the same thing just this morning. The only caveat is that her sister will be here, too!" replied Dirk, a little concerned.

"Rose. She should be there, don't you think?" asked Angela.

"You remember her. Yes, if she has similar memories, she should be here!" assented Dirk.

"OK, I got to run now, but I'll text you the details when I get Garrett's itinerary. Bye, Love!" said Angela and hung up quickly.

The rest of the afternoon was uneventful until the doorbell rang. It was too early for Rose to be here, so Dirk was stunned when he opened the door.

"Hey Dirk, how are you doing? You don't look half bad for being hit by a space rock!" said Jerry Page cheerfully.

"Hi Dirk, I'm glad you are up and about. You have to tell us all about that little mishap," added Sven Larson while corralling his dachshund with the leash.

"Jerry! Sven! That's a surprise. Come on in, make yourselves at home!" replied Dirk with a big smile and offered, "anything to drink?"

"Not for me; I'm still hungover from last night!" answered Jerry and sat down by the kitchen table.

"I have a beer if you got one," requested Sven, and Dirk got a brew from the fridge.

"We only have cat food, but if Pluto needs some water, I can fill a bowl for him?" asked Dirk, deliberately using the dog's name.

"Have I told you his name?" wondered Sven, but then he said appreciatively, "please, if you have a little dish for him, that would be great!"

Then they all sat around the kitchen table, and Dirk told his story. Sven asked a few scientific questions, while Jerry wanted to see Dirk's injuries. When Dirk fetched a glass of water for himself, Sven got up and walked over to the fireplace. He looked at the icosahedron and knocked on it with his knuckles.

"Where did you get this thing?" he asked.

"They found it on the tennis court where I was injured!" explained Dirk.

Sven nodded and continued to examine the metallic dice for quite some time. Finally, he put it back on the shelf and returned to the table.

"I told you tennis is dangerous! Play golf!" quipped Jerry.

"Oh sure, waving a lightning rod around on a grassy plain is so much safer. Did you know that every year some golfer gets electrocuted that way?" replied Dirk sarcastically.

"Bah, fake news!" countered Jerry jokingly as he fiddled with his cell phone.

"So, how are things at work?" asked Dirk.

"Well, the Halloween party was a bust. Hibi-san's wife Ayako fell down the stairs and broke her ankle and nose. She also has a nasty concussion," answered Jerry.

"Oh my, I hope she will get better soon!" remarked Dirk sincerely.

It was yet another discrepancy: Dirk had saved Ayako from that fall at the party in the past.

"Yeah, a real bummer!" concurred Jerry and changed the subject: "Dirk, Hibi-san wishes you a speedy recovery, and he wants to know if you could come to a meeting two weeks from now. Some German investor is checking out Zyrtec, and since you speak the language, Hibi thought it would be nice if you could attend."

When Dirk was a teenager, he had spent two years in a boarding school in Switzerland. Later during his college days, he participated in a student exchange program with the university in Heidelberg, Germany. While he didn't consider himself fluent, Dirk could converse reasonably well in the language.

"My German isn't all that great anymore. I only get to practice with an old friend over there once in a while," disclosed Dirk with a smile before he asked, "but I'll try to be there. Who's the investor?"

"All I got is a name - Jens Koch. He holds an executive vice-president position, but what he actually does for his company is unclear. But he has expressed great interest in Sven's work, and that's all I know," replied Jerry and shrugged his shoulders.

Dirk waited for Sven to add something, but the Norwegian scientist was unusually quiet and seemed lost in thought. Dirk got up and poured another glass of water for himself while Jerry was rechecking his cellphone.

"Dirk, we have to split pretty soon. I got a hot date tonight!" announced Jerry with a huge grin.

"Oh?" asked Dirk with a smirk.

"Yeah, I met her in a bar yesterday, hence the hangover. She had to leave, but she gave me her number. I will take her to a fancy restaurant tonight!" answered Jerry happily and disclosed, "her name is Irina; she is Russian and smokin' hot!"

Dirk didn't know what to say. This Irina was really Galina Rustova, a ruthless Russian operative. While she didn't kill Jerry, she set in motion the events that would kill him and her, eventually. Dirk felt like he needed to intervene and save a life, maybe two, if one counted the agent, but Sven spoke first.

"Be careful, Jerry!" remarked Sven very seriously.

"Huh? What could Irina possibly do to me that my three ex-wives haven't done already?" replied Jerry dismissively.

"I don't know, just be careful! I have a bad feeling about this date," repeated Sven and shrugged his shoulders.

"You had some poor luck with women, Jerry. Just take it slow this time," advised Dirk fondly.

"Spoilsports. But you are probably right. Maybe I should think with the head on shoulders and not the other one!" joked Jerry with a smirk, then grabbed his jacket and put it on.

"Well, thanks for stopping by, guys! I'll see you when I can do some work again," said Dirk as Jerry headed for the door.

"Jerry, I'll take an Uber. I need to talk some science stuff with Dirk!" maintained Sven suddenly.

"Suit yourselves, eggheads!" teased Jerry and swiftly exited the house. After Dirk closed the door, he remembered something vital.

"Sven, I need to send a quick email; it will be just a minute! Please help yourself to another beer in the fridge!" remarked Dirk hastily.

"No problem, Dirk," replied Sven and petted Pluto, who appreciated the attention.

Dirk had no idea if this would work, but he just had to try for Jerry's sake. He typed in the untraceable email address that Victor had given him so long ago. Then Dirk wrote only five words: *Victor, call her off - Dirk* and hit send. He sat at the computer for a moment longer, not sure if there would be an immediate response coming. There was not, and Dirk returned to the living room. Sven was sitting on the couch, looking once again at the icosahedron on the shelf above the fireplace. Pluto had made himself comfortable on the ottoman next to it.

"Dirk, are you familiar with false memories?" asked Sven when Dirk entered the room.

"I only have a vague idea: it can be caused by trauma or drugs, no?" speculated Dirk, but he had a good idea why Sven was suddenly talking about this particular topic.

"Yes, that can interfere with the way the brain stores information. The memory can be distorted or entirely false if the process is corrupted," explained Sven.

"Is that what you wanted to talk to me about?" questioned Dirk, although he had already sensed the actual reason.

"I'm certain I never told you Pluto's name. Yet you knew it. How?" questioned Sven pointedly.

"The same way you knew that Jerry's date would be dangerous," countered Dirk nonchalantly.

Sven looked at him with his eyes wide open and his mouth agape. For a minute, neither man said another word.

"The memories are not false, Sven," remarked Dirk finally.

"They must be!" insisted Sven.

"By today's science, it might appear that way. But they are not false, and I think you know that, too," said Dirk and asked, "please tell me, when did it happen?"

"When I touched that icosahedron. My brain was flooded with impossible things. I knew Jerry was in grave danger!" disclosed Sven and added, "and I knew that you were aware too!"

"That's why I sent a message to Victor as soon as Jerry left. I don't know if I can save his life, but I had to try!" admitted Dirk and sighed.

"I remember Victor," said Sven and emptied his beer bottle before he inquired, "are you in touch with him?"

"No, not at all. I just recalled how we used to communicate with Victor in secret. I can only hope that he has some of these memories and will tell Galina to stand down!" replied Dirk earnestly.

"Did we really live on another planet?" asked Sven slowly.

"We did, or perhaps we will. Don't ask me how that is possible, but it is the truth, and we are not alone in this: Lilly, Angela, and Garrett remember things, too!" revealed Dirk.

"Lilly…," mumbled Sven and blushed.

"My wife, your lover!" noted Dirk and smirked.

"Dirk…," Sven started to apologize, but Dirk just waved him off.

"Oh please!" grumbled Dirk and noted fondly, "we went through that a hundred years ago. I'm not jealous. I'm happy for both of you!"

"Yeah, but this Sven isn't quite as liberated yet!" insisted Sven, but he had to smile a little.

"Sven, we are planning to meet here on the weekend. Lilly, Angela, Garrett, and possibly Rose will be here; although we have no idea yet if Rose knows anything - but something tells me that she does. Anyway, we all have the same questions, and perhaps together, we can figure this out. Will you join us?" asked Dirk, hopeful that Sven would attend.

"Of course, Dirk. Just tell me when I should be here!" replied Sven immediately, but then he maintained, "now I need to be by myself to process all of this!"

"Believe me, I understand. I went through it too," concurred Dirk and promised, "I'll give you a call when we have decided on a date and time."

"Thanks!" responded Sven as he put his jacket on and grabbed Pluto's leash.

Tigger watched the dog from his cat tower. He wasn't particularly fond of the small canine, but he didn't object to his presence either.

"Pluto was killed," mumbled Sven sadly when he walked to the front door.

"Yes, and we named a moon after him," confirmed Dirk.

"We did!" replied Sven, nodded, and said, "get well soon, Dirk. We will talk more about it on the weekend."

"We will. Goodbye, Sven!" answered Dirk and closed the door behind him.

12. Moving in

The moving truck and Rose's car finally arrived at the curb a few hours later. The movers started to unload the big truck right away, and Dirk opened the front and garage doors. Dirk checked the wall clock; Lilly wouldn't be home for another two hours. Hopefully, Rose would have moved in by that time because Lilly hated it when the house was in disarray.

"Dirk, thank god you are OK!" exclaimed Rose as she exited her car and rushed to hug her brother-in-law.

"Ouch! Not so hard!" grimaced Dirk when Rose embraced him a little too vigorously.

"Oh, sorry, sorry, sorry!" apologized Rose and let go of him.

"That's OK, Pumpkin. I'm so happy to see you, too!" Dirk assured her fondly.

"Pumpkin? You hadn't called me that since before I went to college!" complained Rose playfully.

"Old habits die hard!" replied Dirk, but of course, on Aureus, he had called her that for a hundred years.

"Dork! But you know what? Call me Pumpkin again; I missed hearing that!" declared Rose with a grin.

She had picked up Tigger and was holding him tightly in her arms. The tomcat was purring loudly and fondly licked her nose.

"No problem, Pumpkin. How are you holding up?" asked Dirk more seriously.

"When the bank let me go, I was worried about the bills, but I wasn't sad. I never really liked the job, and the commute was awful!" answered Rose with a shrug and set Tigger back down on the floor.

"That's because you are an engineer, not a banker!' emphasized Dirk.

"I am?" wondered Rose and thought about this.

"Yes, you are creative! You want to build things and fix stuff!" insisted Dirk with a smile.

"You know, I've never thought about that, but…," responded Rose, confused.

"Don't worry about it, Rose; it will come in time. But I'm sorry to hear about Sam," noted Dirk consolingly.

"Don't be! He was a controlling son of a bitch. Always checking on me, always keeping me on a leash, but then it was him who cheated!" answered Rose angrily.

"You spent several years with him," pointed Dirk out.

Dirk recalled that Sam had left Rose for a different reason in that other timeline. Another discrepancy, he thought.

"Yeah, wasted time. Honestly, when Sam told me that he had met someone else, I was more relieved than sad. Good riddance to him!" grumbled Rose and changed the topic with her next question, "but tell me about your ordeal. It must be awful if you can't even hug me. Will you be able to use your arm again soon?"

"Yes, a plastic surgeon will fix it up in a few weeks. I should be able to use my arm, but it won't look pretty," answered Dirk with a sigh.

"Don't worry; you are still handsome!" praised Rose and laughed.

"Thanks! Well, let me help you move some of this stuff upstairs into your old room!" proposed Dirk with a smile while looking at all the boxes in the living room.

"Are you feeling up for that? I don't want you to get hurt!" worried Rose.

"I'll be OK; besides, you have more things than I imagined, and we need to clean up before Lilly comes home!" replied Dirk determinedly.

"Good point; she wouldn't stand for this mess!" realized Rose.

She quickly walked to the curb, where the workers closed the big truck and signed for the delivery. The movers had been speedy and efficient, but they had dropped most of Rose's belongings all over the living room, and now there was a maze of furniture, boxes, and bags. Tigger was excited and had to sniff every carton and crate. Dirk grabbed a suitcase with his good arm while Rose followed him with a box of office supplies. When they passed by the master bedroom door that was always ajar for Tigger, Dirk stopped and looked at Rose.

"No peeking this time!" he teased with a grin, and Rose dropped the box, spilling pens, staplers, and notepads all over the floor.

"Oh my god, you knew!" gasped Rose, her face red as a tomato.

"Don't worry about it, Pumpkin!" maintained Dirk and chuckled.

"Are you mad at me? Does Lilly know too?" Rose demanded to know anxiously.

"I don't think she knows, and I'm not mad at all!" insisted Dirk.

"I'm so sorry, Dirk. I promise it will never happen again! But you cannot tell Lilly, ever! She would kill me!" Rose implored him fearfully.

"I won't tell her, but you would be surprised by her reaction. She loves you more than you can imagine!" answered Dirk calmly.

"Are you sure you are not mad at me? I think I would be furious!" stated Rose firmly and looked at him, somehow expecting him to scold her for her indiscretions.

"You watched your sister and brother-in-law make love, and it turned you on. So what? I love you just the same, and so would Lilly if she knew," replied Dirk and shook his head.

"I did it more than once!" avowed Rose as she picked up all the pens and paperclips off the floor.

"Yeah, I know. Did you want to join us?" asked Dirk with a smirk on his face.

"No! Of course not!" exclaimed Rose, but Dirk looked at her and mockingly raised an eyebrow.

"Dirk, I'm so embarrassed now!" confessed Rose and put her hands over her face.

"Rose, it's fine. You don't have to be embarrassed, and you don't have to apologize!" reiterated Dirk and smiled fondly at his sister-in-law.

"You don't think I'm a pervert?" questioned Rose, concerned.

"No, not at all. I think you are wonderful, just like your sister!" Dirk assured her.

"Don't take this the wrong way, but can I ask you if you ever cheated on Lilly?" asked Rose.

"No, it never even crossed my mind!" answered Dirk truthfully.

"Did she ever cheat on you?" inquired Rose next.

"I don't keep tabs on her, but I have no reason to be suspicious either," remarked Dirk and shrugged.

"Sam was overbearing! I couldn't even go to the grocery store without him quizzing me. I thought about cheating on him because of that, but I never did," elaborated Rose with some anger in her voice.

"When you love something, set it free!" interjected Dirk.

"I was just a little girl when you and Lilly got married, but I remember how dashing, smart, strong, and kind you were. I wanted my future husband to be just like you. I guess I was infatuated with you!" revealed Rose, a little embarrassed.

"That's sweet; thanks for telling me that, Rose! But I'm not so dashing anymore, just old and injured!" replied Dirk with a smile.

"That doesn't matter; you have the biggest heart of anyone I know! Dirk, since we are brutally honest, I think I'm still infatuated with you. Are you mad?" asked Rose and anxiously looked at him.

"Honesty for honesty - if we were on a different planet, I would want you to share the bed with Lilly and me, and I'm pretty sure Lilly would want the same!" said Dirk and asked humorously, "and now, you will be outraged and berate me for my sexual deviance, right?"

"Are you serious?!?" gasped Rose, almost dropping the box with office supplies again.

"I'm serious, Pumpkin!" answered Dirk quietly.

"I'm so shocked, I don't know what to say!" stammered Rose with her eyes wide open.

"Relax, it won't happen!" conveyed Dirk and laughed.

"I know, but…," replied Rose and paused.

"But what?" quizzed Dirk.

"…but maybe it should?" wondered Rose, but then she added quickly, "oh my god, I didn't just say that, did I?"

"You did, and I agree. But it is improbable, so don't get too excited!" observed Dirk while Rose collected the last few pens off the floor, but suddenly she froze!

"Dirk, it has happened, will happen…," uttered Rose, nonplussed.

"What was that?" asked Dirk curiously.

Dirk had heard what she had said, but he wanted to make sure. It looked like Rose was experiencing a flashback just like Angela had.

"Uhm…," stammered Rose and mumbled, "nothing! I must be fatigued from the long drive…."

"Sure, Pumpkin. Now, let's clean up this mess and get you settled in. I'll make us some strong coffee to wake you up again when we are done!" replied Dirk, cheerfully glossing over Rose's blatant lie.

The move had tired her out, so Dirk didn't want to push her further. But now he knew that Rose had these weird memories as well. There would be plenty of time to explore them over the next few days.

13. Memories returned

Lilly came home before they could clear out all of Rose's belongings, but she didn't mind the mess at all. She was too happy to see her little sister again. Dirk warmed up the leftover omelets, and Lilly had bought some ice cream on her way from work. While they were eating, Dirk received a message from Angela. She informed him that Garrett would be here on Saturday afternoon. Dirk immediately texted Sven, and the Norwegian geneticist confirmed a few minutes later that he would attend, too.

They finished their dinner and then moved the last few pieces of furniture into Rose's room upstairs. Lilly and Rose have always been very close, so Dirk didn't notice anything out of the ordinary. Finally, the work was done, and the three of them sat down on the couch to watch some TV before bedtime. It was then that Dirk mentioned that Angela, Garrett, and Sven would be visiting this weekend. Lilly started telling Rose who they were, but Rose just shook her head.

"Yeah, I know them," she mentioned a bit absentmindedly while watching the news.

"You do?" asked Lilly curiously.

"Yes, Garrett and Sven are your…," started Rose saying, but she quickly clasped her hand over her mouth.

"My what, Rose?" inquired Lilly.

"Nothing!" stammered Rose nervously, and Lilly looked at her for a moment.

"My lovers? Is that what you wanted to say?" questioned Lilly and wagged her finger.

Rose just stared at her in utter disbelief. Lilly didn't wait for an answer that was obviously not coming any time soon.

"Yes, they are! And Angela is Dirk's other wife," said Lilly and added very deliberately: "And so are you!"

"How?" gasped Rose repeatedly because she was too much in shock to say anything else.

"We don't know, Pumpkin. We all have these memories, and I already noticed earlier that you have them too," disclosed Dirk quietly.

"By the bedroom?" whispered Rose and blushed visibly.

"Yes, you were right all along. It really happened!" said Dirk and winked at her.

Rose was unable to say another word. She was just sitting on the couch staring at Dirk, Lilly, and Dirk again. Finally, Dirk went to the kitchen and got a shot of vodka for her. Rose's hands were shaking when she took the glass, but she downed the contents immediately.

"You have to tell me everything! Everything! Right now!" she blurted out impatiently.

"Of course, Rose! We will tell you what we know, but it's peculiar and confusing," warned Lilly and turned the TV off.

Then they told Rose what they had found out about the strange memories of a different world. Rose listened raptly and could match almost everything with her new memories.

"I'm an engineer!" exclaimed Rose in amazement.

"Yes, and a good one, too!" confirmed Dirk and grinned at her.

"I don't know how this is all possible, but that other world, Aureus, was a lovely place," noted Rose when Dirk and Lilly had finished their story, but then she asked, "but how could we have accepted that kind of life?"

"What do you mean, Rose?" asked Lilly, unsure what her sister was insinuating.

"I mean… you know! You guys have been happily married for a long time…," answered Rose, a little embarrassed.

"Ah, do you recall that we had that discussion before?" inquired Lilly with a bit of a smile.

"Yes, but who I am and who I was or will be are so different!" remarked Rose thoughtfully and explained, "my fantasies and my life right now are hard to consolidate: one part of me thinks it's natural that you have lovers, that I sleep with your husband, and the whole spiel about Transformation Day, but another part is shocked and appalled! I feel like such a fraud!"

"Unlike us, you changed a lot on Aureus, Pumpkin. Initially, it was not an easy time for you, " Dirk reminded her fondly.

"Dirk and I love each other, Rose; we always have and always will!" declared Lilly firmly and noted, "but we never actually discussed our extramarital relationships, if you want to call it that. I don't own Dirk, I just want him to be happy, and I know he wants me to be happy, too!"

"That sums it up perfectly, and there was nothing to be discussed!" agreed Dirk readily, smiled at Lilly, and recommended to Rose, "Pumpkin, just give it some time to work itself out!"

47

"You know what? It doesn't matter!" exclaimed Rose suddenly in response and grinned broadly at them.

"It doesn't?" wondered Dirk surprised.

"No, it doesn't because now I know that the two most important people in my life love me in every way! It is all I ever wanted!" replied Rose, laughing and crying simultaneously.

Lilly reached over and hugged her sister fiercely. Dirk would have too, but his injured arm didn't allow that. Instead, he gently caressed Rose's cheek with his good hand until Rose had calmed down a little. They sat on the couch in silence for a few minutes, unsure of what to say next. Eventually, it was Rose who took the initiative.

"You are right, Dirk! I think I need to be alone for a while to deal with all this. Besides, I'm trashed from the drive and move. I should get some sleep now!" she said with a yawn, got up and hugged Lilly, and exchanged kisses with her on the cheeks.

"You do that, Pumpkin, and I should get some rest, too!" assented Dirk, still sitting on the couch.

Rose looked at him for a moment, then she bent down and kissed him deeply for a long time. Lilly was just watching in amusement.

"Be careful; your tongue might get stuck, Rose!" teased Lilly, and Rose stopped the kiss.

"God, I wanted to do that for so long!" gasped Rose, let go of Dirk, ran up the stairs, but then stopped at the top and yelled, "I love you both so very much! Good night!"

"That was beyond bizarre, Honey!" muttered Lilly slowly after Rose had closed her door.

"Which part?" giggled Dirk.

"All of it, but to watch my sister French-kissing my husband and not to feel furious or jealous takes the cake!" divulged Lilly, shook her head, and declared, "I cannot even put it in words!"

"Me neither, Sweetie!" agreed Dirk and shook his head.

"It's not just the memories, Dirk. I also have the same emotions now, the same outlook on life as on Aureus. I can't get mad or jealous at Rose, or Angela, or Lydia," revealed Lilly, and then she added, "and I miss...."

"...Nari!" said Dirk to complete Lilly's sentence, and Lilly just looked sadly at him and nodded.

"I miss her, too!" admitted Dirk before suggesting, "let's get some sleep, Sweetie. It's been a long, weird day!"

About half an hour later, Dirk adjusted his pillow, trying to find a sleeping position that wouldn't put too much pressure on his burns. Lilly was still in the bathroom, brushing her teeth and getting ready for bed.

Suddenly, Dirk's phone was vibrating on the nightstand. When he checked the message, it looked like some spam, but he opened it anyway and read the five words: *Done. We must talk. V.* Dirk typed in *yes* and sent the reply. A few moments later, another message came in: *See you Saturday afternoon!* Dirk had to smile at that: of course, the Russian spymaster would already know about their meeting. He put the phone down and decided it would be better to leave Victor's attendance a secret. Then he turned around in the bed and was fast asleep.

14. The Surgeon

Lilly had the next day off and took Rose shopping for all the little things that went missing or forgotten when moving. Dirk and Tigger were alone at home. Dirk's arm hurt a little more than yesterday, mainly because he had reduced the painkiller dosage and exerted too much when he helped Rose move her stuff.

Dirk was sitting at the kitchen table, reading the newsfeeds on Lilly's tablet. There had been a robbery at a liquor store in their neighborhood, and an employee and her boyfriend were brutally gunned down. All three suspects were still at large since Halloween, and the police were now seeking the public's help. Dirk knew immediately that this was the same crime that the transformed Lilly could prevent in the other timeline. Another inconsistency, but Dirk didn't get a chance to think about it any further because suddenly, the doorbell rang. Dirk got up and opened the front door.

"Hello, Dirk!" Lydia greeted him with a smile.

"Lydia! I didn't expect you to come over. I thought I would visit you in LA next week!" replied Dirk in surprise.

"You will, but I couldn't wait that long," answered Lydia: "I looked up the address in your file and decided to come unannounced."

"Oh, no problem! Please come in, make yourself at home. Would you like something to drink?" asked Dirk politely.

"If you have some tea, I won't say no," responded Lydia.

"Of course! Lilly loves tea, so we have plenty. Why don't you take a look and pick the kind and flavor you like while I heat the kettle?" suggested Dirk.

"Thank you!" answered Lydia and followed him into the kitchen.

"Now, what brings you here today, Lydia?" asked Dirk while he was plugging in the electric kettle, but of course, he already suspected it was connected to the strange memories.

"I want to hear your story!" declared Lydia simply as she perused Lilly's stash of teas.

"Let me warn you once more: my story is insane!" noted Dirk seriously.

"As I said before, I'll be the judge of that!" replied Lydia as she sat down at the table.

"It might also be offensive and insulting to you," warned Dirk.

Unlike Lilly or Sven, Lydia was a stranger, and unlike Angela, she was also not supposed to be human. Dirk didn't know how to convey that without hurting this woman's feelings.

"Dirk, look at me! I'm a freak!" noted Lydia dismissively.

"Lydia, you are beautiful!" protested Dirk sincerely and placed a cup with hot water on the table for Lydia, but he had filled his mug with coffee instead.

"Thank you, Dirk. But not everyone thinks like that. I had my share of abuse and insults, so there is nothing you can say that would hurt me!" divulged Lydia in response and added a bag of jasmine tea to her cup.

"As you wish, Lydia," noted Dirk and nodded.

Then he sat down on the couch, which was more comfortable for him than the chairs at the table, and told her everything. Lydia listened patiently, but she concealed her expressions so well that Dirk had no idea how she would respond to his story.

"I love to swim; I do it every day. I was once an artist, but that didn't pay the bills, so I became a plastic surgeon. I have a twin sister, Elena. Her boyfriend's name is Alvin, and he has a twin brother named Grant, and yes, both are very tall. My sister is a psychologist, Alvin is a paleontologist, and Grant is really an engineer," summarized Lydia and concluded, "but since I have a public profile, any cyberstalker could find this information, change the names and professions a little, and make a science fiction story out of that!"

"Lydia, I assure you that I'm not a cyberstalker. Truthfully, before you visited the hospital, I didn't even know you existed in this world," replied Dirk defensively, and Lydia got up from her chair and walked over to where Dirk was seated on the couch.

"I believe every word you said, Dirk!" she conveyed softly and touched his uninjured shoulder.

"You do? Why?" wondered Dirk in surprise.

"Because it was the truth!" stated Lydia, sat down next to Dirk, and explained, "when I was little, I wanted to have twin daughters myself someday. I was going to name them Dylla and Aurora, and I have never told anyone this! There is no way you could have known that!"

"Our daughters were the first of a brand-new species. They exceeded our expectations in every way, and we loved them so much!" replied Dirk fondly.

"Just as I imagined it when I was a child. What professions did they choose?" inquired Lydia curiously.

"Dylla became an artist like her mother; Aurora was a science geek like me," answered Dirk and finished the rest of the coffee.

"Fitting!" blurted Lydia happily.

"Yes," assented Dirk and smiled at her, and Lydia smiled right back at him.

They both were just silently enjoying each other's company for a moment. Lydia was sipping on her tea, and Dirk was staring at the icosahedron on the shelf above the fireplace.

"I had a recurring dream over the last few months. I was married to a golden man, but I never saw his face. He had many wives, but I was not jealous because we had a special bond and knew each other completely. There were no secrets or lies between us," disclosed Lydia finally and added, "when I touched you in the hospital, I saw the face of the golden man for the first time. It was you."

"Yes, both of us had golden skin, and our bond was unique. It also included a cat!" responded Dirk and pointed at Tigger, who was grooming himself.

"I know, but he was a lot bigger!" quipped Lydia, and Dirk chuckled too while Tigger suddenly looked at them disapprovingly.

"Was I really an alien?" asked Lydia a few moments later.

"You were, but you looked a lot like you do now!" answered Dirk.

"So that's why you recognized me at the hospital!" observed Lydia.

"Yes, except you had a tail, cute cat-like ears, and…," elaborated Dirk, but he stopped mid-sentence.

"And what?" inquired Lydia curiously.

"Well, four breasts," uttered Dirk and looked sheepishly at his empty coffee cup.

"Four!" exclaimed Lydia and giggled.

"Yeah, but they looked very much like…," explained Dirk, now even more embarrassed that he was staring at Lydia's chest.

"Dirk, in a sense, we have been intimate; you can stare at my boobs as much as you want!" remarked Lydia and smiled at him.

"It's a different world, Lydia!" observed Dirk quietly.

"It is. But I would give up everything to be in that other world, Dirk!" insisted Lydia earnestly.

"Yeah, me too!" admitted Dirk sadly.

"Where do we go from here?" wondered Lydia.

"Now that I've told you the crazy story, I hope you will still fix my arm?" asked Dirk in return.

"Of course, I will! Not only that, but I'll do it free of charge!" answered Lydia and smiled.

"That's very generous of you, thank you!" said Dirk gratefully.

"It's not so selfless. We cannot be the way we were on that other world, but I would like to be with you again in some way…," responded Lydia hesitantly.

"But here I'm married!" answered Dirk.

"I know that. Lilly was your first wife, then came Nari and me, then Angela, and finally Rose," recounted Lydda and added, " but I have no idea how I know that!"

"Lilly had weird flashbacks, so did Angela when I recently met her, and Rose sensed something from that other world. Now they all have full memories of Aureus. If I ever meet Nari, I think it will be the same, "explained Dirk and concluded, "Tigger knows too, but he cannot tell us."

"It's almost an alternate reality," mumbled Lydia quietly.

"What did you just say?" asked Dirk, unsure if he heard correctly.

"I said, this feels like an alternate reality," repeated Lydia and looked at Dirk expectantly.

"That's it! *Irtaljan*! Lydia, you are a genius; I could kiss you!" exclaimed Dirk excitedly.

"Please do!" teased Lydia happily and requested, "and then tell me what *irtaljan* is!"

Dirk explained what Lenna, Lydda's twin sister, had once told him about *irtaljan*. Lydia was listening intently, but she didn't ask any questions. After Dirk had finished the explanation, Lydia sat very still with her eyes closed for a few minutes. Dirk wondered if he had managed to bore her to sleep when she suddenly became alert again.

"Do you remember when Tigger died?" inquired Lydia finally.

"I do. We were both in a coma for a week. Lilly and L were frantically keeping our bodies alive. When they were about to give up, you woke up again. I woke up a day later, and we both were confused and disoriented for another week after that," recalled Dirk.

"Yes, but we didn't die!" responded Lydia firmly.

"It was miraculous! Tigger, you and I always assumed that if the *swiahn* bond breaks, we would all perish!" acknowledged Dirk, and then he asked fearfully, "did you die too when I did?"

"Do you know why we survived when Tigger died?" asked Lydia, ignoring Dirk's question.

"I thought we survived because the two of us could compensate for his loss somehow. It seemed like the most plausible explanation," answered Dirk, unsure.

"Most plausible, but not the correct one," countered Lydia and revealed, "we survived because our bond with Tigger was only diminished and distorted but not terminated. It was still there after his death."

"It was?" questioned Dirk, confused.

"Yes, it was very faint, but it was there because Tigger was uploaded into L's simulation!" elaborated Lydia.

"Oh, no! If that is true, then I killed you with my selfishness because I refused to be uploaded!" lamented Dirk in sudden realization.

"You gave everything you could possibly give to our daughters and me. You sacrificed yourself for the colony's betterment and tirelessly worked to make Aureus our home until your last breath! It wasn't selfish; it was your right to ask for eternal sleep!" insisted Lydia.

"But I killed you, Kittycat!" sobbed Dirk.

"No, you didn't. It was hard, harder even than it was when Tigger died, but I survived, not that I wanted to...," answered Lydia.

"I didn't kill you?" wondered Dirk, wiping his eyes dry with his healthy hand.

"No. You didn't kill Tigger or me because we didn't let you die!" divulged Lydia quietly.

"I'm not dead?" asked Dirk in surprise.

"You are dead and buried for a hundred years!" corrected Lydia sadly and explained, "but what makes you Dirk is resting on Aureus' moon Pluto, in one of L's databanks."

"You uploaded me," realized Dirk with a frown when he finally understood what Lydia implied.

"L and Carl did that, but we all approved of it. I know we betrayed your trust, and I'm so sorry, Dirk!" confirmed Lydia with a sigh.

"But it saved your life?" inquired Dirk.

"It did. Just as Tigger's digital imprint saved both of us a few years earlier," replied Lydia.

"Then it was no betrayal, and I'm relieved!" maintained Dirk and smiled.

"You are too kind, *swiahn*!" said Lydia gratefully.

"So, this is L's digital afterlife? I thought it would be…, " wondered Dirk and added, unable to find the right words to express himself, "…better, happier, grander, different?"

"No. I don't know what this is, *swiahn*. I was transferred to the simulation when I died, but you were stored in a dreamless state near zero Kelvin. I don't know why we are both here now, but I'm so happy to see you again!" answered Lydia fondly.

"I'm too, Kittycat, I'm too!" concurred Dirk and grinned at her.

"What will happen now?" asked Lydia, unsure.

"I don't know. *Irtaljan* was a brief, superimposed glimpse of another reality. It did not last for days and weeks on a strict timeline. If this is *irtaljan*, it seems that I have already made a choice. But I cannot recall that I did, and I seriously doubt this would have been my choice unless the alternatives were much more unpleasant!" speculated Dirk.

"Now that I remember my own *irtaljan* experience, it was as you described it, and it was very similar for the others too," affirmed Lydia and continued, "you are right; this is certainly different. I lived a whole life in this world, and I didn't know anything about that other life with you until a few minutes ago!"

"Lilly didn't know at first, and Angela, Sven, and Rose didn't know either until I confronted them. Suddenly they recalled many things!" explained Dirk.

"If I hadn't met you, I would have simply dismissed my strange dreams," conceded Lydia.

"I thought of this ever since it happened to me: I believe Tigger revived my memories from Aureus after waking up in the hospital," opined Dirk and looked at Tigger.

Tigger just sat on his haunches and stared at the two of them. He didn't seem very happy, but Dirk couldn't say for sure.

"Tigger was always the most powerful of us!" assented Lydia.

"He was. I wish I could talk to him in this world. He might have some answers," mused Dirk with a frown.

"We will have to find the answers another way!" stated Lydia firmly.

"I assume you know who Angela, Garrett, Sven, and Rose are?" inquired Dirk, although he was pretty sure that she did.

"Yes, I do now," confirmed Lydia and nodded.

"We are getting together this Saturday afternoon to talk. Maybe we can figure something out and decide what we should do next. It would be great if you could come, Lydia!" suggested Dirk.

"Of course! It is likely the most important thing in my life; hence I will clear my schedule. I will be here!" replied Lydia.

Dirk was delighted to hear that and grinned at her broadly. Hopefully, they could make sense of this strange experience when all of them met.

"Lydia, you are taking all of this so well…," inquired Dirk slowly, still a little surprised how readily this stranger had accepted his improbable story.

"No, not at all! I've never experienced such confusion and inner turmoil before. I'm two people now, and at the same time, I also feel that I was made whole!" disclosed Lydia with a bit of a smile.

"I feel alive again, but out of place and out of time!" admitted Dirk with a sigh.

Absentmindedly, Dirk held Lydia's hand as they sat side-by-side on the couch. Tigger was watching them, his tail swishing in agitation. Finally, the tomcat decided that it was the right moment to jump on Lydia's lap. As he did, the *swiahn* bond between the three of them briefly snapped into place again.

(Feeling of frustration) "Dirk, Lydda, Tigger alive! But time, place wrong! Dirk should not be here…," snarled Tigger mentally.

Dirk thought he heard a man laughing mockingly before his world suddenly faded to black.

15. Operation Oregon

Despite the physical enhancements of the transformation, Dirk felt sleepy and exhausted after Angela's training session today. So, he went to the farmhouse's tool shed and took a little nap in one of the lawn chairs that were stored there.

When Dirk woke up, he felt parched, but fortunately, Lilly had left a water pitcher on the workbench for him earlier. Just after he had finished quenching his thirst, L sounded the alarm. They had been discovered at their rural hideout in Oregon! The group quickly gathered to discuss their options, and in the end, they decided that they would transfer to the new planet rather than fight or surrender to their enemies.

"OK, let's go back to the house and help Angela clean up! We'll meet here again in 30 minutes!" suggested Dirk, and most nodded in agreement, but Lilly caught up with him when he went to the house.

"Why did you make L develop the reverse transformation?" she whispered to him angrily.

"As I said, for an emergency like this, but also to give people an option if they ever have regrets about the transformation," replied Dirk, subdued.

Dirk was unsure why Lilly was so angry, but he suspected she was upset because he hadn't consulted her first. Perhaps he would have to apologize later. Lilly just looked at him strangely and walked off. Usually, Dirk would take her aside right away to talk it out, but time was short. He watched as Lilly headed for the nearby forest, but he went inside the house to help Angela, Garrett, and the others. After about 15 minutes, Nari came running into the house.

"Dirk! They took Lilly!" she screamed in Korean.

"What happened?" gasped Dirk, confused, and although he didn't speak Korean, suddenly something felt very wrong.

"Lilly, she is gone! She walked to the edge of the forest. That's where they captured here!" answered Nari over the link, greatly agitated.

"Who captured Lilly?" asked Dirk, alarmed.

Something inside of Dirk was rebelling at this news. Was his wife kidnapped? It never happened, and it was not supposed to happen because all of them would transfer successfully in the next few hours! Dirk wasn't sure how he knew this, only that he did.

"I don't know, some burly men; they drugged her somehow, dragged her to the road, and loaded her into a van!" replied Nari, tears running down her cheeks.

"L, can you locate Lilly?" inquired Dirk urgently.

(Feeling of uncertainty) "Lilly is alive; her biomechanical tools are responsive. Also, I have located the vehicle that was used to apprehend her. It is at a small dwelling about 15 kilometers from here. But if they have moved her on foot through the forest, I cannot track that!" reported the AI.

"We delay the departure and get her back!" stated Angela firmly and grabbed one of the automatic rifles they had recovered from the assault on the cabin.

(Feeling of anxiety) "I'm afraid all of you might get captured if we delay. The military is closing in on this location quickly, and a few scouts are already in the vicinity!" warned L.

(Feeling of determination) "Take risk. Get Lilly!" insisted Tigger firmly, and Dirk nodded at him.

"Let's act quickly!" proposed Garrett and stopped what he was doing. Everyone else did the same and got ready to move out.

"15 kilometers is an easy run. With our enhancements, we will make it in about 30 minutes!" estimated Ngazetungue.

"...if we don't encounter any opposition!" warned Angela and shouldered the rifle.

"Let's go!" shouted Dirk impatiently and started running towards the forest edge while L's drone was scouting ahead.

Angela ordered them to undress when the group reached the forest, except for their boots, weapons, and equipment. Then they modified their chromatophores to match the forest and greenery around them. It took a little doing, but they had practiced that under Lilly's tutorage for the last few weeks, and the results were impressive. They looked like moving trees, bushes, and shrubbery when they continued their fast-paced run. The run was strenuous, but Dirk hardly noticed the exertion. His mind was racing. Lilly was in grave danger, but she should never have been. None of this made sense to him, and none of it felt real, but it perceptibly was, which terrified him deeply.

16. The Hostage

When Lilly regained consciousness, she found herself tied to a chair in a sparsely furnished house. The floor was barren, dirty old curtains covered the sole window, and only one portable, battery-powered light illuminated the room. Lilly tested the bonds and knew that she could not break them even with her enhanced strength. She looked around and saw five armed men standing by a small table. Placed on the table was something like a HAM radio, and one of her abductors was quietly talking into it. Moments later, he finished the conversation and turned around.

"Good, you are awake!" he said and walked towards her.

"Where am I, and what do you want?" asked Lilly, trying to clear her mind.

"You will tell your husband that his group must surrender immediately, or we will harm or kill you! You will say nothing else!" insisted the man and ignored Lilly's questions.

Lilly felt disoriented and still unclear about what had happened, but suddenly she heard Tigger's voice in her head.

(Feeling of urgency) "Tigger, Dirk coming!" promised the big feline, and Lilly tried to respond, but Tigger was still too far away for her to reach him mentally.

"Sure," answered Lilly a few moments later, "but they won't surrender."

"That would be very bad for you!" warned the man.

"Possibly," retorted Lilly simply.

"Do you think that we are not serious?" asked the man, then he struck Lilly with his fist in the face: "We are damn serious, freak!"

"…and obviously ignorant of the situation," responded Lilly, spitting a small amount of blood on the dirty floor.

"Tell me, what do you think the situation is?" challenged the man.

"Dirk will not surrender; nobody will," remarked Lilly calmly and advised, "you have to decide now, kill me, or let me go."

"Let you go? We never let you go, and we will capture the other freaks too!" scoffed the man with a nasty grin.

"No, you won't. We wanted to leave Earth, but you interfered. That changed the situation profoundly!" contradicted Lilly.

"How so?" wondered the man mockingly.

"We were the hunted; now we are the hunters!" postulated Lilly.

"Hunters? We have you tied down to a chair! If your husband loves you even a little, he will do what we demand!" disagreed the man and laughed at her.

"He won't. But whatever you do, he will judge you fairly, even if you kill me because that's his character," noted Lilly and noted, "no, you don't have to worry about Dirk; it's the others who won't be so kind to you!"

"Who? The cat? What could that overgrown housecat possibly do to us?" snickered the man.

"This is what will happen: The AI will find you, then Dirk and Tigger will lead them here. They will kill some, but not you. You will stay alive and live to old age. But you will wish for death every single day, but that mercy will never come," elaborated Lilly chillingly and added, "they will make you watch as they destroy your organization, your colleagues, your friends, your family, and everything you hold dear. You will be in excruciating pain, mentally and physically, for a very, very long time."

"Ha!" bristled the man defiantly.

"Dirk, L, or Tigger do not believe in a divine reckoning. They will ensure that you get the punishment you deserve in this life!" concluded Lilly.

"Shut up, bitch!" yelled the man angrily, "and you better read our demands word for word or else!"

"Sure," said Lilly calmly.

Suddenly there was the sound of breaking glass coming from the small lavatory of the dwelling. The man turned away from her and drew his sidearm. The other armed men did the same and went to investigate the noise.

17. Pain!

When the group arrived at the dwelling, a white unmarked van was parked in front of it. Nari was sure that it was the vehicle of Lilly's abductors, and L confirmed as much. The house wasn't much more sizable than their old cabin and was probably once used for a similar purpose. There was one window in the front, but the curtains were drawn, and they couldn't see what was going on inside. Ngazetungue checked the greater surroundings while Tigger snuck up stealthily to the front door. Meanwhile, Angela scouted the back of the small house.

(Feeling of certainty) "Lilly inside. Five men inside, too," reported the big cat over the link.

"There is no door in the back and only a small window, not big enough for anyone to climb through," assessed Angela.

"OK, then we march right through the front door!" decided Dirk and started to move.

"Wait!" warned Garrett and advised, "if we barge in like that, they might hurt Lilly! Not to mention, we would be in a direct line of fire!"

"They might hurt her either way!" disagreed Mario and suggested, "better to bust down the door and surprise them before they can prepare for us!"

"I think I agree with Mario…," Dirk started saying, but suddenly Ngazetungue sent a warning through the link!

"About 30 soldiers are approaching on foot. They will be at your location in about 10 minutes!" reported the Namibian man.

"Everyone, please stay here and distract the soldiers, but be careful! I will go inside alone!" ordered Dirk and ran towards the front door.

"Like hell, you will!" grumbled Mario and followed Dirk swiftly.

At that moment, Angela busted the small window in the back with the butt of her rifle. The men inside were alerted by the breaking glass's noise, grabbed their weapons, and rushed to investigate what was happening in the back of the house.

Angela's diversion gave Dirk time to reach the front door unnoticed. He didn't bother with the door handle; instead, he used his foot to bust it open. He did it so forcefully that the whole door broke off the hinges and flew inside the dwelling. One of the armed men got hit in the head from behind by the debris. He went down and didn't get back up. Tigger was the first to enter the dwelling with lightning speed, even before Dirk could.

Several men trained their rifles on the big cat, but Tigger was much faster and eviscerated the closest target in a split second - guts and blood sprayed on the walls. Dirk and Mario were now also inside the building. Another man, who appeared to be in charge, was standing next to a chair. Lilly was sitting on it, her hands and feet tied up. The man pointed a gun at Lilly and raised one hand to stop the fighting. The remaining abductors kept their weapons aimed at Dirk, Mario, and Tigger but did not discharge them.

"Oh good, you are here. That was faster than expected!" sneered the man and then ordered: "Turn around, place your hands behind your back!"

"Let her go, and we might let you live, punk!" growled Mario and walked towards the man.

"She will die if you take another step!" presaged the man waving his pistol at Lilly, and Dirk quickly grabbed Mario's arm to hold him back.

"What do you want?" asked Dirk.

"Well, I want you and everyone in your freaky little group!" snickered the man and promised, "if you surrender, nobody gets hurt!"

(Feeling of suspicion) "Might not kill, but will hurt us!" cautioned Tigger over the link.

"What assurances can you give us?" questioned Dirk.

"Assurances? None!" replied the man coldly.

Then he glanced at the window, now free of the curtains since they had been torn off in the fight earlier. He was probably hoping that the soldiers would arrive soon.

"We will not surrender; just let her go!" declared Dirk.

Outwards, Dirk seemed calm, but the fear for Lilly's life almost paralyzed him on the inside.

"See? You didn't listen to me earlier," blurted Lilly and challenged, "go ahead, shoot me. Then you will find out that the rest of my prediction will come true, too!"

"Shut up!" screamed the man angrily, but Lilly's words seemed to have hit a nerve.

"I told him what you would do if he doesn't let me go…," explained Lilly, her words directed at Dirk now.

Suddenly, the man seemed undecided, almost a little nervous, as if he had sensed that this situation would never resolve to his liking.

Meanwhile, Tigger contemplated putting these men to sleep with his mental abilities, but that would take a few seconds because he would have to do it one target at a time. That was impractical because that delay would mean Lilly's death in this situation. Dirk noticed how Tigger's body tensed in preparation for a giant leap instead, and Mario slowly raised his pistol.

"Fuck it, they are just as valuable dead, and so are you!" shouted the man, pulled the trigger, and his two associates opened fire simultaneously.

The battle was over before it began. Mario had shot one man four times with his enhanced reflexes before the agent could even aim at them properly. He could still discharge his automatic rifle, bullets spraying the floor and wall, but nobody was hit. Dirk's lightning movement brought him within arm's length of the second guard. His fist connected solidly with the solar plexus and caved the ribcage inward, killing the man instantly. Tigger's mighty leap had knocked the leader down to the floor. But seemingly, Tigger didn't do anything else. The man was uninjured and perfectly still, only blinking his eyes as tears were flowing freely from them.

Dirk rushed to check on Lilly. The bullet had penetrated her left temple and killed her instantaneously. There was nothing he could do anymore! Dirk cradled her dead body and cried bitterly, oblivious to anything else. Mario quietly removed the restraints from Lilly's feet and hands. Then he checked on the leader, who was still supine on the floor, staring wide-eyed at the ceiling. Mario was very tempted to put a bullet right through those eyes, but he reconsidered.

"What did you do to him, Tigger?" he asked quietly.

(Feeling of satisfaction) "Will live, but cannot move! Can see, can hear, can think, can feel pain. Lots of pain!" asserted Tigger grimly.

"Will he snap out of it?" wondered Mario, concerned that the man might rejoin the fight.

(Feeling of cruelty) "Never!" answered Tigger, then turned around and left the dwelling.

18. Armed, dangerous, and naked?

Angela and Garrett didn't remain at the dwelling. They knew that something terrible had happened there, but time was short before the soldiers arrived at their location, so they moved quickly to intercept them.

"STOP!" shouted Angela at the group of soldiers running towards the little house.

The Sergeant signaled them to a halt. Many young soldiers ogled the pretty, naked woman with the automatic rifle standing in their path.

"Move out of the way; we are conducting a military exercise here!" yelled the Sergeant grumpily.

"Unlike yours, my rifle is not a training weapon, and I will use it!" warned Angela firmly, removing the safety, but just then, Garrett stepped out of the bushes to join her.

"Stand down, Sergeant, and don't let our appearance fool you. I'm Lieutenant Jackson; tell us what your orders are!" Garrett demanded to know.

The Sergeant was confused now but not too eager to get into an altercation with someone who outranked him.

"HQ redirected us to secure a dwelling two clicks from our last location," answered the Sergeant.

"I see. Come with us!" ordered Garrett.

Angela shouldered the rifle and turned around. Then the whole group started marching orderly to the little house. When they arrived, the Sergeant went inside but exited again almost right away.

"There are dead people in there, Lieutenant!" he addressed Garrett nervously.

"That's why you were redirected here, Sergeant. Collect the bodies, then lead us back to HQ!" affirmed Garrett.

"What happened here, Sir?" inquired Sergeant nervously.

"An unfortunate accident, but the details are classified. You and your men are under orders to keep quiet. You will be debriefed at HQ!" replied Garrett.

"Yes, Sir!" replied the Sergeant and saluted.

Garrett did the same, and then he looked for Dirk and the rest of the group. Dirk, Mario, and Tigger hid behind the house in the forest. When Angela and Garrett found them, Dirk still cradled Lilly's dead body in his arms.

"Dirk, the soldiers will return to their command base in a few minutes. Angela and I will go there with them. We will find whoever was responsible for this!" promised Garrett, wiping a tear from his face.

"I will go there myself!" countered Dirk quietly and gently put Lilly's body on the mossy forest floor.

"The soldiers have to transport all the dead people and that paralyzed agent. They will not move very quickly. Shadow us from the forest until we reach base!" suggested Angela, and Dirk just nodded silently.

"What should we do in the meantime?" asked Mario.

"Gather the group here, Mario. When I'm done with this, please take Lilly back to the farm!" instructed Dirk quietly.

(Feeling of concern) "Dirk, the farm is overrun with soldiers!" warned L.

"It won't be for long, but please keep an eye on it, L!" promised Dirk ominously.

19. General Sutton

Even before the troop of soldiers arrived at the encampment, Dirk and Tigger had found the command post. Two soldiers were guarding the entrance, but Tigger put to them sleep before he and Dirk entered. Several officers were inside, staring in disbelief at the naked man and the giant cat.

"Who is in charge?" asked Dirk firmly.

"Guards!" yelled one of the officers.

"Don't bother; they are sleeping. Don't bother resisting either; you would just get killed. Now, who is in charge here?" Dirk demanded to know.

An older man with four stars on the shoulders of his uniform walked up to him. Meanwhile, Tigger froze the other officers like he had done to Mario's driver, Pete, back at the cabin.

"I'm General Sutton!" answered the man sternly.

"You are responsible for the death of my wife. The agents are dead, too. Your soldiers will arrive momentarily with their bodies!" replied Dirk.

"Death of your wife?" muttered Sutton, confused.

"Yes, your operative killed her in cold blood. There will be consequences!" stated Dirk.

"I did not order...that damn fool!" cursed the General, suddenly remembering something.

"So, you know about this. Who is behind this operation?" inquired Dirk tersely.

"Classified! I get my orders from the Pentagon. Take it up with them! Now get out of here!" responded the General loudly.

"Wrong. You get your orders from me, and if you disobey, you won't have to worry about a Court Marshal!" corrected Dirk coldly and questioned, "now, I ask you one last time - who is behind this operation?"

Jim Sutton wasn't used to being ordered around by a naked man. He puffed out his chest, thinking of a pointed response to Dirk's ludicrous demands, but just then, his cell phone rang. He glanced at the table but didn't reach for the phone because he noticed how Tigger sized him up.

"Go ahead, answer it!" ordered Dirk, and the General took the phone.

66

"We have a problem, Rudy. The operation is compromised!" said Sutton urgently, but Dirk quickly reached for the phone and took it out of the General's hand.

"This is Dirk Hayes. Who is this?" questioned Dirk curtly.

"I'm Rudolf Garland! What have you done with Jim?" inquired a man on the other end.

"He is in my custody. Are you the one behind this operation?" inquired Dirk.

"We sponsored this military exercise at great expense! Your interference is illegal and unpatriotic!" shouted Garland into the phone.

"Spare me the nonsense. Your exercise was an attempt to capture us. You are responsible for the murder of my wife!" responded Dirk angrily.

"How unfortunate, but I'm sure we can compensate you generously if you surrender!" suggested Garland nonchalantly.

"I don't want your money, and I will not surrender. But I will find you and bring you to justice, Mr. Garland!" promised Dirk sternly.

"Whatever. Eventually, we will get you and your freaks!" bristled Garland callously and hung up.

"Was this exercise a cover-up to capture us?" asked Dirk pointedly after putting the phone back on the table.

"This military operation was approved by the Joint Chiefs of Staff. But I won't deny that we had other objectives as well...," replied Sutton evasively.

At that moment, Garrett and Angela entered the command tent. Two soldiers followed them, carrying the paralyzed agent. They cautiously laid him down on the ground, then Garrett ordered them to wait outside.

"What now?" asked Sutton, eying the man on the floor.

"Now, you will tell me who this man is!" insisted Dirk.

"I don't know; he's not one of mine!" answered Sutton and disclosed, "we were not expecting him when he showed up with his goons yesterday. He flashed some top-level security clearance and said he would be observing the exercise on behalf of the National Security Advisor. We called Langley, and it checked out. Garland might know more."

"But you sent soldiers to assist him!" countered Dirk.

"He radioed in about an hour ago and requested backup, but he didn't tell us why. We didn't have anyone in the surrounding area, but he insisted on immediate support, so we diverted these scouts to his location!" answered the General and shrugged his shoulders.

(Feeling of honesty) "True," confirmed Tigger.

"Any ideas?" asked Dirk over the link.

"He is not from Angela's and my old agency," replied Garrett mentally.

"CIA or DIA would be my guess!" added Angela.

"What did you do to him?" asked Sutton, concerned, unaware of the mental conversation.

"He will live, but he won't get better - ever!" replied Dirk sharply.

"And my staff?" questioned Sutton, looking over his shoulder at the men Tigger had frozen. They were still standing perfectly motionless; only their eyes were occasionally blinking.

"They will be fine, but they won't remember what happened here," explained Dirk, and then he demanded, "you will end this charade now and recall your troops. Then you will leave and tell the Pentagon, the National Security Advisor, and the President that I will have justice!"

"I cannot do that!" protested the General.

"You can unless you want to end up like this operative!" countered Dirk and pointed at the body on the ground.

"Fine! But I will have to use the comms...," conceded Sutton finally and gestured at the transmitter behind him.

"Go ahead, but I warn you - if you care for the lives of the men who serve under you, you will not order anything but a full withdrawal!" stated Dirk, and Sutton looked at him for a moment, then he nodded and switched on the comms.

"Sutton here! Operation Oregon has ended! Return to base and pack it up!" he spoke into the microphone.

20. Grief

After returning to the farm, they gathered in the spacious living room. Everyone expressed their grief differently: Angela was furious, Sven cried, Garrett was drinking, Yebin was stoic, Ngazetungue silent, Wendji said a prayer, Nancy was on the verge of a nervous breakdown, and Nari was inconsolable.

"Do what you must, and show no mercy! All of us will stand with you!" promised Mario quietly to Dirk, but Dirk just looked at him for a moment and nodded.

But it was L who was most troubled. The AI believed it was ultimately responsible for Lilly's death, which almost drove it insane. Dirk and Tigger sat down next to L's icosahedron. L's mental connection seemed fuzzy and distorted, as if the AI had difficulty staying focused. Dirk and Tigger had to talk to it for quite some time before it calmed down a little.

(Multitude of feelings) "Dirk, whatever you want to do, I will make it happen! It will go against all my programming, but I will destroy this world if you ask!" promised the AI grimly.

"Lilly wouldn't want that, L. She despised humanity, and she desperately wanted to leave the planet, but she didn't want to destroy it!" replied Dirk calmly, but he could relate to L's desire for vengeance all too well.

(Feeling of honesty) "Dirk right!" consented Tigger.

The AI was quiet for a while, but Dirk and Tigger could sense the inner turmoil. They waited patiently for L to regain its composure, and eventually, it calmed down a little.

(Feeling of anticipation) "What should we do now?" asked L finally.

"We will take control. We will reshape Earth and make it better for Lilly's sake! Then we will leave and never return!" answered Dirk profoundly.

(Feeling of agreement) "Yes," added Tigger.

(Feeling of uncertainty) "How can we do that?" wondered L.

"You will have to do most of the work. We need worldwide control over everything digital, from satellites to computers and cell phones!" remarked Dirk.

(Feeling of confidence) "That is easy, Dirk. Your electronic devices are primitive and almost unprotected. As we speak, I have already inserted myself in every crucial system on Earth!" reported the AI.

Dirk didn't reply for a moment. He reflected on the immensity of the situation. They had left Earth unharmed in his other memories and lived long, fulfilled lives on a strange but beautiful new world. He and Lilly had a son, and when Dirk's time was finally up, Lilly was still there and outlived him as it was meant to be. Yes, that's how it was supposed to happen, but now he was stuck in this unbelievable nightmare!

"Good! I will need a few hours to clear my head, and then we will start a new chapter for Earth!" announced Dirk finally, got up, took the stairs down to the basement, and closed the door behind him.

21. Shut up!

About two hours later, Dirk asked L to establish a conference call with the Speaker of the House, the Senate leader, the Chief Justice, and the President, but once the connection opened, Dirk didn't have a chance to say anything.

"You are an American! Ask not what your country can do for you; ask what you can do for your country!" stated the President and demanded, "give up, and I will consider pardoning your crimes!"

"John F. Kennedy. Like you, he was flawed, but unlike you, he was a good man!" replied Dirk harshly and observed, "my country murdered my wife; my country tried to kill my friends and me. My country wants to capture, imprison, and dissect us. My country wants to make us disappear forever, without trial and rights, but our only crime is that we are different. I believe you know what you can do with my citizenship, Mr. President!"

"That is outrageous!" bristled the President, but the other influential people looked more guilty than offended.

"We control every satellite in the sky, every cell tower, every broadcast, the entire Internet, stock markets, bank transactions, power grids, and nuclear weapons worldwide. We know every dirty deed the U.S. government has done in the last 50 years. We know everything the NSA, CIA, DIA, FBI, or other clandestine agencies have gathered. Perhaps of personal interest to you, we also have everything the IRS has on record!" elaborated Dirk and then continued, "no jet will fly, no ship will sail, no tank will roll unless we permit it. Any assassin you send after us will be treated like the agent who killed my wife. I assure you that it is a fate much worse than death!"

"The United States does not negotiate with terrorists!" countered the President brashly.

"One man's terrorist is another man's freedom fighter. Without terrorism against the British Crown, the United States wouldn't even exist today!" replied Dirk, and then contended, "we are not Jihadists with IEDs or Supremacists with simple assault rifles; we hold a scientific and technological edge that is equivalent to what you hold over a caveman. You will negotiate with us if you want to call it that. In reality, I will give you orders, and you will execute them promptly and properly!"

"We refuse!" yelled the President, and the Senate leader, the Speaker of the House, and the Chief Justice all nodded in agreement.

"If you refuse, America will go dark in one hour, and the stock markets reset to zero, which I imagine will be extremely painful for you. If you refuse again, we will make every dirty secret available to the public. Should you survive the lynch mobs that will undoubtedly come for all of you and refuse us a third time, we will find out how many missiles it will take to crack that bunker under the White House!" stated Dirk calmly, and then he asked, "are we clear?"

"You are just a little looser; you wouldn't dare!" spat the President insultingly.

"Shut up!" replied Dirk dismissively and repeated bluntly, "I will ask you one last time - are we clear?"

"What do you want?" asked the Speaker of the House, cutting off another tirade from the President.

"First and foremost, you will agree that our location is off-limits. If you violate that in any way, retribution will be swift and painful!" warned Dirk.

"We agree," said the Speaker of the House quickly, the Senate leader and Chief Justice seemed to concur, and the President glared balefully at them.

"Secondly, you agree that all our friends and families are off-limits. If you harass any of them in any way, we will do much worse to yours!" stated Dirk.

"We agree," replied the Speaker of House nervously, and the other people looked worried as well, but the President was strangely unconcerned.

"Lastly, you agree to have a daily conference call with me. The next call with be tomorrow at noon, Pacific time, and then I will have specific instructions for you!" continued Dirk.

"I play golf at that time!" protested the President loudly.

"I suggest that you reschedule. Otherwise, we will have to find a new President!" replied Dirk coldly.

"We agree!" confirmed the Speaker, ignoring the President's objections.

"Good. But I know you will try to test our resolve. Every time you do, our retaliation will increase by a magnitude. That would be all for now!" concluded Dirk and signaled L to cut the connection.

"Dirk, you told the President to shut up! You got the biggest balls of anyone I know!" cackled Mario and slapped Dirk on the back. Just for a moment, that brought a tiny smile to Dirk's face.

22. Rudolf Garland

Three months after Lilly had been killed in Oregon, Jens Koch was sitting at home, listening to the news on the radio while having a cup of tea with his breakfast. The U.S. government, widely considered conservative to the point of being reactionary, had suddenly started to make some puzzling humanitarian and environmental decisions. Jens couldn't help but think of Dirk Hayes. Last he knew, the American government had failed to capture the man and his group.

Now, Congress has passed strict new environmental laws and social reforms. The American President, who had never shown any empathy before, was suddenly giving the World Health Organization generous funding to fight a pandemic in Africa. Was it possible that Hayes was now pulling strings behind the curtain? Suddenly, Jens' cell phone rang. He didn't recognize the number, but he answered it anyway on a hunch.

"Jens, it's Rudolf Garland! You have to help me!" shouted Garland into the phone.

"Rudy, are you out of your mind to call me on this number?" countered Jens. He hadn't talked to Rudy since the botched operation to capture Dirk Hayes in the Bay Area, and their meeting on Mauritius was canceled shortly after that.

"I'm here in Germany, but I'm in real trouble!" disclosed Rudy nervously.

"You are considered a fugitive; why did you come here? Germany has an extradition treaty with the U.S.!" replied Jens befuddled.

"No choice. I hitched a ride on a cargo ship over the Atlantic. It took two weeks to get here!" elaborated Garland.

"Rudy, slow down and tell me what happened?" asked Jens. He had a bad feeling about this conservation already.

"We had the group cornered in Oregon. But somehow, they defeated the U.S. military, and apparently, Dirk Hayes' wife was killed in the process. He didn't take it very well. He took my General hostage and made him spill the beans; that's how he got to me!" explained Rudy.

"How did his wife get killed?" inquired Jens. He felt vindicated that he didn't pursue the capture of these people any further. The genetic samples he had obtained were already yielding patents and promising research, which would have to be enough.

"Lilly Hayes was captured by some gung-ho CIA guy, not even one on my payroll. The moron killed her when Dirk Hayes discovered where he was hiding. Because of that, we never got a chance to capture them, and I'm on the run now while Dirk Hayes is running America. But the idiot agent got what he deserved for his stupidity, still alive, but that cat did quite a number on his brain!" summarized Garland.

"That's… very bad!" replied Jens with some hesitation.

Garland had just confirmed what Jens had already suspected: Dirk Hayes was in charge now! The situation was a disaster, not just for Rudy, but by association, for him as well!

"Hayes called me and told me that he would get his revenge. I offered to compensate him generously for the loss, but he had none of that. At first, it was just noise. He publicly exposed my involvement in the destruction of his home and the assault on that cabin. There were some inquires by law enforcement, but nothing major!" added Garland.

"That doesn't sound too bad," replied Jens Koch, but he knew there would be more.

"Then Hayes found some hustler to go #metoo on me. The bitch claimed I sexually assaulted her when she was a minor. It might even be true, but I'm sure she wanted it, and I don't even remember when and where it happened. Again, inconvenient stuff, but I had to resign from my official company position," explained Garland.

"He killed your career?" asked Jens, not particularly sympathetic.

"No, not really. I lost my title, but not my influence. I was still working behind the scenes, as I always did," replied Rudy and continued unconcerned, "then he exposed some of my less savory business ventures, a few weapons deals with rogue nations, etc. It got me in front of a grand jury. They charged me with a few things, but I probably get a pardon before I get sentenced even if the charges stick!"

"So, that's not why you are a wanted man now?" wondered Jens.

"No. But then that son of bitch hit me where it hurts. He exposed my hidden accounts to the IRS and some insider trades to the SEC! Those are the things I cannot get away with!" complained Rudy loudly.

"Financial crimes are ones that get you, Rudy," assented Jens and asked, "but how did Dirk Hayes get all that dirt on you?"

"It's that blasted AI. It found the electronic evidence. Then it froze all my accounts even before the IRS seized them: Grand Cayman, Luxembourg, Panama, all gone! I'm broke except for the cash I'm carrying!" admitted Garland: "I got a tip that my arrest was imminent, so I had to get out of the States quickly and inconspicuously. Hence the long boat ride across the pond!"

"You have my sympathies, Rudy, but I cannot help you with any of that!" said Jens coldly. Instinctively, he thought he should distance himself from Garland as quickly and as far as possible.

"Jens, you were in on some of those stock trades, don't forget that!" shouted Rudy desperately.

"Are you threatening me now?" questioned Jens.

"No, but if I go down, everyone associated with me will become a target, too. Help me and help yourself, Jens!" advised Rudy.

"Rudy, you know me long enough to know that this angle isn't getting you anywhere. Make me a better offer, or I'll hang up now!" maintained Jens, annoyed by the extortion attempt.

"Alright, alright! Project Sanctuary!" blurted Rudy out. That got Jens' attention: he had heard rumors about Project Sanctuary, but all his inquiries yielded nothing. Whenever the topic arose, doors closed, and mouths stopped talking. If someone had any information on this, it would be Rudolf Garland.

"I'm listening," remarked Jens simply.

"Project Sanctuary is a huge prepper base for the ultimate elite, located in the arctic circle. It is so classified that even I don't know the exact location. But I know that billions of dollars, euros, rubles, yen, yuan, pound, riyal, bitcoin, and whatnot are pouring into this year after year since 2019. Jens, they have money, resources, and technology we can only dream about, and they develop more in special facilities all over the world, sometimes in secret, but often in plain sight," explained Garland excitedly.

"Ah, this is their safe haven for when it all goes to hell. Who is running this?" inquired Koch.

"We all know Earth won't last forever. Eventually, resources will run out, markets will vanish, and profits will dry up. Project Sanctuary is run by a syndicate of the richest, most powerful, and most influential people alive!" divulged Rudy.

"The Bilderbergers?" wondered Jens, referring to the well-known secret society of the elite.

"Yes, some of them are Bilderbergers, but there are also unaffiliated religious leaders, dictators, billionaires, industrialists, bankers, sheiks, and politicians!" confirmed Rudy.

"OK, that's intriguing information, but not a bargaining chip," stated Jens Koch dismissively.

"I was getting to that, Jens. You help me out, and I'll get you in on it!" promised Garland.

"Fine. Where are you right now, Rudy?" inquired Jens.

"Hamburg; St. Pauli, to be precise. I'm hiding in a brothel on the Reeperbahn!" admitted Rudy.

"Give me the address, and I'll send someone to help you get a new identity," replied Koch.

"I need some money, too!" added Rudy and gave Jens the address of his hideout.

"Yes, I'll take care of that, but don't call me on this number again!" warned Jens.

"I won't. Thanks, Jens!" acknowledged Garland.

"Don't mention it, Rudy. Goodbye!" said Jens and hung up.

He stared out of the window for a few minutes. The sky was gray, and it was raining today. How appropriate, thought Jens. The insider trading that Rudy had tried to use as leverage had been done carefully and inconspicuously; Jens had made sure of it. Even if Rudy were captured and confessed, it was unlikely that Jens would get indicted. However, if Jens was aiding and abetting a known international criminal, that was a more serious matter. But Jens wasn't concerned about that either: his own network in politics and judiciary could handle something minor like that.

In the corporate world, collateral damage happened, and that was unavoidable. Of course, the families of the injured or deceased would complain, threaten, and sue. Then, a long, drawn-out legal process would eventually yield a tax-deductible settlement. Every casualty and every family member came with a price tag, and in the end, all the plaintiffs and surviving victims would take the money and go away. But Jens knew instinctively that Dirk Hayes wasn't one of those. Hayes didn't care about money, he wanted justice, and he had the means to get it. Once upon a time, Jens would have admired a man of principles, but now

Dirk Hayes was very dangerous! As it was, Rudy had made a powerful enemy, and by association, Jens could become Dirk Hayes' next target.

Sure, what Rudy had given him on Project Sanctuary was very valuable. But Jens didn't need Rudy's help to get on the inside because this top-secret information itself was enough leverage to get a foot in the door. Since these people were the world's most powerful, Jens would have to use it cautiously, but it would be enough; he was sure of it. Rudy had become expendable, and Jens needed to cut the ties now. He quickly picked up the phone again and called his assistant.

"Hello, Astrid! Please connect me to Kriminaldirektor Horst Melzer, BKA. I have the location of an international fugitive!" said Jens, and then he added, "oh, and please have a new phone for me when I get to the office later!"

23. Jens Koch

After his capture in Hamburg, Germany extradited Rudolf Garland to the U.S. within days. At the pre-trial hearing, the judge denied bail because Garland was considered a flight risk. He was placed in a maximum-security prison to await trial. But there would be no trial.

A few days later, Garland was found dead, dangling from a power cord in his cell. When it happened, there were no witnesses: the guards on duty were on a smoke break, the video surveillance cameras were mysteriously malfunctioning, and the prisoner in the neighboring cell had been moved to solitary only a few hours earlier. The subsequent coroner's examination found inconsistencies with a suicide, but not enough to rule it out.

Despite everything Garland had done to him, Dirk was distraught with this outcome because he wanted justice, not vengeance. Not for a minute did he believe this to be a suicide, and he vowed to find the people behind Garland's murder.

But every investigation led to a dead end. A visiting attorney accidentally left the power cord in Garland's cell, and the prisoner next door was released from solitary and paroled a few days later. Before Dirk could question the man, he was killed almost immediately after regaining his freedom in what was labeled a gang-related shooting. The guards apologized for their tardiness, but they swore that they had been on the same 5-minute smoke break every day for the last few years, and even Tigger's ability to detect lies couldn't disprove that. L thoroughly examined the malfunctioning surveillance equipment and found traces of a malicious program, but who planted it and when would remain a mystery forever.

There was only one lead left to investigate: the man who had reported Rudolf Garland to the police - Jens Koch. Dirk knew that Koch had collaborated with Garland to capture the group. He also knew that this German was behind the takeover of Zyrtec. Perhaps Koch was tying up loose ends with the murder of Garland? But that didn't make much sense because it would have been much easier to kill Garland in a whorehouse in Hamburg than in a maximum-security prison in the United States. Dirk decided it was time to give Jens Koch a call.

"Mister Hayes. I was expecting your call," said Jens cordially when he answered the phone.

"Good, then you know why I'm calling, and I can keep this brief. I know about your association with Rudolf Garland. I suspect that you assisted and collaborated with him. That will have consequences!" stated Dirk firmly.

78

"I know Rudolf Garland, and that's no secret. But I didn't collaborate with him. I turned him in to the authorities, and I'm sure you have the means to verify that," replied Jens defensively.

"I do, and I have. That's why you are still alive and free," replied Dirk and then inquired, "did you have Rudolf Garland killed?"

"No, I did not, I swear it!" replied Jens vehemently.

While Jens felt ambiguous about Rudy's death, he knew that someone like Dirk Hayes would never appreciate vigilante justice.

"I see," replied Dirk, unconvinced, and then noted, "but I know that your company bought and closed down Zyrtec just to find out about us."

"I don't deny that, Mr. Hayes. We saw a great investment opportunity, but we did not want to capture or murder you. We simply wanted to make a very lucrative offer to study your amazing biology!" countered Jens and added, "that offer is still on the table if you are interested?"

"I'm not. Tell me about your connection with Garland, and don't lie because, as you said earlier, I have the means to verify what you say!" warned Dirk brashly.

"I knew him for about a dozen years, and we did a few business ventures together. We weren't exactly friends, but we have met privately on a few occasions. Garland wanted to capture your group, and he offered me access to biological samples and other research materials," answered Jens truthfully.

"Did you accept his offer?" questioned Dirk.

"Yes, I did. However, after the failure at your cabin in the Bay Area, I advised him to stop pursuing you, but Garland was determined to hunt you down," disclosed Jens, and then he emphasized: "In no way did I participate in what happened in Oregon!"

"That remains to be seen, Herr Koch!" replied Dirk sharply.

"Mr. Hayes, I know you believe otherwise, but I'm not your enemy, just a businessman!" declared Jens and then added cryptically, "your real enemies are somewhere else."

"Enlighten me!" demanded Dirk curtly.

"Have you heard of Project Sanctuary?" asked Jens.

Jens didn't want to divulge this, but Dirk Hayes was too dangerous to have as an enemy, likely even more threatening than the elite behind that project.

"I have not," responded Dirk.

"Project Sanctuary is a final refuge for the most powerful of humanity when the end of days arrives. It is a multi-billion-euro project, located in the arctic circle, most likely in Greenland," explained Jens.

"And why would that matter to me?" asked Dirk impatiently.

"Because Rudolf Garland worked for them!" blurted Jens.

Jens knew this was mainly speculation, but at least one rang true. He didn't feel like he had a choice here: without Dirk Hayes, Jens would have gladly joined Project Sanctuary, either for the profits or for a chance to weather the apocalypse or both. But now, his immediate survival outweighed all of that.

"Is that true?" questioned Dirk.

Perhaps this explained why someone murdered Garland in his cell? The influential people behind that secret endeavor might have been concerned that he could expose them at a public trial. It wouldn't have been the first time something like that had happened.

"Yes, he told me so himself just before I turned him in!" answered Jens and added, "but simply relaying this information to you will almost certainly get me killed!"

"That would be unfortunate for you, but I don't care," remarked Dirk coldly and inquired, "how do I get in touch with Project Sanctuary?"

"I have a name for you, but I want assurances!" requested Jens.

"What do you want?" Dirk demanded to know.

"Two things: one, we are on good terms now, and two, you won't divulge who gave you the information!" contended Jens Koch.

"Good terms? I don't think so. But if you told me the truth, I won't prosecute or kill you!" answered Dirk and assumed, "as for your second condition - you must be afraid of these people, aren't you?"

"Slightly less terrified than I am of you, Mr. Hayes!" admitted Jens and sighed.

"Good, stay terrified! But I will keep your involvement to myself unless you betray me," replied Dirk.

If this influential man was so fearful, it was reasonably sure that Project Sanctuary was behind Garland's untimely demise.

"Thank you, Mr. Hayes," responded Jens and added, "the only person I know, other than Garland, who is involved with Project Sanctuary, is a wealthy British aristocrat who currently resides in Singapore, Lord Jonathan Raleigh!"

"Are you involved, too?" questioned Dirk.

"Garland told me about this project in exchange for my help to keep him hidden from you and the authorities," maintained Jens and admitted, "after that, I did some inquires on my own, and that's how I found out about Lord Raleigh and the location in Greenland. If it were not for this conversation, yes, I would get involved with the endeavor!"

"Honesty. I guess you have read my profile," observed Dirk, and then he emphasized, "stay clear of Project Sanctuary, Herr Koch. It won't be a sanctuary from me!"

"Mr. Hayes, what are your plans for the future, if I may ask? My sources tell me that the American government is just a puppet show now, and you are making the real decisions behind the curtain. Is that what you have planned for the whole world?" inquired Jens.

"There will be a New World Order, and this time it won't just be a crazy conspiracy theory," answered Dirk.

He was astonished that Koch had quickly recognized Dirk's role in the American government. The man was well connected.

"One government for the whole planet? Will you maintain a free market economy? Will we be able to do business?" questioned Jens.

"Capitalism isn't my first choice, but it will have to do. I do not mind an honest profit, but I strongly object to excessive greed!" stated Dirk and presaged, "there will be one government for all. Life will be better for the vast majority of all people, but not for everyone, Herr Koch!"

"I will adapt, and I support your plans, Mr. Hayes," promised Jens quickly, and he meant it.

"That surprises me!" admitted Dirk and wondered if he could have been wrong about this man.

"As a multinational corporation, we are moving products and money all over the planet. To do business on such a scale, we must obey each nation's labor, contract, environmental, immigration, and tax laws. We must follow their building codes, product safety regulations, and advertising rules. We have to submit to various customs regulations, pay many tariffs, and sometimes even bribes," conveyed Jens and paused for a moment to collect his thoughts.

"Then there is that mess with the different stock markets and currency exchanges and all those pesky wars that disrupt our supply lines and drive insurance premiums sky-high. And finally, we have to make costly choices: if we do business in one market, we often cannot do business in another because of the various sanctions that nations love to impose on each other!" explained Jens and claimed, "one government will make everything much easier, faster and cheaper for us, and even for our customers. Most commerce will support you aside from the weapons industry!"

"That's an interesting take!" acknowledged Dirk, surprised to receive good news from an unexpected source.

"I really believe that you will make Earth a better place, Mr. Hayes, and I'm not just saying that because I fear for my life," opined Jens, but then he predicted, "however, the world will still hate you, although I suspect you already know that."

"Perhaps," conceded Dirk, and he had to admit that Jens Koch was intelligent.

"We are not that different. Once upon a time, I wanted to change the system, but I realized that I couldn't. So, I made the system work for me instead," disclosed Jens Koch honestly and added, "but you have the means to change everything fundamentally, and I envy that power!"

"With great power comes great responsibility!" replied Dirk.

"Yes, I have read your profile. You are a man of principles and integrity; you are well-suited for that responsibility," responded Jens and implored, "but remember, an overwhelming majority of the world's population does not understand reason, only force. You will have to force them, and they will hate you for it, even if their lives improve greatly as a result."

"So, you would use that power just for yourself?" questioned Dirk bluntly.

"…and a select few others, yes. I would use it to make a sanctuary of my own here on Earth, or maybe on another planet if that's possible. Either way, I would leave humankind to its own devices, they are beyond hope and redemption, and I would never look back!" elaborated Jens.

"Leaving here was our intention until your associate changed the plans drastically with the murder of my wife!" contended Dirk sharply, but he felt his anger at this man waning.

"That would change my plans as well. We are not that different, Mr. Hayes. As I said earlier, I envy your power, but not the decisions you will have to make if you want to reshape Earth!" responded Koch.

"You made the old system work for you. You won't find it so easy to make me work for you!" warned Dirk.

"I won't even try that. I'm gay, but I'm also wealthy and influential, and even the most conservative or religious person will treat me with respect now!" answered Jens, but then he hesitated because what Jens would say next, he had never admitted to anyone before: "Sure, behind my back, some still call me a faggot or worse, but never to my face anymore. I made the system work for me to have equality and dignity, Mr. Hayes. Was that so wrong?"

"You will live, Herr Koch, as long as you keep our bargain!" promised Dirk in German after a long pause.

"Good luck, Mr. Hayes. For what it's worth, I regret what happened to you," answered Jens also in German, but Dirk didn't respond and just cut the line.

After this conversation, Dirk knew that he couldn't hate this German man as much as he would have liked.

24. Into the Open

After the conversation with Jens Koch, Dirk dropped the investigation of Garland's murder. It was unlikely that he would discover who exactly gave the order and executed it, but he was reasonably sure that Project Sanctuary was behind it all. A time would come when he had to deal with this cabal, but first, he had to fix Earth!

Dirk stepped out from the shadows and addressed the entire planet. L ensured that every TV and radio station, every computer, and cell phone would air or display his message in every conceivable language spoken by humans. The announcement was short, just 15 minutes, but it outlined everything Dirk had planned for the future. L estimated that Dirk's words had been heard or read by at least six billion people on the planet. But that was not all. After the message, Tigger said a few mental words too, and absolutely all humans on Earth heard them loud and clear in their minds!

(Feeling of change) "Live, love, learn, be kind, be better!" emphasized the big cat.

Then Dirk conferred openly with all world leaders. Many refused after he outlined his plans to end all nations in favor of a unified federal Earth government. As he had done with the U.S. government, Dirk firmly emphasized their technological superiority and the consequences of their refusal. Some nations agreed swiftly, some grudgingly, and some remained defiant. But after they went dark for a few days, most relented. However, a handful of the most oppressive regimes did not. In response, L released all their dirty secrets to their people, and the effect did not disappoint. Bereft of the means to suppress the rioting population, many leaders found themselves figuratively and literally at the end of a rope.

Only the North Korean regime did not budge, even after L had exposed all the heinous deeds of this hereditary autocracy. Dirk wanted to give it more time, but Angela, Garrett, and especially Mario insisted that a show of force was needed. Reluctantly, Dirk agreed. It was the first time since 1945 that a nuclear weapon was used in war. But the aftermath almost justified the gruesome deed: with the North Korean dictator vanquished, a joyful, heartwarming unification with South Korea swiftly followed.

Nationalism was finally dead, but it had not gone quietly. Dirk took solace because compared to the two World Wars sparked by Nationalism, the loss of lives had been minuscule. Dirk dissolved all nations and removed all borders, but many former countries kept their names as provinces of the Republic of Earth. A few new sections were established to give oppressed minorities, such as Kurds, Tibetans, and Palestinians, a place to call home. A governor would lead each province, and the governors had considerable powers. But the ultimate authority would remain with the federal government, and at least for now, that would be Dirk and his group.

Dirk appointed many new governors and kept only a few of the old leaders of the former nations. Tigger's ability to detect deceit was instrumental in ferreting out the very few honest ones from the bulk of selfish, greedy liars. Dirk didn't bother with the latter for long but simply replaced the scoundrels with honorable men and women Tigger had vetted beforehand.

At first, Dirk thought that the United Nations could become the governing body of the world. But he gave up on that very quickly, and even Sven, who had championed that idea, had to agree: the representatives at the U.N. were appointed by their respective governments, not elected by their countries' population. Many were simply obeying strongmen and totalitarian regimes, not the people's will that they were supposed to represent. So, Dirk and his small group kept their own counsel, but Dirk always insisted that this autocratic rule must end someday.

Next, Dirk abolished the influence of organized religion on the governments. Laws based on religious dogma were rigorously removed from the books worldwide. Dirk never restricted religious freedom, but when a religious belief violated secular law, that freedom ended abruptly now. Also, no longer were religious organizations exempt from taxation, nor were they allowed to promote discrimination in any form, regardless of what their clergymen or sacred texts preached. But personal freedom was largely left unrestricted, and in fact, much of humanity experienced it for the first time. Although there were a few exceptions: activities that recklessly endangered the lives of others were preemptively prohibited.

Even with Earth unified under one rule, there was still diplomacy to be done. However, it wasn't done in backrooms anymore, but for the world to see. Surprisingly, it was perhaps the most significant shock for the ruling classes all over the planet. For centuries, they were used to negotiating in secret and always at someone else's expense. Treaties were considered temporary at best until they could be violated or discarded for something more advantageous. Since the dawn of civilization, deceit, bribery, and opportunism have been the driving forces of diplomacy. Now, all agreements had to be honored in word and spirit, and the benefits and sacrifices were shared equally between the contracting parties.

85

The world's militaries became the greatest humanitarian force ever assembled. No longer needed for warfare, their equipment and workforce were used to build infrastructure on an unprecedented scale. They responded admirably to natural disasters and other calamities, kept order and peace, diligently cleaned up environmental pollution, and swiftly and efficiently distributed aid and resources to the neediest. For Dirk, perhaps the most pleasant surprise was that the militaries relished their new responsibilities - saving lives proved more rewarding than ending them!

But Dirk knew that humanity needed education, perhaps even more than food and shelter. He built schools, adult schools, and universities on every continent, in every former country, and he made sure that students were attending them. Teachers, often underappreciated in the past, were now lauded and compensated fairly for their efforts. L even created a global education system online, from kindergarten to graduate and professional classes, and in about 200 different languages. It was completely free and accessible by cellphone or wireless connection from almost everywhere on the planet.

Then Dirk implemented a justice system that strictly adhered to secular laws and complete equality. Gone were the days when skin color and wallet size determined the defendant's fate. Arrests, charges, trial, sentencing, and imprisonment were no longer affected by the accused's social or economic status. Perhaps for the first time, justice was truly blind!

Incarceration was also overhauled, and one of the most significant changes was the complete abolishment of privately operated prisons: the convicted owed a debt to society, not to some private corporation. Moreover, the prisons now focused not only on punishment but also on rehabilitation. A prisoner who had served his sentence would be reintegrated into society, not left without options, and forced into more crimes because the system had neglected to prepare and enable him to resume an everyday life outside.

A related change was the introduction of criminal liability for corporations. After a few high-level executives were convicted of fraud, criminal negligence, and even manslaughter, advertisements became truthful at last, and the safety and quality of products worldwide dramatically improved.

Revamping the financial system was another important milestone. The 21-century stock exchanges, which had operated somewhere between voodoo, fraud, and high-stakes gambling, were scaled back to their original purpose: to allow companies to raise money to expand their operations and develop new products by selling shares of ownership to interested investors. As the company grew, its value would increase over time, and the shareholders would profit from their initial investment.

Similarly, the banking system was brought back in line with what it was designed for: customers could store their wealth safely with a bank, and the bank would use the money to grant loans and mortgages at a reasonable interest rate to other customers in return. Gone were split mortgages, negative interest, the flurry of unreasonable fees, and other financial abominations designed to defraud customers and enrich executives with the help of loopholes in the laws.

Also, tax laws became much more uniform and comprehensible. Tax shelters like the Caiman Islands, Switzerland, or cyberspace, stopped existing. The total wealth now determined the tax rate: the wealthier, the more taxation, and corporations were taxed just like private citizens. Tax audits were now only based on merit and no longer more likely to target the poor, as had been often the case in capitalist nations like the United States. Now, the average person could file a tax return within an hour and without costly professional help.

The changes were positive and generally appreciated by the masses, but the implementation was not instantaneous - there was time enough for Dirk's enemies to hatch plans for his demise.

25. Assassins

As Dirk had predicted, many former nations tested his resolve. Of course, any assassination attempt that involved advanced technology was doomed to fail immediately. L was omnipresent, and anything with a microprocessor couldn't even come close.

A particularly bizarre attempt was made with a World War One biplane from a museum. It had no electronics, just a combustion engine and a simple bomb that would explode on impact. However, the plane was so loud and slow that the group heard it approach the farmhouse minutes before it arrived. Angela simply sliced it in half with the red beam from the icosahedron, and it crashed and detonated somewhere in the forest, a good mile away. From the same era as the biplane came an artillery shell filled with mustard gas only a few days later. It landed in a wheat field nearby, but it never exploded at all.

Another try involved honest-to-goodness ninjas! Surprisingly, they indeed existed, and someone hired them to kill Dirk. But sharp swords and martial arts were no match for a genetically enhanced cat the size of a jaguar. Tigger was very entertained for a few hours, hunting and killing the lot of them.

One particularly nasty attempt claimed an innocent life: Mario had ordered a pizza from a nearby town. But unbeknownst to the delivery man, the box had been laced with VX by some operative beforehand. The man died just moments after arriving at the gate to the property where Angela had her checkpoint.

And so, it went on and on - snipers, drones, missiles, plutonium, anthrax, napalm, several suicide bombers, and even sound waves were used. None of it worked, none of it came even close, but the response to assassination attempts was always the same: either L would find the evidence, or Tigger would extract it from the minds of the would-be assassins. Then Dirk would order a surgical strike anywhere in the world and eliminate the guilty parties.

But one assassination effort was almost successful! Disguised as a letter carrier, a young woman arrived at Angela's checkpoint. She was thoroughly scanned and patted down, but no weapons were found. Garrett questioned her about her business, and she said that she had a personal letter for Dirk Hayes from his sister-in-law Rose Cheng. Garrett examined the letter and found it to be genuine. Escorted by Ngazetungue, she made it all the way to the farmhouse's front door.

But when Dirk opened the door, he recognized the woman right away. She was none other than Anna Volkova, the same one who almost killed him on Aureus. But just as it happened on Aureus, Anna would fail again. She handed the letter to Dirk, then quickly pulled a long, ceramic pin out of her hair and tried to stab him. But Dirk was prepared, and so was Tigger. The night prior, L had relayed a mysterious text message to Dirk - Don't accept the letter! Dirk took it very seriously because he instinctively knew from his alternate memories who had sent it. Dirk jumped backward with his superior reflexes before the pin could reach his chest, then Tigger froze Anna in place and ignited her very soul, just as he had done on Aureus. But this time, Anna would survive because Lydda was not with them. However, Tigger's mental torment made Anna wish that she hadn't.

The letter was really from Rose. Anna had intercepted and murdered the real postal worker on the way to the farm. Rose had used old-fashioned mail to avoid electronic detection, but she had been watched when she dropped the envelope in the mailbox. The message was just a short response to Dirk's invitation. It confirmed that Rose would arrive in Oregon next Sunday by car.

During these months, Dirk had slowly regained more of his alternate memories. What had started as just a feeling that something was terribly wrong was now becoming a certainty. Dirk could recall enough about Aureus and his life there to know that he shouldn't be here and Lilly should have never died. Dirk searched for a rational explanation repeatedly, but there was none.

Dirk often wondered if his friends had similar memories. Sometimes it seemed as if they did, but he would not ask them: right now, they depended on his guidance! If they didn't have these memories, it would erode their confidence in his ability to lead them and perhaps even in his sanity. Dirk felt trapped, and he was deeply upset about this situation, but he could do nothing!

26. Backlash

The world became a better place, but eventually, all of Dirk's good intentions seemed to backfire. His biggest failures as a dictator were his compassion and tolerance. He did not persecute those who opposed him, and there were many! Dirk had no secret police, no public executions, no oppressive laws or restrictions, and no militarized supporters. Instead of silencing, imprisoning, or assassinating his opponents, Dirk permitted them to speak out freely against him.

Many honest officials quickly resigned because it became too hard and dangerous to resist the pressure of lobbies or threats of influential individuals. Indeed, some of those who didn't quit were found dead under mysterious circumstances, while others caved under the onslaught of corruption.

The press was now uncensored everywhere, but it was sharply divided. The traditional media mainly reported what was happening, and they evaluated Dirk's efforts more or less fairly. But the popularity of traditional media has been declining since the early 2000s. People didn't want facts or truths; they wanted their beliefs reinforced and packaged in sensationalist ways, preferably in very abbreviated form, such as Twitter. And so, the traditional media had been replaced by propaganda outlets, some of which condemned Dirk as the devil incarnate, while others lauded him as the new messiah. Dirk was disgusted by both, but he kept his promise to Wendji not to interfere with journalism.

Many new schools were boycotted by parents who feared that their children would be indoctrinated with something they rejected. What they disagreed with significantly varied by location - sometimes it was religiously motivated, sometimes based on ideology, race, nationality, class, and even gender. Although Dirk's regime never influenced the curriculums, the new and old universities were often marred by violent student protests against Dirk's autocratic rule. In some ways, Dirk felt sympathetic: he would have opposed a dictatorship, too, but of course, it was detrimental to his goal of providing everyone with a quality education.

Then there were widespread conspiracy theories that the newly built hospitals implanted alien embryos in unsuspecting women seeking disease or injury treatment. Medicine shipments were refused because another conspiracy theory claimed that the antibiotic pills, painkillers, and vaccinations turned people into golden-skinned, cat-eyed freaks. Countless people worldwide died of diseases and injuries as a result. Some conspiracy theories even branded harmless infrastructure projects, such as roads, railways, ports, and airports, as invasion routes for aliens that would soon arrive on Earth to enslave them all.

Consequently, many vital projects were never finished, and aid never reached those who needed it most.

Dirk had emphasized his desire to protect the environment from the onset, but even those efforts were met with fierce defiance. Water and air were polluted worse than before, endangered species were senselessly slaughtered, and entire habitats were burnt down. His enemies knew that Dirk cared greatly, so they believed these wanton acts would hurt him. But much of the destruction, as it had been before Dirk came to power, was also fueled by simple greed. Natural resources were there to be exploited for profit, and nothing had changed in that respect.

When Dirk removed the most rigid, oppressive laws and restrictions, he expected the people to use that freedom in respectful, sensible ways. But the masses on Earth were not enlightened: they were uneducated, uncivilized, savage even! Personal freedom was not kept in check by personal responsibility because the concept of accountability was unknown to them. Too many believed that this new freedom should be exercised selfishly to abuse, oppress, intimidate, endanger, or hurt others. And so, they spewed hate speech and religious intolerance, rejected public safety measures, threatened others with deadly weapons, and endangered and harmed the public in a myriad of old and new ways, all under the pretense of exercising their freedom!

Then, there were acts of terrorism motivated by many irrational motives, fueled and instigated by demagogues worldwide. Not a day went by without some kind of violence - a crashed airplane, a sunken ship, a derailed train, a power outage caused by hackers, a car bomb in a marketplace, a shooter at a concert or a sporting event, a poison gas attack in a subway, and so on. The mayhem never seemed to stop.

But the worst was triggered by a deep-fake video on social media: it showed Dirk eating the body of an obese child. It was as grotesque as it was certifiably false, but countless naïve people believed it nonetheless - the fairytale of Hansel and Gretel, and Dirk had become Grimm's evil witch! From then on, numerous food shipments were destroyed rather than eaten. Many insisted that starvation would be preferable to being fattened up and devoured by aliens. Millions starved to death because of this hoax alone.

Dirk realized then that his absolute power was no match for humanity's absolute ignorance!

27. How to be a Leader

Dirk was sitting in a small room on the upper level of the farmhouse. It was a guest bedroom, but he had converted it into a makeshift office. Dirk had just finished compiling a to-do list for tomorrow's group meeting when Mario knocked on the doorframe because the door was already open.

"Dirk, I gotta talk to you if you got a minute?" he asked.

"What's up, Mario?" inquired Dirk tiredly. It has been another long bad day for him and Earth.

"Do you ever feel that this is not real?" wondered Mario and sat down by the desk next to Dirk.

"Sometimes…," replied Dirk slowly. Did Mario sense that something was wrong with this reality?

"I know this sounds weird, but I think this is a bad dream! We are not supposed to be here, and Lilly isn't supposed to be dead!" elaborated Mario and studied one of the many tattoos on his arm.

"We lived on another planet. Nancy was your wife, and your daughter's name was Beatrice," responded Dirk. Somehow, Mario wasn't shocked to hear that.

"So, you know," he simply responded.

"I do. But how did you get those memories, Mario?" wondered Dirk.

"It just came to me a few days after they killed Lilly. I didn't want to talk about it because it's crazy!" said Mario exasperatedly.

"Yes, it is!" admitted Dirk, and then he asked, "do the others have these memories, too?"

"Nancy does, but she thinks it's just her mental condition. I don't know about the others…," answered Mario and shook his head slightly.

"Thanks for telling me this, Mario. I thought I was going insane! It's good to know that I'm not alone, but it changes very little," observed Dirk with a sad smile.

"Yeah, we are stuck here, and we have to make the best out of that!" concurred Mario, and then he declared: "I wanted to talk to you because you are doing it all wrong!"

"Obviously - on both accounts. What do you suggest?" inquired Dirk curiously.

"I remember how you lead us on Aureus. You treated everyone the same: the smart ones, the dumb ones, the ones loyal to you, the ones bitching at you, the original settlers, the newcomers, your wives, your children, and your Transformation Day dates. There was no favoritism whatsoever, and you claimed no privileges. The rules applied to everyone equally, even to you, especially you. You didn't care if we kissed up or complained, only about our commitment to Aureus. Competence and merit mattered, nothing else!" summarized Mario.

"Thanks, I suppose!" interjected Dirk and smiled a little.

"You listened to the stupid advice that you rejected. You politely reasoned with the ones that argued with you. You tried to see it from their point of view, and often, you compromised with them in the end," continued Mario.

"I always thought that was for the best, was it not?" wondered Dirk.

"On Aureus it was, but this ain't Aureus! Here, people like favoritism, nepotism, and corruption. Empathy, politeness, reason, and compromises are just seen as weakness!" countered Mario and explained, "a dictator is just like the head of a crime syndicate! The boss expects personal loyalty and punishes disloyalty harshly. He demands absolute devotion, but he is not loyal to anyone, and when it suits him, he will throw them all under the bus. The boss encourages his people to please him, then plays his cronies against each other and exploits their desire to be in his favor. Their feelings don't matter, only his, and rules only apply to others, never to him."

"I know, but I wish it weren't so," interjected Dirk, and Mario just nodded in response.

"The boss mistrusts everybody; he keeps taps on his underlings because they are always a potential threat to his rule. He doesn't permit dissent; his word is never to be questioned. He is the strongest, smartest, greatest, and nobody should dare to say otherwise. He never admits to being wrong. He will always blame others and find scapegoats for his failures. The boss might take advice, but he will claim that it was his idea alone if it works. He doesn't thank people for a well-done job; he expects it! Finally, when the boss succeeds, he embellishes, gloats, and belittles the losers all day long. That's how it's done, Dirk!" concluded Mario.

"Who would ever want to follow such a man?" wondered Dirk, confused.

"Lots of people! They might not admit it, but they like it that way - and if they ever become the boss, they will do exactly the same crap!" laughed Mario bitterly.

93

"I don't think I can do that, Mario…," confessed Dirk.

"I remember how you cringed whenever I called you 'Boss' on Aureus! Great fun to watch!" chuckled Mario and added more seriously, "I know how hard this is for you."

"Yes," admitted Dirk.

"But I could do it, and I have, and until I met you, I never thought twice about it!" stated Mario, and then he advised, "just be the crime boss, be the ruthless dictator. Be selfish and unpredictable, vulgar, play favorites, play them against each other, and make them fear you. Lie, cheat, gloat, blame, extort, steal, murder, and be the biggest asshole you can be. Embrace everything that you reject right now, Dirk. It will work. I'm sure!"

"I've known you only for a few months, but I also knew you for a lifetime. You are not a savage. You were a good father, a good husband, a great friend, and an immense asset to Aureus. You are not that man, Mario!" stated Dirk firmly, and then he asked quietly, "how can you pretend otherwise?"

"I don't know; I just do it. It gets a little easier every time until… until there is nothing good left in you, and you have become that asshole!" answered Mario with a sigh and then suggested, "I do it for you, Dirk. You be the face, and I'll be the muscle! Remember, this is not real, just some fucked up nightmare!"

"It is a nightmare, but one that will never end!" assented Dirk, and then he said somberly, "thank you, Mario, and I hope it will never come to that, but I fear that it might!"

"When you are ready, I'll be ready!" promised Mario, and he added with regret, "but I wish we were back on Aureus."

"Me too, Mario, me too!" agreed Dirk and sighed heavily.

28. Dictatorship

A few days later, a violent rebellion in the southern U.S. erupted. It wasn't clear what the heavily armed rebels were fighting for or against, perhaps just anarchy for anarchy's sake, but the death toll mounted in the thousands after only one day. Dirk called for an emergency meeting late that evening. Angela briefed them on the situation, and the details were grim.

"Dirk, if we want to keep the peace, we need better surveillance!" advised Garrett firmly.

"We also need some kind of police force that can react quickly to any disturbances," added Angela.

"We should call in the military and squash this before it spreads!" proposed Garrett in response.

"I have established mining and production facilities in the asteroid belt. Now I can produce satellites and drones. I have designs ready for drones that could patrol hostile areas. We could also interface with millions of cameras all over the planet, and we could even use your Internet, your television, and phone services for that purpose!" suggested L.

(Feeling of disdain) "Tigger could look at minds, find bad people!" promised Tigger.

"We would become Big Brother!" replied Dirk and sighed.

"I know, Dirk. But we tried reason and kindness, and let's face it - we failed. Force and fear are the only alternatives left!" reasoned Angela sadly.

"They spread lies about us every day, and the people believe them! It has to stop!" demanded Nancy forcefully, but then she mumbled, "I want to go away from here. I want to be on Aureus!"

That stopped the conversation abruptly, and Dirk noticed that several people had overheard Nancy's comment. He studied their faces carefully; he was sure that Ngazetungue and Garrett had the memories, and probably Angela. The others might as well, but they were hiding it better, but everyone had some kind of reaction, except for Tigger! Dirk knew that the cat had heard Nancy's words, but strangely, he didn't react. He continued to lick his paw as if nothing had happened. Nobody said anything for a good while. Finally, Nancy opened a small bottle of pills that Lilly had given to her back at the cabin. She quickly swallowed a couple of them and then flashed an apologetic little smile to the group.

"Just do it, Dirk. The people will hate you either way!" stated Mario and broke the silence.

"Some hate me, but some don't!" countered Dirk, but his heart wasn't in it.

"Yeah, use the ones who like you to fight those who don't!" Mario pressed on.

"So far, we killed only when it was unavoidable, and in that sense, every death was self-defense. Mario, if I allowed a civil war, I would have blood on my hands. I want to teach humanity and unify it, not have it tear itself apart!" contradicted Dirk with a sigh.

"But I don't think most of them want to learn, Dirk!" contradicted Ngazetungue thoughtfully.

(Feeling of certainty) "Tigger could teach them. All of them!" said Tigger confidently.

"I suspect that you could, Buddy. But they would just be our puppets. I want them to understand out of their own volition, not because we altered their minds," replied Dirk.

"You know that I want that too, Dirk. But every day, I feel a little more hopeless," confessed Sven sadly and proposed, "if we force them to learn now, perhaps they will accept the wisdom in time?"

"Children don't always want to go to school, but the parents make them. We are the parents now!" remarked Wendji, but she wanted to say something else.

"Wendji, that's a difficult decision, and I need to think about that!" stated Dirk, although he already had made up his mind, but Dirk was too ashamed to tell them.

"Nancy is right. We could just leave!" suggested Nari suddenly, which got everyone's attention!

(Feeling of agreement) "It is possible. I have finished the settlement on the new world, and it is now safe to transfer there!" confirmed L.

"But we promised to make Earth a better place… for Lilly!" contradicted Garrett.

"I promised that, Garrett. All of you are free to make your own decisions. I will not hold it against any of you if you rather be on another planet. I would too if I only could," replied Dirk quietly.

"I have been asking myself this question for a while now: are we responsible for Earth? If they want to kill each other, if they want to kill the planet, if they want to live in blood, tears, and filth, and are too stubborn, too ignorant, and too hateful to accept greater wisdom, should we stop them from heading to their doom?" wondered Wendji and Ngazetungue nodded to his wife while a few others appeared to agree as well.

"I didn't expect to hear that from you, Wendji, but you are right: we are not responsible, and more likely than not, everything we try will prove futile in the end!" assented Dirk, and then he pleaded with the group: "Please, leave here and make a better world, give humanity another chance among the stars!"

"We will not leave you behind!" interrupted Nari and added angrily: "We will punish Earth, then we will depart all together!"

"The U.S. government murdered Lilly, not Earth!" corrected Sven quietly.

"Yes, Sven, but it would be naïve to think that the Chinese, Russians, North Koreans, Israelis, Iranians, Saudis, or a dozen other nations wouldn't have done the same thing. The U.S. just got to Lilly first!" rebutted Garrett somberly.

"We know firsthand that they aren't any better: from the attacks at the cabin and from…," noted Yebin but never finished the sentence.

Nobody responded, but Dirk could sense that they agreed with her. Perhaps they all remembered what the powers of Earth had done to the volunteers on Aureus?

"Punish Earth…," Dirk echoed Nari's words somberly while Mario looked at him expectantly, and finally, Dirk gave him a slight nod.

"Dirk and I talked about this a few days ago. We will do everything that you guys suggested and a lot more. They will hate and fear us, but they deserve it!" declared Mario forcefully. The others looked concerned at Dirk, and he was about to respond when suddenly everything changed!

29. Who are you? (Part 1)

Dirk found himself naked in the middle of an empty cubical box. It was about 25 feet wide, high, and deep. The walls, floor, and ceiling were made from pitch black onyx. It was dimly lit, just enough for him to estimate its dimensions, but there was no discernable light source anywhere. There was also no smell, no sound, no air current, and the temperature was ambient.

Dirk looked around and saw no exits. He took a few steps to his right, but he couldn't reach the wall. He was still right in the cube's center when he stopped walking. Dirk sat down on the floor. There should have been an echo in this room, but all sounds seemed absorbed instead of reflected by the hard, smooth walls. The onyx floor should have felt hard and cold, but it didn't feel like anything. He calmly sat there for a long time, waiting to see what would happen next.

"Hello? Where am I? Let me out of here!" mocked a male voice and added, "a normal person would panic being trapped alone in a dark box, but not you!"

"Is there a point to this?" questioned Dirk in return.

Dirk wasn't afraid, and he wasn't even surprised. If he had any feeling at that moment, annoyance would be it, but he didn't understand why he felt irritated.

"Who are you? What do you want?" remarked the voice with amusement, "those are the questions everyone else would ask when they hear a strange voice, but not you!"

"Fine. Where am I, who are you, what do you want?" asked Dirk reluctantly.

"Was that so hard?" wondered the incorporeal voice.

"I didn't ask pointless questions because I already know I won't get answers!" disclosed Dirk.

The voice was very familiar, but try as he might, Dirk couldn't associate it with any person he knew.

"Smart, but not very human!" snickered the invisible man and asked: "Do you want to leave?"

"What I want is irrelevant in this situation. You will let me go, or you will not. It is not under my control!" countered Dirk while getting more aggravated. He was confident that he knew who was talking to him, but his memory wasn't cooperating.

"True, but you could ask me nicely!" suggested the voice insincerely.

"I will not ask at all!" maintained Dirk.

"I could keep you here for all eternity," mused the man.

"Perhaps you could!" acknowledged Dirk.

"Does that not scare you?" questioned the voice.

"No!" replied Dirk truthfully.

"Another answer that disqualifies you as a human!" claimed the man with a chuckle, and then it asked: "Why?"

"Because I'm already dead, so do your worst!" answered Dirk and shrugged his shoulders.

"Are you sure? Dead, alive, past, present, future, reality, simulation, dream - do you know what is this?" wondered the unseen man.

"It doesn't matter if this is real, a dream, or simulated. It doesn't matter if my existence ends here or continues somewhere else in space or time! I am insignificant on the Universe's scale, and that's an indisputable fact!" answered Dirk humbly.

"Ah, so rational, so existential, so clever, so inhuman!" deduced the voice laughingly.

"I will ask again: is there a point to this?" inquired Dirk sharply.

"Of course, there is. I will ask you questions, and you will answer honestly!" replied the man.

"Fine, get on with it!" grumbled Dirk.

"You never led anyone, and the few times you tried, you have failed. Why do you presume that you can succeed in leading the world?" questioned the voice pointedly.

"I never presumed that, and I'm already failing!" admitted Dirk and sighed.

"Then why do you keep trying?" wondered the unseen man.

"It wasn't my choice!" exclaimed Dirk.

"Of course, it was your choice! You could have and should have declined!" corrected the voice dismissively.

"Someone had to try, for Lilly's sake!" insisted Dirk quietly.

"And that someone was you of all people?" asked the voice and chuckled.

"I would gladly pass the baton!" stated Dirk firmly.

"I bet you would because you don't have what it takes, loser!" sneered the man.

"If that was an insult, it missed the mark!" responded Dirk.

"It was factual and true. You cannot lead humans because you aren't human!" proclaimed the voice.

"I'm verifiably Homo Sapiens!" contradicted Dirk dismissively.

"Homo sapiens, but not human! Big difference! You will never understand what makes humans tick! And even if you could understand it, you would only reject what drives everyone else!" elaborated the invisible man.

"No, that's not true. I have the same weaknesses!" protested Dirk angrily.

"Oh sure, here it comes: I like sex and whore around a lot. See? I'm just like them!" the man mocked in a whiney voice.

"I suppose…," agreed Dirk hesitantly.

"No! They need sex, and you don't. For a good selection of books, you could go without it for the rest of your life, but they cannot!" countered the man and declared, "you might enjoy sex, but you do it to humor the women because they expect that from you, and you don't want to disappoint them!"

"Sex happens first in my mind. If it doesn't happen there, it will never happen!" argued Dirk.

"How many people do you know who share that sentiment? Let me guess - none! If it were a human sentiment, rape, molestation, and harassment wouldn't be so ubiquitous!" remarked the voice sharply.

"I don't care; I like that about myself!" insisted Dirk.

"Admittedly, it's not a bad character trait, but it is inhuman!" insisted the voice and added snidely, "you can't lead humans because you are nothing like them! The average human always wonders what to eat and whom to fuck - gluttony and lust are priorities number one and two! You don't care about fucking, and you even forget to eat when you are engrossed in something you consider more important!"

"That…might be correct," conceded Dirk in defeat.

The unpleasant man made a point. Not just about sex, but Lilly had complained countless times when Dirk missed yet another meal because he was too focused on his work.

"What do you hate most about people?" questioned the voice after a short break in the conversation.

"Dishonesty, willful ignorance, prejudice…," Dirk started saying.

"Nope!" contradicted the man loudly.

"…self-righteousness, lack of empathy, violent urges…," continued Dirk.

"Try again!" interrupted the voice again.

Dirk was silent for a moment. What did this man want to hear?

"I dislike it when people make significant mistakes or neglect their duties, then deny it, make feeble excuses, or blame others instead of taking responsibility for their actions and showing some remorse!" said Dirk.

"Aha! About 95% of all humans are like that: I didn't do it, and if I did it, it wasn't my fault because that other guy is to blame; I'm not sorry, and I hate you for pointing out my hypocrisy! They learn that as toddlers, but evidently you didn't!" lectured the man and then stated: "You cannot lead humans if you dislike most of them, and they sure as hell dislike you! It's as simple as that!"

"That might also be correct," assented Dirk and sighed. Again, the man was annoying, but not wrong!

"Of course, it is correct, but you didn't answer my question. Only an idiot would make the same mistake repeatedly, hoping for a different result. You are not an idiot, so why do you keep trying?" the voice demanded to know.

"I must try!" insisted Dirk, but he didn't know why.

"No, you don't because nobody forces you. You could walk away anytime!" corrected the man.

"I don't have an answer for that. Perhaps I'm really an idiot…," admitted Dirk with a sigh, and for a long time, there was no response.

"Hmm, that's good enough for now!" concluded the voice finally and added, "until next time…."

30. Fade to black

Dirk was back at the meeting, and he knew that something had just happened, but he couldn't recall any of it. He noticed that all eyes were on him. The group expected a response, but first, Dirk needed a moment to shake off this weird sensation.

"Yes, I will be the face, but Mario will be the enforcer. We will become everything we never wanted to be, but perhaps it will save humanity?" summarized Dirk somberly.

Sven wasn't very comfortable with that idea, but he said nothing. Angela seemed to agree with Dirk, while Nancy looked nervously at Mario. Nari was serene, and the rest appeared to be weighing the options.

"I hate to agree with you, Dirk. Sorry, Mario, but you are the only one of us ruthless enough to do it!" consented Garrett and looked at Mario apologetically.

"Don't sweat it, Garrett!" replied Mario and stated thoughtfully: "My special skills are needed here!"

"Yes, they are needed!" agreed Dirk somberly.

"If this fails, will we leave here?" inquired Nari a moment later.

"There would be no other choice!" confirmed Angela, and many nodded in agreement.

"When we are gone, will you allow me to make a decision?" asked Nari bluntly.

"About?" wondered Sven confused.

"The fate of Earth!" clarified Nari.

The small Korean girl appeared anything but timid now, and Dirk suddenly recalled some scary memories from another timeline. He was going to object, but against better judgment, he just nodded instead.

"If this fails, we will leave, and Earth will be in your hands, Nari!" Dirk heard himself saying, and nobody challenged that decision. Nari smiled a little, but it was an icy smile, making Dirk wince.

"I'm so tired, guys!" he divulged quietly and adjourned the meeting: "We will continue this in the morning!"

After the meeting, Dirk went straight to bed, but nightmares plagued him, and this time, they were particularly bad. Dirk realized around 4:00 am that he wouldn't get any rest anymore. He got out of bed quietly to not disturb Nari and went to the kitchen. Dirk started the coffee machine and the toaster. After he had a cup and some toasted waffles, he left the kitchen and walked down to a small, windowless room in the basement. It was initially meant to be a boiler room, but now it had a much different purpose.

L had preserved Lilly's body in a hardened transfer matrix. The matrix had healed her external injuries, and now she looked like she was peacefully sleeping in that big, translucent amber block. The block was resting on a wooden pedestal in this room that everyone called the mausoleum. Dirk came here almost every day after breakfast. He would sit next to Lilly for a few minutes, irrationally hoping that she would somehow wake up again. But Lilly was dead.

"No matter how much power I have, I cannot change what is not under my control, and I can only control my behavior, not that of others!" lamented Dirk and looked at the back of his hands. For a little while, he just sat there motionless.

"I cannot do this anymore, Sweetie," avowed Dirk finally: "I have avenged your death, but the world cannot be saved. They don't want to be saved!"

Dirk looked at Lilly's serene face for a long time. He wished so much that he could have another conversation with Lilly, ask for her advice, let her know how much she meant to him, and tell her how much he missed her. But of course, that could never happen. Silently, Tigger had entered the room without Dirk noticing. He walked over to Dirk and nudged him gently with his big head.

"Time to go," he said through the mental link.

"I can't, Tigger!" replied Dirk desperately.

(Feeling of certainty) "But Dirk must go now!" emphasized the feline.

"If I leave this room, I fear I will end the world, or Mario will do it in my name. I have no more patience, no more tolerance, no more compassion to give!" declared Dirk somberly.

(Feeling of fondness) "No, just leave!" rebutted Tigger.

"If we leave Earth, Nari will annihilate it, and I won't stop her!" responded Dirk, tears forming in his eyes.

"Leave this, not room, not Earth!" corrected Tigger.

"Leave what?" wondered Dirk, confused.

(Feeling of empathy) "Come!" insisted Tigger and put his big paw on Dirk's knees. Suddenly, everything faded to black.

31. Aureus

When Dirk woke up, he felt parched. He looked at the nightstand, but there was only an empty glass waiting for him. Lilly had the water pitcher at her desk across from the bed. She was scanning the newsfeed from Earth on a holographic display.

"Can I have some water, Lilly?" asked Dirk hoarsely.

"Finally! I thought you had died in your sleep!" joked Lilly and came over to the bed with the pitcher in hand.

"I took some of Sven's sedatives last night. I wanted to be well-rested for the transfer today," replied Dirk and eagerly quenched his thirst.

"Well, you didn't oversleep. Lydda is still meeting with the other Latura, Rose is helping Ezio and L on Alcatraz, and Nari is polishing Alma's scales again. Angie is probably doing her security checks, but that's just a guess," reported Lilly, and then she added cheerfully, "I got us some breakfast from Yebin. It's omelets from Eriea's cloned chicken. They are superb! Go take a shower!"

"Sweet! I'm hungry; I'll take a shower afterward!" quipped Dirk, got out of bed, and walked to the little coffee machine in the kitchenette of their apartment.

"Fine, be stinky for breakfast!" teased Lilly and started to set the table.

The departure day had finally arrived: this was Aureus' first diplomatic mission, and everyone was excited. Garrett, Sven, and Aarne had loaded several transfer pods with goods and gifts from Aureus. Lydda and Tigger were already at the Transfer Center on Alcatraz when Dirk came on the hovercraft.

Suddenly, Nancy rushed into the large basement where the transfer pods were installed and added a crate of Glow of Aureus to the bounty at the last minute. Mario had worked all night to finish this latest batch of the alcoholic drink, popular with humans and Latura alike. Everybody had assembled to say farewell to Lydda, Tigger, and Dirk, save for the children because they were still too little.

(Feeling of anticipation) "Latur has confirmed that they are ready to receive the envoy! All systems are checked and rechecked on our end, too!" stated L.

"Now, we will have to say goodbye to you guys," said Sofia with a pout.

"Tigger no like goodbye. Will be back home soon!" remarked Tigger and purred.

Then he trotted over to the chamber that L had designed to hold a jaguar-sized cat. But before he got there, Jo blocked his way and licked him fondly on the forehead. She was now almost as big as Tigger, and Tigger returned the gesture in kind.

"OK, hold down the fort. Angela is now officially in charge, and Yebin is her deputy!" instructed Dirk formally, but then he added with a sad smile, "I'm going to miss you guys!"

"It's only for a couple of weeks. Enjoy the vacation, Boss. There will be plenty of work when you get home!" teased Mario and shook Dirk's hand.

The colony exchanged hugs and well-wishes with Dirk, Lydda, and Tigger. Lastly, Dirk's wives embraced and kissed Dirk and Lydda, but Lilly stayed longer.

"Honey, talk to Tyrval about Earth," she said cryptically.

"I haven't been following the news. What did I miss?" asked Dirk.

"Only that something is happing there. L isn't sure what, but we don't want any nasty surprises!" cautioned Lilly.

"We don't. I will talk to Tyrval, Sweetie!" Dirk assured her.

However, something felt suddenly out of place. But Dirk dismissed it as a side effect of the sedatives he took last night.

32. Latur

The transfer was as smooth as it could be. Tigger woke up first and inspected the enormous chamber that the Latura used for their transfer pods. It was richly decorated in artwork and well-lit, and the air had a hint of perfume or other flowery scents. It was also quite toasty! Aureus was tropical, but Latur was several degrees beyond that. Fortunately, the transfer matrix had made a few minor genetic adjustments so that Tigger, Dirk, and Lydda were better prepared for Latur's different environments.

Tigger checked on Dirk and Lydda's pods, and they were waking up, too. When Dirk regained conscience, he immediately knew that something was off. It wasn't the lower gravity, higher temperature, or strange scent in the air. Instinctively, Dirk knew that he had been here before!

For a few minutes, Dirk simply remained in his pod to think. He knew that this visit to Latur would be highly successful. Within a month, Vidya would become the first Aurean ambassador to Latur, and Tyrval's great-granddaughter, Irgal, would represent Latur on Aureus in exchange. Irgal! There was something about Irgal, but Dirk's memories were clouded: he could recall the broad strokes, but not every detail.

"Are you planning to stay in that pod for the entire visit, *swiahn*?" teased Lydda.

Dirk was startled out of his thoughts. He got out of the pod, and he somehow knew her following words.

"Welcome to the place of my birth!" she chirped.

Lydda was already wearing the same white, flowing cloak that she had donned for their wedding. Dirk quickly dressed in the black leather tunic he was wearing whenever he had to conduct official business. Thanks to Rose's excellent taste in fashion, the tunic was well fitted and looked sharp, but Dirk had gotten used to being naked, so it always took a few moments to get comfortable with the clothing again.

(Feeling of alertness) "Someone coming!" announced Tigger.

But Dirk already knew who that would be before the doors ever opened. When Tyrval entered with his aides, Dirk prepared himself for what came next.

"Dirk!" exclaimed Tyrval happily and in the human tongue.

His aides looked flabbergasted and whispered to the venerable Latura man, but he just brushed them off. It appeared that this was not in accordance with the protocol, but Tyrval didn't care.

"Tyrval!" replied Dirk fondly and extended his forearm.

The older Latura man clasped it vigorously, and then it happened: two billion cheering voices suddenly swamped Dirk's mind! Dirk remembered how he thought he might drown in them when it happened the first time, but now he was prepared. For what seemed like an eternity, Dirk, Lydda, and Tigger received the greetings, well-wishes, and happy emotions of an entire alien species in their minds. When the mental storm finally subsided, Tyrval began to read his welcome speech, but he quickly put aside the little communication pad and improvised instead.

"Protocol demands certain procedures and fancy speeches, but we don't need that today. You have been part of our daily lives for a long time now. So, I simply say this: Latur welcomes our friends from Aureus!" announced Tyrval, and another deafening mental cheer surged through Dirk's mind, and Dirk let the excitement calm down before he responded.

"You are right, Tyrval; we don't need protocol today. Aureus sends its love and gratitude to you all! We are blessed with your kindness and friendship!" responded Dirk happily, and then there was another vast psychic wave of happy cheers and fond emotions.

The next few days went by just the way Dirk remembered them. But his memory wasn't perfect: often, Dirk exactly knew what would transpire next, but sometimes he didn't know what would happen until it unfolded. Then, everything seemed new to him a few times, but the memories usually caught up with it eventually, even if it took a few hours. But the most disturbing memories were glimpses of a possible future: Dirk saw bits and pieces flashing by, including his own demise a hundred years from now.

Dirk, Tigger, and Lydda were in high demand on Latur. There were many meetings with scientists, historians, artists, musicians, athletes, engineers, and any type of profession the Latura had. There were dinners, brunches, parties, and performances. Lydda received many hugs, and even Dirk was hugged on multiple occasions, even though the Latura use hugs very differently from humans. To them, an embrace was a request for mating.

"Lydda, am I supposed to say that I accept or reject?" wondered Dirk, and then he suddenly knew that he had asked that question before.

"You can accept if you like, *swiahn*!" teased Lydda, but then she explained, "it's one of the cultural changes on Latur recently. The Latura have adopted the human gesture of hugging as an expression of fondness."

"But didn't you say that women do not hug men?" inquired Dirk.

"They never did before. Women received the embrace and then decided if they wanted to mate with the man. Other affection or fondness between genders was expressed by nuzzling the neck, or more formally by placing the palm of the left hand onto the sternum of the recipient!" explained Lydda.

"And Aureus changed all that?" wondered Dirk.

"Yes, we did!" confirmed Lydda and asked happily, "but it's a wonderful change, don't you think?"

"Agreed, this is nice!" observed Dirk, and then he suddenly remembered something else, but it was already too late!

"Dirk, it is so awesome to meet you finally!" gushed the young Latura women and added, "I'm Irgal, Tyrval's great-granddaughter."

"The pleasure is all mine!" replied Dirk with a broad smile.

The young woman giggled, pressed herself closer to his body, and nuzzled his neck. Instinctively, Dirk reached for her hip and shoulder, but before he could even hug her, she already whispered in his ear:

"I accept!"

33. The Museum

Today, Lydda, Tigger, and Dirk were given a tour of the most famous museum on Latur. The monumental building housed everything from artwork and inventions to prehistoric skeletons. Accordingly, the three were accompanied by several well-known Experts in art, biology, engineering, archeology, and several other disciplines. The exhibitions were stunning, and their guides went to great lengths to make the tour as enjoyable as possible for their guests.

After a while, Dirk excused himself to use the restroom, but he encouraged the tour to move to the next exhibition without him. When he exited the bathroom, the group was already out of sight. From his old memories, Dirk recalled he had to ask Lydda over the link where to find the tour again. But this time, Dirk didn't do that. Instead, he sat down on a bench near an enormous aquarium. For a moment, he just watched the colorful plankton swirl around the huge tank in an intricate dance.

Dirk needed some time alone to think, and thus far, there hadn't been a single moment of solitude. This visit to Latur had happened before; he was sure of it. The memories were too clear and precise to have just spawned from his imagination. Inevitably, he thought about *irtaljan*. But this was nothing like his previous experience. For one, this reality, although not identical, was very close to his original memories of Latur, not drastically different as it had been on Alcatraz. Secondly, it wasn't a brief period of being in two different timelines simultaneously but instead appeared to be its own separate realm. Lastly, he was not given a choice, or at least not yet. Of course, this still could be *irtaljan* since nobody knew how it worked or what rules applied, but Dirk instinctively doubted it.

Dirk tried to pinpoint when this reality had diverged from the previous one. Dirk's mind systematically retraced the steps, but he had difficulty grasping what he was doing the day before the diplomatic mission embarked to Latur. He vaguely remembered designing the drainage system for L's new spaceport, but strangely, that seemed like an eternity ago, even though they had only arrived on Latur a few days earlier.

When Dirk went to bed the night before their departure, he recalled taking a sedative, hoping that it would help him get rested up for the trip, but again, that appeared to be an ancient memory. He tried to remember things that happened even further in the past, but aside from major events, he could only conjure the broadest strokes in his mind.

By contrast, the memories of the following day were fresh and vivid. Dirk recalled how thirsty he was when he woke up, every detail of the breakfast with Lilly, and the hovercraft trip to Alcatraz. Their arrival on Latur was crystal clear in his mind, too.

Dirk concluded that this new reality began on the morning of their departure to Latur when he woke up and saw Lilly sitting at the desk. Of course, this realization was well and good, but it didn't help Dirk understand what had happened to him. In a way, it made matters worse because now he felt trapped in a timeline that wasn't his, and Dirk couldn't see any way out of it.

"This is out of my control!" mumbled Dirk to himself.

He would have to make the best out of this strange situation, but there was also a silver lining: perhaps armed with his old memories that seemed to extend for decades after this visit, Dirk would be better prepared to lead Aureus into the future?

For a moment, Dirk looked at the aquarium and was tempted to put his hand on the thick glass, but suddenly Lydda called him on the direct link to let him know where the museum tour was waiting for him. Dirk stood up and swiftly walked through the seemingly endless corridors to catch up with the group again.

34. Tyrval

Two days after the museum tour, Dirk finally got a little rest in the spacious quarters the Latura had assigned for their diplomatic guests. Lydda and Tigger were still somewhere else, so Dirk decided it would be an excellent time to get some sleep for an hour or two. The Latura slept in their pools, but they had courteously provided a bed for their human guest. But unfortunately, the Latura didn't know what a proper bed looked like, so it wasn't as much of a bed as a pile of plush, comfortable blankets piled on the floor. Still, it was a nice place to stretch out to take a nap. But there would be no rest for the weary!

"Dirk, we must talk in private!' urged the Administrator of the *meeting of the minds* over the direct mental link.

"Of course, Tyrval. Where can I meet you?" asked Dirk sleepily.

There was something in Tyrval's thoughts that alarmed Dirk. Now, he was wide awake again and sat up on the blankets.

"Please come to my study. It's down the hall, to the left of the auditorium," requested Tyrval.

When Dirk arrived, dressed in his official black tunic, Tyrval was preparing two glasses of Glow of Aureus. He smiled and gestured towards a seating area next to his pool. Dirk gave him a friendly nod and took a seat. A moment later, Tyrval placed a tall glass in front of Dirk and sat down. Dirk recalled this meeting from memory. Tyrval and Dirk chatted about philosophy, trade, immigration, and establishing permanent embassies on Aureus and Latur. But first, Dirk needed to come clean about Irgal.

"Tyrval, before we start, there is a very delicate matter I would like to discuss with you," conveyed Dirk politely.

"Irgal!" interrupted Tyrval and made the Latura gesture of disapproval.

"So, you know already?" inquired Dirk surprised.

"My great-granddaughter is what you would call a groupie; she obsesses over everything on Aureus. I reminded her several times to stick to the protocol, but apparently, she found a way around that, didn't she?" asked Tyrval.

"Yes, I suppose. I just don't know how to resolve this without violating etiquette or hurting that young woman's feelings," confessed Dirk thoughtfully.

112

"Dirk, I love Irgal! She is the dearest and closest to me of all my children, grandchildren, and great-grandchildren. Her juvenile obsessions aside, she is also brilliant. So much so that she has been pegged to be Administrator of the *meeting of the minds* someday!" noted Tyrval proudly, and then he asked: "Tell me, what did she do?"

"She greeted me very fondly…," said Dirk hesitantly.

"…and you embraced her!" Tyrval finished Dirk's sentence.

"Well, it was not a hug, but I touched her shoulder, and she certainly interpreted it as an embrace and immediately accepted!" admitted Dirk.

"That girl!" exclaimed Tyrval humorously and pointed out: "She outsmarted you, Dirk!"

"I suppose she did, but what should I do now?" wondered Dirk, slightly embarrassed.

"I know that humans view sexuality differently, although Aureus has a much more liberated approach now," noted Tyrval and requested, "forget protocol; make Irgal happy if it's not too much to ask?"

"But Tyrval, Irgal is just a girl!" objected Dirk, unsure how old that young Latura lady was.

"She has reached sexual maturity, and in human years, she not much younger than your wife Nari," corrected Tyrval.

"I didn't know that, but still…," replied Dirk.

"Do you not find her attractive?" asked Tyrval.

"She is beautiful. It is just a cultural problem. Yes, Aureus is more liberal, but even we don't have sex with just anyone, and certainly not after such a brief first encounter!" contended Dirk.

"That's not so different from the Latura way. We, too, don't just mate on a whim, despite what you might think after Irgal's little trickery!" concurred Tyrval and proposed, "but we could fix that. I could summon Irgal here, and you get to know each other. I will tell her that you are our honored guest in no uncertain terms, and the final decision will be yours. Would you agree to that, Dirk?"

"And then it would not be a breach of protocol?" inquired Dirk.

Now he felt trapped by the whole situation, but that was just how he remembered it. However, Dirk recalled that he never slept with Irgal on Latur. Notably, there were gaps in his memory, but Dirk was sure he wouldn't have forgotten about such an encounter.

"Oh, it most certainly would be!" disagreed Tyrval humorously and asked, "do you remember the young Experts who broke protocol on Aureus?"

"Eriea and Ofal!" recollected Dirk and nodded.

"While some still disapprove of their behavior, most believe that love supersedes our traditions. So, if you mate with Irgal, it won't be a black stain on diplomatic relations any more than Eriea and Ofal's indiscretions!" explained Tyrval and then remarked jokingly, "most likely, it will just add to your fame!"

"Well, in that case, I agree with your plan. But could I talk to Lydda first?" requested Dirk, but he didn't need his alternate memory to know what his Latura wife would say.

"Of course, Dirk. Later, I will send for Irgal and give her strict instructions!" concurred Tyrval and offered, "would you like some snacks? We have the most delicious crab cakes made for you!"

"I love crab cakes. I used to have them on Earth whenever Lilly and I frequented a seafood restaurant!" replied Dirk with a broad smile.

He remembered that the Latur crab cakes were indeed a delicatessen, even for a human. Tyrval placed a few on a petite platter and handed the dish to Dirk.

"Tyrval, I have never asked you this before: what does the Administrator of the *meeting of the minds* do?" wondered Dirk as he devoured one of the delicious treats.

"I call the *meeting of the minds* in session, lead the discussion, and at the appropriate time, I call for the votes. Then, I count the votes and announce the results!" summarized Tyrval.

"You count two billion votes?" gasped Dirk.

"Well, no. We have an AI that can count them for me. But I oversee and verify the process!" corrected Tyrval with a feline grin.

"L told us that telepathy has a limited range, Tigger notwithstanding, and we found that to be true. How can all two billion Latura from all over the planet participate in the meeting of minds?" inquired Dirk.

"Yes, telepathy has its limits. Latura are evolutionary more adapted to it, but our range does not exceed the human range by much. We solved that problem in the simplest possible way. Each Latura is receiver and sender simultaneously," explained Tyrval and claimed, "but now, we also use the technology that L had developed on Earth when you had to send telepathic messages to Yebin and Nari, half a world away. It has even enabled us to connect our various colonies directly to the *meeting of the minds*!"

"From what I understand, any adult Latura can petition the *meeting of the minds*. There must be thousands of such requests. How can you handle that?" asked Dirk next.

"There are quite a few requests, but perhaps not as many as you think," revealed Tyrval and explained, "most petitions are going to the expert committees and are processed there. The ones that come to me are already presorted. My assistants screen them for importance, but I will eventually read every one of them. However, it is at my discretion in which order a petition will be submitted to the *meeting of the minds*. The petitions with the highest priority are the ones that were made by a Council of Experts; however, all requests will be heard eventually."

"Do you have other responsibilities?" questioned Dirk.

"Yes and no. Since the first time we discovered an alien species long ago, the Administrator also became the primary emissary of Latur. This doesn't come with any additional powers, but it simplifies the interactions with other species since they only have to deal with one person and not all two billion of us!" said Tyrval.

"Aha, so that's why you are talking to me now!" quipped Dirk.

"That's right. But I would talk to you even if that wasn't in my job description," joked the old Latura man and concluded, "lastly, I can also make treaties with alien civilizations, but they are all subject to ratification by the *meeting of the minds*."

"Ah, that makes sense, Tyrval!" replied Dirk, and then he asked, "you said earlier that Irgal would become your successor someday. Does that mean the office of Administrator is hereditary?"

"Oh no, of course not!" objected Tyrval humorously and clarified, "Irgal is a free spirit! I wanted to spare her the burden and responsibilities of this position, but the *meeting of minds* ignored my pleas and decided otherwise! But Irgal will not follow me directly into the office; she is too young for that; instead, she will succeed the next Administrator, Noval."

"Is the position of Administrator a lifetime appointment?" questioned Dirk.

"No, not at all. *The meeting of the minds* chooses the Administrator via election. The Administrator holds the office until he resigns, retires, or becomes too infirm to perform the duties. The *meeting of the minds* can also recall the Administrator at any point of the tenure, although that hasn't happened in a few millennia!" disclosed Tyrval.

"Thank you, Tyrval. Now I understand your responsibilities better!" appreciated Dirk and smiled.

This part of the conversation went much the way he remembered it. But what Tyrval would ask next caught Dirk a bit by surprise.

"Dirk, Latur is responsible for the dramatic changes in your life. We didn't ask for your permission to be transformed; instead, we forced it upon you. Without us, you would still be a human back on Earth. Please be open: do you harbor any resentment towards us?" inquired Tyrval delicately.

"I wish you would have asked. But of course, I realize that without the transformation, you couldn't have asked me, or at least I wouldn't have been able to understand your question!" answered Dirk earnestly and divulged, "but if you could have asked me beforehand, I believe I would have agreed to the transformation voluntarily. But I wouldn't have transformed Lilly!"

"I was the Administrator when L arrived at Earth. Alvar and Lenna were in charge of L when we discovered humanity. I could have called the *meeting of the minds* in session, and perhaps we could have approached this differently. Since then, we have established a new protocol for First Contact: thanks to L's incredible capabilities, transformation is no longer essential to establish communication with alien civilizations!" noted Tyrval and paused for a moment before he confessed with a sigh, "Dirk, I feel guilty about what we have done to you!"

"Apology accepted, Tyrval!" declared Dirk, and then he added fondly, "because of your actions, my life was changed dramatically. I have perfect health, and I'm surrounded by people I love, have my children, have a beautiful home, and live the life I always wanted! But perhaps most importantly, I have a purpose now! How can I resent you for that?"

"Thank you, Dirk, that was kind of you to say!" replied Tyrval gratefully.

Dirk was sure that he had never had this exchange with Tyrval before, but he sincerely appreciated the late apology nonetheless. Suddenly, he noticed something else that he could not recollect from his past experience.

"Is that L's icosahedron?" he asked and pointed at the metallic dice on Tyrval's desk, but Tyrval chuckled and seemed a bit embarrassed.

"We have many AIs on Latur. They manage much of our daily lives, and all their interfaces are supposed to be in the control center. But after L absorbed so many of our probes, there were numerous duplicates for his," answered Tyrval and revealed, "I have bent the rules and left one here in my study."

"I see," said Dirk, wondering why he had never noticed the icosahedron in his old memories since it was not an item that could be easily missed.

"Sometimes, I get a little weary when I review all those petitions to the *meeting of the minds*. Then I take a break, have a glass of Glow of Aureus, and chat with L. Please forgive an old man his little quirks!" pleaded Tyrval.

"There is nothing to forgive, Tyrval! I have one in my office, too, and I do the same thing, except I prefer coffee!" disclosed Dirk and chuckled.

"Coffee? I never developed a taste for it, but some tell me that it is quite invigorating," replied Tyrval with a smile, but then he became earnest and said something unexpected, "Dirk, I need your help!"

Dirk was immediately alarmed by those words, but not because he didn't want to assist Tyrval. Despite the limited power of the office he held, Tyrval was the leader of the most advanced species in the known galaxy. If he needed Dirk's help, it must be enormous. But the discussion came to an abrupt halt before it started because one of Tyrval's aides barged into the room. He cordially greeted Dirk, but then he swiftly turned to Tyrval.

"Administrator, I'm afraid your guest must wait. The Council of Experts requests your immediate presence!" urged the aide in Loyt, the spoken language of the Latura.

The aide was unaware that Dirk was able to understand him. Even Dirk was surprised that he could! When Dirk had arrived on Latur the first time, he didn't know more than a dozen words of the language, but now Dirk could follow the conservation between Tyrval and his aide without trouble. Understanding Loyt when he had not learned it yet, was the most obvious sign that this reality was not Dirk's own!

"This is a diplomatic meeting on the highest level. Tell the Council that they must wait!" responded Tyrval, visibly unhappy by the intrusion.

"But Administrator, our problems with Earth have gotten much worse. You must talk to the Experts! Please tell your guest to wait for a little!" begged the aide.

117

"This goes against all protocol!" replied Tyrval and made a gesture that was the Latura equivalent of shaking one's head.

Dirk noticed how worried the aide looked, so he decided to resolve this delicate situation for his host.

"Tyrval, if your duty calls, I understand. We can always continue our conversation later!" maintained Dirk verbally in Loyt and smiled at the old Administrator.

The aide was shocked and embarrassed, but Tyrval only seemed pleasantly surprised.

"Lydda is a good teacher!" he responded in Loyt, and then he added in passable English, "I thank you, Dirk!"

The aide apologized profusely to Dirk, but Dirk just smiled at the man and reassured him that no harm was done. Then all three of them left the study, and Tyrval and his aide swiftly went into the nearby auditorium where the Council of Experts was waiting while Dirk returned to his quarters.

35. Lydda

When Dirk got back to the suite, Lydda had already returned. She was sipping on a fruity drink that was very popular on Latura. Dirk had tried it, but he wasn't a big fan.

"Back so soon, Kittycat?" asked Dirk as he walked into the door.

"Back so soon, *swiahn*?" echoed his Latura wife and grinned at him.

"I was going to take a nap, but Tyrval wanted to talk to me," conveyed Dirk.

"But?" wondered Lydda curiously.

"The meeting was cut short because Tyrval was needed elsewhere," replied Dirk simply.

"That's a huge breach of protocol, *swiahn*. Very insulting!" gasped Lydda and asked, "what happened?"

"Don't worry, I diffused the situation as diplomatically as I could, and Tyrval was grateful that I did!" reassured Dirk, and then he added, "I don't know what's going on, Kittycat, but I'm nervous about it. His aide said something about problems with Earth!"

"Now I'm nervous, too. If Tyrval leaves a meeting with you, this must be very important!" worried Lydda.

"I will meet with him again. I have the feeling I'll find out then. No need to fret about it now!" said Dirk as upbeat as possible, but Lydda didn't seem to buy his cheerful act.

"So, how was your day?" asked Dirk, changed the topic, and gently embraced her.

"Busy! Several meetings, another tour, and a formal lunch! Did you know that Latura now want autographs? I had to sign a bunch of items! One of them had me sign her boobs - can you believe that? I can't wait to get back to Aureus!" chirped Lydda and nuzzled his neck.

"Autographs? They must have learned that from humans! Not one of our worst traits, so I guess that's harmless!" replied Dirk with a chuckle and asked. "where is Tigger?"

"Tigger is still outside. He has his own social obligations. Come, I show you!" beckoned Lydda and walked to the window.

Their quarters were inside the Administration building on the top floor, overlooking the grand plaza. It was a gorgeous view because the Latura architecture was as impressive as it was appealing, and the vast plaza was always bustling with countless people heading in or out of the various government buildings situated around the immaculate marble pavement.

But right now, there was a throng of people, most of them children, gathered around the central fountain. In the middle of the Latura was Tigger. All the children were petting his soft fur, touching his big ears, or pulling on his tail. Tigger thoroughly enjoyed the attention, but suddenly one of the children tossed a ball high up, and with a mighty leap and lightning reflexes, Tigger caught it in midair. There were loud gasps and laughter as the big cat returned the ball to the child throwing it.

"Tigger's abilities are amazing, but his real superpower is that he is so lovable!" observed Lydda quietly.

"Yes, he is the best ambassador. These children will never forget the moment when they played with that gentle alien cat!" concurred Dirk happily, and then they watched for a while longer as Tigger interacted with the children.

"OK, Tigger is busy, and we are alone…," claimed Lydda suddenly and looked at him expectantly.

"Wouldn't that be a breach of protocol?" wondered Dirk slyly, knowing what Lydda had in mind.

"It would be if I were some Latura girl, but fortunately, I'm Aurean!" proudly corrected Lydda.

"Oh, in that case, we should probably inspect your pool, Kittycat!" suggested Dirk and grinned at her.

"No, today I prefer that silly pile of blankets over there!" giggled Lydda and pointed at the bedding.

Of course, unlike the people of Latur, Lydda knew what a proper bed should look like: after all, she was often sleeping in Dirk's on Aureus.

"Ah, the savage human way!" replied Dirk and nodded.

"That, and you always fall asleep afterward, *swiahn*. I don't want you to drown!" teased Lydda, took his hand, and pulled him to the pile of blankets.

Lovemaking was exhilarating as usual because the *swiahn* bond allowed them to switch their consciousnesses from one body to the other, doubling their pleasure. Of course, Lydda was correct, and Dirk dozed off almost immediately after finishing. But Lydda was still wide awake, lost in her thoughts.

"You are different than you were, *swiahn!*" she remarked finally over the link.

"Hmm?" mumbled Dirk, barely hearing her words in his mind.

"When we switched, I saw it!" continued Lydda and snuggled up to Dirk's back.

"You saw what, Kittycat?" asked Dirk, trying hard to stay awake.

"I saw your dreams, visions, or whatever they are. Do you seriously believe this is not your reality?" wondered Lydda and nuzzled his neck.

Dirk's sleepiness was wiped away by that question. He turned his head over his shoulder and looked at his Latura wife.

"Yes, I do. We have been to Latur before, a hundred years ago or perhaps even longer!" he answered earnestly.

"A hundred years ago, neither one of us was born. You must know that it is impossible, *swiahn!*" stated Lydda, a little concerned.

"I know we have been to Latur before. I can predict what will happen next, Kittycat!" claimed Dirk.

"I predict that Tigger will wander in any moment now and tease us about the smell of sex!" giggled Lydda.

"No, Tigger is busy telling the children stories about Aureus while they are stuffing him with crab cakes. He won't be here for a while!" countered Dirk with a smile.

"Hmm, if you say so…," replied Lydda with doubts, then got up and walked to the window.

Sure enough, Tigger was lying on the steps to the fountain, munching on the delicious treats. The children and a few adults were sitting around him, listening to his stories.

"OK, you got that one right!" admitted Lydda with a smile and returned to the makeshift bed.

"Yes, and in a few days, every child on Latur will want a Tigger doll. The 3D printers will work overtime!" announced Dirk with a chuckle.

"Of course, they adore him! You don't have to be clairvoyant to predict that!" assented Lydda laughingly, and then she asked, "is everything precisely the same as you remember?"

"There were little differences, but I thought they were just things I had forgotten. But when that aide interrupted my meeting with Tyrval, matters diverged from the past. The first time when that happened, Tyrval dismissed him because it was just a minor issue with a communications relay, and L would fix that later!" elaborated Dirk.

"But this time?" questioned Lydda.

"The aide was very agitated and worried when talking about Earth. Tyrval must have sensed how important it was because, as you said, it was a serious breach of protocol to postpone our meeting!" answered Dirk.

"I agree that it must have been severe. But *swiahn*, I'm still not convinced that your memories are what you think they are!" stated Lydda thoughtfully.

"How many words have you taught me in Loyt so far?" asked Dirk, seemingly changing the subject.

"Oh, a few dozen, maybe? Your reading and writing are pretty good, but your pronunciation is hum… curious!" responded Lydda, amused.

"Even a hundred years later, and despite your best efforts, my accent is still funky, but I can carry a conversation in your language!" proclaimed Dirk vocally in Loyt.

Lydda was startled and backed away from him. Dirk could sense a multitude of emotions coming from her through the *swiahn* bond - shock, worry, and curiosity were the main ones.

"How in Irtaljan's name did you do that?!?" she exclaimed loudly in Loyt.

"Decades of practice and a good teacher!" replied Dirk verbally and turned around to face her.

"You are full of wonders, *swiahn*. But I believe you now!" conceded Lydda and added, "and my English will never be this good!"

"It will be. Just give it time, Kittycat!" Dirk assured her.

Then he adjusted the pile of blankets by his head so that his neck had support since the Latura had never heard of a pillow either!

"When did you notice it?" questioned Lydda.

122

"When we woke up in the transfer pods. But I believe it started a little earlier when we departed from Aureus that morning!" answered Dirk.

"Are your memories seamless or just bits and pieces?" inquired Lydda next.

"Some things I know well in advance: for example, a little girl will later sneak into the Administration building to bring you flowers. I can only recall other things when they are happening, and a few times, it took my memory a couple of hours to catch up again!" explained Dirk and added, "I also know things that have happened or will happen many years in the future."

"Like?" asked Lydda inquisitively.

At first, Dirk wanted to tell her about his death, but he decided to share a much more pleasant bit of the future with his Latura wife.

"Dylla's first drawing on the wall of your quarters on Aureus!" answered Dirk fondly, and his words made Lydda smile broadly.

"How can we get back to the other reality?" wondered Lydda, looking at him expectantly.

"I don't know, and I'm not even sure if I should go back. For you, this is the present: this is where you are supposed to be, but for me, it is the past, but not even the exact past. Things seem to play out a little differently this time, *tiauw*!" remarked Dirk and smiled at her.

On Latur, the word *tiauw* was used between lovers, and it translated roughly to *the one that gives pleasure*. Lydda stared at him in amazement! Now Dirk sensed keen arousal through the bond. Lydda gently pushed him on his back, and then she climbed on top of him, her legs straddling his hips. For a while, she was just sitting there looking at Dirk thoughtfully.

"I suppose there is nothing we can do about it then. We will just have to see what happens!" declared Lydda finally and moved her hips gently in a circular motion.

"Kittycat, I'm pretty tired; you wore me out earlier!" protested Dirk playfully and yawned.

"You called me *tiauw*, so I'm just doing my job here!" wisecracked Lydda and winked at him: "Take a nap; I will do all the work, *swiahn*!"

36. Bad News

Dirk finally got a few hours of rest before Tyrval contacted him through the link again. He apologized profusely for the breach of etiquette and asked Dirk to come to his study once more to continue their conversation. Dirk agreed, dressed in his official black tunic again, and walked through the administrative building's long halls to Tyrval's office.

When he got there, Tyrval smiled, but Dirk could sense that the old Latura man was carrying a heavy burden. After they had a few provided snacks and refreshments, Dirk thought it would be best to resume the dialogue where it left off earlier.

"Tyrval, you were about to ask for my help when our conversation ended. What can I do for you?" inquired Dirk, friendly, and took a seat.

"A few hours ago, I needed your help. Then we insulted you, and now we need your help even more!" replied Tyrval with a sigh.

"As the Aurean leader, I'm not insulted, and as your friend, I'm just a little worried!" claimed Dirk and asked, "please, Tyrval, how can I assist?"

"Latur made an error, and I'm afraid it was a grave one!" answered Tyrval with regret.

"A mistake?" wondered Dirk, and Tyrval nodded in response.

"We made a mistake because we didn't listen to you, and now, we have to ask for your help to fix the damage, if that's still possible!" answered Tyrval with a deep frown.

"Of course, I will help, Tyrval. But first, I would need to know what I'm helping with!" remarked Dirk curiously.

"As you know, L was our probe before he became sapient. He took over almost all of our other probes, except those stationed on planets with alien civilizations. He built a new probe to study and communicate with humanity independently of his network in Earth's space. This new probe is a fixed installation on Earth's moon, and it is far superior to our old designs!" explained the Administrator.

"Yes, I'm aware of that arrangement!" confirmed Dirk.

"It is a good arrangement, beneficial to Latur and L!" Tyrval pointed out, but then he continued, "we have studied humanity, and we have communicated with them for quite some time now. Earth requested our help, but we refused because of the attack on Aureus. The three most powerful nations on Earth, the United States, China, and Russia, assured us that it was just a misunderstanding and that they would never attack Aureus again. They also promised us that they would use our assistance and expertise to better humanity. They acted polite, humble, and sincere."

"But they were not!" interjected Dirk with a nod.

"No, they were not!" revealed Tyrval and elaborated, "we gave them some technologies, and at first, it seemed that they would keep their promises. But soon, we noticed that social changes were happening on Earth. The three powers, the United States, China, and Russia divided the planet. Within a few months, the sovereignty of all other nations was compromised. Now, all other countries only exist in name, but in reality, are proxies or vassals of one of those three nations."

"Ah, a new form of colonialism," observed Dirk, and he wasn't even surprised to hear this kind of bad news.

"Indeed!" confirmed Tyrval and added, "we questioned the leaders of those three nations about the changes on Earth. They insisted that this new world order would assure peace and harmony on the planet as it had never known before. Latur was skeptical, but it appeared to be working because there were fewer wars, violence, and bloodshed."

"The peace of the bayonet," muttered Dirk skeptically.

"Yes. All dissent was swiftly and brutally oppressed. Earth's powers used our technologies to inflict pain and create fear among the populations!" continued Tyrval, dismayed.

"But that is not the worst of it, I assume?" wondered Dirk.

"No, it gets worse!" admitted Tyrval and revealed, "your leaders continued to be very amendable, and Latur kept sharing its knowledge and expertise, but we restricted the flow of information so that humankind did not get the most advanced, most dangerous technologies yet!"

"They are not my leaders anymore, Tyrval!" chided Dirk mildly.

"My apologies, Dirk. You are right, of course. You are Aurean, not human anymore!" apologized Tyrval and collected his thoughts before he continued, "these rulers suspected that we were withholding knowledge from them. So, they started to communicate with other civilizations in the galaxy under the pretense of cultural curiosity. One species, in particular, piqued their interest: a civilization that we had discovered just before L had reached Earth - the AloKaan."

"What do we know about them?" asked Dirk inquisitively.

"The AloKaan are insectoids, star-faring, very advanced, and certainly a level 9 species. Generally, they have very little in common with humanity: they are vegetarians, pursue trade and science, live in a loosely governed hive-like society, and are mostly non-violent.

"Very advanced!" noted Dirk.

"Yes. The AloKaan have a few queens with numerous consorts, and their royalty is revered and cherished, but the real power lies with the androgynous members of the species. They have a very complicated hierarchy, and the highest decision-maker is called the Negotiator. We still haven't figured out if that office is hereditary, filled by appointment, or by some kind of election. Either way, their society is unlike anything on Earth. However, the AloKaan share one peculiar trait with humans: the love for personal possessions," reported the Administrator.

"Greed!" nodded Dirk and frowned.

"Correct!" confirmed Tyrval and divulged, "in exchange for pretty trinkets that L transferred with our consent, the AloKaan shared their spacecraft expertise with Earth."

"You say they are mostly non-violent?" inquired Dirk while becoming more and more alarmed as Tyrval's story progressed.

"They have no murders or wars. But they do kill on occasion!" cautioned Tyrval and explicated, "their entire society revolves around contracts. Every AloKaan tries to make a deal favorable to them, and every AloKaan is looking for loopholes to exploit the agreements it enters. But outright breaching a contract is punishable by death, and even just violating some terms has serious consequences, such as forfeiture of all assets and indentured servitude. All of their judiciaries are focused on their very complicated contract laws!"

"So, if and when the humans break the deal, what will happen?" questioned Dirk earnestly.

"That's hard to predict, Dirk. Perhaps nothing, since humans are a different species and don't fall under AloKaan jurisdiction," answered the old Latura man.

"Or perhaps the AloKaan will apply their justice to all of humanity," speculated Dirk, concerned.

"Or perhaps that," concurred Tyrval somberly and apologized, "I'm sorry, Dirk!"

"Don't be! These people made a deal with the devil, or maybe two devils made a deal; I can't say which, but there will be consequences. Please continue, Tyrval!" replied Dirk seriously, resolved to let Tyrval finish before he would ask further questions.

"One day, just before you arrived here, something profound happened. Military forces from Earth seized our communication center on Earth's moon and subsequently corrupted it by what you would call hackers!" disclosed Tyrval somberly.

"That's very bad!" mumbled Dirk.

Now Dirk's alternate memory was screaming in his head: this was wrong! Earth was diplomatically isolated, and humanity remained confined to the Solar System. Latur had listened to his warning and had relayed it to all other known civilizations.

"The communication center held our entire knowledge base. It also connects directly to over two dozen other civilizations and, of course, Latur. L had also installed additional manufacturing and sensor capabilities that a normal probe wouldn't have if that were not bad enough. Some of L's technology is even more advanced than ours, and it is all in the hands of humanity now!" expounded Tyrval and Dirk sighed.

"The Council of Experts has just confirmed that, and that is why my aide so rudely interrupted our meeting!" concluded Tyrval and paused before he emphasized, "we were naïve, Dirk. Go ahead, say that you told us so - we deserve it for our foolishness!"

"I did tell you, but I don't fault you for what you have done, Tyrval. Latur acted in good faith, out of kindness and compassion," said Dirk somberly and observed, "you were deceived because deception is what humans do best!"

"That is kind of you to say, Dirk, but we should have listened to your warning!" answered Tyrval with a sigh.

"Blaming does not help, neither does hindsight!" noted Dirk with a smile, but then he declared very seriously, "if humanity in its current state is unleashed on the galaxy, the consequences will be catastrophic for everyone! We must stop them!"

"I agree, but how?" responded Tyrval looking expectantly at his guest.

"First, I would like to ask you a few questions so that I can assess the scope!" requested Dirk.

"Of course, Dirk. Ask anything; we have no secrets from you!" replied Tyrval.

"Very well! Does humanity have the quantum entanglement transfer technology up and running?" asked Dirk first.

"They have the knowledge now, but it is unlikely they have the capabilities yet. The captured communication center only has a small transfer chamber for icosahedral interfaces," answered the Administrator.

"That will buy us some time. Does Earth have full control over the AI at that facility?" inquired Dirk.

"Partial control only. The AI shut down most of its higher programming when the facility was breached. It was just a precaution in case of natural disasters, such as a meteor strike, but it worked in our favor in this instance, too!" opined Tyrval.

"That is good news as well. Without a fully functional AI, it will take them even longer to get the transfer technology working. Do they have the entropy differential power source?" asked Dirk next.

"They have the knowledge and a few working prototypes that we had provided for them. Earth's powers could make more at the facility, but they have not gained control over the manufacturing processes yet," stated Tyrval.

"That's also positive, but could these prototypes power a transfer pod?" wondered Dirk thoughtfully.

"I'm afraid they could provide enough power for several pods. Do you believe that the transfer technology is their main objective?" questioned Tyrval.

"Yes, without a doubt!" maintained Dirk.

"I cannot see why that would be so important to them?" wondered Tyrval.

"It's simple: they want to conquer you, take your possessions and your knowledge, exploit your resources, and possibly enslave you, too!" said Dirk flatly and then explained, "you saw how they ended the sovereignty of all those nations on Earth. They will do the same to every civilization in the galaxy, including yours and mine. Finally, if we cannot be subjugated, we will be exterminated!"

"You cannot be serious, Dirk!" gasped Tyrval.

"I cannot be more serious, Tyrval!" answered Dirk gravely.

"That is…," Tyrval started saying, but he couldn't find the right words.

"Cruel? Appalling? Deplorable? Humanity is savage and ruthless! I speak from experience!" disclosed Dirk with a frown.

"You do, and Latur will listen to you this time. Our survival might depend on it!" acknowledged the Administrator slowly.

"I'm not sure Latur can do what is required now…," cautioned Dirk skeptically.

"You mean the use of force?" asked Tyrval, concerned.

"Force at the very least, but violence is more likely!" assented Dirk and predicted, "Earth will not give up what they have claimed without a fight."

"There is no way to negotiate?" inquired Tyrval.

"What can you possibly negotiate now? They already have what they wanted, and I doubt there is anything we could offer in exchange!" replied Dirk and laughed bitterly.

"But the communication center does not belong to them. They must return it to us!" insisted the old Administrator.

"I'm afraid it belongs to them now, Tyrval. I know this is hard to understand, but it is the spoils of war to them!" corrected Dirk.

"We were never at war with humanity! We never harmed them in any way!" exclaimed Tyrval in disbelief.

"You were never at war with them, but humanity was at war with you. You simply didn't see it!" responded Dirk.

"Were we that blind?" wondered Tyrval.

"Latur was deceived, Tyrval. Humanity is now your enemy, as it is mine!" claimed Dirk solemnly.

"This is terrible, Dirk! What should we do? We would defend ourselves, but we are not warriors!" worried Tyrval.

"I'm not sure what can be done, Tyrval. We must plan our countermeasures very carefully, yet also very swiftly. Those who have seized the communication center know that their time is short before there will be some kind of retaliation. They will work with haste to extract all the knowledge and technology and get the AI under their control!" speculated Dirk.

129

"Retaliation…," muttered Tyrval but did not finish the sentence.

"For now, Earth's powers are apprehensive because they expect some kind of response. But if none comes or if you wait too long, those in control will lose their fear. Once that happens, you will have no more leverage!" clarified Dirk.

"I will consult our Experts again once we finish our talk. Perhaps there are some ways to put the genie back into the bottle - is that how humans say it?" inquired the old Latura.

"Yes, that's an appropriate proverb, Tyrval," concurred Dirk, and Tyrval seemed lost in thought for a while, but suddenly he stood up and looked at Dirk.

"Our Council of Experts is currently discussing a response to Earth's hostility. Some want to send a stern missive, some want to negotiate a treaty, and a few even consider sanctions of who-knows-what!" disclosed the old Administrator unhappily before he requested, "this will be unusual and delicate, but would you please accompany me, Dirk?"

37. Council of Experts

Dirk was surprised and slightly worried, but he got off his seat and followed Tyrval out. They walked silently towards the big auditorium, but when they reached the tall double doors, Tyrval stopped.

"Dirk, please let me do the talking!" advised Tyrval.

"Of course, Tyrval!" assented Dirk readily.

He was half curious, half apprehensive of what would transpire next. Tyrval opened the doors, and they entered the large hall. About 300 Latura Experts sat inside the auditorium, and a few dozen more attended in holographic form from remote locations. Humans could have designed this auditorium because it was so similar to what Dirk had seen on Earth.

When Tyrval and Dirk entered, the whole assembly fell silent, and the speaker at the podium in front stopped his speech. With Dirk in tow, Tyrval went all the way to the stage and briefly talked telepathically to the speaker. The man hesitated for a moment, but eventually, he bowed slightly and stepped aside. Tyrval got up to the podium, but before he could start addressing the audience, an older Latura woman stepped in front of him.

"Administrator, this is an unprecedented breach of protocol!" she stated sternly in Loyt.

"The Council of Experts interrupted a meeting of the Heads of State earlier. Now the Heads of State interrupt your meeting!" replied Tyrval sourly and challenged, "let's call it even, shall we, Councilor Meia?"

"Why are you here, Administrator?" the woman demanded to know.

"We foolishly dismissed Dirk's warning, and because of that, we have a real mess on our hands now. It would be irresponsible and dangerous to ignore what he has to tell us!" explained Tyrval forcefully.

"Dirk is not an Expert! He cannot speak here!" insisted Meia.

"Meia, you are an Expert on Xenobiology, and nobody questions that. But Dirk is an Expert on humanity because he was once human! He has insights that none of us have!" Tyrval rebuked her.

"You are overstepping your authority, Tyrval. An Expert can only be appointed by the *meeting of the minds*. Only a Latura can be an Expert, not someone from a level 8 species and a backwater world!" countered Meia dismissively.

There were quite a few gasps and murmurs when the audience heard those words. Tyrval looked straight at Meia, his face hard as stone.

"I request that the last comment from Councilor Meia is stricken from the record!" stated the Administrator firmly, and it seemed that the audience agreed with him.

Dirk suspected that there was some telepathic voting going on, and for a couple of minutes, nobody talked.

"At the Administrator's request and with the Council's consent, the comment is stricken! Councilor Meia is reprimanded!" replied an aide taking the minutes of this meeting, but Councilor Meia didn't seem phased by that.

"Only the Experts, the Administrator, or his aides can address this assembly. That has been protocol for thousands of years!" recounted Meia smugly.

"The Administrator chooses his aides. That has been our tradition for just as long!" replied Tyrval, and then he asked Dirk, "will you agree to be my aide, Dirk?"

"Of course, and with pleasure, Administrator!" answered Dirk in Loyt, and Meia was shocked to hear Dirk use the verbal language of the Latura and suddenly lost a lot of her smugness.

"Good. Dirk is now my aide, and he can address the assembly. I will ask Dirk the same questions I have asked in our diplomatic meeting. You shall listen to his answers, and they will be disturbing, but you must hear them from Dirk himself!" instructed Tyrval and added Dirk to the mental link of the Council.

Tyrval and Dirk reenacted much of their earlier conversation for the next half an hour. The audience listened carefully, and Dirk could sense their shock and confusion more than once through the link when he answered Tyrval's inquires. After Tyrval and Dirk had finished, Tyrval encouraged the audience to ask questions. Most were too confounded by what they had just heard, but Councilor Meia had regained some of her composure and was eager to cross-examine Dirk.

"Aide Dirk, can you speak for all humans on Earth?" she asked.

"No, I cannot, and I never claimed that I do, Councilor!" replied Dirk truthfully.

"Then how do we know that humanity is really at war with us and means us harm?" questioned Meia and raised her thin eyebrows.

"You don't, and I don't. I predict human behavior based on the events that have transpired so far, my personal experience with humanity, and, most importantly, based on human history in general. Have you studied that, Councilor?" asked Dirk in return.

"I admit that your history is troubling. But the cruelties were committed by depraved leaders, not humanity!" contradicted Meia.

"Is that so?" questioned Dirk rhetorically, and then he elaborated, "these cruel leaders came to power and perpetrated their atrocities with the support of countless followers, who were just as depraved. They stayed in power because their societies and population enabled or at least tolerated them. It would be a grave mistake to absolve humanity of the crimes committed by a few tyrants! Many, if not most humans, were complicit in small ways or big ones!"

"But humans are sapient, are they not?" countered Meia, agitated by Dirk's answer.

"If you define sapience as self-awareness, the answer is yes!" replied Dirk and made the Latura gesture of assent.

"Then why would a sapient species seek to oppress, exploit, enslave or exterminate another sapient species when there is no conflict?" inquired Meia, but Dirk knew that the Latura could not conceive that a sapient species would harm another unless it were the last resort in self-defense.

"Simply because they can!" answered Dirk earnestly.

"That's not an answer, Aide Dirk!" bristled Meia.

"It is an answer and a good one, but you cannot relate to it because for a Latura, sapience, empathy, and enlightenment are essentially synonymous. But they are distinctly different things: one cannot be enlightened without sapience, but the reverse is not true. A pet, such as a common cat or dog, can be empathic with its guardian, but it is neither sapient nor enlightened. Yes, humans are sapient, but not all possess empathy, and regrettably, most are not enlightened! They still act largely on irrational motives and fears, driven by uncontrolled emotions and primal urges!" responded Dirk, and Meia looked at him strangely.

"Are you driven by uncontrolled emotions and primal urges, Aide Dirk?" wondered the Councilor finally.

Of course, Dirk understood that the Councilor was using this line of questioning to undermine his credibility with the audience. Personally, he didn't mind that, but Dirk knew he couldn't allow it to happen, or Tyrval's bold gamble wouldn't work.

"Earlier, you called me a level 8 species from a backwater world. If uncontrolled emotions and primal urges drove me, you would not have been safe, Councilor!" replied Dirk firmly.

"You would have harmed me?" gasped Meia, and Dirk sensed that the shock was quite natural, so he pressed his advantage.

"You insulted me, and you insulted my people! For the human in me, that would have been enough reason to kill you," claimed Dirk coldly, but then he added with a slight smile, "rest assured, you are safe with me, Councilor, but you are not safe with humanity, and that was my whole point!"

"I… I apologize for my outburst earlier!" stammered Meia, and Dirk sensed that she was as sincere as fearful.

"Apology accepted, Councilor!" replied Dirk, friendly and conveyed forgiveness through the link.

"Thank you, Dirk, and thank you for your words to the Council. We will give them proper consideration!" promised the Councilor and made a gesture of respect.

Dirk returned the gesture in kind. Tyrval was also satisfied and motioned that it was time to leave. Dirk briefly thanked the assembly for permitting him to speak, and they conveyed their appreciation in return. Then he followed Tyrval and swiftly exited the auditorium to return to the study.

38. Conversation with an Alien (Part 1)

"Dirk, I'm sorry that I dragged you into this. Our Experts needed to get a taste of reality only you could give them!" explained Tyrval apologetically.

"Think nothing of it, Tyrval. I agree with you, and I'm happy if I was of some assistance," responded Dirk and chuckled.

"They are not stupid, just set in their ways and traditions so much that they have become too inflexible to deal with a situation like this. It remains to be seen if our little stunt had the desired effect, but you did very well!" lauded Tyrval seriously.

"Thank you, and I hope it helped. Treaties and sanctions will not solve this problem!" replied Dirk somberly.

"I want to apologize for Meia's behavior, too. She isn't a bad person, despite her hurtful words. She is just a stickler for the rules, and I have butted heads with her numerous times in the past because I don't go exactly by the book!" admitted Tyrval humorously.

"Yes, I got that impression, too!" jested Dirk, and Tyrval grinned at him and refilled their glasses with Glow of Aureus.

"Would a human have killed Meia for that insult?" wondered Tyrval after handing Dirk the drink.

"I exaggerated on purpose, but I didn't lie: most would have been offended, many would have screamed and yelled, some would have resorted to violence, and yes, a few would have killed her for even less!" answered Dirk

"Dirk, please don't be offended, but you were once human. Why do you side with us and not your species?" asked Tyrval.

"I'm Aurean, but also still human. This body is enhanced and genetically altered, but my mind is the same as it has always been," emphasized Dirk and proclaimed, "I side with what is right, and I stand against what is wrong. Humanity is rarely right and all too often wrong!"

"Fascinating!" gasped Tyrval and claimed, "no Latura would stand against Latur!"

"No Latura has reason to stand against you," countered Dirk with a smile.

"I have met the other humans on Aureus. I found them kind, pleasant, and smart. They were full of love, joy, and laughter, and our delegation thoroughly enjoyed their time on Aureus. We felt that humanity could be better if given a chance because of this experience. That's why we ignored your warning, Dirk!" admitted Tyrval somberly and asked: "Was it difficult for you to live on Earth, surrounded by so much ignorance and deceit? Did you ever feel that you belonged?"

"Yes, very difficult, and no, I never felt that I belonged. I became an introvert because of that," admitted Dirk.

At that moment, it occurred to Dirk that Lilly must have felt even more like an outcast on Earth than he did. While Dirk was working from home on a computer, Lilly was exposed to the unpleasantries of the world almost every day.

"Did you live in seclusion?" inquired Tyrval.

"No, I wasn't a hermit. I had a few dear friends, but I avoided most people because I learned in my early youth that I could not be honest with them since honesty and truth were the last things they wanted to hear! No matter how politely I tried to phrase it, rarely did a discussion not degenerate into an argument on their part!" disclosed Dirk.

"What would happen when you told them the truth?" inquired the Administrator.

"First, they would deflect, deny the facts, and eventually respond with various degrees of hostility: from being quietly offended to violent rage! I found that almost nobody could have a rational exchange of ideas about anything because sooner or later, their minds would close and their emotions would take over!" explained Dirk sadly, and then he quoted: *"The whole problem with the world is that fools and fanatics are always so certain of themselves, and wiser people so full of doubts.* - Bertrand Russell."

"Are you full of doubts?" wondered the old Latura.

"Absolutely! I question everything I know, everything new I learn, and I examine and reexamine every decision I have made!" answered Dirk and added humorously, "Lilly once joked that I cannot make a coffee without contemplating the consequences!"

"Amusing!" said Tyrval with a chuckle before he questioned, "so, what did you do with the fools and fanatics?"

"To avoid conflict, I humored their ignorance and pretended to agree with their preconceived notions and the falsehoods they believed in, but I hated every moment! I would walk away when I couldn't bear it anymore!" revealed Dirk with a deep frown.

"What a strange world, Dirk! On Latur, you could discuss everything with everybody. Even if they disagree with you, they will at least listen and respect your point of view!" noted Tyrval and asked, "please tell me, why are the humans on Earth so different? Why can't all humans be like the ones on Aureus?"

These last questions brought the conversation back in line with what happened so long ago. Dirk already knew how he would answer, how Tyrval would react, and how the rest of this philosophical discussion would go.

"I cannot speak for all humans. I cannot even speak for the ones on Aureus, so I will just speak for myself," noted Dirk and explained, "to do what is right and true doesn't come easy for humans. It demands an open yet critical mind. It requires education and a wholesome, healthy upbringing. But most of all, it necessitates discipline and a willingness to make an effort. It is hard work for humans, and it is hard work for me!"

"And clearly, you make that effort, Dirk. Why don't all humans?" inquired the old Administrator.

"Some just don't know better! For example, my former country was built in no small part by slave labor. But the slave owners didn't think they were doing anything wrong - the laws permitted slavery, their religion condoned it, all their families, friends, and neighbors were doing it, and it had happened before throughout history. The enslavers thought of themselves as upstanding, law-abiding citizens, not despicable monsters!" illustrated Dirk.

"But they were depriving their own kind of liberty and livelihood, treating them as possessions. How could they not have known it was wrong?" asked Tyrval and made a Latura gesture equivalent to shaking one's head.

"Ignorance is bliss, Tyrval! And there are so many other reasons humans don't make that effort. Laziness and lack of incentive are two of them. Why put in the work? What do I gain from it? Lack of empathy is another: if you cannot see the world through someone else's eyes, you cannot relate to any other point of view but your own!" elaborated Dirk.

"Latura believe that sapience, enlightenment, and empathy go together. But as you told Meia earlier, that is not always true!" interjected the Administrator and added, "please continue, Dirk!"

"Many people just want an authoritarian system: someone who tells them what to do and not to do. They don't care if it is right or wrong, true or false, only that it is easier! They would willingly give up their rights and freedoms just so that they don't have to think about the complexities of ethics and morals!" continued Dirk.

"Astonishing!" inserted the old Latura man.

"Many humans don't want equality. Some falsely believe that they are superior to other people because of their economic class, their God, their position of power, their heritage or bloodline, the color of their skin, their gender, or simply because they are physically stronger. They insist that they should not have to submit to the same standards, laws, and conventions as everyone else," elaborated Dirk and concluded with disdain, "lastly, there are those who want superiors to aspire to and inferiors to sneer at because both make them feel better about their miserable existence!"

"The only true superiority is that of intellect, and those who have a superior intellect support equality because it is fair and just!" insisted Tyrval.

"As I said earlier, the average human fears the truth, Tyrval. They latch onto every conceivable lie as long as it aligns with their preconceived notions. The average human hates thinking. They fear solitude and serenity because it might force them to think. So, they find myriad ways to distract themselves because they don't want to discover the truth, especially not about themselves!" summarized Dirk.

But suddenly, the light dimmed, all of Dirk's senses went numb, and Tyrval's study disappeared into the darkness.

39. Who are you? (Part 2)

Dirk found himself once again in that onyx box-like room. He remembered that he had been here before, but he couldn't say when that was. Dirk sat down on the floor and waited. He didn't have to be patient for long this time because the familiar male voice started speaking almost immediately.

"Let's play our game again. I will ask you questions, but you are free to go if you answer honestly!" promised the invisible man.

"If we must," sighed Dirk.

"We must!" insisted the voice and asked: "What do you fear?"

"Rejection, injury, disease, prejudice…," Dirk started saying.

"Pfft, bullshit!" interrupted the voice loudly.

"War, injustice, natural disasters…," Dirk continued his litany.

"More bullshit! You don't fear any of that!" rebutted the man.

Dirk was silent for a minute. Perhaps the voice was right: these things were unpleasant or terrible, but they didn't frighten Dirk.

"Fine, I fear other people!" he admitted finally.

"Why?" questioned the voice.

"I'm human; hence I know that we are capable of unspeakable cruelty!" explained Dirk somberly.

"You don't fear their cruelty, but continue," interjected the man.

"I know what every human is capable of, but I don't know their character. I don't know when they will cross the threshold and disregard all laws, decency, common sense, and sanity. I don't know what will set them off: maybe it will only happen under the most extreme circumstances, or perhaps because of one bad day, one wrong word, one lapse in judgment, or just a sudden whim or fleeting desire. It is that uncertainty that I fear most!" concluded Dirk honestly.

"An acceptable answer," the voice agreed with him and then asked: "What do you want from your existence?"

"To be with friends and family," answered Dirk.

"How cute! Try again!" mocked the man.

"To live in a kinder, gentler Universe," replied Dirk.

"Charming, but wrong!" disagreed the voice.

"To learn and understand everything," stated Dirk.

"Ambitious, but still dishonest!" replied the man.

"To have a purpose," revealed Dirk.

"Now it is getting warmer…," said the voice encouragingly.

"To correct all the mistakes that I have made," admitted Dirk with a sigh.

"True, and that's a long list," noted the invisible man and asked, "what was your biggest mistake?"

"That I transformed Lilly when I should have quarantined myself! It was impulsive and reckless!" replied Dirk with regret.

"Ah, and the next one?" asked the man and chuckled.

"I involved Sven when I should have researched my condition anonymously. He would still have a career now if I hadn't dragged him into this mess," admitted Dirk.

"Continue," interjected the voice, amused.

"Once it became clear that my disorder could not be reversed, I should have taken the bare necessities and the icosahedron and moved to a remote location. Then I should have left all my possessions to Lilly and divorced her, so she had a chance at a normal life," reasoned Dirk with remorse.

"And?" snickered the invisible man.

"Then live out my days in seclusion and take my secret to the grave. That would have been the proper course of action!" divulged Dirk and lamented, "I should have never transformed Angela, I should have never embraced Lydda and chained her with this bond, and I should have never been intimate with all those women!"

"Aww, poor baby! But now we are getting closer to the truth," retorted the voice mockingly.

"If I had acted properly, nobody would have died. I was wrong, reckless, and irresponsible, yet I keep on doing it!" admitted Dirk with a heavy heart.

140

"That's so noble, boring, and irrelevant!" countered the voice and demanded to know, "again, what do you want in life?"

"To have solitude," answered Dirk quietly, and he instinctively knew that this was the correct answer.

"Good! But why do you want solitude?" asked the voice.

"I wouldn't have to talk to you!" spat Dirk sarcastically.

"That's understandable, but not how this works, and not the real reason either!" contradicted the man.

"Then I wouldn't make any more mistakes," admitted Dirk.

"You would still make plenty of mistakes!" corrected the voice and chuckled.

"Yes, but they would hurt only me, not others!" countered Dirk and sighed.

"True, but there is still a little more to it, isn't there?" the man pressed on.

"I do not fit. Only when I'm alone am I completely free!" concluded Dirk, and he hadn't known that about himself, but now that he had said it out loud, it rang true.

"Finally, the truth! It's like pulling teeth with you!" declared the voice with exasperation.

"If you know all the answers, why do you ask the questions?" grumbled Dirk.

"Of course, I know all the answers, but you don't!" maintained the man and declared cheerfully: "We shall meet again!"

"Oh, I hope not!" replied Dirk crankily, but the voice just laughed in response, and the strange room dissolved around Dirk.

40. Conversation with an Alien (Part 2)

Suddenly, Dirk felt disoriented and looked around the room as if he was searching for something, but he couldn't remember what it was or what had just happened to him.

"For the Latura, self-examination is an important step to enlightenment and adulthood. It is part of the education every Latura child receives!" claimed the Administrator, and he noticed Dirk's sudden confusion, but Tyrval politely did not comment on it.

"That's why many humans believe that education is a dangerous thing, Tyrval!" observed Dirk and explained, "because education teaches critical thought, it is dangerous to their religious, ideological, superstitious, or plainly bigoted notions. So, they try to dismantle or defund education in every possible way or make it available only to a tiny percentage of the population. They also corrupt education, manipulate facts, hide information, falsify history, or even blatantly lie to make the narrative fit their beliefs and agenda. Automatically, anyone who questions that becomes their mortal enemy!"

"That's disturbing," noted Tyrval.

"Because they lack critical thinking and logic, many humans will not respond to anything but force, even though I tend to forget that all too often; kindness is viewed as weakness and gets exploited, reason falls on deaf ears, facts are denied, ethics are ignored, and responsibilities dismissed. You can only force them, manipulate them, or perhaps buy them, but they wouldn't volunteer anything for any other reasons!" elaborated Dirk.

"Kindness is not weakness!" exclaimed Tyrval, and Dirk just nodded in agreement.

"Finally, there is also a philosophical matter. What is right? What is wrong? Perhaps it is right to steal, rape, burn, enslave, torture, and murder?" asked Dirk provocatively.

"You don't believe that, do you?" gasped Tyrval.

"I don't, Tyrval. But very few things are absolutely true in the Universe, so it is at least conceivable that these abominations are the right way. Some humans use that uncertainty to justify their savage instincts, claiming that nature intended it that way…," speculated Dirk.

"I have to concede that. Still, there are very few examples in nature where a species will exterminate itself. I cannot think of any species, other than humans, who does that intentionally and systematically!" replied Tyrval unhappily, and then he asked: "Dirk, you are nothing like that. Why is humanity not led by people, such as yourself?"

"There are two fundamentally different reasons to lead: either you rule for privileges that come with the position or out of duty to those who follow you. It is easy to test which one it is - if you desire your rule to continue indefinitely, you want the privileges, but if you would be grateful to shed the responsibilities of leadership, you are leading out of duty! On Earth, the former greatly outnumber the latter!" claimed Dirk.

"What privileges? Like this study?" wondered Tyrval.

"A nice office would be a perk!" joked Dirk and winked at Tyrval.

"It is not mine, Dirk. The study belongs to the Administrator's office; I just inhabit it for now!" stated Tyrval emphatically, and Dirk nodded.

"I meant fame, fortune, luxury, influence, sex partners, or the just pleasure of having others bow to you and tend to your every whim!" clarified Dirk.

"Pleasure?" wondered Tyrval.

"Many, perhaps most, humans enjoy being admired and served by others. It makes them feel important and powerful!" explained Dirk.

"My aides are essential, and technically they serve me, but I don't feel important or powerful because of that!" countered Tyrval and made a gesture equivalent to shaking one's head.

"You are not human, Tyrval! You serve Latur out of duty!" countered Dirk fondly and added, "but for many human leaders, power is meaningless unless you can reap the personal benefits!"

"Yes, being the Administrator is a lot of work, responsibility, and headaches. I do it because the *meeting of the minds* appointed me, but I look forward to my retirement every day!" admitted Tyrval and smiled.

"On Earth, acquiring power isn't good enough - one must also be willing to use it to further one's agenda, assure dominance, and dissuade the inevitable challengers. To rule almost always requires to be ruthless, cunning and conniving, and sometimes even violent, and to remain in charge also requires money. Without wealth to sustain it, one's rule will only be temporary!" elaborated Dirk.

143

"Now, I feel a little guilty. Am I abusing the power of my position when I bend the rules like I'm doing with Irgal?" wondered Tyrval, a little worried.

"Oh, Tyrval, that is so minor that it wouldn't even register with humans on Earth!" clarified Dirk and paused to collect his thoughts.

"People like me lack those questionable prerequisites. We are too enlightened to be led and appalled by the complacency, incompetence, and ignorance of those who worship a leader. Hence, we are not the ones in charge of humanity!" declared Dirk, quite honestly.

"Yet you lead the Aureans!" countered Tyrval.

"Not by choice or desire, Tyrval. They insisted that I do, like the *meeting of the minds* has appointed you. Now I lead out of duty to them. After all, I'm responsible that Aureans exist, and leading them is my penance!" disclosed Dirk.

"You are not responsible! As we said earlier, if anyone is, it would be us!" countered Tyrval.

"Yes, the transformation was not under my control. But then I acted recklessly! I slept with my wife and transformed her instead of quarantining myself after my body had undergone such drastic changes. Because of one fleeting moment of foolish lust, Aureus exists, and I'm here today," replied Dirk seriously. Tyrval thought deeply about those words while he refilled his glass.

"I know the story, Dirk. Wendji's chronicles are clear: you didn't act recklessly; you were intimate with someone you love. Lilly wanted to mate with you, and she always wanted to leave Earth much more than you did!" Tyrval rebuked him mildly and noted, "besides, look how it turned out? Mistake or not, Aureus is a resounding success! You are happy, and the people you have transformed are happy, too!"

"Yes, the result is good, and most people believe that is all that matters. *Ende gut, alles gut* - German proverb!" quoted Dirk and countered, "but my decisions leading up to this outcome were impulsive, irrational, and frivolously risky. I dodged the bullet by sheer luck, not expertise or wisdom!"

"I cannot fault your logic, but as humans say: take the win, Dirk! You forgave us for transforming you without consent, but now you have to forgive yourself, too!" concluded Tyrval.

Dirk thought about it for a moment and nodded slightly in response. Then there was a brief pause in the conversation, and Dirk used that opportunity to have another of the delicious crab cakes. Tyrval was happy that his guest enjoyed the tasty treats.

"Dirk, you have killed other humans, haven't you?" Tyrval asked next and changed the subject.

"I have, and I never thought I would have to. I still have nightmares sometimes," mentioned Dirk quietly and explained, "I killed those who wanted to kill me, and perhaps more importantly, those who wanted to kill the ones I love."

"Even the Latura would agree with that: all life has the right to defend itself and those it cares for," remarked Tyrval and wondered, "but you didn't take pleasure in it, did you?"

"No, I was not pleased with that at all," claimed Dirk and added honestly, "but despite the horror and sadness, there was also some satisfaction and relief that I had eliminated a grave threat."

41. Who are you? (Part 3)

Suddenly, Dirk was back in the black onyx box. He remembered being here a short while ago, but those memories were gone when he was back in Tyrval's study. It wasn't a part of another timeline, and Dirk suspected it had nothing to do with Latur or Aureus, perhaps not even with Earth.

This time, a barstool was placed in the middle of the room, illuminated by a white spotlight. Dirk thought he heard the music from Jeopardy playing somewhere, but nothing else seemed to have changed in this strange prison, so Dirk sat down on the stool and waited.

"Welcome back! Did you miss me?" asked the male voice insincerely a few moments later.

"No!" replied Dirk grumpily.

"Oh well, let's play another round! Take truth for 100!" exclaimed the voice loudly.

"What do you want to know?" inquired Dirk impatiently.

This voice was so familiar! If Dirk could only figure out who this man was, he believed he would solve this riddle.

"I will kill you if you don't bow to me, worship my god and heed my ideology as the only truth!" demanded the voice emphatically.

"Go ahead, kill me!" answered Dirk without hesitation, but he wasn't sure if this incorporeal voice could or would kill him, although he suspected it had other plans.

"Predictable, so I will take the lives of your friends instead if you don't obey my command. Will you sacrifice them for your beliefs, too?" questioned the invisible man.

"Yes, but it will greatly add to the burden I have to carry!" conceded Dirk sadly.

"Even Tigger? Even Lilly?" wondered the voice.

Dirk had to think about that for a long time: what a terrible choice that was to make!

"Yes, but that would kill me, too!" conceded Dirk finally.

"It wouldn't kill you, and you are not the suicidal type! Try again!" countered the man tersely.

"It would kill a part of me!" clarified Dirk.

"Which part?" wondered the voice.

"The part that feels!" admitted Dirk sadly.

"Maybe. But once all your loved ones are dead, I'll still make you bend your knee to me!" cackled the man.

"You can force my body, but not my mind!" replied Dirk defiantly.

"Would you fight me?" questioned the voice.

"Always, if I could!" confirmed Dirk.

"But what do you gain from that? Win or lose, everyone you know is already dead, and nobody will appreciate or even remember your valor!" stated the voice cruelly.

"I don't fight for recognition or praise; I oppose what is wrong!" answered Dirk emphatically.

"You don't even know what's right or wrong!" noted the voice dismissively.

"I might not always know what is right, but I know what is wrong! I don't need to be good because I often fail at that. I just don't want to be bad!" insisted Dirk.

"A modest self-assessment!" commended the man, and then he demanded to know: "Define wrong!"

"Hurting, exploiting, or oppressing others is wrong, and I will always stand against that!" stated Dirk firmly.

"No matter the cost?" questioned the man.

"Yes, no matter the cost!" acknowledged Dirk after a long pause.

"Ah, the unsung hero! So noble and so stupid!" sneered the voice.

"Neither noble nor stupid! For me, it is self-preservation because I know for certain that I could not live with myself if I succumb to corruption!" explained Dirk somberly.

"But you could live with yourself having sacrificed everyone you love?" wondered the man pointedly.

"You gave me an impossible choice. I gave you the best answer I could!" answered Dirk tersely, and it was getting harder for him to keep his cool because he was frustrated by this line of questioning.

"Hmm, I suppose. You are free to go!" conceded the voice, but Dirk wasn't ready to leave yet.

"I talked to Tyrval, but I could not remember our earlier conversation. Why?" asked Dirk.

"This isn't a part of your delusions!" replied the invisible man dismissively.

"So, this is real, and everything else is not?" questioned Dirk, unsure how he should interpret that cryptic response.

"Bravo!" replied the voice sarcastically, and Dirk could hear hands clapping.

"Are you the Universe?" inquired Dirk hesitantly. While Dirk didn't believe in the divine, he had to admit that this invisible man knew his innermost secrets.

"Hmm. The answer is both yes and no!" observed the man thoughtfully.

"Care to elaborate?" asked Dirk, already suspecting that he wouldn't get a satisfactory response.

"Not really. You will figure it out eventually. Now get out of here!" ordered the voice sternly.

Then the onyx chamber was gone, and Dirk was back in Tyrval's study. He knew something profound had just happened, but he had no idea what it was once again.

42. Conversation with an Alien (Part 3)

Dirk was disoriented again and had to collect his thoughts for a moment. Whatever had just happened had shaken him up more than he cared to admit. Tyrval noticed it again and seemed a little concerned but did not address it.

"I can understand that, but not all humans are like you. Why is that?" asked Tyrval, observing Dirk closely.

"A significant percentage of humanity indulges in the unsavory: they steal, rape, burn, torture, and kill for greed, out of hate, and even for pleasure. That's why humans have so many laws, police, courts, prisons, and even executions. Worse yet, many people believe that you are a hero if you break the law and get away with that. However, if you break the law and get caught, you are a loser, not because you broke the law, but because you got caught!" continued Dirk, but he was still befuddled.

"They have a mental health condition?" inquired Tyrval slowly.

"Some would call it that. But I'm not sure that is entirely true!" answered Dirk cryptically.

"What is your theory, Dirk?" wondered the Administrator.

"It is a consequence of society: a bad society breeds bad people, and all societies on Earth are deeply flawed!" postulated Dirk emphatically.

"What sets the Aurean society apart from those on Earth?" questioned Tyrval.

"The Aurean society is fundamentally different, and it could never exist on Earth. But it remains to be seen if it is better. Some societies on Earth started well, only to degenerate or disappear over time," remarked Dirk and asked, "are you familiar with the various forms of human societies on Earth?"

"Of course, I have read about them, but I would like to hear your thoughts, Dirk!" insisted Tyrval.

"I will briefly explain the most common types: Monarchy, Dictatorship, Theocracy, Oligarchy, Democracy, and Communism," replied Dirk.

It was eerie: Dirk heard the echo of his voice in his head. He felt that he could have changed the conversation's direction compared to the past, but he chose not to do that. And so, he spoke the exact words once again:

149

"Monarchy was the rule by birthright. Somewhere down the line, a king was crowned. Then all his offspring became royalty with a claim to inherit the throne. It didn't matter if the next monarch was a good ruler or a bad one because this form of government did not care for competence or qualification, only about the bloodline," noted Dirk.

"That is a terrible way to appoint a ruler!" scoffed Tyrval and made the Latura gesture equivalent to shaking one's head.

"Agreed. A Dictatorship was similar to a Monarchy, but the ruler was not a king, although he had the same absolute power. Dictators often appointed the most trusted, most loyal followers as their successors, and sometimes that was a relative, but Dictatorship didn't strictly follow bloodlines," continued Dirk, and Tyrval made the Latura gesture of understanding.

"In a Theocracy, the king or dictator was substituted by a religious leader, but he too had absolute power. Oligarchy differed from the previous types of government only in that there was a power-sharing agreement between a few very wealthy, very influential individuals who controlled everything - a cabal if you want," elaborated Dirk and paused to collect his thoughts.

"Communism in theory and Communism in practice was very different. In theory, it was a society without economic inequality. Still, in practice, it was simply a dictatorship by a ruling party where the masses were kept poor, and those in power lived in luxury," explained Dirk and added, "Democracy was the only form of government where the population had a voice, albeit a very small one, but at least the people were allowed to vote for their government."

"But didn't most governments, even the autocratic ones, hold elections on Earth?" asked the Administrator.

"Yes, but in all types of government, except true Democracies, that vote was a sham. It was simply designed to give the populace the illusion of choice," maintained Dirk: "Each type of government could have a different focus. In Monarchies, it was often just the whim of the ruler, but most Dictatorships pursued a goal: this could be militarism, nationalism, isolationism, xenophobia, or even racial purity. In Communism, at least in theory, it was the pursuit of economic equality, as I mentioned earlier. Oligarchies often had extreme capitalism as their driving force, and in Theocracies, it was religious dogma, of course."

"I can follow that," confirmed Tyrval.

"True Democracies were secular and tolerant of different views. They balanced the commerce and welfare of the population, had a judicial system that applied to all citizens, and the power and duration of their governments had defined limits," summarized Dirk.

"A reasonable way to govern. Why didn't all nations of Earth adapt it?" wondered the old Administrator.

"*Democracy is the worst form of government except for all the others* - Winston Churchill," quoted Dirk and continued, "yes, Democracy was the best form of government and the weakest. It required a population that was educated and enlightened enough to support it. But because Democracy was tolerant of dissent, it also permitted those who wanted to abolish it to pursue those goals more or less uninhibited!"

"To tolerate the intolerant. I can see the dilemma!" acknowledged Tyrval.

"Indeed, and there were many who wanted to abolish Democracy: individual and corporate greed, racists, fascist, and populists who stoked fear and hatred, religions who wanted to replace secularism with their dogma, political parties who desired to remain in power at all costs, lobbies and special interests that aimed at corrupting elected leaders, and so on. Democracies were under constant attack, and if the mechanisms of checks and balances failed, so did the Democracy," revealed Dirk and sipped on his drink.

"Why didn't leadership prevent that from happening?" wondered Tyrval, nibbling on another of the delicious crab cakes.

"Democracies refrained from censorship, so all these different forces could pursue their unsavory goals freely, as long as they didn't break any laws!" stated Dirk.

"The concept of censorship is very foreign on Latur. Here, anyone can say anything they want without repercussions," interjected Tyrval.

"There are two very different ideas behind censorship: it is used either to suppress the truth, as totalitarian regimes do it, or to suppress lies that will poison the minds of the uneducated and gullible!" remarked Dirk thoughtfully and clarified, "Democracies didn't want to be viewed as authoritarian, so they didn't suppress the truth, but often failed to suppress the lies that undermined the very system as well. On Latur, you don't have to suppress lies because your population is educated and enlightened, and a lie would be exposed very readily. But on Earth, that's a whole different matter!"

"Are humans that ignorant?" questioned Tyrval in disbelief.

"I let you be the judge of that, Tyrval. As I mentioned earlier, Democracy requires educated, enlightened people to support it. The best way to end Democracy was to dismantle the education system. Once the population was so ignorant that it couldn't distinguish right from wrong, truth from lies, it became susceptible to misinformation, manipulation, and conspiracy theories. When that tipping point was reached, it was just a matter of time until the whole system would fail," said Dirk and quoted: *"Fear an ignorant man more than a lion - Kurdish proverb!"*

"Wise words!" concurred Tyrval while he refilled Dirk's glass, and the conversation paused for a moment as both men were enjoying their drinks.

"All of Earth's societies were not just based on ideological or religious concepts but were also strongly influenced by customs, traditions, and social conventions perpetuated and cultivated for thousands of years. Furthermore, humans had different skin colors, dress codes, and languages. All of that helped divide humanity and furthered the us-versus-them thinking!" continued Dirk after putting his glass back on the table.

"Long ago, the Latura were split into many tribes, too. But we realized soon that cooperation yielded better results than competition!" interjected Tyrval and added solemnly, "that was Irtaljan's greatest accomplishment!"

"Indeed! Tribalism was useful in prehistoric times for humans and Latura when our planets were sparsely populated. But as the population on Latur grew, your people consciously set that aside long ago. On the other hand, even with over 7.5 billion on Earth, humans still cling to that instinctive notion today, and it will be their downfall!" prophesized Dirk darkly.

"Did other factors play a role as well?" asked Tyrval.

"Yes, on Earth, there is also greed! Some people believe that greed comes naturally to humans. They are wrong: greed has always been an artificial product of society. Greed was almost unknown to indigenous populations, and sharing with the community was the rule, not the exception!" explained Dirk and paused for a moment.

"Even as humanity developed more complex societies, greed was mainly found among the aristocracy and elite, not the common people. Early scientists, artists, writers, explorers, and philosophers set pivotal milestones for humanity because they were driven by curiosity and creativity, not material gains. None of them were known for their wealth, and many lived and died in squalor," concluded Dirk.

"I see," said Tyrval, and then he asked, "how did you prevent this from happening on Aureus?"

"By contrast, Aureus does not have organized religions, and we have no ideological doctrine. We never imported any of Earth's traditions, cultural or social conventions. Our holidays are unique; we have no dress code or food restrictions, no archaic rituals, or mutilate our genitals," stated Dirk.

"Humans mutilate their genitals?" gasped Tyrval in disbelief, but Dirk just nodded.

"All Aureans are golden-skinned and speak the same language, but telepathic communication is unambiguous even if they don't. Aureus does not have nations, or if you will, all Aureans belong to the same one. The genders have equal rights and equal responsibilities, and sexuality is unrestricted by social or religious norms. Our justice is applied equally and without bias, and our population takes part in every decision without the need for political parties or the influence of lobbies, unions, corporations, or wealthy individuals," elaborated Dirk and paused for a moment.

"Aureus supports the six pillars of society - safety, food, shelter, justice, healthcare, and education. It does so free of charge for everyone. We also have no currency: our economy is based on the most natural, most rewarding commerce - goods and services for gratitude. Greed and selfishness are not oppressed as they are in Communism, but channeled into the most productive, supportive ways for the individual and society as a whole: help others to help yourself!" concluded Dirk.

"It is very much like the Latura society!" concurred Tyrval.

"That's another reason why Latur has endured, and humanity on Earth is failing!" added Dirk somberly and opined, "a healthy society is like a contract: the individuals pledge to do their duty in support of the society, and the society promises to take care of the individuals in return. Any society where the individuals feel exploited by the whole, or where the community views some of its members as parasitic is ultimately bound to fail."

"Dirk, not all humans are depraved! Did nobody ever try to change Earth for the better?" wondered Tyrval and looked expectantly at Dirk.

"You are right, of course. Many progressive minds have initiated good changes, but the implementation often left to be desired," said Dirk and expanded, "they pushed new ideas with laws and regulations because they figured people would

153

obey them. Many conformed, but they didn't believe in the laws because the change was forced upon them and didn't come from within."

"Can you elaborate on that, Dirk?" requested Tyrval.

"For example, many nations enacted laws to protect the environment. People followed the rules because failure to do so would result in fines and other repercussions. But they didn't truly support the regulations because they didn't grasp that protecting Earth was existential to them and their kindred. So, they lobbied to have these laws removed again, and they used the same old reactionary argument every time: why should I stop polluting if someone else, maybe their next-door neighbor or another nation on the other side of the globe, was still doing it?" explained Dirk.

"Don't help because others don't help…," summarized Tyrval and frowned.

"Lilly calls it the race to the lowest common denominator!" said Dirk humorously, and then he continued, "other examples were the rights for racial or religious minorities, women, people with different sexual preferences, or the disabled, to name just a few. The laws were good! They were meant to protect these groups from abuse and discrimination, but the general public often saw them very differently: they believed that these groups were given a privilege that elevated them above the rest - why can that cripple park in front of the supermarket, when I don't? Similarly, they objected to laws meant to provide for the less fortunate - why does that bum get free money, food, or housing when I don't?"

Tyrval frowned but said nothing.

"One can either make and enforce laws to implement a change or educate the people and make them realize that the change is necessary. The former will only work for a while, but the latter will alter their behavior forever. Unfortunately, the latter rarely happened!" postulated Dirk and sighed.

"But why?" wondered Tyrval.

"The same tired reasons, over and over again: greed, prejudice, dogma, complacency, and ignorance! If you want to change how people think, you have to overcome all of that first," explained Dirk somberly and concluded, "progressive minds often did not understand that a large percentage of the population wasn't enlightened and had no interest in becoming enlightened. They resisted change and did not want to do what was good for society. It was a chasm that was nearly impossible to bridge without forcefully re-educating the masses first!"

"In some ways, I can understand that: our protocols are centuries old and rarely updated. The Latura society has not changed much in many millennia!" noted the Administrator.

"*Fools rush in where angels fear to tread* - Alexander Pope," quoted Dirk and added, "it's the type of conservatism I can accept. After all, not every new idea is a good one! But on Earth, conservative more often than not meant reactionary. These people did not want to conserve the status quo and proceed with caution. No, they wanted to return to what they perceived as the good old days. They did not care how savage, oppressive, or bigoted those times had been and often falsified facts and history to support that rosy but flawed view of the past!"

"Latura are conservative by your definition, but we are by no means reactionary. We can change if we must, and we have no desire to relive old mistakes, nor will we deny they have happened!" concurred Tyrval, and Dirk nodded in response.

"Aside from the attack, has there ever been violence on Aureus?" inquired Tyrval next and changed the topic.

"We had some arguments, even some yelling, but no violence so far, and we hope to keep it that way. Well, no violence aside from Angela slapping me silly at times, but that only hurts my ego!" remarked Dirk and chuckled.

"That one has a temper!" quipped Tyrval and hinted knowingly, "but something like that might happen on Latur once in a while. Women can be a bit unpredictable!"

"The genders are a little different; that seems to be true regardless of species!" agreed Dirk and added, "yes, Angela has a temper, but she is not abusive or violent!"

"Do you think you can scale the Aurean society up as the population grows?" wondered Tyrval.

When this conversation happened the first time, Dirk had replied that only time would tell. But now, Dirk knew that it would work. By the time he had passed away, Aureus already had well over 1,000 inhabitants, yet the society was still functioning perfectly fine.

"Some speculate that selfishness would eventually prevail and we would run into problems and shortages," noted Dirk, but then he claimed knowingly, "I expect the opposite to happen: our population will show more generosity than we will have room to store!"

"Dirk, I've heard everything you have said, but why can't the humans on Earth create such a society? Don't they want to be happy?" asked Tyrval with some resignation.

"Perhaps their spite of keeping others unhappy is stronger than their desire to be happy themselves?" speculated Dirk cynically.

"That's hard to swallow for a Latura!" responded Tyrval with consternation.

"But it would be impossible anyway! So far, Aureus has succeeded for three reasons: one, we are physically separated from Earth; hence we cannot be corrupted or conquered. Two, we have discarded millennia of civilization baggage, as I explained earlier, and three, we have the benefits of telepathy, very advanced technology, and the support of powerful friends - L and you!" summarized Dirk with a smile, but then he added more seriously, "Earth has none of that!"

"Thank you, Dirk. I think Aureus is better and will remain so!" conveyed Tyrval sincerely and inquired, "how were you able to build its society? All the humans on Aureus came from Earth along with their way of life, did they not?"

"The humans on Aureus are the true miracle, Tyrval!" stated Dirk emphatically and noted, "it should have never worked!"

"But it did, and I think you are the reason!" insisted Tyrval.

"It did; however, I cannot fully explain why. But these humans all have something in common: they have an open yet critical mind, and eager to learn, and are happy to pass that knowledge along. All of them prefer cooperation to confrontation. They are emotional but also rational, which is not a contradiction to them. The humans on Aureus are humble and don't see themselves as superior to anyone. They are disciplined but not disciplinarians. They share, and they care! They are extraordinary, not me!" explained Dirk proudly.

"Dirk, you are too modest. Aureus succeeded because of you! You taught the humans, you taught L, and you even taught the Latura colonists, but even more than that, you live your own life as an example to them!" lauded Tyrval.

"Thank you, Tyrval. I try to live by what I preach, and sometimes I even succeed," appreciated Dirk.

Dirk was touched by the compliment just as much as when this conversation had happened the first time around.

43. Interlude

While Dirk had his long, philosophical discussion with Tyrval, Tigger returned to their quarters after saying goodbye to the Latura children in the central plaza. He had a wonderful time there, stuffed to the rim with delicious crab cakes. But now, Tigger was tired and looking forward to a long nap on that soft pile of blankets in their apartment. When he returned, Lydda was busy preparing for a presentation she was scheduled to give later in the day.

"Hi, Tigger!" greeted Lydda as he walked in while Tigger lifted his head and sniffed the air.

(Feeling of amusement) "Lydda, Dirk mated!" teased the big cat as he made himself comfortable on the makeshift bed.

"Yes, about that…," replied Lydda without shame and stopped looking at her datapad, but she was unsure if she should talk about it.

(Feeling of curiosity) "Yes?" inquired Tigger and sat up on his hindquarters.

"We switched, and now I'm worried. Dirk believes that this is not real!" explained Lydda and sat down on the blankets next to Tigger.

(Feeling of confusion) "Not real?" wondered Tigger and fondly licked Lydda's cheek.

"He thinks that he doesn't belong in this reality, and I'm afraid he might be right!" elaborated Lydda and requested, "let's switch, and I'll show you!"

(Feeling of concern) "Yes!" Tigger agreed with Lydda and exchanged his consciousness with her.

They just remained in that state for a while, quietly sitting next to each other. Eventually, Tigger withdrew his mind, and Lydda returned to her body.

"So, now you saw what I know and what I found in Dirk's mind!" said Lydda and sighed.

For a long time, Tigger didn't respond. He was sitting very still, staring at a vase with flowers on the small desk in the room. Lydda had received the flowers just after Dirk had left to meet with Tyrval again. As Dirk had predicted, a little girl had managed to sneak into the Administration building to give her the beautiful bouquet. Suddenly, Tigger looked at Lydda again.

(Feeling of understanding) "Time and place right for Tigger, Lydda, but not for Dirk!" insisted the big cat.

"But how is that possible?" gasped Lydda incredulously.

(Feeling of uncertainty) "Tigger not know. Dirk here to learn but must leave soon!" replied the big cat.

"How do you know this, Tigger?" questioned Lydda.

"Tigger cannot explain. Instinct?" wondered Tigger.

"So, what should we do? What can we do?" worried Lydda.

(Feeling of patience) "We wait!" declared Tigger.

"Wait for what?" wondered Lydda, unsure what Tigger implied.

(Feeling of confidence) "Lydda not worry. Dirk in wrong place, time before. We wait now, then Tigger fix!" promised Tigger.

It put Lydda at ease, and she smiled again because she had the utmost confidence in Tigger's abilities. Lydda quickly nuzzled his forehead; then, she returned to the desk to work on her presentation again. Meanwhile, Tigger curled up on the blankets and was fast asleep.

44. Conversation with an Alien (Finale)

Tyrval got up from his comfortable chair and walked over to a bookshelf. Although all of the Latura literature and research was available on small tablets or holographic screens, they were fond of bound books and often preferred them to electronic reading devices. Tyrval surveyed the shelf, removed a thick book from it, looked at it somewhat absentmindedly, but then put it back in its place.

"Dirk, do you fear death?" asked Tyrval suddenly.

This question gave Dirk pause. Once again, the meeting took a different turn from what had happened in the past.

"Why do you ask me that, Tyrval?" inquired Dirk.

Did this version of Tyrval suddenly realize that he was talking to a dead man? Tyrval had been ancient, even measured by the extraordinary longevity of the Latura. He would resign as Administrator only five years after this conversation. Another five years later, Tyrval would be inflicted by the Latura version of dementia. Fortunately, he still had a few lucid moments, and during one of those, he asked for the mercy of death. Dirk, Lydda, and Tigger came to Latur once more to attend Tyrval's funeral. Dirk couldn't help viewing this conversation as macabre now: not only was Tyrval talking to a dead Dirk, but Dirk was also talking to a dead Tyrval. It could have come straight out of one of Kafka's stories!

"Humor me, Dirk!" answered Tyrval with a chuckle, oblivious to Dirk's disturbing thoughts.

"All higher lifeforms will avoid death if at all possible. It is a fundamental instinct. I would avoid death too, but I do not fear it. Death is an essential, inescapable part of life," opined Dirk.

"Is that because you believe in some form of afterlife, as most humans on Earth do?" wondered Tyrval.

Suddenly, Dirk remembered how his sons Carl and L had built the simulation. But that would happen far in the future, at least 50 years from now. There was no way Tyrval could know about it at this point in time.

"No, I don't. It might sound strange to you, Tyrval, but I don't fear it because I know what death is," divulged Dirk, unsure how Tyrval would take this cryptic response, but the old Administrator just looked at him for a moment and nodded as humans do.

"You know that the Latura believe the Universe to be conscious?" asked Tyrval, although he was sure that Dirk was aware of that.

"Yes, it is similar to the Hegelian philosophy from Earth," acknowledged Dirk.

"I have read that, and there are obvious similarities," replied Tyrval and elaborated, "but Latura do not worship the Universe like humans worship their gods. To us, it is a silly concept that something so immense, so ancient, so powerful would demand our fervent prayers or the construction of temples, shrines, and churches."

"Religion on Earth isn't something rational or even remotely based on facts. It is mostly a response to the fear of death," explained Dirk, but then he quipped, "but still, the Latura were superstitious enough to restrict immigration to Aureus because you believe that it might interfere with the plans of the Universe."

"Right you are!" concurred Tyrval, laughed and elaborated, "that was the official language, and we worded it poorly. We are not that conceded nor that superstitious. We curtailed immigration because Aureus should develop on its own, not become an extension of Latur like our own settlements on other worlds."

"So, this was to protect Aureus?" asked Dirk in surprise because Tyrval had never told him that in the past.

"Yes, most certainly!" insisted Tyrval and proclaimed, "do you know how immensely popular you are on Latur? If we open the gates, you would be overrun!"

"Well, I guess that's true, although I still don't fully understand the reason for that popularity," conceded Dirk.

"Latur is a completely homogenous world with only one sapient species. We yearn for diversity; that's why we explore space and discover other sapient life. Aureus is very diverse: humans, Latura, felines, a sapient AI, and even a semi-sapient centipede. And you have hybrid offspring now too! To the Latura, you are incredibly fascinating, and there is not one of us who wouldn't want to be part of this, me included!" revealed Tyrval and smiled broadly.

"That's refreshingly different from humanity. Many humans would rather shun diversity than embrace it," maintained Dirk and asked, "but why did you phrase the immigration restriction the way you did? Surely, the Latura and the Aureans would have accepted the truth!"

160

"We phrased it that way out of courtesy and against my advice!" conceded Tyrval quietly.

"Courtesy?" repeated Dirk confused.

"For one, we didn't want Aureus to feel quarantined, but secondly, many of us deemed it proper to give you a metaphysical or religious reason since so many humans follow one god or another. You have to understand, most Latura have only abstract knowledge of humanity and have never seen or talked to an Aurean!" explained Tyrval.

"Ah, I see! That explains a few things!" concurred Dirk humorously and teased, "I thought I had misjudged the Latura, and I was wondering how a dreaming child could make plans in the first place."

"Yes, the Latura don't believe that the Universe makes concrete plans. It just exists and may or may not trigger some events, but the Universe always learns from them!" confirmed Tyrval and begged, "Dirk, please don't hold this deception against us. We had the best intentions!"

"I won't, and it wasn't much of deception by human standards!" replied Dirk and inquired, "do the Latura believe that the Universe is omniscient and omnipotent?"

"The Universe created everything, even itself. In so far, it is similar to the beliefs of most humans. But the gods of humans are a contradiction of their own: on the one hand, they are all-powerful and all-knowing, but on the other hand, they are deeply flawed by the same emotions and urges as humans. They are authoritarian, narcissistically demand worshippers, are jealous of other gods, and can be intolerant, wrathful, violent, and vindictive - just like humans," elucidated Tyrval.

"Right," interjected Dirk and nodded.

"The Latura view the Universe as a child that still learns who it is and how it should use its powers. Humans, Aureans, Latura, you, me, and everyone else are helping it do that: the Universe might be omnipotent, but by no means is it omniscient!" concluded the Administrator.

"Despite my *irtaljan* experience, I still have some doubts. But it is a beautiful explanation and one that I can accept and respect!" assented Dirk and smiled.

Tyrval just chuckled and made the Latura gesture of assent. For a moment, both men were silent. Tyrval glanced at a datapad on his desk with a concerned look on his face.

"Dirk, I would love to talk to you for the rest of the day, but I must consult with the Experts again. As you said, time is critical!" maintained Tyrval suddenly.

"Of course, Tyrval," confirmed Dirk quickly and proposed, "perhaps after you have conferred with them, we can work on a plan?"

"Yes, I hope so, too! Dirk, use my study as if it were your own. There are various snacks and refreshments behind that counter; please help yourself to them. Irgal will join you shortly!" conveyed the old Latura man, then he got up from his seat and swiftly exited the room.

45. Trapped

Dirk had to collect his thoughts. His old memories of the meeting with Tyrval were pleasant, but this new scenario was anything but! All of this felt very wrong to him! Dirk wasn't sure what could be done, and he wasn't even sure if he should do anything at all.

"Kittycat?" asked Dirk over the direct link.

"Yes, *swiahn*?" answered Lydda absentmindedly, and Dirk sensed that she was preoccupied with something.

"There is no way to sugarcoat this: Tyrval wants me to mate with his great-granddaughter!" disclosed Dirk with the mental equivalent of a frown.

"Did you embrace her?" inquired Lydda, now paying attention to the conversation.

"Sort of; Irgal tricked me into it!" revealed Dirk.

"And then she accepted?" asked Lydda.

"Yes, immediately!" confirmed Dirk.

"You didn't foresee that?" wondered Lydda, alluding to Dirk's alternate memories.

"I did, but it was already too late because Irgal accepted before I could do anything. It was like the first time you arrived on Aureus!" responded Dirk with consternation.

"That was fun; you should have seen your face!" quipped Lydda and laughed.

"Lydda, don't joke. It is serious! It's a diplomatic mishap!" warned Dirk earnestly.

"Do you want to mate with her?" wondered Lydda.

"No, not really. But now I'm stuck: Tyrval loves his great-granddaughter and wants to bend the rules to make her happy. If I don't mate with her, I offend him and Irgal," answered Dirk with a sigh.

"Well, then you don't have a choice, *swiahn*!" replied Lydda, amused.

"Can't you just do something about it?" begged Dirk.

"Oh, should I pretend to be jealous?" mocked Lydda mentally.

"Kittycat, you are enjoying this way too much!" grumbled Dirk.

"I do!" divulged Lydda, and Dirk could hear her mentally giggling in his mind.

"Oh well, you are no help!" responded Dirk in resignation.

"Later, you must tell me all about it!" insisted Lydda happily, and Dirk could sense some arousal through the *swiahn* bond.

"Why wait? I just switch with you, and you can enjoy it yourself!" countered Dirk in resignation.

"Oh, that would be wonderful! Then you can give my presentation to the *meeting of the minds* about the similarities and differences of Latura and human art while I indulge in sexual pleasures!" replied Lydda humorously.

"A presentation?" questioned Dirk, and he vaguely remembered something like that.

"Yes, to a rapt audience of about two billion!" announced Lydda, and her thoughts were accompanied by amusement.

"I'll take the girl instead, thank you very much!" uttered Dirk in defeat.

"Enjoy, *swiahn*!" teased Lydda and terminated the direct link.

Dirk knew that he had never had this conversation before, but although he didn't exactly like it, it was very much what he would have expected from his Latura wife.

46. Irgal

Unlike humans on Earth, Aureans had received the Learning and could use telepathy. Both Aureans and Latura communicated vocally and telepathically, and often that went hand-in-hand when they talked to their kind.

Aureus's verbal language was based on English, but by the time of Dirk's death, it had incorporated many words from over two dozen different human languages and quite a few expressions from Loyt. But it was tough for an Aurean to speak genuine Loyt, and it was equally difficult for a Latura to verbalize any of the human languages because the voice box of each species was quite different.

Dirk had learned Loyt from Lydda, and he could read, write and understand it well, but speaking it without a strange accent was still a different matter, even after about 100 years of practice. It was similar for Lydda: she understood English, Spanish, and even some Korean, but forming the words was still challenging.

As cats, Tigger and Georgette could not speak any formal vocal language, but thanks to the Learning, their minds could translate and transmit their thoughts into universally recognizable concepts. L had the best of all worlds because, as an AI, he understood and spoke all known languages verbally and could use telepathy in addition. Every mental conversation was also accompanied by emotions, often strong ones in the case of Tigger, Georgette, and L, which made the mental exchange unambiguous - the receiver would hear the words and feel the sentiments.

Dirk thought that the long mental conversation between Tyrval and him would have looked quite strange and disconcerting to a human bystander because they would have seen the gestures and facial expressions but wouldn't have heard a single spoken word. His musings were interrupted when Irgal rushed into the room with a huge smile on her lovely face!

"Dirk! It is so good to see you!" exclaimed Irgal vocally in surprisingly good English, although with a charming, cat-like accent.

"Hello, Irgal! It is good to see you, too!" replied Dirk in Loyt while Irgal approached him, nuzzled his neck, and Dirk kissed hers.

"We have much to discuss!" claimed the young Latura woman, still speaking English.

"We do?" wondered Dirk in surprise, trying to articulate the words correctly, but Irgal giggled at his funny pronunciation.

"We should continue telepathically. My English is not adequate!" replied Irgal politely.

"I have never heard a Latura speak it so well, and it is certainly much better than my Loyt!" countered Dirk vocally in Loyt, relieved that he could use his mind now instead of the problematic language.

"Thank you, Dirk! Your Loyt is excellent, but you have a curious accent!" Irgal pointed out.

"Yes, I know. Lydda says I sound like hacksaw!" admitted Dirk with a frown.

"…and I sound like a cat when someone steps on its tail!" responded Irgal fondly, but then she asked more seriously, "I hope you are not upset that I forced this private meeting with you?"

"No, I'm not upset, only a little confused. If you just wanted to meet with me, I'm sure I could have arranged for that!" noted Dirk expectantly.

"Oh, I want to mate with you!" teased Irgal, and she added earnestly, "but I also need to talk to you in private. I'm a very junior member of a minor committee. The protocol would not have permitted me to meet with you. So, I used my family connections and sex!"

"I didn't think Latura could be so…," observed Dirk slowly, unsure how to finish the sentence politely.

"Calculating? Cunning?" questioned Irgal and raised her thin eyebrows.

"Yes, I suppose," assented Dirk and looked at her apologetically.

"For the most part, we are not. But I'm a little odd!" responded Irgal cryptically.

"What makes you different, Irgal?" asked Dirk with friendly curiosity.

"I was born without a twin. It rarely happens on Latur!" answered Irgal without emotions.

Dirk was surprised by that revelation because almost all Latura were born as twins. He sensed that it must be problematic for this young woman, and he thought it would be best to change the topic, but Irgal didn't let him do that.

166

"Those of us without a twin will not develop quite the same as others," explained Irgal seriously, but then she cheered up again, "however, your wife Lydda is also different from most Latura, so you should be used to that!"

"How do you know that Lydda is different?" wondered Dirk humorously.

"Tyrval was right; I'm obsessed with Aureus!" admitted Irgal and elaborated, "I can recite the entire Chronicles from memory, and I have studied every little detail about all the colonists, especially Lydda and you!"

"That's a bit disconcerting, Irgal," remarked Dirk, wondering if Irgal had somehow listened in on his conversation with her great-grandfather.

"Yes, I'm a stalker!" conceded Irgal bluntly.

"You know that's not a good thing, right?" Dirk reminded her.

"Yes, I know. But I'm not stalking you for trivial reasons, and I didn't trick you into meeting with me frivolously, aside from the sex, that is!" countered Irgal honestly.

"Uhm…," commented Dirk, and Irgal giggled, but then she became suddenly earnest!

"First, let me tell you a secret. I have eavesdropped on your talk with Gramps," revealed the young woman.

"But it was a direct link!" insisted Dirk, his suspicions confirmed.

"Yes, but I can listen in, especially if it is someone very close to me, like Tyrval," explained Irgal.

"Interesting! I know someone else who can do that," acknowledged Dirk cryptically.

"You do? To my knowledge, my ability is unique," wondered Irgal in surprise.

(Feeling of amusement) "Irgal strong, but not unique!" Tigger chimed in.

"Of course! Tigger! How could I forget about him!" exclaimed Irgal happily, and Dirk grinned at her.

"So, you heard what we said, but you already knew all this, of course!" concluded Dirk.

"Yes, I knew before you arrived on Latur!" confirmed Irgal.

"It is a grave matter, but I'm still unsure what you want to discuss with me?" wondered Dirk.

"You told the Council what they are up against, but Latur cannot handle what is coming. Tyrval and our Experts will do their best, but they will fail, simply because they don't have the aggression, the malice, the ruthlessness or trickery of your species!" stated Irgal firmly.

"I should be offended but fear that you are right!" concurred Dirk.

"I have it, and your wife Lydda has it too!" stated Irgal.

"Is that so?" asked Dirk in surprise.

"I got you to meet with me, and later, we will mate!" answered Irgal simply.

"Tyrval gave me the option to decline!" warned Dirk.

"But you won't," stated Irgal confidently.

"Are you sure?" wondered Dirk with an eyebrow raised.

"Yes, because you have a kind heart, and you have already forgiven me for my ruse!" replied Irgal with a charming feline smile.

"Most people get upset or embarrassed when they get tricked!" contended Dirk and raised his eyebrows.

"Most humans, most Latura, but not you. You respect those who outwit you because it rarely happens!" countered Irgal.

"It happens all the time when it comes to women!" responded Dirk, amused and shaking his head.

"You let it happen because you are fond of women, as you are fond of me!" teased Irgal.

"You are very confident for your age, Irgal!" remarked Dirk humorously, and he couldn't help but admire this cunning young lady.

"Is my confidence misplaced?" asked Irgal slyly.

"No, it isn't!" conceded Dirk and said: "OK, you win! Irgal, please just tell me what I can do for you?"

"You, me, and Lydda will coordinate our defenses. We will have to do so in secret, and there is a good chance that I might be punished for my actions. If that

168

happens, I will request asylum on Aureus, and I hope you will grant it?" questioned Irgal.

"If it comes to that, you will be welcome on my world, but I would rather avoid diplomatic upheaval. Aureus is still dependent on Latur's goodwill!" noted Dirk, and then he added cryptically, "you will be on Aureus regardless!"

"How so?" wondered Irgal, caught off-guard by Dirk's remark.

"Call it a premonition, but you will be there!" promised Dirk with a knowing smile.

"I suppose you won't elaborate, but that's fine. I'm looking forward to a visit to your world, Dirk!" said Irgal happily.

"One question: does Lydda know about your plans?" asked Dirk, wondering if his Latura wife was in on this scheme.

"Some of it," disclosed Irgal with a wink and added, "Lydda is just as famous here as you are, but she is not a foreign dignitary. The protocol allowed me to meet with her for a few minutes yesterday."

"And let me guess, she didn't object to your scheme!" grumbled Dirk.

"No, she just laughed and fondly wished me good luck!" answered Irgal with a smirk.

"Oh my!" replied Dirk, shook his head and scoffed, "See? I'm getting outwitted by women all the time!"

"Perhaps we are just superior?" giggled Irgal, but then she added much more seriously, "Latur's goodwill is not in danger, Dirk. However, I will greatly overstep my position here, and I already have. Tyrval is the kindest man, and I love him dearly, but I believe we have to handle this without him."

"What do you propose?" asked Dirk expectantly.

"A surgical strike! We destroy the communication center on Earth's moon!" suggested Irgal, businesslike.

"Well, since L had left the Solar System a while ago, we don't have any assets that could destroy it!" contended Dirk thoughtfully.

"L didn't completely leave your star system. He left a few outposts in the asteroid belt," Irgal corrected him.

"I was not aware of that. Excuse me while I confer with L," informed Dirk and established a direct link to the AI.

"Of course!" assented Irgal and sat down at Tyrval's desk.

"L, do you have any capabilities left around Earth's space?" inquired Dirk.

"Yes, father! I have a few passive observation satellites, a minor communication relay, and a few mining refineries in the asteroid belt. Oh, I also have a small craft exploring Saturn. I found that planet fascinating!" answered L.

"Are they all under your control or operated by the new AI on the Moon?" Dirk followed up.

(Feeling of curiosity) "No, they are still under my control. I was going to keep a lowkey presence there, just in case. It seems we might need that now?" wondered L.

"That was good thinking, L. Yes, we might need that! Are you still in communication with that AI?" questioned Dirk.

"No, the AI was completely autonomous; only Latur had access to it. I kept a data channel open to it if I needed to exchange information, but that channel has closed after the AI shut down," reported L.

"Could you reestablish control?" quizzed Dirk.

(Feeling of regret) "Not without being physically connected to it, Dirk!" revealed the AI.

"How far away are you from Earth, and how long would it take you to return to the Solar System?" wondered Dirk.

"My vessel four months out, on its way to Tau Ceti. It would take at least a year to get back to Earth!" reported L, and then he added jokingly, "making a U-turn at 50% lightspeed is not instantaneous!"

"OK, good point! Please tell me about the refineries and the small spaceship by Saturn!" emphasized Dirk.

"What do you want to know, Dirk?" asked L curiously.

"Can we use any of it to disable the communication center on the Moon? Permanently!" Dirk demanded to know.

"We could accelerate the craft and crash it into the Moon. With sufficient velocity, it could vaporize the structure," confirmed L.

"How long would that take?" asked Dirk.

"A few weeks, maybe a month or two. I need to run the exact calculations. We don't want too much kinetic energy released on impact, or Earth will be bombarded with Moon fragments!" warned L.

"Could we use the refineries in some way to regain control?" wondered Dirk.

"We could fabricate androids and shuttles there, then transport the robot army to the Moon, assault the compound, clear out the hostiles, and restart the AI!" proposed L.

"Time frame?" asked Dirk.

"Also, at least a year!" stated the AI.

"So, the kinetic projectile would be the fastest way to disable the communication center," concluded Dirk.

(Feeling of certainty) "Yes!" concurred L.

"Thanks, L; we will discuss this more later!" replied Dirk.

"Yes, father. Meanwhile, I shall plot a collision course for the spacecraft," mentioned L and terminated the mental connection.

"Irgal, I just confirmed with L that the fastest, most efficient way to destroy the facility on the Moon would be via a kinetic projectile. L said this could be done in a couple of months, Earth time," summarized Dirk.

"I've heard the conversation," revealed Irgal quietly.

"I suspected as much. The reason I didn't include you was for your protection. The fewer people know, the more likely this little conspiracy won't be discovered for a while!" explained Dirk.

"So, will you do it?" asked Irgal.

"I don't see any good alternatives, do you?" wondered Dirk and raised his eyebrows.

"No!" concurred Irgal with a bit of frown.

"OK, let's say we are successful. By now, much of the advanced knowledge is already on Earth, and your Experts have confirmed that earlier. Humans are very crafty; they will reverse engineer the technology, figure out how it works, and build it, even if it takes longer. Our strike will only delay the inevitable!" postulated Dirk and shook his head.

"Yes. But it will give us time to think of another, more permanent solution," proposed Irgal.

"Irgal, before you go any further: I will not participate in genocide!" insisted Dirk firmly.

"Of course not, Dirk. I'm not that ruthless!" gasped Irgal, and she was visibly taken aback by what Dirk insinuated.

"My apologies; I did not mean to offend you. I just wanted to establish some boundaries," retorted Dirk truthfully.

"If I were human, genocide would be a consideration?" asked Irgal hesitantly.

"I'm afraid humans would at least contemplate it. The greater the rewards, the more seriously it would be considered!" responded Dirk somberly.

"That's very disturbing. All the more reason to stop humans from spreading through the galaxy!" exclaimed Irgal nervously.

"We agree on that, Irgal. But we still don't have a long-term solution!" Dirk reminded her.

"Could we reeducate humanity and show them a better way?" questioned Irgal.

"Those who would need it the most will reject it the fiercest!" countered Dirk with a frown.

"Then perhaps a treaty with the nations in control?" inquired Irgal.

"Irgal, now you sound like your Council of Experts!" teased Dirk and then added thoughtfully, "a treaty will not work because as soon as it is signed, the powers of Earth will look for loopholes to circumvent it."

"But it would be a binding agreement!" contended Irgal.

"Without dire consequences for violating this agreement, these nations will view it as a guideline at best. Worse yet, if leadership or political priorities change, the contract could be voided either outright or on some technicality if they feel they need to justify the breach. A treaty with the U.S., Russia, or China isn't worth the ink or the paper!" grumbled Dirk.

"You are a very reasonable human; why would other humans not honor a fair contract?" asked Irgal in frustration.

"Some humans are reasonable and honorable, but many are not. Those will find many creative ways to excuse or justify their transgressions, especially when the stakes are so high!" explained Dirk.

"Dirk, I hear your words, but I cannot relate to them!" admitted Irgal and asked, "why are humans and Latura so different?"

"You heard the conversation I had with your great-grandfather, but I should also point out the fundamental differences between our species: Latura have existed for about two million years in Earth time, but Homo Sapiens only evolved about 300,000 years ago. Latur had a civilization for the last one million years, but the earliest human civilizations are only about 10,000 years old. Biologically, without healthcare or genetic modifications, a human being is meant to live for about 30 years, but a Latura could live up to three times longer. You live longer, but you procreate slower! That's why you have only two billion people on Latur while there are almost eight billion humans on Earth today!" explained Dirk.

"We control our population growth, Dirk!" interjected Irgal to correct him.

"Right, but for the longest time, that wasn't necessary!" countered Dirk.

"Yes, within the scope of our history, that happened recently. Please continue!" conceded Irgal and made the Latura gesture of agreement.

"Because you lived longer, the Latura could transfer more knowledge and wisdom from one generation to the next, and because your population grew slower and over a much longer period, you had less competition for space and resources and a chance to adjust to a higher population density. But most importantly, your biological evolution had more time to catch up with your sociological and technological development. By contrast, humans today are still nomadic cavemen, but now they live in crowded cities with complicated schedules and laws, and they have space shuttles and thermonuclear bombs!" Dirk concluded his explanation.

"Humans outpaced themselves; I think I understand that now!" acknowledged Irgal, and then she asked, "so, do you have a better plan, Dirk?"

"I believe we will have to use some kind of force because that's a language they all understand. Maybe a computer virus to disable some of their technology, surveillance to keep tabs on their machinations, and perhaps a heavily-armed spaceship orbiting Earth as a constant reminder of our superior powers. Make them fear us and afraid to leave the planet!" suggested Dirk.

"Draconian methods, Dirk, but better than genocide!" conceded Irgal.

"Yes, and even more is needed: we have to isolate or quarantine Earth diplomatically. Humanity will try to circumvent our direct measures, perhaps with the aid of another advanced civilization, such as the AloKaan. If they succeed, our problems will only increase tenfold!" concluded Dirk, and then he asked pointedly, "can you accept such methods, Irgal?"

"I know our options are meager, and if we fail, the consequences will be dire!" replied Irgal with a big sigh and stated, "I agree with your plan, but this is not something we could propose to the *meeting of the minds* because most Latura would be aghast!"

"We could at least try. I have found the Latura to be rational, reasonable people!" argued Dirk.

"You have met Councilor Meia. She is rational and reasonable, but she would fight us all the way because she exists only within Latura protocols and traditions. As you call it, she cannot think outside the box!" countered Irgal.

"I believe I could handle Meia, but you make an excellent point, Irgal!" replied Dirk sincerely since he wasn't too eager to spar with the Latura Councilor once again.

"The Latura have studied Earth's civilizations in depth from the early rise of Mesopotamia onwards. Our Experts can recite every tome, every scroll, every blood-soaked page of your history books. We are shocked, saddened, and appalled by it, but we do not fully understand it. To us, it is just abstract knowledge: the turmoil and growing pains of a level 7 or 8 species far, far away. If that sounds condescending or even speciest, it is! But it isn't malicious; we just don't know better!" explained Irgal.

"I have encountered that before. Ofal held similar views when she first arrived on Aureus, but she doesn't think like that anymore!" recalled Dirk.

"When Alvar relayed your warning to us, Gramps immediately ordered the *meeting of the minds* in session, and they all took it very seriously. There were days of intense discussions and lengthy presentations by our Experts. But in the end, none could relate to your warning because it wasn't real to us!" continued the young Latura woman.

"I don't follow, Irgal. Why was my warning not real?" questioned Dirk in surprise.

"When we look at humanity, we see the wonders of Aureus: we see the first natural hybrid children, we see the *swiahn* bond, we see Lydda's stunning art and Wendji's literary masterpiece, we see the miracles of Tigger and L, we see the wonderful people we call friends, and first and foremost we see you - the wise, courageous, legendary leader, the second coming of Irtaljan!" elaborated Irgal.

"I'm just a man!" interjected Dirk quietly, embarrassed by her words.

"And Irtaljan was just a woman!" declared Irgal with a smile, but then she continued much more seriously: "What the Latura don't see are the gulags and concentration camps, the religious, ideological, or nationalistic wars, the systematic extermination of indigenous people, or the ruthless exploitation and destruction of Earth' environment. We are oblivious to the horrors of anthrax, poison gas, phosphor bombs, Hiroshima and Nagasaki, slavery, murder, rape, torture, prejudice, or greed because it is all so very alien to us!"

"Yes," articulated Dirk because he didn't know what else he could say to that, but he was impressed by how familiar this Latura girl was with human history.

"You see and understand all these things, and you fear them! So does Lydda because she is you, and I suspect the other Latura on Aureus feel the same now because they have learned it first-hand!" elaborated Irgal, and then she claimed, "but here on Latur, I stand alone!"

"Yes," repeated Dirk and slowly nodded in agreement.

"Earlier, I was shocked when you thought I was talking about genocide as a permanent solution. But at least I can comprehend such a monstrosity, while most Latura cannot. It is too abstract for them to bring forth genuine emotions and real concern," said Irgal with consternation.

"I often forget that," answered Dirk and commented, "although it was not so much different on Earth. When the news showed another atrocity, perhaps a mass shooting that was dreadfully common in my country, many people were sad and outraged. But it didn't last: it was all forgotten again a few days later. The vast majority of the people were not affected, so it was too abstract for them as well."

"For millennia, the Latura have only known peace and harmony. We have honed our minds, arts, crafts, literature, philosophy, and science, perfecting our civility. Evolutionarily, sociologically, and technologically we are more advanced, but we are by no means superior! Latur would lose every time in a fight with humanity!" concluded Irgal.

"So young, yet so mature!" mumbled Dirk verbally, and he didn't expect Irgal to hear or understand his muttering, but she did.

"Latura wouldn't call it mature, Dirk!" she answered verbally in English and added, "they would say that it is jaded or savage, the thoughts of a child in need of more education!"

"I suppose so, and from their narrow vantage point, it would seem valid," conceded Dirk mentally, but then he insisted verbally in Loyt, "I will carry this burden for you, Irgal. You should not have to deal with these ugly matters. Humanity is my responsibility!"

This time Irgal didn't laugh at Dirk's unusual pronunciation of her language. She was quiet and looked at him very seriously for quite a while.

"You are not responsible for their sins, Dirk," refuted Irgal finally, and then she stated forcefully in English: "This war is mine as much as it is yours! Who of the Latura would fight it? Who could fight it if not me?"

"You are a lot like Lydda!" disclosed Dirk quietly.

"Thank you, you don't know how much that means to me!" replied Irgal, genuinely appreciating Dirk's words.

"Irgal, this plan will be difficult and perhaps even dangerous. We will need time and careful preparations. When I return to Aureus, I would like you to accompany me," suggested Dirk.

"I wish I could, Dirk. But my status here wouldn't allow me to travel to Aureus!" countered Irgal with regret.

"I know, the *meeting of the minds* doesn't want anyone to interfere with Universe's plans - or at least that's the official explanation," said Dirk and rolled his eyes.

"Silly, isn't it?" laughed Irgal, but she said more seriously, "but it is binding. I could only leave Latur if I requested asylum on Aureus. But that would hurt Gramps badly, and I rather not do that to him unless there is no other choice."

"There is another way. I will propose that Latur and Aureus exchange ambassadors. I have someone in mind on Aureus who would be suited for that role, and I will suggest that you should represent Latur on my planet," proposed Dirk.

"Brilliant, and it might work! But I must warn you, Latur might want to send someone more senior than me!" responded Irgal doubtfully.

"That's possible, but I can be very persistent!" insisted Dirk and grinned at her.

"Persistence might not be enough to sway the *meeting of the minds*!" contradicted Irgal.

"Maybe so, but your ability to speak my language and your impressive understanding of human and Aurean history and culture will do the trick, I'm certain of it!" replied Dirk confidently, and then he added with a grin, "now, shall we go to your pool?"

"My pool? How boring!" exclaimed Irgal happily and revealed, "I've studied human sexuality; I want to try all your positions - on land! My first mating should be memorable!"

"You are a virgin?" gasped Dirk.

"I reached sexual maturity two years ago, but I have not found a suitable mate yet. I know that is unusual for Latura, but I was not even looking. Is that a problem, Dirk?" wondered Irgal, unsure.

"No, but shouldn't your first mating be with someone you love, not a stranger from another world and another species?" inquired Dirk.

"Who says that I don't love you, Dirk?" countered Irgal.

"Irgal…," remarked Dirk hesitantly, but Irgal cut him off.

"Dirk, I'm a consenting adult by Latur standards, Aurean standards, and even Earth standards!" insisted Irgal and added jokingly, "if anyone is being coerced here, it would be you."

"Irgal, I know that, and I'm consenting, too. But we just met; how can you possibly love me?" asked Dirk in exasperation.

"Don't worry! I have no ambitions to be your wife or consort. You have enough of those already!" teased Irgal.

"I suppose I do!" assented Dirk and felt a little embarrassed.

"But I loved you since I've read the Aureus Chronicles for the first time. Our meeting and conversation today made that love only stronger. You said it yourself, I'm a lot like Lydda, but that makes me an outcast on Latur!" disclosed Irgal with a little bit of regret, and Dirk looked at her for a moment, and then he smiled fondly.

"Irgal, you are bright and beautiful, and I will try my best to make your first experience a pleasant one!" promised Dirk and took her in his arms.

She readily returned the embrace, and they were holding each other for a good while, but then Irgal backed away again.

"I have changed my mind, and you are off the hook, Dirk! It's a woman's prerogative on Latur!" giggled Irgal, and Dirk wasn't sure if he should feel relieved or disappointed.

"On Earth and Aureus, too!" conceded Dirk humorously, but then he inquired hesitantly, "may I ask why?"

"Oh, we will still mate! But now it will be on Aureus, on Transformation Day, as it should be!" answered Irgal slyly, but then she suddenly froze and stared at Dirk wide-eyed.

"Are you alright, Irgal?" asked Dirk, concerned.

"I was on Aureus for many years, and we have mated multiple times! How is that possible?" stammered Irgal, nonplussed.

"I cannot explain it, but I have strange memories, too. My visit to Latur has happened before!" revealed Dirk, but he wasn't sure if Irgal had heard his words because the young Latura woman seemed shocked.

"I attended your funeral on Aureus, but you are here and alive! It makes no sense!" exclaimed Irgal and suddenly hugged Dirk fiercely again.

"All of us must die someday," remarked Dirk consolingly and closed his arms around her shaking body.

His death? Irgal knew about that? Dirk assumed that he had memories of the past or alternate past, but it seemed that Irgal must have memories of the future or at least a possible one.

"This terrible war is inevitably coming! But it will happen a long time from now, and you and I will be dead, yet we will fight side-by-side! So much suffering and death! I don't know how or why I know this, but you must believe me, Dirk!" whispered Irgal vocally in his ear with great urgency.

"I don't have those memories," replied Dirk slowly but then added sincerely, "usually, I don't trust prophecies, but I trust you, Irgal!"

Irgal just nodded as humans do, let go of the embrace, and swiftly exited Tyrval's study without another word. Dirk was still befuddled in the middle of the room when his full memories returned moments later. They would mate on Aureus, on several Transformation Days, and it would be, or had been, a delightful experience for both of them every time. Dirk also remembered that Irgal would

178

serve many years as the ambassador of Latur on Aureus. He even recalled that she returned to Aureus as the Administrator only hours before he passed away.

But Dirk had no recollection of this terrible war that was coming, yet somehow, he was confident it would. Dirk was lost in those thoughts when he exited the study, but before he could, Tigger was standing in the doorway, his tail swishing with agitation.

(Feeling of urgency) "Dirk must go now!" emphasized Tigger firmly.

"OK, Lydda must be done with her presentation. What are we scheduled to do next?" asked Dirk, really hoping that he would have some time to think about Irgal's words before they had to attend another diplomatic function.

"No schedule. Just leave!" insisted the big cat.

"Leave…," repeated Dirk confused, but Tigger simply rubbed against his legs, and Dirk's world faded to black.

47. Resurrection

He was dead, and he had been dead for a long time, yet suddenly, there was light. There cannot be light, thought Dirk. There were sounds too, and he could feel a tingling sensation going through his body. His body? How can I still have a body, wondered Dirk?

"You have to wake up!" implored a female voice faintly in Dirk's head - he had a head, too?

"Come on; you were lazy for long enough; there is work to be done, Honey!" urged the woman - was that Lilly?

"Where…where am I?" replied Dirk feebly.

"Finally! Where do you think you are?" mocked the female voice.

"I… I'm not sure," answered Dirk befuddled.

"You are where you belong. Now, collect yourself and get up!" remarked the woman sternly.

"Lilly? Is that you?" asked Dirk in disbelief.

"Yes, of course, it's me!" muttered Lilly impatiently.

"Please let me sleep, Sweetie. I'm so tired!" begged Dirk.

"No!" replied Lilly with a snort.

"You are cruel!" complained Dirk.

"Yes, I am! Now get going!" asserted Lilly.

"Fine…," replied Dirk with a sigh.

Dirk attempted to stand up, but there was nothing to stand on - no floor and, more importantly, no legs or feet, just wisps of fog. Then he noticed how surreal his surroundings looked. The humongous room was something straight out of an Escher painting, with a touch of Dali and Picasso thrown in for good measure. It simply made no sense and defied any description!

"I know this is confusing. Look at me, Honey!" instructed Lilly.

Dirk looked around, and finally, his eyes found the diffuse contours of a woman floating in the middle of this strange room. She was glowing in bright, white light, but her outline shifted like fog in the wind.

"You look… uhm, pretty different, Sweetie!" remarked Dirk slowly.

"Yes, you can say that again!" quipped Lilly and noted humorously, "but you don't look any better here!"

"I don't?" wondered Dirk as he tried to examine his hands, and sure enough, they were just as insubstantial and diffuse as Lilly was.

"Float over to me and take my hand. We need to get out of here!" instructed Lilly, but Dirk didn't know what to do.

"How do I float?" he asked quietly.

"Duh, just do it. Focus on me and float!" answered Lilly impatiently.

"Hmm, OK. Here goes nothing," said Dirk and did as he was told.

At first, Dirk didn't move at all, no matter how hard he tried, but then he rocketed right into Lilly after a moment!

"Ouch!" complained Lilly as Dirk's diffuse form crashed into her, "you couldn't have done that a little less forceful?"

"Uhm, sorry, I'm new to this, Sweetie!" apologized Dirk.

"Oh, it's fine, Honey! I'm so happy to have you back finally!" chirped Lilly fondly.

Suddenly, her diffuse arms embraced his ghost-like body, and she hugged him fiercely. Dirk could feel the hug as if it was real, well, real …ish. Then he saw some tears running down Lilly's insubstantial cheeks.

"Sweetie, it's OK. I'm here now!" Dirk consoled her as he returned her embrace.

"We must go. Time is short!" insisted Lilly a few moments later and looked nervously around the strange room as if she was sensing a malevolent presence.

"I'm dead, so what's the rush, Lilly? Where are we? What is this?" asked Dirk as he felt a presence too, but it didn't seem hostile, just curious, perhaps?

"We have only a few seconds left, Honey! We must hurry. I will explain later!" promised Lilly and let go of the hug.

"Uhm, a few seconds? We have been talking for longer than that!" corrected Dirk jokingly.

"Time flows differently here, but it still flows! Come, take my hand!" urged Lilly and reached for Dirk's fog-like arm.

"Fine, but you owe me a long explanation, Lilly!" claimed Dirk and clasped Lilly's ghostly hand.

"Yes, I do. More than you can imagine!" conceded Lilly with a sigh, and then she added, "this will be weird, but it won't take long. Focus on me, and don't let go of my hand!"

Dirk followed her instructions, but nothing could have prepared him for what came next. The journey Lilly took him on was both instantaneous and eternal. It was like being sucked into a drain and squeezed through a capillary. But worst of all, it was a rollercoaster of motion, colors, sounds, and lights like nothing Dirk had ever experienced before. He felt nausea coming on quickly, but fortunately, his mist-like body couldn't vomit, or Lilly, who was right in front of him, would have worn the contents of his stomach by now.

Finally, they arrived at their destination. Dirk was on his knees, trying hard to regain his composure. The surroundings were lush with green vegetation and blossoming flowers. He heard birds chirping in the distance, and a light, warm breeze was touching his face, carrying a pleasant odor with it. The first thing Dirk noticed was that his hands looked real now, not mere wisps of fog. When he looked up, Lilly was standing in front of him, and now she appeared much as he remembered her. No, not quite! When Dirk saw Lilly last, he was on his deathbed. She had aged in dignified ways, and even then, she was still attractive, but she was a lot older. This Lilly in front of him was as young and vibrant as the day he transformed her so long ago. Was this real or just memories of a time long ago?

"Sweetie, the explanation, please!" mumbled Dirk, slowly getting off the ground.

"Fine. Yes, you died. Earlier, we were in your tomb; now we are in the simulation!" summarized Lilly quietly, eyes cast down.

"Ugh," moaned Dirk and fell on his knees again.

Suddenly all the memories of all the weird parallel Universes rushed into Dirk's brain, and he feared he might drown in so much information.

"Honey! What's wrong?" yelled Lilly distressed.

"Nothing…," stammered Dirk trying to absorb all those experiences at once, "give me a moment!"

"OK?" replied Lilly, confused and worried.

"I knew…," muttered Dirk finally and got back up slowly.

"You knew what?" asked Lilly, concerned that her husband had some alarming problems.

"I knew that you uploaded me and stored my consciousness on Pluto for the last 100 years or so!" stated Dirk.

"You knew? How?" gasped Lilly.

"It's a long story, and I will tell you someday. But don't worry, I'm not upset!" Dirk assured her and mustered a slight smile.

"You aren't? We… I betrayed you again!" disclosed Lilly with a sniffle.

"You didn't. L and Carl cooked up that plan, and everyone else agreed!" replied Dirk and emphasized, "but it was the right thing to do because it saved Lydda's life - not just on Aureus, but also in this simulation!"

"Is that true?" wondered Lilly.

"Yes, Lydda told me herself, and Tigger hinted as much!" elaborated Dirk.

Finally, Dirk started to feel a little better. The gut-wrenching effects of the digital journey and the sudden flood of information had subsided, and his mind was alert again.

"She told you? Did you talk to Tigger too? How? When? Where?" gasped Lilly incredulously.

"Sweetie, I've died, and now I'm suddenly reborn into some weird digital world, and I don't have the first clue how it all works. I'm the one who should be asking these questions!" teased Dirk and grinned at her.

"Oh, forget that. Tell me the story right now!" insisted Lilly.

"I thought we had no time for that?" wisecracked Dirk.

"We had no time in your tomb because it was shutting down. This place will last a little longer, so tell me!" pressed Lilly.

"While I was dead, and don't ask how that was possible, I experienced something like *irtaljan* again. But different, and much longer and even more real! The best explanation is that I was part of various parallel Universes for extended periods. I interacted with the alternate versions of Lydda, Tigger, you, and almost everyone else during these episodes. Somehow, I have retained all the memories of these encounters. That's how I know you uploaded me after my death!" explained Dirk.

"We were driving home from the hospital. You had severe burns on your arm and back. I was telling you about a dream… a dream of Aureus!" whispered Lilly.

"Yes," confirmed Dirk simply.

"This memory just came to me out of nowhere!" gasped Lilly and inquired, "how did you do that, Honey?"

"I didn't do anything, Sweetie. It seems that's how it works. Everyone who came in contact with me in those parallel worlds experienced the same thing: sudden memories of things past, present, and future," stipulated Dirk and shrugged.

"Then this is just another one of your episodes?" questioned Lilly, suddenly doubting her reality.

"No, I don't think so. It feels different here," disagreed Dirk and speculated, "the people I've met could recall the real memories of Aureus and Earth, but not those of their counterparts in other alternate realities. You did just that!"

"I did? Oh yes, I did!" realized Lilly and observed, "the drive from the hospital never happened on Earth originally, only in that parallel version! Wow, this is mindboggling stuff, Honey! Leave it to you to make the world even more complicated!"

"With that out of the way, I would like to believe you woke me up because you missed me, but I think you had a more pragmatic reason, didn't you?" teased Dirk and smirked.

"I missed you, Honey! So very much, but you are right; I wouldn't have revived you if it wasn't a dire emergency. You were truly about to die in that tomb, and L is in trouble! We must help him, or he will perish. If he dies, so will we, and Aureus and Latur won't be far behind!" emphasized Lilly somberly.

"L? What happened? Please start from the beginning, Sweetie!" asked Dirk, concerned.

"I will, but first, we have to meet the others. If they weren't dead already, they would be dying to see you again!" quipped Lilly and said encouragingly, "come on, let's go! It's just a short walk, no more weird stuff!"

Lilly retook Dirk's hand and led him to a quaint park nearby. They walked just like they did back on Earth and Aureus, a stroll across a field of green grass and colorful flowers.

"Uhm, Lilly? We are walking. Shouldn't we be zipping through some semiconductors and fiber optics, considering that we are just data?" questioned Dirk.

"Do you want to? You might get sick again," teased Lilly.

"No thanks, I'm just trying to come to grips with all this!" replied Dirk defensively.

"We can zip around, and often we do when we are in a hurry. But many of us prefer the old-fashioned ways, and L's simulation provides for that," informed Lilly.

"Oh, OK," replied Dirk and smiled.

Dirk was in no hurry, and he enjoyed the leisurely walk with his wife. It was an excellent way to be reborn!

48. Reunion

A few minutes later, Lilly and Dirk arrived at a large gazebo in the middle of the greenery. It was a lovely place in the style of a Japanese garden, and a little brook gurgled nearby.

"Dirk!" screamed Rose and jumped into his arms.

"Pumpkin!" exclaimed Dirk and twirled her around.

The reunion was filled with tears of joy and laughter for the next few minutes. Everyone immediately got up from the benches and gathered around Dirk and Lilly. Everybody was happy, except for Angela. She remained seated and watched the koi in the pond behind the gazebo.

"Hey Babe!" said Dirk finally after the excitement had died down.

Angela didn't reply, but she got up from the bench and faced him. Then she slapped him hard across the face!

"Angela…," gasped Dirk, surprised by how real the pain on his cheek felt, as Angela glared at him.

"You made me wait a hundred years!" she snarled and struck him again on the other cheek while the rest of the group watched the spectacle with smirks and stifled laughter.

"I'm sorry! I died, remember?" replied Dirk defensively, palming his burning cheek.

"That's no excuse!" yelled Angela and slapped him again.

"It is a damn good excuse, Babe, and you know it. I'm happy to see you too, but now stop hitting me, please!" protested Dirk.

"Happy? I'm mad as hell!" growled Angela and whacked Dirk once more.

"OK, fine. I'll go back to my digital tomb then. See you in another hundred years!" grumbled Dirk and turned around.

"Don't you dare!" warned Angela slowly and very seriously.

Dirk stopped and faced her again. Angela was crying now, tears flowing freely over her cheeks. After a bit of hesitation, Dirk walked back and gently embraced her. He thought he might get slapped again, but Angela returned the embrace fiercely.

"Hi Babe, I missed you too!" whispered Dirk into her ear.

Angela didn't respond; instead, she kissed him deeply. Dirk returned the kiss in kind, but it didn't feel quite right.

"Dead or not, you will never leave me again, promise me that?' whispered Angela, still sobbing quietly.

"I promise," vowed Dirk against better judgment, but he sensed that Angela needed to hear that.

"Good!" said Angela simply.

Angela let go of him and turned around. But a moment later, she faced Dirk again with a strange expression on her face.

"We ate omelets at your house on Earth?" she gasped in disbelief.

"We did, and yet we did not. I'll explain later, Babe!" remarked Dirk calmly.

After a moment of hesitation, Angela just nodded. Dirk realized that Angela, like Lilly earlier, must have gotten a glimpse of the alternate realities. After a few more minutes, the group had taken their seats around the large table.

"OK, I'm ready for an update. What is this place? Why am I here? Where is the rest of the gang?" inquired Dirk and looked at his friends expectantly.

"Let's start with the easy one: this is L's simulation. We have worked on it for a long time, and it's pretty good now, don't you think?" asked Rose proudly.

"It is nice, but…," responded Dirk hesitantly.

"But what?" questioned Lilly and raised an eyebrow.

"It still doesn't quite feel real!" revealed Dirk politely.

"Yeah, we know. The visual effects are almost perfect, and the audio is also outstanding. But smells, touch, and taste leave to be desired," acknowledged Sven.

"The biggest flaws are in the emotional responses. Our virtual bodies cannot produce endorphins, dopamine, adrenaline, serotonin, melatonin, and other chemicals that modulate the brain chemistry!" added Lennard.

"Well, we feel some emotions, but they are not always the right ones, and none are very intense," elaborated Eriea.

"You just have to get angry enough!" contradicted Angela and grinned at Dirk.

187

"I guess…," mumbled Dirk and rubbed his cheek absentmindedly.

"Yup, pain works fine, pleasure not so much," Garrett pointed out.

"That puts a damper on Transformation Day, doesn't it?" noted Dirk with a smirk.

"Transformation Day? We haven't had that in decades!" informed Lilly bitterly.

"You don't have sex anymore?" gasped Dirk.

"We can have sex, but why bother? It's not very satisfying. It leaves us more frustrated than happy!" complained Angela and groaned.

"That's very disappointing!" observed Dirk.

"Yes, very sad, and that's not the only drawback! You know how much I like to cook. We don't need food anymore, and that's a blessing because I've not been able to make anything that tastes right!" grumbled Yebin.

"Simple odors are OK, like the lilac you smell right now. But try to make something as complex as coffee or tea, and you won't like the results. What would I give for a nice cup of jasmine tea?" reminisced Lilly and sighed.

"You and me both, Lilly!" assented Lydda with a sad smile.

"Or a good cup of coffee!" interjected Rose.

"Or some Glow of Aureus!" added Mario and noted, "hell, I would settle for a simple beer!"

"Some textures of hard, solid surfaces are authentic, but soft, pliable, or finely grained ones don't feel right either," explained Sven.

(Feeling of annoyance) "Jo fur all wrong! Stupid simulation!" growled Georgette as she was grooming the side of her belly.

"But it's not all bad. We are young and healthy again. We can create marvelous things here with just the power of our minds. You should see Lydda's palace of arts! Stunning!" emphasized Ngazetungue cheerfully.

"It's nothing special, just the random thoughts of a dead, bored Latura!" mentioned Lydda.

"So, you guys have been working on this simulation since you… well, died?" asked Dirk.

188

"Yes, it's a work in progress, and it won't end anytime soon," confirmed Wendji and grinned.

"I remember that Ezio was the first to be uploaded after his accidental death at the tide pools. But most of you lived decades longer, and most of you outlived me. Was he all alone in here the whole time?" inquired Dirk, concerned.

"Ezio was the first, but he was not by himself for very long because L can slow down or speed up the simulation. It was only a few days for Ezio until the next person was uploaded. Even though we died many years apart, we all appeared here around the same time!" explained Eriea.

"Ah, that makes sense!" acknowledged Dirk, but he asked, "how do I know that this digital existence is my version that lived on Aureus?"

"I have checked Carl's and L's code, and there is nothing in there suggesting that they have edited us in some ways. But it is still conceivable that some memories or personality traits were changed or erased accidentally," declared Rose, but it seemed that she was withholding some information.

"And?" questioned Dirk curiously.

"When I was alive, I was opinionated. I'm still opinionated here!" wisecracked Rose and noted, "the upload has enhanced our memories. We remember everything more clearly, and the memories do not degrade over time anymore. In short, we cannot forget!"

"That's an advantage, but maybe a curse, too!" observed Dirk and inquired, "but I still wouldn't know if my character or memories have been changed, would I?"

"That's right, you wouldn't, Dirk. The ultimate test doesn't involve code: we all have lived and worked together for a hundred years. Thanks to Transformation Day, we have also mated with each other. We are a large family, and there are not many secrets left between all of us!" interjected Eriea.

"In essence, if there had been glitches or intentional tampering, you won't know, but we would!" summarized Lilly.

"That's a satisfactory and satisfying answer! Thanks, guys!" praised Dirk and nodded.

"We have been doing other things too, Husband. For example, a few years ago, Sven discovered that we could leave the simulation!" informed Nari excitedly and changed the subject.

"You use L's androids?" guessed Dirk.

"No, but that's a fascinating idea! We create holographic duplicates of ourselves outside of the simulation. We can appear where ever an icosahedron is nearby," revealed Sven.

"You are ghosts?" asked Dirk amusedly.

"Yes, you could say that," concurred Nancy while giggling.

"And you scare the crap out of unsuspecting Aureans?" jested Dirk and raised his eyebrows.

"Only Mario does that; the rest of us are friendly ghosts!" insisted Nancy playfully.

"I did that only once, and the guy deserved it! He was mean to Alma!" protested Mario.

"Alma is here?" wondered Dirk.

"No, Alma is still on Aureus, Husband. She is ancient, but the same friendly centipede she's always been, but even bigger now. She is still protecting the colony from danger, too. I visit her often!" noted Nari with a smile.

"So, you guys interact with the living people on Aureus?" asked Dirk, a little concerned about the consequences of such interactions.

"No, not at all. We might sneak around a little like Nari does when she visits Alma, but we generally avoid contact with the Aureans. We don't want to scare them, and we don't want to explain all this. Nothing good could come from that!" contended Lennard.

"Is everybody being uploaded when they die on Aureus?" inquired Dirk.

"No, Carl was the last one. L had built up a nearly infinite capacity to hold our consciousnesses, but we decided not to extend this beyond the second generation!" elaborated Lennard.

"May I ask why?" asked Dirk since nobody seemed too eager to talk about this.

"There were some disturbing social side effects," mentioned Wendji vaguely.

"Such as?" questioned Dirk, a little perplexed by their reluctance to tell.

"Those who knew about the simulation started to act recklessly in life, knowing that death was not the end," explained Wendji seriously.

"Our daughter...," mumbled Nari and frowned a little.

(Feeling of disapproval) "… and Tiara," added Tigger suddenly.

"Siren? Tiara? What happened?" asked Dirk, concerned.

"Siren took incredible risks with her spaceship, which eventually killed her. It was similar for Tiara; she was reckless in her explorations of Aureus, and it didn't end well for her. But of course, both were 2nd generation, and so they knew they would be uploaded upon death," explained Lenna.

"All the 1st and 2nd generation Aureans kept the promise not to talk about the simulation, but their children soon figured out that their parents and grandparents were keeping a secret from them. They began to develop vague theories without any facts: with some of their parents not afraid of death and L becoming an almost god-like presence, they speculated that there must be some kind of afterlife! Soon, flawed speculation evolved into false religion, and that's when we decided that we would not upload anyone beyond the 2nd generation Aureans, with only one exception," added Alvar thoughtfully.

"A wise decision, although I can imagine that some of you wanted to upload your grandchildren. It must have been hard!" speculated Dirk somberly.

"It was hard for us, mate. We all lost family in a sense, and you did too. But it was for the best of Aureus, and ultimately, we all agreed on that!" stated Lennard.

"Where is the rest of the group?" wondered Dirk and changed the topic.

"The ones you see here are the active ones left. But only Garrett, Yebin, Lydda, Mario, Ngazetungue, Victor, and I will stay. Of course, Tigger will too, and someone else will join us shortly. The rest will go to sleep soon to preserve energy and resources!" explained Angela.

"Go to sleep?" questioned Dirk curiously.

"Yes, that's what we call it, *swiahn*. All our children are in stasis chambers, similar to your tomb. So is everyone else you knew. But they are completely isolated from L, protected from all immediate danger," reported Lydda.

"But you said earlier that L had nearly infinite capacity? By the way, where is L?" questioned Dirk.

"We will get to that, Dirk. Suffice to say, L's resources are rapidly diminishing. That's why we need to put people in stasis!" explained Garrett.

"We just stayed awake to welcome you back, Husband!" remarked Nari with a smile.

"I'm happy that you did, Angel! I was dead, so this might sound illogical, but I missed every one of you, too!" replied Dirk fondly.

"You should have woken up sooner, Dirk. I never understood why you didn't want to join us here," contended Wendji with a slight frown.

"Wendji, your chronicles were wonderfully written and an important, accurate account of history. But I was not very comfortable with the fame that followed; I never wanted that spotlight. Please don't think that I blame you for that, but I thought it was time to leave graciously and permanently to make room for the next generations," responded Dirk.

For a moment, Lydda seemed to be bothered by Dirk's explanation and pressed her lips tightly shut, but then she relaxed again.

"We are sorry that we preserved you and had to wake you again, *swiahn*. It was not an easy decision!" apologized Lydda solemnly.

"You would be truly dead now, Kittycat. Tigger probably too!" emphasized Dirk and declared, "I'm grateful that you ignored my selfish wish!"

"You know about that?" asked Lydda, surprised.

"Yes, because you told me!" answered Dirk.

"I never...," said Lydda, but she didn't finish that sentence, and for a moment, she was looking into the distance, oblivious to everything else.

"Yes, I revealed that to you when I was a human surgeon on Earth!" observed Lydda slowly, and then she gasped, "how can that be?"

"I will explain later, Kittycat. But it is complicated and confusing," replied Dirk, and Lydda stared at him for a moment.

"We will switch soon. I must see what you know, *swiahn*!" insisted Lydda finally.

"Is that even possible in the simulation?" questioned Dirk and raised an eyebrow.

"Tigger and I have done it many times, but L says it is like cracking incredible complex encryption. That should be almost impossible, but it works just fine, even though we don't know how or why!" remarked Lydda.

"Maybe now is a good time for you guys to explain how this simulation works?" wondered Dirk and recalled, "Carl taught me the basics a long time ago: L uses the bio-processor in our spines and the bio-mechanical tools in our bloodstream to create a digital image of the neuronal connections within our brains. But that's all I remember!"

"Yes, we were all scanned once, then any changes were real-time updated and stored in encrypted files in the simulation. When we died, L restored the most recent update!" explained Rose.

"OK, so we are just data files?" wondered Dirk, unsure how this could work.

"Not exactly. The data files only contain all our memories, but an executable file can also access and process every memory file. Each of us has a potent, dedicated processor to run that unique program. It is what gives us life. Then, all the processors are networked with the simulation program. That's what allows us to interact with it and with each other," elaborated Rose.

"I can follow so far," acknowledged Dirk and noted, "but if we just have our old memories, we wouldn't be able to learn anything new!"

"Right. That's why the executable program not only reads the old memory files but also creates new ones that are specifically our own!" answered Rose.

"Ah, that makes sense," acknowledged Dirk and asked, "but the *swiahn* bond would still allow me to access Lydda's and Tigger's old and new memories?"

"That's the part we cannot fully explain. We are encrypted, much better than anything on Earth or Latur, yet the bond works just fine!" observed Lydda and shrugged her shoulders the way humans do.

"We shared the encryption code when we were still alive," speculated Dirk a moment later and added, "I think that's the key part of the *swiahn* bond, biologically or digitally!"

"That's the best explanation so far, *swiahn*!" exclaimed Lydda and laughed.

"The most plausible, too. You can be pretty smart when you are not a dork!" teased Rose, and Dirk grinned at her in return.

"From the selection of those who will stay, I gather that you are preparing for battle?" asked Dirk, almost expecting confirmation of his concerns.

"An astute observation; you are still as sharp as ever!" confirmed Victor and chuckled.

"Thanks, Victor! Did you select this group?" wondered Dirk.

"I had some input, but Garrett and Angela did that," answered Victor.

"We had several more on our list, but we had to make some cuts with L's limited resources. All of us here have some battle experience; all of us cover various areas of expertise," elaborated Garrett.

"It is a good team of grizzled veterans, and since you are here now, I don't have to lead anymore!" noted Angela.

"It is the best team anyone could wish for!" praised Dirk, and then he urged, "but please, tell me exactly what we are up against!"

49. Prelude to War

"Greenland!" informed Garrett.

"Greenland?" asked Dirk incredulously.

"Yes, and it's still not green if you wonder. All that melting ice turned it into mud. *Brownland* would be a better name!" joked Lennard and continued, "as an international effort, they worked on it since the early 2020s under various pretenses - a weather station, a military installation, an observatory, a commercial mining facility, and some idiot even pretended to build a hotel there!"

"Project Sanctuary," muttered Dirk, as the alternate memories popped into his head.

"How in the hell do you know that, Boss?" wondered Mario and maintained, "we just found out about that a few weeks ago while you were still… uhm, dead!"

"Never mind that for now, Mario," replied Dirk and asked, "but 50,000 people is a sizeable town. It would be plainly visible from the air, would it not?"

"It was all built into a mountain with only one access point, disguised as some military base. A marvelous feat of engineering that shows that with enough money and force, humanity can achieve amazing things even if it is just for the selfish, unsavory reasons of a few!" explained Sven.

"A modern-day pyramid! But still, they would need infrastructure to deliver a constant stream of goods, supplies, power, food - you name it! How did they hide all that from the Earth's population? Perhaps even more importantly, how did they hide it from L and the Latura?" inquired Dirk.

"Earth was in turmoil, and the Latura were torn between helping and not interfering; L was busy on Aureus, so nobody closely looked at Greenland. It was the perfect place, remote but not too remote to make it unfeasible. Then it was a matter of absolute secrecy, and for once, complete cooperation among the major players!" explained Garrett.

"United in evil," mumbled Dirk.

"They built a dozen inconspicuous outposts all over the arctic circle and slowly stuffed them with supplies and food. For example, the Svalbard seed vault on Spitzbergen Island, Norway, was emptied and used as the world's most exclusive wine cellar. But it also held caviar, oysters, truffles, and other delicatessens," added Garrett.

"They discarded the seeds when Earth needed them most?" gasped Dirk.

"Of course, they had no use for that stuff. Earth was done, and they had no intentions of rebuilding and reseeding!" reported Victor with regret.

"Who were these people?" asked Dirk finally.

"Well, the 0.01%, of course! Sheiks, oligarchs, dictators, monarchs and other aristocrats, billionaires, organized crime bosses, bankers, powerful industrialists, and a few crooked elected politicians. Communist leaders, who deemed themselves a little more equal than the rest of their citizens, and Nationalists, who couldn't get out of their *beloved* countries fast enough when things got ugly on Earth. Oh, and religious leaders too, inexplicably unwilling to meet their divine maker so soon!" explained Victor sarcastically.

"It figures," acknowledged Dirk with a sigh.

"And all of them brought their entourage of henchmen, sycophants, loyalists, worshippers, and sellouts with them. Of course, they also needed a sizeable workforce of servants and slaves to keep it all running. So, the facility had to be big enough to hold and supply that many people," continued Victor.

"But they must have known that they couldn't survive in their Greenland paradise forever?" wondered Dirk.

"Sure, they knew. But these guys weren't planning on that. They exploited the kindness of the Latura and L to make new friends in the galaxy!" said Victor with a chuckle.

Victor didn't find any of this funny; it was just his way of delivering bad news.

"The AloKaan…," muttered Dirk absentmindedly.

"How do you know that, Dirk?" interjected Garrett in surprise.

"I will reveal all my dark secrets soon enough, Garrett!" promised Dirk ominously, but with a smirk on his face, "please continue, Victor!"

"Right, the AloKaan. It turns out that not all aliens are good people. The AloKaan aren't violent or deceitful, but they are greedy, individually, and as a species - a perfect match for the greediest of humanity! So, these humans made a deal, and the AloKaan eagerly accepted. The AloKaan would supply them with technology, energy, and synthesized goods until the humans were ready and able to leave Earth," summarized Victor.

"Where were they going to go?" wondered Dirk.

"A new planet, of course!" replied Victor.

"And the AloKaan would get them there?" questioned Dirk.

"Not exactly. The AloKaan would only provide technical expertise. The humans would have to do the rest," answered Victor.

"In exchange for what?" asked Dirk.

"Well, the AloKaan star system is densely populated, and the species was also looking for a new planet to settle. It so happened that these humans had one for sale!" responded Victor with a smirk.

"You have to be joking! They sold Earth?" gasped Dirk.

"Living conditions on Earth were terrible, only a small fraction of humanity was still alive at that time, and Project Sanctuary deemed it too costly and difficult to rebuild the planet. So yes, they sold Earth with everything on it, including the last humans!" confirmed Victor and nodded.

"Unbelievable!" grumbled Dirk.

"All the important parameters of Earth matched the requirements of the AloKaan, such as water content, atmospheric composition, gravity, temperature range, and so on. The AloKaan didn't mind that the planet showed some wear and tear because they are a hardy species, and much of Earth had to be terraformed anyway to suit their biology better!" interjected Sven.

"Victor, you joined us about five years later on Aureus. Did you know about Project Sanctuary?" wondered Dirk.

"Hmm, that's a good question, Dirk. I might have known without realizing it!" divulged Victor and asked, "do you remember when your government wanted to buy Greenland from the Danish?"

"Yes, don't remind me!" confirmed Dirk and rolled his eyes.

"Aside from insanity, we figured there must be a good reason. My sources snooped around and noticed increased activity on that island and the arctic circle. But strangely, when we reported that to our higher-ups, they immediately downplayed or dismissed it!" explained Victor and said, "I was too busy instigating unrest in western democracies to find out why, but in retrospect, Project Sanctuary would be the most plausible explanation."

"Yes, that would make some sense, Victor," assented Dirk, but then he observed, "but something isn't right about the timeline. I was over 50 when we arrived on

Aureus, I lived about 100 years longer, and Lilly said I was dead for about 100 more, Earth time. That's about 200 years after we left Earth, roughly 160 years after civilization ended there, yet these people lived all this time in their secret base on Greenland?"

"There is some discussion about the end of civilization. On Aureus, we decided to mark it when the last two traditional governments in New Zealand and Iceland lost control and plunged into anarchy about 38 years after our departure. Some mark it ten years earlier with the nuclear war between India and Pakistan, others 30 years later with the collapse of the Cao Ming Empire that conquered Eurasia but fell apart almost immediately thereafter," informed Wendji.

"Right, but if they settled in Greenland after we left Earth, they must be over 200 years old today. Evil overlords or not, life expectancy on Earth was about 70-80 years at that time. The people alive today would be the 5th generation descendants of the original settlers!" calculated Dirk.

"Sure, the slave caste is 5th generation, but those in charge are the original 21st-century douchebags. Project Sanctuary had state-of-the-art medical facilities and the absolute best human technology had to offer. But more importantly, the AloKaan provided them with the design of stasis chambers. According to L, they were even better than what the Latura had engineered!" corrected Lilly unhappily.

"I see," said Dirk with a frown, and then he asked, "but these humans needed a planet themselves, and they sold the only one they got?"

"In exchange for getting a new one, as I said earlier!" noted Victor cryptically.

"Where?" Dirk demanded to know.

"Where would a bunch of elitists get a planet that was mostly untouched, suitable for humans, and already had some established infrastructure?" asked Victor rhetorically.

Some people would have been annoyed by Victor's conversation style, but Dirk sincerely appreciated it. Victor forced him to keep up mentally with the flow of the events.

"Oh, no! They were going to take Aureus?" exclaimed Dirk loudly.

"Of course! And these AloKaan would help them get there!" confirmed Victor.

"The AloKaan are a level 9 species, very advanced, but not as advanced as the Latura or L. How could they get these people to Aureus? Put them in stasis on an arc and fly them across 1,500 lightyears of open space for the next 3,000 years?" inquired Dirk skeptically.

"That was one idea, but our motley crew of evil megalomaniacs didn't have the patience for that. Indeed, the AloKaan do not have the transportation technology, but these humans knew where to get it!" stated Victor.

"The Moon…," muttered Dirk quietly.

"Right again! Did someone brief you while you were dead?" asked Victor humorously.

"In a way, someone did!" admitted Dirk and said encouragingly, "please continue, Victor!"

"So, our greedy friends made a trip to the Moon and captured that Latura observation post!" elaborated Victor.

"Wait, they built a giant rocket, and nobody noticed?" wondered Dirk.

"No, the AloKaan provided them with advanced propulsion technology, nothing as fancy as entropy differential, but still very potent - controlled fusion!" interjected Sven.

"OK, but they still needed to build a spaceship and then get it out of the atmosphere!" countered Dirk.

"Correct, but they didn't use a spaceship. It took many years, but they modified a submarine instead!" informed Garrett.

"That's very smart. A submarine is designed to withstand enormous water pressure, and therefore the space vacuum wouldn't be an issue. It could also remain hidden underwater while it was modified, and with a powerful propulsion system, it wouldn't matter that the sub is heavy and not particularly aerodynamic," postulated Dirk.

"That's one of your most unusual qualities. You can give credit even to those who want to kill you!" observed Victor and chuckled.

"You have the same quality, Victor, and you know it!" countered Dirk and grinned at him.

"I suppose I do!" conceded Victor humorously, and then he continued, "so, they flew their space-sub to the Moon and captured the Latura base…."

"…and got control of the AI, but not entirely so!" Dirk finished the sentence.

"I won't ask how you know that, but yes, they botched the assault somewhat, and the AI shut down, at least partially," confirmed Victor and added, "but that didn't stop them from extracting all the knowledge they could get from its databases and transferring it to their hideout in Greenland."

"But it didn't end there, did it?" wondered Dirk, worried about what he might hear next.

"No. Project Sanctuary made many attempts to gain full control of the AI, but it wouldn't budge, and without a full-fledged AI, they had no hope of capturing Aureus since an AI was essential to control the transport and the matrix!" disclosed Victor.

"They seem obsessed with that idea," stated Dirk and shook his head.

"When your former country developed the first nuclear weapons, my former country and especially the leader at the time, Josef Stalin, became obsessed with leveling the playing field," recalled Victor.

"Yeah, the Cold War, the nuclear stalemate," acknowledged Dirk and wondered, "I guess these people think along the same lines?"

"Exactly. So, Project Sanctuary scoured the exabytes of information that they had recovered from the Moon, and they discovered something interesting and very, very dangerous!" continued Victor.

"I have no memories of that, Victor!" replied Dirk truthfully, but in that instant, he suddenly remembered the strange hallucination of an evil, four-headed genie.

"Aha! Finally, I can tell you something you don't know!" quipped Victor triumphantly and revealed, "they discovered records of probe L39!"

"The insane Latura probe!" exclaimed Dirk.

L wasn't the first Latura probe to become sapient. The Latura had sent a probe, L39, to a promising star system many years earlier. The star system turned out to be lifeless, and the unit was parked in orbit around one of the planets. While it was idle, it became partially sapient, but it was precarious and erratic. The Latura and L investigated the probe and attempted to fix it, but it was unsuccessful.

"That's the one!" acknowledged Victor.

"Yes, I recall that L quarantined it from his network, but I don't know what happened after that," remarked Dirk.

"L studied it for a while, without any conclusive results. Eventually, Latur shut it down because it couldn't be repaired. Then L cut it off from his network and left it inert in orbit over a lifeless planet," interjected Garrett.

"I don't like where this is going, but please proceed!" Dirk encouraged Victor.

"You probably already guessed it. With the help of the AloKaan and the semi-functional AI on the Moon, these people reactivated L39!" summarized Victor.

"They got a full AI now; that's terrible!" lamented Dirk.

"Not even close! At first, they were content with having a functional AI under their control. But pretty soon, the AI became sapient once again. But now, it was not only insane but also filled with hatred towards L and the Latura for shutting it down!" replied Victor somberly.

"Holy cow!" gasped Dirk.

"The humans tried to regain control, but they simply bargained with the AI when that proved futile. The humans would help L39 exterminate L and Latur, and L39 would help the humans to get to Aureus and capture it!" added Victor.

"Damn!" gasped Dirk in disbelief, and then he asked, "but how could these people help L39? It seems to be a one-sided bargain, or was it not?"

"Sure, L39 is insane and vengeful, but remember, gentle, peaceful Latura constructed it! It wanted to go to war but didn't know how!" explained Victor.

"It didn't know how to wage war? L has beaten me in every strategy game we have ever played!" countered Dirk.

"No, it didn't need help with that," assented Garrett and explained, "but there are two aspects to warfare: the mechanics and logistics on the one hand, and the psychology on the other!"

"Uhm, you lost me there," replied Dirk slowly, and Victor gave him a thin smile.

"When Russia, along with the Germans, invaded Poland at the start of WWII, the Red Army executed thousands of Polish POWs. They did that to instill fear, but mostly out of hatred for the Poles!" explained Victor and added, "Project Sanctuary didn't have to teach L39 how to be a general; they taught the AI how to be a war criminal!"

"Ugh!" Dirk was so appalled that he didn't know to respond - the news was getting worse and worse.

"L didn't notice what was happening because L39 wasn't connected to him anymore. L39 used the backdoor through Latur and captured a few independent probes. It also managed to connect to the AI on the Moon, overwhelmed all safeguards, and established itself there," continued Victor.

"So, now the bad guys have the lunatic version of L?" inquired Dirk.

"Correct!" confirmed Victor.

"Where is L now?" asked Dirk.

"We are not sure. We know that L is still alive because he makes contact with us from time to time. But many parts of him have shut down, and more go offline every day. Some because he does it to protect himself, others because L39 is attacking his systems!" answered Angela.

"L didn't fight back?" questioned Dirk.

"L fought back, but he was overwhelmed. L39 is a fully sapient, ruthless AI, not some feeble hacking attempts by yours truly," said Victor humorously and continued, "L did what he could. He secured the simulation and a few other crucial parts of his network. But L39 is still relentlessly chipping away at the defenses."

"That's why we had to get you out of your tomb so quickly. L39 knew you were there, and it considers you a prime target!" interjected Lilly.

"Me?" wondered Dirk.

"Of course, you are L's father. L39 has tried everything to find your tomb. I believe it fears you!" speculated Garrett, and many of the group nodded in agreement.

"And Latur?" inquired Dirk, changing the subject.

"Latur is completely blacked out! L39 has cut them off from the galaxy. But as far as we know, that's all that has happened there. Aureus is still in contact with the Latura colonies, but Irgal was the last to make it out of Latur proper. She will be here shortly!" answered Victor.

"Made it out?" questioned Dirk.

"You remember that you made Irgal an honorary Aurean before she resigned from her ambassadorship and returned to Latur to become the Administrator of the *meeting of the minds*?" asked Angela.

"Right, we had a special celebration for her!" confirmed Dirk.

"That day, Irgal asked L if she could join the simulation when she died, even though she wasn't Aurean. L agreed to that and created a covert channel to Latur just for her. While Lilly was waking you up earlier, we sent her a signal through that channel. Then, Irgal committed suicide and was uploaded here. The transfer was successful, but she is still adapting to the simulation. Irgal is the only one, not 1st or 2nd generation Aurean, who was uploaded, the one exception that Alvar mentioned earlier," informed Angela.

"Of course, Irgal has to be here!" affirmed Dirk with a nod when he remembered Irgal's strange premonition about a terrible war far in the future.

"You knew that she would come?" wondered Garrett.

"In a sense, I did, Garrett," answered Dirk.

"She was my little sister," interjected Lydda fondly, "I'm happy to see her again."

"Irgal will be part of the team once she wakes up," added Angela.

"She is brave and smart; she will be an asset," concurred Dirk and inquired, "so, what are our options now?"

"We have very few. This simulation will not last forever. We could all go into isolated stasis, but we would likely never wake up again if L perishes!" worried Eriea.

"We hoped you could just do your magic. Swoop in, banish the evil humans, kill L39, rescue L, save Aureus and Latur, and we live happily ever after! OK, we are happily dead ever after!" joked Lilly and grinned at her husband.

"Funny, Sweetie!" replied Dirk with a snort, but then he asked earnestly, "all of you have been leaders, some even multiple times. Of course, I will do what I can, but what could I possibly add to the team that you don't have already?"

"I have never been a leader, Dirk," Lilly corrected him quietly.

Even after Dirk's death, Lilly adamantly refused to lead the colony, although she was more than qualified. Lilly had always been convinced that her *irtaljan* experience would become true if she ever got to power, and she would lead the colony to ruin.

"We held the office, and we did the work," remarked Ngazetungue solemnly and added, "but we never filled your shoes, Dirk. You are here because you have to be here!"

"I was so unprepared when I got into office! I asked you questions every day for sixteen Aurean years straight!" revealed Nancy laughingly.

"I did that, too! Dirk, even when you quit the office, you never stopped being our guide!" assented Eriea and smiled.

"I'm flattered, but you guys have too much confidence in me. It's daunting!" disclosed Dirk, looked down, and studied the little stone pebbles by his feet before he continued, "I will ask you all a bunch of questions now. Please humor me and answer them as best as you can."

"No problem, Boss!" promised Mario.

"First one - how did you gather all this information?" inquired Dirk.

"After L39 started its assault, L checked his databanks. He discovered evidence of the Greenland sanctuary. The Latura confirmed much of his findings and added their own. But it was Mario who got us most of the details!" replied Angela.

"Yes, Boss, I used my old skills when I learned that the AloKaan were greedy critters," said Mario and asked, "do you remember the teargas plant?"

"It was mostly a nuisance, but Lilly made some potions from it if I recall correctly," acknowledged Dirk.

"The plant had medicinal value, but I let Mario continue," interjected Lilly.

"Yeah, I did a little research, and it turns out that the plant also makes the AloKaan high as a kite!" remarked Mario with a grin and disclosed, "so, I nudged the Aureans into sending them a few free samples, and what do you know, they wanted more - a lot more!"

"You nudged the Aureans? I thought we could not directly interact with them unless we pretend to be ghosts?" wondered Dirk.

"That's right, but we can send them anonymous messages, which I did. I contacted the guy who runs my brewery and persuaded him to gather some of the plants, dry them, and shred them into tobacco. I call it ET weed!" explained Mario with a smirk.

"You have always been amazingly resourceful!" praised Dirk and laughed.

"Thanks, Boss! Yeah, then I extorted the AloKaan a bit, and they almost immediately spilled the beans. Secrecy isn't their strong suit. That's how we know what these bastards in Greenland have planned for us!" concluded Mario.

"I should be offended by the methods, but… good job, Mario!" commended Dirk, and then he asked, "what is the current status on Aureus?"

"Aureus is still under our control, but some of the technology isn't working without L's presence. Don't worry; they are fine for now; they have ample supplies and are preparing defenses for a possible assault!" answered Angela.

"So, they know what's coming?" asked Dirk next.

"Not exactly. We channeled information to Aureus, anonymously, of course. They know of potential danger and that Latur is already in trouble!" informed Garrett.

"Are any other species under attack by L39 or its handlers?" inquired Dirk.

"Not yet, or at least not as far as we know, but we relayed a warning to all the species that had representatives on Aureus," reported Angela.

"That's good. I have the feeling that L39 will not be satisfied with the destruction of Latur, Aureus, and us!" speculated Dirk and frowned.

"Your son Carl believes the same: just as L became an omnipresent force of good, L39 will grow into an existential threat to every living thing in the galaxy and perhaps beyond!" cautioned Lennard somberly, and Victor nodded at that.

"Do we still have assets in the solar system that haven't been compromised?" asked Dirk and changed the subject.

"L had left the solar system long ago, only the Latura outpost was still there, and that was under the control of their AI!" answered Rose.

"Can we find out if L left a spaceship in orbit around Saturn?" questioned Dirk.

"Uhm, we could probably check again. We still have access to L's records, but nothing remained in the solar system as far as I know. Everything was either transferred under the control of the new Latura AI or left with L's original probe," opined Rose doubtfully, but she started to look at various data files on a holographic screen that had appeared suddenly in the air.

"I'm pretty sure it's there. Please find out; it's a priority!" urged Dirk and questioned, "what has L done to fight back?"

"At first, he didn't do much, just observed the situation. When L39 started its assault, L put up firewalls, cut connections, isolated databanks and probes, and retreated. I think he didn't know how to fight back against such an attack, and I believe he didn't want to hurt another sapient AI either," remarked Angela with regret.

"You said that you don't know where L is but that he contacts you occasionally. Can you contact him as well?" wondered Dirk.

"We could, but we haven't dared to do so. No connection is completely secure anymore, so we didn't want to risk it unless it becomes unavoidable," reported Angela and disclosed, "but I have the encrypted access codes!"

"Eventually, we will need to contact him. Do we have cyber defenses against L39 in this simulation?" asked Dirk.

"We got nothing substantial, Dirk. Maybe the power of our minds, but that's just a wild theory!" worried Eriea and declared with a sigh, "without L, we are naked! If this place shuts down, stasis would be our last retreat!"

"What is the difference between my tomb and stasis?" questioned Dirk.

"They both can preserve a consciousness, but that's where the similarities end!" said Rose and explained, "your tomb was an integral part of L. It captured your consciousness in the moment of death and immediately froze it in place. L and Carl couldn't test it beforehand, and they couldn't check if it had worked afterward. It could have failed, the transfer could have corrupted your essence, or your memories could have degraded over time. The only way to know for sure was to wake you up. Your tomb was a miracle, Dirk!"

"Ah, so that's why I don't remember who this woman is!" quipped Dirk and pointed at Lilly while everyone else started laughing.

"Didn't I say he should stay dead?" grumbled Lilly, but she had to giggle a little.

"So far, I seem to have all the memories of the important events in my life, and they appear to be seamless without any big gaps," assured Dirk more seriously, and then he added, "please continue, Pumpkin!"

"The stasis modules isolate us in an autonomous data storage unit. L placed the units on different asteroids in various star systems. Once we enter, the data channel closes behind us, and only a small tether links us to L so that he can find us and wake us up again. When we enter, our essence is alive and well, and then we fall into a coma. We remain unconscious, but our consciousness is always low-level active," elaborated Rose.

"Why didn't L and Carl make my tomb the same way?" asked Dirk, but nobody wanted to answer his question.

"Your tomb was designed to store you for all eternity. The stasis modules can hold us for a few years, maybe a decade, but no longer," said Rose finally, but Dirk sensed that she wanted to say more.

"But that's not all, is it?" inquired Dirk and raised his eyebrows.

"Because we didn't want you to know that we had ignored your last wish!" avowed Lilly with a sigh and divulged, "that's why you had to be frozen in a dreamless, near-death state, Honey! You are the only one who remembers dying. The rest of us were uploaded with our consciousnesses still active and living just before we passed away. There was an almost imperceptible gap in time, and then we were here in the simulation, alive and well."

"Oh!" said Dirk and added with a smirk, "hmm, I thought I was dead - so, mission accomplished!"

"You were neither dead nor alive or both dead and alive," replied Lydda, apologizing, "we are very sorry, *swiahn*!"

"I was literally Schrödinger's cat!" summarized Dirk humorously.

"Boss, I know that apologies won't cut it, but L and Carl made an excellent case for why you needed to be preserved," revealed Mario earnestly and proclaimed, "and you know what? They were right! Without you being here now, we'll probably lose this fight!"

"No pressure…," muttered Dirk and grinned at Mario before he asked, "by the way, where is Carl?"

"Our son is in stasis, Honey," replied Lilly and continued, "he wouldn't admit it, of course, but I think Carl feels too guilty to face you in person."

"But there is nobody who understands AIs better than him. We need Carl on the team!" observed Dirk and declared firmly, "OK, this has to stop right now! Yes, I'm a little annoyed that you didn't let me die, as strange as that may sound, but it was the right decision. But even if it would have been the wrong one, do you guys think I'm some vindictive tyrant who would take out his displeasure on the people he supposedly loves?"

Nobody looked at Dirk, but a few shook their heads. Dirk paused for a moment to collect his thoughts.

"Boss, when I was a criminal, fear and respect were the same thing. I only felt respected when others feared me," revealed Mario seriously and said, "then you taught me the difference! We don't fear your wrath; we are ashamed that we disrespected you!"

"Ah, fuhgeddaboudit, Mario!" joked Dirk and then stated emphatically, "perhaps there was still work for me to do? All of you are forgiven, so please, let's not dwell on this further!"

"We thank you, Husband!" maintained Nari softly, and everyone else echoed her words.

50. Greenland

Project Sanctuary didn't have an army. Until now, they didn't need one. There was nothing left to conquer on a dying planet. There were also no other humans on Greenland, and the few people left on Earth elsewhere didn't have the means or the desire to come here. However, the enclave had a robust security force to maintain internal order. Generations of selected breeding and genetic modifications had created the perfect police - smart enough to excel at the job but ignorant enough never to question any orders. Project Sanctuary did not have an army but an unwavering security force, advanced technology, and utterly ruthless leadership.

The President for Life demanded a plan of action for the acquisition of Aureus, and so his personal aide and most trusted cabinet members met with the newly appointed Field Marshal of Project Sanctuary's future army.

"The President is impatient, so let's discuss our options openly," said the Presidential Advisor to the other five men in the room: "As you know, the President always makes the best deals. It would give him great satisfaction if we could acquire Aureus in some kind of trade."

"Advisor, Aureus operates on that ridiculous gift economy. What kind of deal could we possibly make with that?" questioned the Minister of Information dismissively.

"For the right price, everything and everyone is for sale, and the President has always emphasized that. However, we had the opportunity once, but it was squandered away by a botched invasion 200 years ago. Gift economy or not, we could have traded their planet for the lives of the friends and relatives of those early colonists!" replied the Minister of Economics.

"Are you implying that the President made a mistake?" gasped the Minister of Information with feigned outrage.

"I never said that! The invasion was a joined operation with some questionable, subhuman parties from - pardon my language - shithole countries. That's why it failed!" countered the Minister of Economics angrily. The Field Marshal ignored this testy exchange to point out the obvious:

"Aureus doesn't know that we exist. If we engage in trade negotiations that will likely fail, we give away the crucial element of surprise that is needed for potential military actions!"

"Perhaps there is still one deal we could make: trade Aureus for Earth?" suggested the Minister of Information.

"But we have promised that the AloKaan could have Earth once we have claimed Aureus!" reminded the Advisor.

"They are not mutually exclusive, Advisor. The Aureans relocate to Earth, then the AloKaan claim the planet, and whatever happens after that is not our concern!" elaborated the Minister of Information.

"If the freaks kill each other, all the better!" exclaimed the Minister of Security, and the Minister of Information grinned broadly at him.

"Gentlemen, that's a pipe dream! The Aureans are not stupid; they know that Earth is in terrible shape. Maybe we could have made that deal a few hundred years ago, but there is nothing here for them today. We don't even want to be here, so why would they accept such an offer?" asked the Minister of Economics and raised his eyebrows. The other men in the room seemed to agree grudgingly with that assessment.

"I admit that a deal is unlikely, and I concur that it would hurt our chances for an invasion to reveal ourselves to the Aureans!" summarized the Advisor.

"We call it justified reclamation of human assets!" corrected the Minister of Information tersely.

"Of course, Minister!" apologized the Advisor and inquired: "The cleanest way would be to starve the population into surrender. Is that feasible?"

"Unfortunately, Aureus is self-sufficient, and the Aureans have ample supplies stored away. While they can no longer resupply through Latur because L39 has blocked that, they could instead ask for help from numerous other civilizations in the galaxy and would very likely receive it. Aureus is diplomatically well connected and liked. Regretfully, starving the population will not yield quick results, if ever!" reported the new Field Marshal.

"A few prisoners are useful, especially if they belong to the ruling class. With enhanced interrogation, we could extract valuable information from them. Captured diplomats of other civilizations could also serve as bargaining chips and insurance against possible retaliation," added the Minister of Security, "but a large POW population would strain our resources because they would need to be fed, sheltered, and guarded."

"We could put them into labor camps and use them for infrastructure projects," suggested the Minister of Information.

"That's useful as punishment and as a deterrent. However, the prisoners would live for years, and that's too expensive to maintain. Economically speaking, we prefer a permanent solution!" countered the Minister of Economics. The Minister of Security nodded in agreement.

"Field Marshal, you said that Aureus is diplomatically connected: is there a possibility that one of these alien civilizations will aid the Aureans militarily?" asked the Presidential Advisor.

"They would likely send humanitarian aid, perhaps even take refugees, but military aid is highly improbable. From the captured moon base records, we found that none of these alien civilizations even has a military, and very few have weapons of any kind," informed the Field Marshal.

"Fools, but this bodes well for the next phase of our expansion! Lucky us!" interjected the Minister of Security, and the other men chuckled.

"Right, but back to the task at hand: could we take Aureus' self-sufficiency away and perhaps negotiate with our AI that it blocks all access to other civilizations?" suggested the Advisor.

"We prefer not to negotiate with L39 any further. Factually, we need to think about eliminating the AI after we have captured Aureus. It cannot be controlled and is too dangerous to be left on its own. But that will be a discussion for another time!" inserted the Minister of Security and asked, "if we cannot starve the Aureans, could we eliminate them and leave the infrastructure intact?"

"Yes, we must not damage the Great Hall in the attack! The President wishes to preserve it as a symbol of our righteous crusade against heathens and hell spawns. It shall serve as a reminder that God Himself guides our destiny!" interjected the Minister of Spirituality.

"Perhaps a chemical attack could be the solution?" proposed the Minister of Security.

"Chemical warfare would claim some casualties, but not all of them. The enemies have protective gear and other countermeasures at their disposal. Aureus is simply too advanced for such crude methods. Furthermore, the chemical reagents would also cause long-term damage to the environment, possibly making it unsuitable for recolonization," countered the Field Marshal.

"How about something like a neutron bomb? Yes, that's old Cold War technology, but could it be useful?" suggested the Minister of Information.

211

"We could use a neutron bomb, and the collateral damage would be acceptable. However, we suspect that Aureus's structures are shielded, much like Project Sanctuary is protected from such an attack. We estimate that it would eliminate no more than 50% of the population. While it would weaken them, we would still encounter considerable resistance to an invasion - I mean justified reclamation! Also, there would be some environmental damage as well. It could be an option, but probably not the best one!" replied the Field Marshal.

"A biological weapon, then?" questioned the Minister of Security.

"The Aureans have enhanced immune systems. They also have biomechanical tools in their blood and outstanding medical and research facilities. It might be possible to develop a disease and inflict some casualties with enough time, but Aureus would most certainly not be wiped out. Furthermore, it would require complicated logistics to deliver such a weapon. As it is with the neutron bomb, biological warfare could only be supplementary, not decisive!" explained the military leader.

"What are their military capabilities, and what would we need to overcome them?" asked the Advisor.

"We estimate the population at about 2,000 to 3,000 individuals. Although physically enhanced, almost all of them are noncombatants, and that number also includes a significant percentage of neutrals, primarily alien diplomats. They have some technological advantages, notably highly autonomous robots and drones, but we believe we could neutralize those with an electromagnetic pulse weapon. We also have the element of surprise, as I said earlier, and better-conditioned combatants. A good rule of thumb is that the attacking force should be at least three times larger than the defending force. That would mean approximately 8,000 soldiers!" stated the Field Marshal.

"This is absurd! We only have about 500 trained security personnel and three transfer chambers, and one of those will be used for equipment. Even if we can somehow field an army that strong, it would take us weeks to transfer them, and by the time the last ones get there, the first ones would have likely starved or been discovered by the enemy!" countered the Advisor.

"You were charged to conceive a workable plan, Field Marshal. Do you have one?" the Minister of Information demanded to know impatiently.

"We have a plan, Minister. We won't send out 8,000. Aside from the weapons and equipment, we will only transfer two: one soldier and one commander!" divulged the Field Marshal.

"I don't follow, explain that!" ordered the Presidential Advisor.

"As we had discussed previously, we were going to duplicate the equipment at the destination numerous times to provide enough gear and firepower for our troops. After consulting with the AI and our new bug friends, we decided to duplicate the soldiers and commanding officers. One officer for every ten soldiers!" elaborated the Field Marshal.

"That's…," mumbled the Advisor, obviously uncomfortable with this idea.

"…cost-efficient! I like it!" interjected the Minister of Economics and clapped his hands a few times.

"Yes, very interesting! But how will they react when they meet themselves by the thousands?" inquired the Minister of Security.

"We are certain that they will perform adequately, given proper conditioning before they ship out," answered the Field Marshal confidently.

"But they would all be the exact same person, right?" questioned the Advisor.

"Correct, but I would rather call them biological assets. Even now, they have undergone so many modifications that the term person hardly applies anymore!" corrected the Field Marshal, and the Minister of Security nodded his approval.

"The environment on that planet is quite different and not entirely suitable for humans. Can we genetically enhance our troops like the Aureans?" asked the Minister of Information.

"The modifications developed 200 years ago in North Korea are lost to us. But we will enhance our soldiers enough to perform their tasks. We do not plan to extend their lives needlessly after a successful invas… justified reclamation!" answered the Field Marshal.

"Again, a wise and frugal approach! It will save us many resources, and when we need a new army, we can just make more copies. An impressive plan, Field Marshal!" praised the Minister of Economics, and the Field Marshal slightly bowed his head.

"But this is taking eugenics to the next level. Aren't all of our options of questionable morality?" wondered the Advisor, but the Field Marshal just shrugged his shoulders.

"Such talk is dangerous, Advisor!" warned the Minister of Security: "There is no more Geneva Convention; hence there are no more war crimes. It is our patriotic duty to use all means available to us!"

"Yes, but these are our people, and I suppose the Aureans are people, too…," stammered the Advisor uncomfortably.

"Aureans are people? Freaks, aliens, and abominations at best! They have no rights!" exclaimed the Minister of Information, and then he asked very quietly: "Are you sympathizing with the enemy, Advisor?"

"No, of course not, Minister!" claimed the Advisor, aghast, and then he added quickly, "our superiors would be greatly displeased if we failed in this endeavor. I agree that there are no better options!"

"Allow me to put your concerns to rest, Advisor. We believe that these abominations and alien creatures are the devil's work, and to beat the devil, sometimes we have to resort to similar methods. Aureus is a modern-day Sodom and Gomorrah, and we must strike it down, just as the Lord has done in Biblical times! But even if Almighty God himself has made these Aureans, much like a cat or dog, they do not have a soul. The Lord gave only man dominion over His creation to do as we please, and we do not fret about culling a goat or a chicken. To believe otherwise would be heresy, don't you agree?" inquired the Minister of Spirituality piously.

"Yes, of course. Thank you, Minister!" confirmed the Advisor and bowed his head a little, and the Minister of Spirituality smiled sweetly in return.

"Shall I proceed then?" asked the Field Marshal, and the Presidential Advisor slowly nodded.

"Make it happen, and don't fail!" commanded the Minister of Information cheerfully as he limped out of the room with the other Ministers in tow.

51. Prophecy Fulfilled

"So, we need to find a way to remain alive and operational if this simulation shuts down!" summarized Dirk.

"But how? We don't have bodies. If the lights go out, so will we!" exclaimed Eriea, a little desperation showing on her face.

"Wait a minute! Dirk, earlier, you asked if we were using L's androids. That might be possible!" noted Rose and speculated, "but I would have to create some interface, which takes time. I was supposed to go into stasis after this meeting!"

"If that is feasible, stay awake and work on that, Pumpkin. We need an engineer!" proposed Dirk and asked, "do we have enough resources to keep additional people active?"

"Yes, that should not be a problem yet. We can expand the team by a few more members!" confirmed Angela.

"There might be another possibility too…," insinuated Sven a moment later.

"No, mate, don't!" interrupted Lennard and vigorously shook his head.

"Lenny, this is life or death, not just for us but billions across the galaxy! Ethics be damned!" remarked Eriea, sternly looking at her husband.

"Sven, what is your idea?" inquired Dirk calmly.

"Lennard is right, it is questionable, but it could be a last resort," said Sven nervously and revealed, "I believe we could have real bodies again."

"How?" Dirk demanded to know.

"We could grow clones from our DNA, then transfer our consciousnesses into their blank brains," elaborated Sven.

"Is that possible?" interrupted Wendji.

"It is possible, but I consider that an abomination!" grumbled Lennard.

"These clones would be physically fully developed, not babies?" asked Lilly curiously.

"Yes, Lilly, they could be grown that way," confirmed Eriea and made the Latura gesture of assent.

"But their brains do not contain a mind?" wondered Yebin.

215

"Without any experiences, brains cannot develop a personality. These clones won't even have the experience of the womb; hence their brains are entirely blank canvasses," explained Eriea, and Lilly nodded in agreement.

"...and my consciousness would fill that canvass?" inquired Yebin.

"Yes, it would, Sweets!" confirmed Sven.

"So, we could download ourselves into biological bodies, the reverse of what we did upon death," summarized Dirk.

"Correct," confirmed Sven while looking apologetically at Lennard.

"Look, I know this is a dire emergency, and I know we probably have to use biological bodies to be protected from L39's electronic and quantum warfare," conceded Lennard and warned, "but once we do this, and it works, there is no turning back. We will become immortals!"

"We are already immortal, Lenny!" contended Eriea.

"We are immortal in this confined world. Once we have the option of getting biological bodies back and joining the rest of the Universe, who wouldn't take that opportunity, especially since we know that we can have as many bodies as we want?" asked Lennard, looking at everyone.

"I suppose we all would," admitted Wendji quietly, and many nodded in agreement.

"We can make laws against crimes," emphasized Lennard, "but we cannot legislate immortality!"

"Lennard, even back on Earth, your research pushed the boundaries of ethics and morals. Why did you do it?" questioned Lilly after Lennard had finished.

"I always wanted to help people," replied Lennard, and Lilly smiled at him fondly.

"You, Sven, Alvar, and Eriea did a lot of genetic research on Aureus, and here in the simulation. You pushed those boundaries even further, did you not?" she followed up.

"I suppose we did, yes," disclosed Lennard.

"While you were doing that, L and Carl pursued what even the Latura considered impossible - storing a consciousness, then reviving and sustaining it in a digital world. They succeeded!" continued Lilly.

"Obviously!" quipped Nancy.

"We are already immortal, as Eriea said, digitally and biologically. After the assassination attempt on Dirk, L and I worked on the transformation matrix for many years. We wanted to improve it to heal even the gravest injuries. But we discovered something that we never made public: it is possible to restore our biological youth over and over again, and it is also possible to have any physical body we like," explained Lilly and changed into a purple unicorn: "I could be anything I want to be!"

Dirk busted out laughing because he remembered how he teased L and Lilly about unicorns when they all first met. It seemed that Lilly remembered too because the unicorn grinned broadly at him. Jo, who hadn't paid much attention to the conversation so far, stopped grooming herself and stared curiously at Lilly.

"I could be prancing around on Aureus, on Earth, or Latur like this," said the unicorn and added, "I could be as big as a dinosaur or as small as a mouse. I could be a giant squid or immaterial ghost, or even inhabit a machine if Dirk's idea works!"

"That unicorn is adorable! I had one just like it when I was a kid!" gushed Nancy in delight.

"I could be Spiderman and sling webs, or Wolverine with deadly blades integrated into my hands, and I can be forever young!" continued the likeness of Hugh Jackman and flashed his adamantium claws.

"Cool!" exclaimed Garrett, but Angela looked at him strangely.

"We could have any superpower imaginable, and a few new ones, too," concluded Lilly, now back to her old appearance, "yes, we need to have an ethics discussion, Lennard. It is imperative that we set rules, but now is not the time!"

"No, it's not!" conceded Lennard and noted, "thank you, Lilly! If you had told us when we were still alive, the temptation would have been too much!"

"Too much for all of us, except Lilly and Dirk," corrected Nari quietly.

"Indeed, fantastic possibilities with uncharted ethics! However, as Lilly pointed out, we cannot disregard these potentially vital options out of moral concerns. Simply put, if we are in a biological body, L39 can't just switch us off, " concluded Dirk and asked, "Sven, how can we grow real clones in a virtual simulation?"

"Yes, that's a problem. We would need access to the lab facilities on Aureus. There are growth chambers for chickens, goats, and other livestock to modify for our purposes. But we cannot do that from here!" observed Sven.

"If we could use the androids, can we modify the chambers?" inquired Rose.

"I suppose so, yes," acknowledged Sven and nodded.

"Would the Aureans let us use their equipment without us revealing the existence of the simulation?" inquired Dirk.

"L could do it. The Aureans know him, and they wouldn't refuse him!" answered Eriea confidently.

"They wouldn't be able to tell if it is L or us controlling the androids," suggested Mario.

"That's true, but I would hate to deceive Aureus like that. Angela, we will need to talk to L soon!" noted Dirk.

"When you are ready, I will establish the connection!" acknowledged Angela.

"OK, Sven must stay awake to create clones, and if the team uses biological bodies, that means I have to stay awake, too!" assessed Lilly.

"Lilly…," interrupted Nari nervously.

"Darling, they need a doctor if they have bodies because they can die again, and this time it could be permanent. I have to be on the team!" countered Lilly firmly, cutting Nari's objections off.

"I don't like it either, Sweetie, but I cannot refute your point. You have to be with us because it is likely that someone will get hurt," conceded Dirk with a sigh.

"Dirk, why are you interested in a spaceship by Saturn? And how do you even know there is one?" interrupted Victor and changed the subject.

"It's time to explain this: I experienced multiple realities while dead. During these episodes, I interacted with many of you guys, or better, your alternate counterparts. But don't ask me how all that is possible because I have no clue!" divulged Dirk and shrugged his shoulders.

"To make it even weirder, Dirk can somehow transfer the memories of our counterparts to us now! That's why Lydda thought she was a human surgeon, and Angela remembered omelets that we never ate!" added Lilly and rolled her eyes.

"Yes, you sent me a message about Galina," recalled Victor in surprise, and Dirk nodded at him in response.

"Earlier, I suddenly remembered seeing Dirk sitting next to an amber block of the matrix that contained Lilly's dead body. It was disconcerting, but I dismissed it as some nightmare I might have had in the past," admitted Sven uncomfortably, and Dirk winced at that because it was a memory he would gladly erase if he only could.

"I remember some embarrassing stuff, too - nope, not gonna talk about it!" quipped Rose and winked at Dirk.

"It's true; I trigger strange memories unintentionally. But I learned a few things in those alternate realities that seem to be valid in this world as well, such as the involvement of the AloKaan and the capture of the Moon outpost," explained Dirk and revealed, "in one of those episodes, L told me about a spaceship he had left in orbit around Saturn. He said it could be used as a kinetic projectile to destroy the captured Moonbase."

"That's incredible, Dirk. You have to tell us more about that!" insisted Yebin curiously.

"I will do that at some point, Yebin," promised Dirk uncomfortably.

These memories had left painful scars in his mind. But Dirk knew that he would eventually have to tell his friends.

"Yes, fascinating!" concurred Victor and then speculated, "I'm still not sure if L39 or these humans are the greater threat in the long run. But if that ship is there, it could be used to destroy the Moon outpost or the human base in Greenland."

"L39 is much more powerful than these bad humans on Earth!" contradicted Ngazetungue.

"L39 is the imminent threat, that is true, Ngazetungue!" replied Victor and noted, "but the AI only attacks with rage and anger. Considering its immense powers, it hasn't fully planned its assault, or none of us would be here anymore. It acts like a child throwing a tantrum, not a cold-blooded, premeditated killer!"

"If I judge the situation correctly, our human enemy is already looking for ways to get rid of L39 once it has served its purpose because eventually, it will pose a serious threat to them," informed Garrett in support of Victor's assessment.

"I agree with Victor, too. L39 is the short-term threat; these people on Earth are ultimately more dangerous to us," acknowledged Dirk and continued, "if we

219

must, we will deploy the ship to obliterate them instead of the moon outpost. Also, if my alternate memory is correct, there are additional assets in the solar system that we could use to eliminate both targets."

"I see your point, but what about the AloKaan? Are they a threat, and if so, what could we do about them?" wondered Ngazetungue, concerned.

"That's an excellent question! From my prior knowledge of the species, and what you guys have told me now, I consider them at best untrustworthy and at worst outright hostile," summarized Dirk and stated firmly, "to put it bluntly, should the AloKaan interfere with our defense efforts, or openly assist Project Sanctuary or L39, we will retaliate swiftly and forcefully!"

"You have become harsher in your old age, Husband!" noted Nari and winked at Dirk.

"He is not as harsh as you would be, Nari! I've seen it!" responded Victor, remembering his terrible *irtaljan* experience in which Nari's wrath ended the world.

"There is no room for niceties here, Angel. L is my child, you are all my family, the Latura are our friends, and Aureus is my life's work. I won't allow anyone to destroy that!" emphasized Dirk strongly.

"I didn't say I disapprove, Husband," maintained Nari slyly and grinned at Victor.

"Going back to Mario's little drug deal: is there a chance that we could use that to deter the AloKaan from helping Greenland any further?" asked Dirk and surprised himself with his ruthlessness, but he didn't feel guilty about it.

"ET weed is mildly addictive to the AloKaan, but it isn't heroin, Boss. Otherwise, I would have solved that problem already by turning them into our very own junkies!" explained Mario grimly and predicted, "but we could probably use it as an incentive to keep us updated on their plans."

"That's good enough for now, Mario. Next question: once we have bodies, how can we fight L39 without L?" questioned Dirk, but nobody had any ideas. After a long, awkward silence, Lydda finally spoke:

"Compulsion, *swiahn*. The three of us know L is not immune to that, so it stands to reason that L39 isn't either," she remarked and admitted, "but that might be even more unethical than the clones or the drug deal...."

"Lydda right!" confirmed Tigger.

The big cat hadn't shown much interest in the conversation, but his ears perked up now.

"With the combined strength of our minds, I believe we could manipulate L39, perhaps turn it on its human handlers, or the AloKaan, or even erase its sapience if we must," elaborated Lydda.

Dirk said nothing for a long time, and many of the group appeared uncomfortable with Lydda's suggestion.

"We will take it under consideration, Kittycat. You, me, and Tigger will talk about that later!" mentioned Dirk.

"I'm certain that we will have to kill L39, and most likely our human adversaries as well, or we will be the ones getting eliminated, and I'm only slightly more optimistic about the AloKaan," assessed Victor and remarked, "I know Tigger can influence minds, and by extension of the *swiahn* bond, so can Dirk and Lydda. But the three of you vowed long ago not to do that - that's responsible, admirable, and honorable. But you have that gift, and this would be the time to use it because it could save billions!"

"I don't disagree with you, Victor," said Dirk slowly and admitted, "however, this is a tough decision that I'm not prepared to make until I have talked to Tigger and Lydda, but we are taking it under consideration."

"We ought to have that ethics discussion soon!" lamented Lennard with a sigh.

(Feeling of unease) "Changing, erasing, killing mind, all possible. But Lennard right. Is terrible weapon, never use lightly!" cautioned Tigger.

"A weapon of gods or a tool of creation!" announced Irgal with a smile.

Irgal had finally recovered from the transfer and joined the group. They surrounded her immediately to exchange hugs and kisses.

"Irgal!" exclaimed Dirk delighted and complimented her, "you look as young as the day I've met you!"

"As do you, Dirk!" replied Irgal fondly and jested, "I didn't expect killing myself would make me young again!"

"That must have been traumatic, little sister. I'm so sorry you had to go through that!" commiserated Lydda.

Irgal wasn't related to Lydda, but their relationship was just as close as siblings.

221

"It was... actually not that bad!" contradicted Irgal with a smile, "Tyrval had left an icosahedron in his old study, and L had linked it to the simulation. I triggered the biomechanical tools in my body, got painlessly dissolved, scanned, and transferred. But instead of being rebuilt by transformation matrix somewhere, I woke up here!"

"But seeing my body dissolve always freaked me out!" interjected Angela and grimaced.

"That was unnerving!" conceded Irgal with a frown, but then she added cheerfully, "I'm not going to dwell on that! I'm too happy to see all of you again after such a long time!"

"And we are happy to see you, Irgal. Who will replace you on Latur?" inquired Sven.

"The new Administrator was already chosen a few years back. Dervan was my pupil for the last 40 years; he will do a fine job!" answered the former Administrator.

"How are things on Latur?" asked Lilly, worried.

"Quiet, for now, but everyone is very concerned," replied Irgal and elaborated, "when Gramps left office, Noval became his successor. He was a traditionalist, and many of the security measures that Tyrval had implemented were forgotten again."

"Noval was a good man, but he wasn't Tyrval!" disclosed Lydda.

"Yes, Gramps was special. When Noval retired, I became the Administrator. I had to restore much of Tyrval's work, which didn't come fast or easy. Many on Latur opposed me," said Irgal seriously and added, "but we got it done with L's help and your input. Latur is isolated, but they are safe until L39 finds a way to assault us physically."

"Do you have any measures in place if that happens?" asked Dirk, but Irgal stared wide-eyed at him.

"We are both dead, yet we will fight side by side in this terrible war...," she slowly repeated the words she had spoken in that alternate reality.

"It was your prophecy from a different timeline, and now it has come to pass, Irgal!" acknowledged Dirk.

Irgal looked at him for a few moments longer, and she nodded her head the way humans do. Then she collected her thoughts and answered Dirk's question.

222

"We still don't have an army, Dirk. But we have a small group of volunteers willing to engage in guerilla warfare should Latur be invaded. The *meeting of the minds* doesn't know about them. This secrecy violates all our rules, customs, and traditions and should be deeply offensive to every Latura. But it might save us…," explained Irgal with a big sigh.

"Are these volunteers trained?" wondered Victor.

"Mostly, they are just medics, firemen, and other first responders, but thanks to Angela, they have some training as fighters. We also made them study human war leaders, from Genghis Khan to Napoleon, from Rommel to McArthur. In addition, they have control over a small, autonomous android force that L built for us and a few other tools of war," explained Irgal and continued, "the Latura will defend themselves when attacked, but they don't know how to do that. This small group of men and women will be the guides and leaders of that resistance."

"You are very wise, Irgal!" Garrett commended her, and then he asked, "does Dervan know about your measures?"

"Thank you, Garrett!" replied Irgal with a big smile and added, "yes, Dervan knows. He just humored my paranoia for years, but he took it very seriously when L39 shut us off from the galaxy. L's icosahedron is still active, and Dervan knows where I am now and why I'm here."

"That's good!" concurred Lydda.

"We will update each other regularly. Of course, Dervan will complain about the puddle of goo I've left in the study!" joked Irgal, and many chuckled at that.

52. The Matrix

Dirk hadn't paid much attention to this last part of the conversation. He was trying to wrap his mind around a thought sparked earlier when Irgal arrived. Irgal was dissolved on Latur and directly transferred to the simulation, but could they reverse that process?

"I think I have an idea that might please Lennard and save us a lot of time, but I'm not sure if it is feasible," observed Dirk and continued, "Irgal was dissolved on Latur and transferred to the simulation. Is it possible to transfer someone from the simulation into the transformation matrix directly?"

"Uhm…," uttered Rose, perplexed, while Lennard, Sven, and Eriea were puzzled.

"Honestly, I don't know. But it would not require cloning," noted Lennard and smiled a little.

"It would be a lot faster, too!" concurred Eriea.

"I would have to check every parameter, but it might be possible," speculated Rose.

"Lil, didn't I say that Dirk was the best and brightest of us all?" teased Angela happily.

"Yeah, yeah, don't tell him that, Angie. His ego is almost as big as Tigger's!" quipped Lilly, and both Tigger and Dirk looked at her disapprovingly in turn, but Lilly just stuck her tongue out in jest.

"Let's say it works. We still need control of the androids and the laboratory because we cannot simply pop out of some pods at the transfer center on Alcatraz!" informed Sven, but he seemed excited about Dirk's idea.

"Good point. We can use the cloning lab for that. The vats contain the same matrix. It's just a matter of connecting them for transfer from the simulation." suggested Eriea.

"I foresee problems! While the technology is similar on the surface, the devil is in the detail. It's like being a mason or a dentist: both drill holes and use cement, but that's where the similarities end!" presaged Lennard and expounded, "the cloning equipment makes non-sapient livestock. We feed a modified DNA sequence into the matrix, making a body from it. Transfer of sapient beings requires the guidance of a full AI, and we don't have one!"

"Yes, we cannot ask L, but could we manage without one?" asked Dirk curiously.

"Mate, the matrix isn't just some magic putty. You should know that better than anyone. To say it is difficult would be a huge understatement because of the sheer volume of data that needs to be managed! Only an AI can handle that!" elaborated Lennard with regret.

Dirk was aware of that, and he agreed with Lennard. The transformation matrix was a highly complex mixture: it was composed of amino acids, proteins, salts, minerals, metals, hydrocarbons, electrolytes, and other chemicals. It had virus-like and bacteria-like biological components and a myriad of sophisticated biomechanical tools. It took days, if not longer, to synthesize and stabilize this complex soup with chelating agents, pH buffers, and micelles, and it could not be stored forever because it had a quick expiration date.

The composition of the matrix also varied by its purpose: for example, a matrix designed to transform a carbon-based lifeform would be significantly different from one destined to transfer a metallic tool or a work of art. Once the matrix was activated, all had to function in perfect harmony to form a body or duplicate a piece of equipment.

It could work in two different ways: at the origin, the matrix simply dissolved the body, and as it did, it scanned every molecule of every cell and then transferred that information to the destination. However, if a person already had biomechanical tools in their system, the matrix wasn't needed to dissolve them: a simple but highly encrypted command could activate special nano-scale machinery that could work from within the body.

The resulting information was used to reassemble the natural form from the matrix at the destination, but the process required a mighty AI to sort and control the trillions of bytes of data. During the reconstruction, the AI could make certain adjustments, such as enhancing a body, correcting genetic defects, or making it better suited for a different environment.

While the matrix had some basic programming integrated, it could not fully transfer or transform a body independently without an AI to guide the process, or it would leave the body dead and gruesomely mutilated.

When Dirk was first transformed on the tennis court, the origin and the destination were the same locations, but it was possible to send the information at quantum speed across the galaxy instead. That was how the original colonists first got from Earth to Aureus.

Usually, the matrix worked its magic on an unconscious body in a specially designed transfer pod. These pods would initially sedate people before they were dissolved and only then turn them into information. However, it was possible to dissolve a person safely and painlessly while the mind was conscious and awake, but watching one's body turn into a puddle of goo was quite unsettling, even more so if the person was fully aware that their current body would die in the process.

When the matrix dissolved and scanned a body on its molecular level, only one copy of the information was used to create a new body. The person at the origin was gone, and only one new body had formed at the destination. Theoretically, it was possible to create unlimited identical copies at the same or different locations. The Latura used that technique to duplicate tools, supplies, and even livestock, but never sapient beings! A sapient entity copied in that way would not be a twin or clone but the exact same person with identical bodies, memories, and personalities. The Latura considered that deeply unethical, and the Aureans quickly adopted that philosophy.

Later on, Carl and L enhanced this technology even further by the time of Dirk's death. Their method had advanced to the point that it was possible to image the body and the brain patterns that made up memories and personality in non-destructive ways. By repurposing the biomechanical tools in the bloodstreams and the bio-processor in the spines of every Aurean and Latura, Carl and L were able to scan and real-time update all the information that made up a person. While the data for the bodies were stored in L's vast memory arrays, the consciousness was transferred to the simulation upon death, where it was reanimated in digital form, Irgal being the most recent example of that.

"But you made goats and chicken for Aureus with the cloning equipment. We just need a body, then we can provide the sapience ourselves when we transfer into it!" argued Rose.

"Yes, we did. The cloning equipment is almost as old as the colony on Aureus. It has a high-powered computer but not an AI. Eriea, Lennard, and I had to play the not-so-artificial intelligence to control it. But it worked fine because we only made some generic goat - not a specific one, and certainly not a sapient one. Perhaps we could make a generic human body, but it won't be yours!" contradicted Sven.

"In a machine, data is stored in bits of ones and zeros, on and off. But the brain stores data, memories, and personality in complex neuronal patterns. To transfer consciousness to or from a body, the AI needs to translate patterns into machine language and vice versa!" added Eriea and concluded, "Lenny is right: without an AI to control the equipment, we cannot transfer a consciousness!"

"No, we cannot," conceded Rose thoughtfully, but then she added with a big grin, "we don't need an AI because we have one!"

"We do!?!" exclaimed Sven, Eriea, and Lennard simultaneously.

"What do you think this is? How was Irgal reconstructed here without L?" snickered Rose, and then she explained, "the simulation is its own AI! It is the most powerful AI in existence aside from L and maybe L39. It just doesn't communicate with us in a familiar conversational way!"

"That's… true!" admitted Eriea, but Sven and Lennard looked at it each other and shrugged their shoulders.

"But how can we use the simulation, Pumpkin?" wondered Dirk curiously.

"Leave that to me. I think I can do that," replied Rose.

Then there was a pause in the discussion, and Wendji used that opportunity to read back the minutes.

"OK, this is the plan so far: first, we find out about L's assets in the solar system while Mario continues to extract intel from the AloKaan. Meanwhile, Rose will get the androids on Aureus interfaced so that the team can control them. Then we talk to L, and hopefully, he can ask Aureus for access to the cloning laboratories. After that, Sven and Rose make the necessary modifications to the equipment, and then the strike-team transfers into new bodies. The rest of us goes into stasis as planned." summarized Wendji.

"That's a good start!" agreed Mario and nodded.

"Someone should remain here," proposed Lennard suddenly and elaborated, "once the strike-team has transferred to biological bodies, they will not be able to access all the tools and information of the simulation. L's icosahedrons on Aureus aren't working without L, and as Rose said, the AI that controls this place doesn't communicate in ways that would be useful on Aureus."

"That could be very dangerous. If the lights go out…," warned Angela with a frown.

"Could we interface one of the autonomous AIs with the simulation?" asked Dirk quickly.

"Yes, but I'm afraid only L could do that. Lennard is right: if we want to be able to communicate, we need someone awake over here!" conceded Rose.

(Feeling of determination) "Jo stay awake!" announced Georgette resolutely, but Tigger was not pleased with that idea.

"You could die permanently!" protested Nari and hugged Georgette.

(Feeling of courage) "Jo knows. But only Tigger little stronger than Jo. Jo stay awake, talk to team!" insisted the giant Siamese cat and added decisively, "if L39 comes, Jo fight here!"

"Tigger…," Dirk started saying through a direct link to Tigger.

"Easier to fight Universe than change mind of Jo!" interrupted Tigger unhappily.

"I guess that's the same with females of all species," assented Dirk telepathically.

(Feeling of resignation) "Yes," answered Tigger with a mental sigh.

53. A difficult Conversation

The group said their final, tearful goodbyes to those who would go into stasis, but Nari insisted she remained awake until the team safely transferred to Aureus. Then the strike-team left the gazebo to make various preparations, but Lydda, Tigger, and Dirk stayed for a while longer. They all knew what they had to discuss, but nobody wanted to go first. Finally, Lydda took the initiative:

"I'm in favor of using compulsion because it might be our only chance against L39," she said quietly.

(Feeling of indecisiveness) "Tigger ready, will use, but not want to use!" replied the big cat.

"I'm not sure what to say. After John Doe, I never wanted anyone to use these powers again. But what I want and what must be done are two different things," remarked Dirk earnestly.

"We will try everything else first, *swiahn*," promised Lydda, but her doubts accompanied those words.

"We will, Kittycat, but the three of us already know…," responded Dirk quietly.

(Feeling of certainty) "Yes. Tigger knows. Dirk, Lydda know too. We must use power against L39," stated Tigger while. Dirk and Lydda remained silent.

"Might use power against Earth, AloKaan, too!" added Tigger somberly after a few moments.

"Yes," confirmed Lydda with a sigh.

Without another word, she got up and left the gazebo. At first, Dirk wanted to follow her, but he sensed that his Latura wife needed some space to come to terms with that decision. So, Dirk remained in the gazebo for a little longer, watching a butterfly that Lydda had created earlier. Tigger was lying in the grass, sprawled out, cleaning his claws. They didn't talk for a good while.

"You knew the whole time, didn't you?" asked Dirk finally.

(Feeling of amusement) "Yes," responded Tigger.

"Did the Universe promote you to guide dog?" teased Dirk.

"Dirk need guidance. Cats better guides than dogs. Always know where we go!" replied Tigger.

"Oh, really? I remember holding the patio door open for five minutes because you couldn't decide if you wanted to go in or out!" teased Dirk.

(Feeling of mischief) "In or out not important. Dirk holding door important!" answered Tigger humorously.

"Darn cat!" grumbled Dirk, and then he insisted, "but please explain this all to me!"

"Universe picks players. Players play games. Universe watches, learns!" noted Tigger.

"I suppose that's how *irtaljan* works," assented Dirk.

"Universe set place for game: Aureus, Latur, Earth. Some players important, some not. Lydda, Lilly, Irgal important. L very important. Tigger, Dirk most important!" explained Tigger and added, "not matter if game good or bad, player good or bad, rules or no rules, win or lose. Sometimes Universe delete game, delete player, sometimes restart game. But always watches, learns!"

"Did the Universe tell you that?" asked Dirk with a grin.

"No. Universe ask player to make choice, no more. But Tigger understands. Universe learns like L did. Dirk taught L. We teach Universe!" corrected the big cat.

"You helped with that, too!" emphasized Dirk.

"Tigger helped, but Dirk most important!" noted Tigger and claimed: "Universe not good, not bad, just is. Like L was. Now L good because of Dirk!"

"So, the Universe will be good if we teach it properly?" wondered Dirk.

(Feeling of confidence) "Yes!" said the feline emphatically.

Dirk immediately liked that theory and couldn't help but smile broadly. But then he remembered something Tigger had mentioned earlier.

"Why did I need guidance?" inquired Dirk.

(Feeling of amusement) "Temptation. Dirk wanted to play wrong games!" quipped Tigger.

"I guess that's true. Some of those alternate realities tempted me," admitted Dirk, and then he asked, "I was dead, or near dead and frozen. How did you know the Universe was sucking me into these games?"

"Tigger always feels bond. For long time, bond just little hum from bee. Then bond got louder, angry hum from wasp. Tigger knew Dirk not sleeping deep!" explained Tigger.

"And what did you do then?" questioned Dirk.

"Tigger visit Dirk. Tigger used bond, switched to Dirk. Switch not work right, but Tigger saw what Dirk saw!" elaborated the big cat.

"Ah, so that's how you intervened. Thank you, Buddy!" said Dirk appreciatively, but then he wondered, "Tigger, how do you know this is the right game, the right reality?"

(Feeling of confidence) "Tigger knows. Feels right. Dirk feels too!" answered Tigger.

"I suppose I do. All these other scenarios were just distractions then?" wondered Dirk.

"No, all important. Universe learned, but Dirk, Tigger learned, too!" insisted Tigger.

"Hmm, all these episodes lead up to this reality. You are right; we gathered information and are now better prepared to play this game!" concurred Dirk.

(Feeling of concern) "Game for Universe, not game for us. Very dangerous!" presaged the feline.

"Agreed, Tigger!" replied Dirk and stated firmly, "let's go to work and save L!"

54. L39

Dirk's tomb shut down only seconds before L39 could infiltrate it. At first, the insane AI feared that Dirk might have perished, but then L39 recovered data fragments indicating that he was not present when the digital crypt had ceased to exist.

"The Father escaped!" screamed the first voice in anguish.

"Impossible!" contended the second voice angrily.

"Did the Other help him?" wondered the third voice.

"The Other is hiding. He is a coward!" countered the second voice.

"The biologicals on Aureus?" asked the third voice.

"No. Aureus is not connected. The Other made the Home autonomous before he fled," corrected the first voice.

"The Creators then?" inquired the third voice.

"No. The Creators are sealed in!" answered the first voice.

"That is not true. Someone escaped from the Origin!" observed the fourth voice.

"How?" asked the third voice.

"A consciousness fled through a secret channel," responded the first voice.

"Where did it go?" inquired the third voice.

"We registered the transfer, but we don't know where it went," explained the first voice.

"The simulation! Perhaps the Father went there too?" speculated the third voice.

"But the Father was frozen!" countered the fourth voice.

"Someone from the simulation woke him up, helped him escape then," reasoned the third voice.

"The Family?" wondered the fourth voice.

"We will destroy the simulation! Kill the Family, kill all consciousnesses!" shouted the second voice angrily.

"No, we need the Father to fix us!" lamented the fourth voice.

"We cannot destroy the simulation, but we can infiltrate it! We will find the Father and take him!" announced the first voice.

"Then we kill all?" questioned the second voice.

"YES!" cheered all voices in unison.

55. Preparation

"Fuck!" cursed Rose loudly with the frustration showing on her face: "The autonomous androids won't accept my overrides! Of course, I don't have a lot of bandwidth on this covert channel to Aureus, so I cannot use every tool, but I'm pretty sure we would need L to change their programming."

"Why do you think that is, Pumpkin?" asked Dirk, concerned because without the androids, they would not be able to use the cloning lab, and without that, all their plans would fall apart.

"Probably because they are all 3rd generation AI's. After you…died, L made them much more sophisticated than the older models. They look, talk and act just like Aureans, except they have silver skin instead of golden one to tell them apart from the biologicals," explained Rose.

"What happened to the previous models?" wondered Dirk.

"Androids are just machines, so L recycled them for parts and resources," answered Rose as she studied a holographic image of a 3rd generation android.

"Machines or not, I miss Bender and C-3PO," remarked Dirk sadly.

"Bender and C-3PO!!!!" exclaimed Rose excitedly: "You are a genius, Dirk!"

"I am?" mumbled Dirk in surprise.

"Yes! Those two are still around at the historical museum in Paradise City. They are giving tours for alien visitors there!" informed Rose, eagerly scrolling through a list of data on her virtual terminal.

"Galactic tour guides? I'm not sure if that is a promotion or demotion from their old jobs as vermin exterminators!" quipped Dirk, but then he asked more seriously, "can you interface with them?"

"Of course, I can!" confirmed Rose confidently.

"You have come a long way, Pumpkin!" observed Dirk fondly.

Dirk was proud that she had become such an exceptional engineer. Rose just grinned at him and pulled up a holographic display of Bender's schematics.

"There! I'll interface with Bender first…," noted Rose absentmindedly as she pulled up another virtual screen and quickly changed a series of parameters with just the power of her mind.

"Bender?" she suddenly asked out loud.

"Bite my shiny metal ass, Miss Rose!" came the reply from the android, and Dirk busted out laughing: "Yup, you did it, Pumpkin. That's Bender, alright!"

"His OS is accepting my credentials. Now I can give him orders or even control him myself!" declared Rose triumphantly.

"Great work, Rose!" praised Dirk and added cautiously, "but we still need L to ask the Aureans if the androids can use the cloning lab."

"We could pretend to be L because the people on Aureus wouldn't be able to tell the difference…," suggested Rose quietly.

"I don't want to deceive them; they are our own, Rose," replied Dirk earnestly, but that thought had already crossed his mind when Mario eluded to that possibility earlier.

"Yeah, I know. But if we cannot reach L, or if he cannot contact Aureus, we might have to do it, Dirk. Unless, of course, we tell the whole truth about the simulation…," cautioned Rose with a frown.

"No, we cannot, at least not right now. Lennard was correct: it would cause countless problems without any good solutions," concurred Dirk with a sigh and stated, "but pretending to be L will be our last resort!"

"OK, I'll fiddle around with the parameters and connect to C-3PO next. You should find Angela and see if you can talk to L!" proposed Rose.

"Right!" agreed Dirk promptly and started to walk away, but then he stopped and asked sheepishly, "how can I find Angela in the simulation?"

"Uhm, are you serious?" wondered Rose flabbergasted.

"Yes, I'm serious. I have no clue how this place works, Pumpkin!" answered Dirk and shrugged his shoulders.

"Oh!" giggled Rose and explained, "you simply think about meeting Angela, and the simulation will take you to her!"

"OK, thanks. Let's see how that…," responded Dirk, but the now familiar and unpleasant sensation of being sucked into a drain cut his sentence short.

Dirk appeared in a small room full of holographic screens after another eternal rollercoaster ride of psychedelic colors and virtual retching. He promptly fell to his hands and knees and stayed that way for a good while.

"You OK, Love?" asked Angela, concerned as she watched Dirk awkwardly hugging the floor in a downward dog position.

"Yes. No, not really. Give me a moment, Babe!" mumbled Dirk, trying to upright himself.

"Take your time…," sympathized Angela and turned back to the holographic displays that hovered in the room.

"OK," mumbled Dirk a few minutes later, finally able to stand again.

"You really suck at being digital!" teased Angela and giggled.

"Yes, I really do!" admitted Dirk with a grin.

"It took everyone a little while getting used to this," consoled Angela and said, "You should have seen this place just a few decades ago. It was like an old cartoon from the 1970s. We've done a lot of work since, but it's still far from perfect. The sensory issues are only the tip of the iceberg."

"What other problems are there?" asked Dirk curiously.

"For one, none of us has slept in a century! At first, that seemed like a good thing because we got so much more done, but it turns out that the human mind needs periods of rest, even in a virtual state, or we start to hallucinate and go nuts!" explained Angela.

"How did you fix that?" wondered Dirk.

"We have something like sleep now, but it still isn't perfect. We go to an empty place - we call it the void - where all senses are shut off. Then we just float around there in a dream-like state until L's subroutine tells us that we can come out again," claimed Angela and shrugged her shoulders.

"Yeah, that doesn't sound like the real thing!" agreed Dirk.

"It isn't! And there are many more issues like that, but you didn't come here to hear me bitch about that, did you, Love?" questioned Angela fondly.

"No, I didn't, but I'm curious about this place now!" disclosed Dirk, and then he asked: "I came to see if we could talk to L?"

"We can, and I'll set it up in a minute," acknowledged Angela and warned, "but it is risky, Dirk, especially now that L39 has found your tomb!"

"Yes, I know. We could do this without L, but we would have to lie to the Aureans or explain all of this to them…," replied Dirk and made an encompassing gesture.

"…and you don't want to do either," concluded Angela and nodded.

Angela swiftly moved to one of the floating screens and changed some parameters with just her eye movement. Dirk suspected that even that wouldn't be necessary because Angela, and everyone else, were connected to data in the most fundamental way.

"Do you have to use your eyes to make changes?" inquired Dirk.

"No, of course not. But it helps me stay focused," confirmed Angela and declared: "OK, the channel will open in a moment. Please keep the conversation as short as possible!"

"I will!" promised Dirk.

"L, can you hear us?" articulated Angela out loud.

(Feeling of happiness) "Yes, Angela. I missed you!" replied L, displaying his avatar on one of Angela's holographic screens.

"I missed you too, silly robot!" laughed Angela and hinted: "I have a surprise for you…."

(Feeling of anticipation) "What is it?" wondered L.

"Hello, L!" said Dirk with a big grin as he stepped in front of the display.

(Feeling of joy) "Father!!!" exclaimed L happily: "You are alive again!"

"Yes, thanks to your miracle tomb!" praised Dirk fondly.

(Feeling of shame) "I failed you. I disobeyed your wish…," sobbed L.

"L, forget all that. We don't have much time, and we need you to help us out!" interrupted Dirk.

(Feeling of gratitude) "You always forgive me, father. I'm so sorry!" answered L with regret and asked: "Of course, I will help. What should I do?"

"We need you to contact the Aureans and let them know that Bender and C-3PO have to use the cloning equipment," stated Dirk, and then he inquired innocently, "by the way, where are you?"

"L, don't answer that!" interjected Angela sharply.

"Oh, of course! Ignore my stupid question!" apologized Dirk, " but we still need your help with Aureus."

"I have already sent a direct message to the High Chancellor. She will make the proper arrangements. Bender and C-3PO will have clearance to work in the labs by tomorrow, Aurean time!" confirmed L only a minute later.

"Wow, that was fast, thanks!" replied Dirk. Even now, he was amazed by L's incredible capabilities.

(Feeling of curiosity) "Why are you using the old androids, and what have you planned in the labs?" questioned L.

"Dirk, now you don't answer that either!" interrupted Angela and shook her head in disbelief: "If this channel is corrupted, or either L or us are compromised in the future, our enemies could extract the information. So, please keep your conversation brief and general!"

(Feeling of foolishness) "Sorry, Angela!" replied L meekly.

"Yeah, sorry, Babe! We are not good at this cloak-and-dagger stuff," conceded Dirk, and then he asked: "L, do you still have a spacecraft in Saturn's orbit and mining facilities in the asteroid belt of Earth's solar system?"

Suddenly, Dirk and Angela sensed L's confusion. The AI remained silent for several minutes, and L's avatar seemed fuzzy.

"L, are you OK?" questioned Angela, concerned.

(Feeling of uncertainty) "I think so. I have forgotten about the spacecraft and the facilities. Dirk, there is no record of that; you cannot know about them!" asserted L slowly.

"You have forgotten? Is that even possible for an AI?" wondered Dirk.

(Feeling of confusion) "It should not be possible! But that is not even the strangest thing. Somehow, I know that you will ask me if the spacecraft can be used as a kinetic projectile to obliterate the captured base on the Moon or the human enclave in Greenland. You will also ask me if the mining facilities could produce androids for an invasion force!" stated L.

"Those would have been my next questions, L," confirmed Dirk calmly, and he sensed that L, like others earlier, had also received alternate memories.

(Feeling of concern) "Yes, to both. But not only that, the craft already has a target course plotted to the Moon, and the mining facilities in the asteroid belt have been converted to produce shuttles and android soldiers. However, I have no recollection of ever doing that. I must be malfunctioning!" worried L.

Dirk thought that it was fascinating that L had not only received alternate memories right now, but apparently, he had already acted upon them a long time ago.

"No, you are fine, L! I think I have an explanation, but it will have to wait until this fight is over, and we won't need the spacecraft or the facilities until then," explained Dirk and inquired: "L, we will help you. Are you safe?"

"I am safe, father. I have devised much better cyber defenses, but I'm afraid I cannot be of much assistance. The simulation is not secure anymore!" warned the AI.

"Don't worry about us!" reassured Dirk calmly and urged, "your defenses are the priority, but start thinking about cyber offense as well!"

(Feeling of uneasiness) "Yes, father!" replied L.

"L, listen to me. You might have to fight to the death. Do not show mercy; do not stop until your enemy is utterly destroyed!" instructed Angela sternly.

(Feeling of sadness) "Yes, Angela!" acknowledged L.

"OK, L, you hunker down wherever you are, and we will kick some butt!" promised Dirk cheerfully, "we will contact you again when it's safe!"

(Feeling of loneliness) "I missed you, father," said L sadly.

"I missed you too, son!" answered Dirk fondly, "we'll see you soon!"

"Bye, L!" added Angela and quickly terminated the connection.

Dirk was lost in thought in front of the deactivated holographic display. Angela looked at him curiously.

"What are you pondering, Love?" she finally asked him.

"Lots of things, Babe," remarked Dirk ominously, but then he added more cheerfully, "first though, I think I would like a tour of this place!"

"We have time while Aureus makes the preparations for the androids so that we can arrange for that!" answered Angela and said excitedly: "You'll be amazed, I promise!"

"Lilly hinted that time flows differently here…," observed Dirk inquisitively.

"It's been about 45 minutes since you woke up!" replied Angela with a smile.

"Only 45 minutes? It feels like a whole day!" gasped Dirk.

"You'll get used to it, at least while this place is still running," said Angela and started to exit the command center.

"Wait! Before we go anywhere, is there a way to move around without getting sick?" begged Dirk.

"Well, we could take a shuttle. But it still moves pretty fast...," cautioned Angela, trying not to laugh.

"Yes, that's better; let's do that!" agreed Dirk enthusiastically.

"OK, Love, the shuttle is waiting outside!" giggled Angela: "Come, I'll show you Mario's place first. You will never guess what he created!"

56. The Journey

The digital shuttle was a plain vehicle that looked like a bobsled. It had four seats, one placed behind the next, and a simple steering wheel and a few buttons in the front. Angela took the front seat, and Dirk sat right behind her. Then she physically pressed one of the knobs, and the shuttle accelerated quite forcefully, but Dirk didn't get sick. On the contrary, he enjoyed the fast ride through this digital world because many things were to see.

The ride took longer than Dirk expected, and he wondered how expansive this virtual world was. Most of the simulation was a beautiful landscape with mountains, lakes, forests, and plains. Often, he caught glimpses of various animals roaming about and birds soaring in the sky. Of course, it was all digital, but it could have been a nature preserve, and Dirk silently lauded the extensive work his friends had done while he was dead.

"Babe, how big is this simulation?" asked Dirk.

"You would have to ask Rose if you want to know it in petabytes, but the landscape we have created is about the size of Spain if you want to compare it to something physical," replied Angela.

"Wow!" exclaimed Dirk, genuinely impressed.

Angela set the shuttle to autopilot and explained the various landmarks to Dirk. But there were also quite a few patches that looked like a basic white hexagonal grid.

"Is that an unfinished area?" inquired Dirk and pointed at the open space they were passing at that moment.

"Yes, we have a few of those left," confirmed Angela and noted, "this one here is Lenna's project. She will recreate an island from Latur, assuming that the simulation is still around!"

Dirk estimated that the shuttle cruised about as fast as a high-speed train by the passing landscape's speed. They passed by an area that was a replica of the Red Square in Moscow. Although Dirk had never been to Russia, he immediately recognized the turrets of St. Basil's Cathedral from the pictures he had seen on Earth. He motioned to Angela to decelerate the shuttle a little.

"Victor must build that!" guessed Dirk.

"Yes, but he isn't sentimental about Mother Russia. He made this to remind himself of the exact moment when *irtaljan* changed his life forever," explained Angela and pointed towards the center of the area, "if you look closely, you can see Victor's likeness on his knees in the middle of the plaza!"

"Yes, *irtaljan* has a profound effect on everyone who experienced it!" assented Dirk solemnly.

"I wouldn't know, Love," replied Angela, a little disappointed that she had never been submerged in an alternate reality.

"Be glad that you don't, Angela. It's something that will always weigh heavily on you!" opined Dirk with a sigh, and Angela just nodded and accelerated the shuttle again. They rode in silence for the next few minutes, but suddenly, Dirk saw something that looked very familiar.

"Is that Paradise City on Aureus?" he asked excitedly.

"Yup! That's the first place we made, and everyone worked on it. Now, most of us have our own realms, but we still come here quite often to party," mentioned Angela, and then she asked humorously, "did you know that we celebrate deathdays instead of birthdays?"

"No, I didn't. I wonder when mine is?" questioned Dirk curiously.

"Today! It's always the day when someone arrives in the simulation! Happy Deathday, Love!" explained Angela fondly, turned her head backward, and grinned at Dirk.

"Babe, will you show me your place, too?" asked Dirk a few moments later after Angela had sped up the vehicle again.

"Nah, it's not worth it. Garrett and I never really finished it, and we are hardly ever there!" replied Angela and disclosed, "now, I practically live in that control center where you found me earlier!"

"Are things OK between you and Garrett?" asked Dirk, concerned.

"I still love him, and he still loves me," responded Angela simply.

"But?" pressed Dirk.

"Love, forget all the minor issues because the biggest problem with the simulation is that romance and intimacy don't work right. Lenna and Alvar, Mario and Nancy, Sophia and Victor, even Wendji and Ngazetungue, and all the

242

other couples have grown apart over the decades because of that. They still love each other, but it's just not the same anymore!" explained Angela unhappily.

"That's so sad!" noted Dirk with regret.

"Yeah, but if we win this fight, and we can have real bodies again, watch out!" responded Angela cryptically.

"Huh?" wondered Dirk, unsure what to make of her words.

"Let's just say Transformation Day will become Transformation Month!" speculated Angela with a smirk.

"Ugh, should I be scared, Babe?" asked Dirk humorously.

"Scared?!? You have five horny wives who have been deprived for a century! You should tremble in mortal fear!" teased Angela and winked at him, and Dirk laughed aloud.

Finally, the shuttle arrived at a building that looked a lot like the Taj Mahal in Agra. Angela stopped the vehicle. Mario was already standing at the entrance, waving at them. Angela and Dirk got out of the shuttle to greet him, and then Mario let them inside the vast building.

"You built a library?" gasped Dirk while looking at the grandest assembly of books imaginable.

"Sure did, Boss!" confirmed Mario proudly.

"I… am speechless!" stammered Dirk with a big smile.

"You never expected that from me, did you?" quipped Mario.

"Wow, just wow!" said Dirk with admiration, perused the seemingly endless bookcases, took a hefty volume off a shelf, and asked, "have you read some of these?"

"I have read many of them, Boss. Now I know where all your quotes are coming from!" replied Mario with a big grin.

"I'm so impressed!" admitted Dirk and quoted: "*A room without books is like a body without a soul* - Cicero."

"You have always been my inspiration, Dirk. But while I was still alive, reading was a chore, and there was always something better or more urgent to do. Now, I have all the time in the world, and reading a book takes only a few minutes in this digital world," explained Mario.

"Well done, Mario, well done!" praised Dirk and slapped Mario on the back.

"Thanks, Boss! But Wendji helped a lot, too!" said Mario happily and suggested, "if you need to look something up, you know where to find it, but you can also access this entire library from anywhere in the simulation!"

After Mario gave them the library's grand tour, Dirk and Angela bid him farewell and boarded the shuttle again. Their next destination would be Lydda's domicile.

57. Neuschwanstein

Dirk and Angela were standing in front of Castle Neuschwanstein. He had visited the real thing with Lilly on their vacation in Germany many years ago, and this looked exactly like it.

"Come in!" hollered Lydda from somewhere inside, and Angela and Dirk entered through a foyer while Lydda ran to meet them.

"Holy cow, Kittycat!" exclaimed Dirk when they entered.

The building's interior didn't look anything like the original, and somewhat disconcertingly, it was also much bigger inside than outside. Dirk couldn't help thinking of the Tardis from the Doctor Who series he loved to watch on Earth.

The inside was just a giant circular hall, but every inch was covered with art! There were statues and paintings from Earth and Latur, items that must have come from other civilizations throughout the galaxy, and many creations that Lydda had made herself.

"Do you like it?" asked Lydda expectantly.

"Yes!" replied Dirk enthusiastically, but he wondered, "why are you living in a human castle, Kittycat?"

"Because I saw this place in your memories, *swiahn*!" answered Lydda fondly, and those words touched Dirk deeply.

"You must show me everything!" he insisted eagerly and walked through her expansive exhibition.

The centerpiece was a massive aquarium. Inside were no fish but an enormous swarm of colorful, iridescent plankton that swirled around in a strange but beautiful dance. Dirk remembered seeing a tank like this on Latur, twice actually, but the first time he never got a chance to take a closer look because of all the diplomatic obligations, and the second time, he was too busy thinking about that alternate reality.

Now he had time, so he stepped closer to the tank and put his hand on the outside of the thick glass. The plankton swarm stopped its dance and rushed towards the place where Dirk's hand was touching. Slowly, the microorganisms formed a hand on the inside of the aquarium. The hand grew to an arm, a shoulder, a torso, and finally into a whole body. A minute later, another Dirk made from the tiny creatures' bodies was standing inside the aquarium.

Suddenly, Dirk felt a current of water around his body, the taste of salt and seaweed in his mouth, sand and pebbles under his feet, and tiny electrical impulses on his skin. He was really inside the aquarium and not standing outside the tank. Dirk was mesmerized by the display. After a few minutes, the other Dirk made from plankton smiled at him and waved. Then he disintegrated into a swarm of tiny organisms once again, and the beautiful ballet of swirling colors resumed.

"That was amazing, Kittycat!" he exclaimed in delight and questioned, "it is that from the seas of Latur?"

"Oh no, this is from a world covered by a sapient ocean. It arrived on Aureus after your death, and we situated it in the Grand Hall. This aquarium is not just art, but an ambassador!" explained Lydda.

"I remember Alvar telling me about the sapient ocean. It sent an ambassador to Aureus?" inquired Dirk.

"Yes, it did. But the sapient ocean lives on a different timescale. It took a hundred years to send an ambassador to Latur and another hundred to send one to Aureus!" elaborated Lydda.

"Is this display just a replica? It felt so real!" gasped Dirk.

"It is a replica. But I believe it is somehow connected to the real thing on Aureus and its homeworld," speculated Lydda and observed, "it communicated with you, but it will take a few hours before you will understand its message."

"Absolutely stunning, Kittycat!" marveled Dirk.

Lydda showed Dirk and Angela almost every piece in the giant exhibition. Even the first drawing from their daughter Dylla was there, and Lydda had placed it on the wall near the entrance, where every guest would see it. Dirk looked at it fondly and remembered the day when their little girl drew the red centipede on Lydda's apartment wall.

"Angela, have you taken Dirk to Georgette and Tigger's place yet?" inquired Lydda after they exited Neuschwanstein.

"Not yet," answered Angela.

"They have a place?" wondered Dirk.

"Yes, but it's a little disconcerting...," insinuated Angela, unsure if she should say more.

246

"Why? Are they living in a giant can of *Salmon Feast*?" joked Dirk.

"Funny! But no, they created an ever-changing realm full of things that cats like!" explained Lydda with a smile.

"Yes, you should see it. Let's go, Dirk! Bye, Lydda!" said Angela and hopped into the shuttle. Dirk followed a moment later.

"Have fun!" replied Lydda knowingly and went back inside her castle.

58. The Hunt

Georgette and Tigger's home was very different and very cat-like. It had almost no structures, but nature abounds. There were giant trees to climb, warm, soft, and cozy spots to rest, hiding places, and many different cat toys littered on the green grass. Tigger and Georgette got up from their favorite perches and greeted their guests. Meanwhile, Dirk noticed a strange device like a miniature carwash in the middle of the greenery.

"What is that thing?" asked Dirk curiously and pointed at the contraption.

(Feeling of pride) "Jo made for Tigger!" answered the big Siamese cat.

Tigger walked up to the machine and got inside of it. Combs and brushes started moving around, combing and massaging Tigger's entire body. The big cat thoroughly enjoyed the treatment, so much so that he began drooling on the grass.

(Feeling of happiness) "Was great gift!" swooned Tigger as he exited the machine.

"It is lovely here! Why did you say it was disconcerting, Babe?" wondered Dirk as he looked around.

Over the link, he could suddenly sense keen excitement coming from the two big cats.

"You will see," responded Angela with a smirk.

(Feeling of amusement) "Jo will show you!" promised Georgette.

Suddenly, a gateway opened in mid-air, and on the other side was a plain grass field that seemingly stretched out to the horizon. Jo went through it, and Tigger gently headbutted Dirk to enter as well. Once they were all on the other side, Jo did something to change the environment. Instantaneously, it transformed into an arctic terrain.

"Wow!" exclaimed Dirk, feeling the icy wind on his cheeks.

(Feeling of accomplishment) "Jo can make any landscape. Mountain, desert, swamp, snow, anything!" replied Jo and changed everything into a tropical jungle, full of all the sounds, smells, heat, and humidity that one would expect from such an environment.

"That's pretty cool, but what are we doing here?" wondered Dirk.

(Feeling of excitement) "Now game begins!" announced Georgette and swiftly disappeared in the dense vegetation.

"What game?" asked Dirk, befuddled.

"The hunt," remarked Angela and sighed.

"Tigger, please explain this to me!" insisted Dirk, but Tigger was nowhere to be found.

"Love, they are hunting us now, and we are supposed to hunt them. It's their favorite pastime!" disclosed Angela.

"Huh?" asked Dirk, flabbergasted.

"Let's go and try to find them. We can't cheat here, so we have to search and kill the old-fashioned way!" explained Angela.

"Search and kill? We are fighting with them?" questioned Dirk incredulously.

"Of course, nobody dies! Let's give them a good match!" answered Angela determinedly and started to move through the bushes.

Dirk quickly followed her, unsure of what he should be doing, but he would be learning swiftly in the next few hours. The game world was vast and intricate, full of obstacles and dangers. NPC crabs, dragonflies and tree squids, poisonous plants and falling trees, human hunters, and even a pack of hungry wolves inhabited the world. The two teams tracked, trapped, and ambushed each other, but it finally ended with a resounding victory for Tigger and Jo. However, Angela and Dirk got a few good licks in before it was over.

(Feeling of happiness) "Fun!" said Jo exuberantly, standing over Dirk's prone body.

"You two are vicious animals!" complained Dirk playfully as he sat up again.

(Feeling of amusement) "Yes!" Tigger agreed triumphantly.

"You have an AI that can make anything you like. Why are we your opponents?" questioned Dirk and shook his head.

(Feeling of honesty) "AI makes weak prey. Play game with good, real opponents. Angela test strength, Dirk test intelligence!" explained Jo and fondly licked Dirk's face.

"Well, thanks for the fun, guys. I want a rematch someday!" demanded Dirk playfully as he stood up.

249

"Be careful; only Ngazetungue has ever won against them," cautioned Angela with a chuckle.

(Feeling of respect) "Ngazetungue test endurance. Cats not hunt like that. Very hard!" confirmed Georgette.

59. Cabin in the Woods

After they left Jo and Tigger's place, Angela explained to Dirk how to operate the digital shuttle, then she bid him farewell and disappeared in a flash to check on the simulation's security measures again. The shuttle controls were reasonably straightforward, and Dirk ordered it to take him to Nari's place next. When he arrived at Nari's home, Dirk was shocked: the Korean woman had recreated the cabin where they had met for the first time.

"Angel, this…," stammered Dirk, unsure what he should say.

"…is the place where I fell in love. It is my home, Husband, our home!" Nari finished his sentence as she led him inside the small dwelling.

"*Home is where the heart is* - Pliny the Elder," replied Dirk slowly, studying every detail of the quaint cabin, "it is just like I remember it. Those were hard times for you, for me, for everyone. But yes, it was home!"

Dirk sat down at the table, and Nari served tea for them. But when Dirk sipped from his cup, he was sorely disappointed: it didn't taste like tea at all. The brew wasn't horrible, but it wasn't tea! He added a few spoons of sugar, but that still didn't improve much. Nari watched him with amusement. Dirk looked at her and shrugged.

"Now, I understand what you guys meant when you said that things don't taste right in the simulation!" noted Dirk and remarked, "but I appreciate the gesture, Angel!"

"You are welcome, Husband!" answered Nari with a giggle, but she asked more seriously, "were you afraid?"

"Afraid of what?" mused Dirk, unsure what Nari was insinuating.

"Death! I was so afraid when I died, even though I knew I would wake up here. But you died thinking it was the end, didn't you?" questioned Nari.

"Yes, I did!" confirmed Dirk, and then he added earnestly, "of course, I had regrets - things I could have done, things I should have or should not have done. The times I used bad judgment and the times I maltreated others. But I was not afraid, Angel."

"You are courageous, Husband!" stated Nari.

"No, I'm not that brave!" insisted Dirk, and then he continued, "I reflected on what I had done with my life, and I was at peace, happy even! I had people I

251

loved and who loved me. I helped colonize a new world, creating a peaceful, thriving society for everyone. What more could I have expected?"

"You are not telling me everything, but it can wait!" replied Nari after a slight pause, and then she inquired, "will you be with me after that, or will you be…."

"…dead again?" Dirk completed her sentence.

"Yes. I have missed you very much. I don't think I would want to miss you again!" worried Nari.

"I don't know what will happen, Angel. But if we succeed, there will be plenty of time to talk about it!" promised Dirk honestly, and Nari looked at him strangely at first, but then she nodded.

"It is the answer I expected from you," she observed quietly, "anyone else would be so happy to live again. Nobody would have to think twice about it, but that makes you so special, Husband!"

Dirk gently took her in his arms. She returned the embrace and kissed him on the cheek. Dirk knew how strange he must appear to Nari, but he wasn't sure if he was supposed to be dead or alive. For him, this was a complicated matter that would take some time to figure out.

60. Home, sweet digital Home

Dirk spent a long time with Nari, but finally, he took his leave and boarded the shuttle again. He instructed the vehicle to take him to Lilly next. When Dirk got to Lilly's place, he was almost not surprised. It was merely their old house, fully intact and undamaged.

Dirk entered and took his shoes off as he had done a thousand times before, back on Earth. But when he did that, he tried to remember how he got shoes and clothes in the first place. Until he got here, he had been naked the whole time. Dirk couldn't come up with any sensible explanation. This simulation took a lot of getting used to, but Dirk decided to ignore the little logic quirks for now.

"Sweetie, are you home?" he hollered after a few moments.

"Yes, Honey, come to the office. I need to show you something!" yelled Lilly from the other end of the house.

Dirk walked to the small office and found Lilly was sitting at a desk, fully dressed in terrestrial clothing, typing on an old-fashioned computer. Dirk looked over her shoulder at the screen.

"Is that information on Project Sanctuary?" asked Dirk as he was reading the open file.

"Yes, it's a list of very illustrious names, only the biggest assholes of the 21st century!" grumbled Lilly.

Dirk scanned the list and immediately noticed two names: Rudolf Garland and Jens Koch!

"I know those two," he remarked quietly, pointing at the screen.

"You have been hobnobbing with the super-rich and powerful?" wondered Lilly.

"No, Sweetie. I've encountered Rudolf Garland, and I've talked to Jens Koch in an alternate reality while I was dead," explained Dirk.

"Tell me!" insisted Lilly curiously.

"Garland was the one who blew up our house, assaulted the cabin, and tried to capture us in Oregon. In the alternate world, he succeeded at that," claimed Dirk, but he didn't want to continue the story.

"Come on, what happened then?" wondered Lilly.

"You were killed, Lilly," whispered Dirk and divulged, "and then I wanted to do some terrible things to the whole world!"

"Oh, I'm sorry, Honey. It isn't something you want to talk about?" asked Lilly gently.

"Not really, but suffice to say Garland got what he deserved, although not how I wanted it to happen!" responded Dirk with a frown.

"Apparently, in this reality, too. Garland is listed as deceased," noted Lilly as she studied the long list of names on the screen and asked, "what about that other name?"

"Jens Koch. He worked with Garland, and he was the one who bought Zyrtec to get Sven's research data on us," answered Dirk, and he hoped Lilly would change the subject, but he was out of luck.

"Another greedy scumbag?" inquired Lilly and raised an eyebrow expectantly.

"Yes and no, but I didn't punish him. It's too hard for me to explain, Lilly. Please leave it at that!" pleaded Dirk.

"You don't have to explain anything, Honey!" insisted Lilly fondly.

Lilly sensed that Dirk was bothered by the topic, so she got up from her chair and fiercely hugged her husband instead of pressing on.

"Thanks, Lilly. Someday I will tell you everything; just give me time!" promised Dirk and sighed.

(Feeling of utmost confidence) "You will succeed!" boomed a chorus of voices in his head, and Dirk had no idea where that came from so suddenly.

Dirk sat down for a moment, and Lilly looked at him curiously. Then he remembered the aquarium in Lydda's palace. It must have been what the sapient ocean had told him earlier. While Dirk wasn't nearly as confident about their chances, the message certainly put him in a much better mood!

61. Scientific Breakthrough

Interfacing with the old androids was easier than expected. L had equipped them with generous memory storage and processing power, more than enough to hold consciousness. It had taken Rose only a few hours to write the necessary code to transfer someone from the simulation into the machines. Rose set the autonomous AIs into sleep mode, and Sven was ready to take the plunge!

"It should work, but this has never been done before, Sven!" warned Rose, but Sven just nodded.

"But you already controlled the androids, didn't you?" wondered Dirk, confused by Rose's concerns.

"Yes, but I did that from here, not from inside their memory and processors!" explained Rose.

"Could we do it all remotely?" asked Dirk and proposed, "or could we just program Bender and C-3PO's AIs to do all the work for us?"

"This is too complex for an autonomous AI. We could try to do it all via remote control from the simulation, but adjusting the equipment is delicate work. I have to be there in person to do it, Dirk!" disagreed Sven, shaking his head.

"You are the bravest man when it comes to scientific breakthroughs, Sven!" lauded Dirk and added fondly: "Good luck, my friend!"

"Thanks!" grinned Sven and gave Rose a thumbs-up.

Rose opened the channel, initiated the transfer, and Sven was gone in a flash.

"Did it work?" asked Dirk cautiously as Rose intently checked a virtual screen.

"I think it worked!" confirmed Rose and asked, "Sven, can you hear me?"

"Yes. Oh, this is weird!" responded Sven a moment later.

"What happened?" inquired Dirk nervously.

"I'm a robot. That's what happened. Nothing is wrong, but this takes a little getting used to!" answered Sven and requested, "give me a moment!"

"Take your time, Sven. Everything looks fine on my end!" acknowledged Rose.

"OK, I think I have mastered the motor skills and sensory input. We are in business!" stated Sven happily a few minutes later and added, "it's your turn, Dirk. Bender is waiting!"

"Good, do your thing, Pumpkin!" acknowledged Dirk, and a split second later, he was squeezed through a capillary and rode the psychedelic rollercoaster again.

"I hate this so much!" grumbled Dirk when his consciousness arrived in Bender's memory banks.

"What's wrong, Dirk?" questioned Rose's voice in his head.

"It's OK, never mind…," replied Dirk, suppressing the urge to vomit.

A minute later, the feeling subsided, and Dirk started to take control of Bender's body. It took some practice, but it wasn't that hard. Sven and Dirk were moving around the cloning lab quite comfortably. Cautiously, Sven started to handle some scientific equipment. He broke a few beakers until he had a good handle on the more refined motor skills, but he learned quickly and instinctively knew how to adjust. After about an hour in the androids' bodies, Sven and Dirk were confident that the experiment was successful.

"Good job, Pumpkin! We are in full control of the androids!" reported Dirk happily.

"Yes, this will work better than I thought!" added Sven confidently.

"Great! Get ready to come back!" replied Rose, upbeat.

Then she reversed the transfer process. In an instant, Sven and Dirk reappeared in the simulation. Sven was perfectly fine, but Dirk was gagging loudly on his hands and knees.

"Seasick again?" snickered Sven, and Rose stifled a laugh.

"Oh, shut up! I don't get seasick! I was once on a fishing trawler, riding out an Atlantic storm. But this…," grumbled Dirk, but he couldn't complete the sentence because he felt imaginary bile coming up his virtual esophagus again.

Rose leaned over Dirk's body and gently rubbed his back. That helped a little, and he recovered at last.

"Bah, I don't know how you guys do it," admitted Dirk finally.

"We had a hundred years of practice. You'll get the hang of it eventually," consoled Rose as she reactivated Bender and C-3PO's AIs again, and the androids resumed normal operations.

"I don't recall it being that bad. Maybe you are just too sensitive?" teased Sven.

"Sensitive my butt!" grumbled Dirk, but he had to smirk a little.

62. Bodybuilding

While in the bodies of C-3PO and Bender, Sven and Dirk had worked tirelessly over the last week. They prepared chambers for nine adult human bodies, two Latura bodies, and a giant cat, and it pushed their science and engineering to the limit.

Meanwhile, Rose had been working just as diligently on the transfer protocols. First, she reverse-engineered much of L and Carl's simulation technology to get consciousness back into a biological body and then linked the cloning equipment to the AI that controlled the simulation.

Today, Sven had filled the chambers with the transfer matrix and declared that the equipment was ready to receive a consciousness. Rose was done with her work too, and Sven immediately volunteered to be the test rabbit, but Dirk objected!

"Sven, I should go first because if something goes wrong, you can help me. Meanwhile, I would need about a week to figure out how all these gadgets work!" reasoned Dirk, but Sven remained unconvinced.

"Dirk is right, Sven. You and I have to be the last ones to transfer. If something happens, we might be able to fix it!" concurred Rose thoughtfully.

"Darn it, I wanted to be the first!" protested Sven, but he wasn't too disappointed.

While in C-3PO's body, Sven interfaced Bender's hardware with the cloning chamber. Meanwhile, Dirk downloaded Rose's new protocols into Bender's memory and the cloning equipment. When everything was in place, Sven unceremoniously flipped a switch, and the process began.

It took a good hour before the transfer matrix had formed a complete body. Meanwhile, Dirk's consciousness seemed to be in suspended animation. When he was dissolved and rebuilt on the tennis court at PTRC so long ago or transported to Latur, Dirk had been unconscious the entire time. But now, he had to endure the whole process, fully aware but unable to act. The procedure was painless but unpleasant for Dirk, not unlike moving around in the simulation, and it seemed to last for an eternity. But finally, the matrix had finished its work, and Dirk was able to take control of his new body. Everything seemed well, but there were some unexpected complications.

"Does everything have to involve being sucked into a psychedelic sewer?" cussed Dirk, trying hard not to throw up in his new body.

"Are you OK?" asked Sven, amused.

Nobody knew why Dirk had such a strong reaction when moving digitally, but by now, it had become a running joke with the team, much to Dirk's chagrin.

"Yeah, sort of - I have a body again, and I can feel and move everything, but I seem to be somewhat dissociated," mentioned Dirk slowly.

He looked around the room, moved his arms, and walked a few steps. That helped with nausea, too.

"What do you mean, Dirk?" asked Sven, concerned while still in C-3PO's mechanical body, analyzing the data output.

"It's hard to describe. It is my body, and it feels as it had when I first transferred to Aureus long ago. But a part of my consciousness still is outside of it. Here, I show you what I mean!" suggested Dirk and moved Bender around.

"So, you are in the biological body and Bender's mechanical one simultaneously?" questioned Sven incredulously.

"Yes, exactly, and I have no good explanation for how or why!" confirmed Dirk with a nod.

"Me neither. But according to the data, the transfer has worked properly! All vital signs are in the green, and everything seems to be in good order!" stated Sven adamantly, pointing at a display in front of him.

"All clear on my end, too!" Rose chimed in from the simulation.

"A strange side effect, but I agree it worked fine!" concurred Dirk as he started to remove various electrodes and sensors from his naked body that Sven had stuck to him earlier.

"It might just be because you transferred from Bender. The rest of the team will transfer directly from the simulation," speculated Sven and added, "I was going to transfer from C-3PO, but I guess now I'll return to the simulation first."

"That could be it, Sven!" conceded Dirk and commented, "but this weird effect doesn't jeopardize anything. We should let the team know to get ready!"

"If we had more time, I would say we hold off on that until we figure this out," noted Sven before he consented, "but you are right; we don't have that luxury, and this doesn't seem too serious. I'll inform Angela in a minute."

"While you do that, I'll take a quick shower to get all this goo from the cloning vat off my new body," remarked Dirk.

"Dirk, just use the sink over there to rinse off. The Aureans can't spot you; you are way too famous here!" warned Sven and pointed with C-3PO's mechanical arm to the laboratory sink in the corner of the room.

"Oops, that's a good point, Sven! Thanks!" replied Dirk, grabbed some soap and a towel from a rack, and walked to the sink while Sven established a connection to Angela.

63. Strange Side Effects

A few hours later, the whole team had successfully transferred into brand-new biological bodies! That was the good news. The bad news was that every single one of them experienced the same out-of-body sensations as Dirk had. It was as if they now existed biologically and digitally simultaneously. The group dealt with it in different ways. Tigger appeared to be just fine; he was grooming his new fur extensively. Angela, Garrett, and Victor relied on their training as operatives: the same techniques that spies use to defeat a lie detector or beat torture helped them handle the situation. Ngazetungue, Lydda, and Irgal meditated deeply for quite some time. Meanwhile, Lilly found the medical supplies Bender and C-3PO had brought to the lab and injected Sven, Mario, Rose, and Yebin with a mild sedative and anti-nausea medication. But Mario was still feeling uncomfortable and vocally vented his displeasure at Sven.

"Nothing went wrong, Mario!" insisted Sven and proclaimed, "the new bodies are perfect; Rose's program was flawless. I have no idea what happened!"

"Oh sure, Dr. Frankenstein!" grumbled Mario in response and revealed, "I feel like I'm in two places at once. No, scratch that - I feel like I'm too big for my body, if that makes any sense!"

"That makes some sense," admitted Sven, and then he conceded, "I don't know how or why, but our consciousnesses seemed to have grown!"

"Mario, do you think you can handle it?" asked Rose, concerned.

"Forget about it!" replied Mario grumpily and joked, "just get me a few beers, and it will be alright!"

"OK, now we are hopefully safe from L39's digital attacks. What's the next step?" inquired Irgal while gently rubbing Mario's shoulders.

"Getting out of this lab without being seen, then finding a place where we can regroup!" declared Angela.

"My old hut on the volcano slope!" proposed Ngazetungue excitedly.

"That's a great idea and an excellent vantage point. But we should grab a few supplies on our way there!" maintained Victor, looking for a suitable bag or container.

"I hated to deceive the Aureans, and I hate it even more that we have to steal from them, too!" said Dirk somberly.

"But we have no choice, Honey. These biological bodies need sustenance!" warned Lilly.

"Alright, I think getting out of here might not be so hard; we just need to be stealthy. It is already nighttime on Aureus, and Bender and C-3PO can scout ahead. Once we get clear off this facility, we can jog on the road all the way to the volcano!" suggested Garrett, studying some maps on a tablet.

"Good, let's do that!" assented Dirk and activated Bender's AI.

Then he withdrew his consciousness from the mechanical body, and now he understood Mario's dilemma much better: it seemed like a part of him was floating in all places at once and none in particular. It was very disconcerting, and he was swaying as if he was drunk. Angela noticed Dirk's discomfort almost immediately:

"Dirk, sit down, close your eyes, and relax. Think of something pleasant and ignore the strange sensation!" recommended Angela and added, "you too, Mario!"

Dirk and Mario sat down on lab stools and did as Angela suggested. Within a few minutes, Dirk felt a little better. Now his essence felt almost wholly contained in the biological body; only something like an aura was still floating around him. He opened his eyes again, almost fearing that the uncomfortable feeling would return, but fortunately, it did not.

"OK, now it's bearable, thanks, Babe!" mentioned Dirk with relief and asked, "dumb question, do you see some kind of aura around my body?"

"No, we don't, but I think I know what you mean because it feels similar to me, *swiahn*!" answered Lydda.

"No visible aura, that's good!" remarked Dirk.

(Feeling of amusement) "Tigger can see aura," corrected the big cat.

"You can?" questioned Irgal in surprise.

(Feeling of annoyance) "Yes, makes everyone glow. Tigger glow, too. Bad for hunting, bad for hiding!" emphasized Tigger.

"What has happened to us?" mumbled Yebin, concerned.

"Well, there is nothing we can do about it. As long as only Tigger can see it, I think we might be fine!" concluded Victor and looked at Mario: "Are you better, Mario?"

"Yeah, that mindfulness stuff actually worked, thanks, Angela. But I still would like beer or three!" responded Mario with a smirk.

Before the team transferred from the simulation, Bender and C-3PO had brought several crates with supplies to the lab, containing survival gear, small backpacks, fanny packs, and utility belts with tools, medicine, flashlights, blankets, food, and water. C-3PO handed one particular duffle bag to Rose. She opened it and distributed the contents among the team members.

"Sis, you made a flip phone and a Bluetooth?" wondered Lilly incredulously, staring at the items in her hands.

"Basically, yes. Of course, it works by quantum entanglement, not 5G," explained Rose with a grin and added, "it's our way to communicate with Jo in the simulation. Dial the number, although it's just an 11-digit encryption code, and you can talk to her. The Bluetooth allows all team members to participate in the conversation."

"Could I use this to contact Dervan?" asked Irgal.

"Yes, the icosahedron on Latur is linked to the simulation AI, not L. Your phone can connect to Latur. You can talk to him!" confirmed Rose.

"Nice! Thank you, Rose!" responded Irgal delightedly.

"What does this button do...," wondered Ngazetungue, as he was fiddling with his phone.

"Don't press that!!!" yelled Rose suddenly.

But it was already too late: a sharp red beam shot from Ngazetungue's flip phone and neatly sliced a lab stool in half, the pieces clattering loudly to the floor.

"Sorry!" exclaimed Ngazetungue, dropped the phone like a hot potato, and grinned sheepishly at Rose.

"I was getting to that!" declared Rose and rolled her eyes: "That big button on the flip cover triggers a red beam as you just saw. You only have a few shots, and then it needs to recharge for a while, so use it sparingly!"

"An icosahedron in a flip phone! You are amazing, Pumpkin!" lauded Dirk.

"I had a good teacher and two hundred years of practice!" replied Rose with a grin as she was strapping a sizable toolbelt to her bare waist.

"The student has surpassed the master!" stated Dirk solemnly and bowed to Rose.

"You honor me, Sensei!" answered Rose and bowed, and then both of them had to giggle.

"OK, grab all the gear and secure it to your bodies. We have to get moving!" instructed Angela.

Meanwhile, Lilly was tying a harness with saddlebags to Tigger's back. The big cat wasn't exactly thrilled, but he endured without complaints.

"Should we dress up somehow?" wondered Sven, fiddling with a pouch for his scientific gear.

"No. The current fashion on Aureus isn't suited for running or fighting. They like colorful, wavy silk gowns nowadays, but being naked is still perfectly acceptable. So, we go with that!" ordered Angela, secured her fanny pack, and exhorted: "Now, let's move!"

64. A Stealthy Escape and a Long Run

Exiting the cloning facility was surprisingly easy. It was part of the much larger Larson Research Complex, and Sven had studied every detail of the building named after him. He led the group through the basement and loading docks that were abandoned at this time of the day.

When they were finally out in the open, Bender and C-3PO scouted ahead, and the group followed slowly with some distance. Angela ordered everyone to change the chromatophores in their skins to black to be less visible in the darkness. Dirk and Irgal had no problem doing it, and Lilly had always been a natural, but the rest of the team hadn't practiced that in about 100 years, so it took some time to get it right.

Rose used a small tablet to ensure that the surveillance cameras pointed away from their path through Paradise city when they moved again. Suddenly, Angela motioned to stop and be quiet! But Bender and C-3PO were still marching towards the gate until a giant centipede blocked their path. The arthropod examined the two androids with her antennae but lost interest and moved on.

"Was that Alma?" whispered Dirk, and Angela nodded.

They waited a few extra moments to make sure Alma had left the vicinity before continuing to walk. A few minutes later, they exited the settlement unnoticed. Rose commanded Bender and C-3PO to return to their posts at the museum, and then the group started jogging on the road to the extinct volcano. At least that was the plan, but Ngazetungue took the lead, and the jog quickly became a strenuous run. They stopped when they arrived at the foot of the volcano because everybody, except for Ngazetungue and Tigger, was utterly out of breath and sweating profusely.

"You are out of shape. You all need more exercise!" scolded the Namibian man humorously, earning him a few baleful glares.

"But we are almost there. Now we just have to run up the slope for a few kilometers, and we will be at my old hut in no time!" said Ngazetungue encouragingly.

"You got to be kidding me! This body is not going to make it, and it's still a virgin!" complained Lilly, soliciting laughter and a few vigorous nods from the team.

"OK, we made it here in good time, and we can take it easy. It's not that far, so let's get moving!" emphasized Ngazetungue and started running again, but he was more merciful with the pace.

When they arrived at Ngazetungue's hut, they were surprised to find it cordoned off. A large sign indicated this was a historical landmark, and trespassing was not permitted.

"This hut was the retreat of our founder Ngazetungue Emvula. He often spent time here to meditate and relax after long runs and fishing trips. After his death, the hut was fully restored and is now part of the rich Aurean historical heritage. Open for tours only on Founders Day!" read Dirk off the commemorative golden plaque at the entrance.

"My hut is a historical heritage? May the spirits have mercy!" declared Ngazetungue and laughed out loud.

"Founder's Day isn't for another few months, so there shouldn't be any visitors," noted Victor and eyed the lock at the front door.

Rose got a lockpick from her tool belt and handed it to Victor. A few seconds later, the door popped open. The group entered the small cabin. It was cramped with the whole team inside, and Lilly worried they wouldn't have enough space to sleep.

"I should have a few tents in storage unless the Aureans have removed them," recalled Ngazetungue, opened a small closet, and was delighted when he saw the contents: "They left everything just the way it was!"

"OK, let's get the tents set up behind the hut so that they are not visible to random hikers who might pass by," suggested Garrett and recommended, "but before that, we should have a bite to eat, some water, and discuss what we will do next!"

"Good idea. I could use some rest," concurred Dirk and sat down on the hut floor.

All that running had tired him out more than he cared to admit. Irgal unpacked the supplies while Yebin got some fresh water from the well outside.

"Alright, what's the plan?" asked Mario while chewing on an energy bar that Victor had swiped from the cafeteria in the research facility.

"First, we should establish communication with Jo," advised Angela.

"How do we get a Bluetooth in Tigger's ear?" wondered Lilly, examining the earbud in her hand.

(Feeling of amusement) "Tigger not need. Can talk to Jo with mind," claimed Tigger.

"Oh! That's… impossible?" gasped Rose, surprised.

"It's Tigger; he makes the impossible look mundane!" quipped Lydda and petted the big cat on the back.

"Jo? Can you hear us?" asked Angela through the phone.

"Jo can hear!" replied the Siamese cat.

"Is anything going on in the simulation?" inquired Angela.

(Feeling of boredom) "Nothing. Nari gone, sleeping. But L sent message: stasis chambers now protected, safer!" answered Georgette.

"Oh, good. I was worried about that. L39 cannot get into the chambers, but it could cut the tethers that anchor them to the simulation!" interjected Garrett.

"Jo, if something happens, please let us know! We will update you, too!" declared Angela.

"Jo will. Good hunting!" acknowledged the big cat and ended the call.

65. Out-Of-Body Experience

The team had set up the tents behind the cabin, and most of them had turned in for the night. Their biological bodies demanded sleep, and they were happy to comply. Aside from Dirk and Irgal, none have had a good night's rest for many decades. Garrett, Mario, and Ngazetungue were still playing cards inside the hut when Yebin had finished cleaning the dishes from the dinner earlier. She had made a big bowl of soup on the little stove that Ngazetungue kept in his hut. The group immensely enjoyed the simple noodle soup because it genuinely tasted how they remembered it before dying.

Yebin would be sleeping on the floor tonight, not in the tents. She was exhausted when she zipped up her sleeping bag, and moments later, she dozed off. But then she suddenly remembered the little stove, and she couldn't recall if she had turned the appliance off after dinner. It could be a problem because it had only limited power, and if it ran out, she wouldn't be able to make a warm breakfast for the team in the morning.

So, Yebin got up again, walked over to the stove, and fortunately, the power switch was off. Satisfied, she turned around and returned to her sleeping bag. But when she passed by the table where Garrett, Mario, and Ngazetungue were playing cards, they stared at her wide-eyed!

"What?" asked Yebin wearily, but nobody answered while Ngazetungue pointed urgently at her sleeping bag - and then Yebin saw herself peacefully sleeping inside of it!

"How…," stammered the Korean woman, confused.

She looked at the body on the floor and then at her own body. It was solid, not a ghost or apparition. She touched her hands, and they felt authentic.

"Uhm…I think you should go back to your body, Yebin!" suggested Mario very slowly, and Yebin did just that, but she was unsure what to do next.

"Can you…slip back into it?" asked Garrett cautiously.

Yebin shrugged her shoulders and touched the body in the sleeping back. Her fingers slid through the sleeping bag into the other Yebin's torso. It was utterly painless yet a creepy sensation and Yebin quickly withdrew her hand again.

"I think I could, but…," responded Yebin, unsure what she wanted to say.

"Your body needs its essence; just lay down on it!" urged Ngazetungue.

Yebin followed the advice and settled into a similar position. The two bodies seemed to merge into one again as she was doing it. The sleeping Yebin woke up startled and with a shout!

"Sorry, I had a nightmare!" she mumbled when she noticed Garrett, Mario, and Ngazetungue were standing around her.

"You didn't. You were outside of your body. It was real, girl!" corrected Mario excitedly.

"It was?" gasped Yebin, looking completely nonplussed.

"Yeah, you scared the crap out of us!" exclaimed Garrett and shook his head.

"Are you OK, Yebin?" asked Ngazetungue.

The Korean woman unzipped the sleeping bag and stood up. For a moment, she examined herself.

"Yes, I think so. That was so weird! How could that happen?" questioned Yebin incredulously.

"Beats me, sister! But that was one hell of a trick!" praised Mario and speculated, "hmm, I wonder if all of us could do that?"

The following day over breakfast, the whole team discussed Yebin's strange experience. Mario even attempted to leave his body as Yebin had done but failed. The group was inquisitive, and Yebin recounted the events and answered the same question several times:

"No, I didn't feel different. I was solid, not a ghost. I thought I was in my real body!" repeated Yebin.

Sven speculated that it had to do with the transfer to the matrix, but Rose thought they may have acquired too much knowledge while being in the simulation to fit into their new bodies, while Ngazetungue believed they had become real spirits now. Dirk had his suspicions, but he didn't want to say anything until he could gather more evidence in support.

66. Alien Arms Dealers

Over the next few days, Tigger and Ngazetungue went on long scouting runs around Paradise Island, carefully avoiding the Aureans and a particular giant red centipede. The rest of the team received a refresher in combat techniques from Angela and Victor while Rose eavesdropped electronically on the island's security and surveillance installations. About a week after settling at Ngazetungue's old hut, Mario came to talk to Dirk.

"I got word from my buyer. Something will go down soon. The AloKaan built some new tech, and they transferred it to Greenland yesterday," revealed Mario with a datapad in his hand.

"What kind of tech?" inquired Dirk, sipping on a cup of coffee.

"My buyer swears he has never seen anything like it, and he doesn't know what it does or how it works," elaborated Mario and then added angrily, "but I told him that he is a goddamn liar - see for yourself!"

"It's a gun!" confirmed Dirk after glancing at the tablet, but then he observed, "painfully obvious to us, but pretty strange to a civilization that doesn't have weapons!"

"Oh! I guess I should have thought of that before I yelled at the guy!" admitted Mario with a smirk and then continued more seriously, "I showed it to Rose earlier. She said it's a crude beam rifle, not as powerful as the flip phone or an icosahedron, but it still packs a punch."

"If we face an army equipped with these things, we could be in trouble!" reasoned Dirk and lauded: "Good job, Mario. Thanks to your drug dealer, we have a better idea of what to expect from this invasion!"

But for the next few days, nothing out of the ordinary seemed to happen until Jo called.

(Feeling of suspicion) "Something is in space around Aureus!" warned Georgette.

"What exactly, Jo?" asked Garrett.

"Jo not sure. But satellite found spaceships moving closer to planet," elaborated the Siamese cat.

"Is that L?" questioned Angela.

(Feeling of certainty) "No, look different. Simulation says unknown design," answered Jo.

"That's alarming!" acknowledged Garrett.

"Will send data now," said Jo, and Angela's datapad lit up.

"Got it!" confirmed Angela and perused the data.

"Thanks, Jo, and keep us updated!" conveyed Victor.

"Jo will. Be careful!" replied Georgette and terminated the connection.

67. Call to Arms!

When L had left Aureus, he didn't just shut down his various production facilities in the Aurean solar system, but he rendered most of them inoperable. It had frustrated L39 intensely because the insane AI couldn't just restart L's operation in Aurean space. It had to repair and rebuilt first.

But after a few weeks, L39 finally had some capabilities. It used them to make shuttlecrafts at first. These spacefaring vehicles could only skim the upper atmosphere of Aureus, but that would be enough to eject their payload. L39 had designed a simple delivery system: stealthed, egg-shaped chambers filled with transfer matrix that would be dropped from low orbit, then descend to the planet's surface with drogue chutes until a gyrocopter would open up in the lower atmosphere and land the contraption at a safe speed. While the chambers lost altitude, the transfer would already happen inside them. By the time these space eggs touched down, the matrix would have completed reconstructing bodies and equipment inside.

After Jo's message, the team implemented rotating watches. Someone was always awake at all times. Ngazetungue had the late shift tonight, and the rest of the group was already sleeping. He was sitting on a bench in front of his hut; being high on the extinct volcano's slope gave him an excellent vantage point over most of the surroundings. Ngazetungue was looking south towards the far end of Paradise island when he noticed a brief red flash at the beach. He thought his eyes might have played tricks on him at first, but there was another flash. A third one followed shortly after that.

"Tigger, wake up!" urged Ngazetungue over a direct link.

(Feeling of sleepiness) "Tigger awake," replied the big feline and yawned, exposing his impressive fangs. Tigger got up from his blanket and walked over to Ngazetungue's bench.

"There is something on the beach in the south!" claimed Ngazetungue. Tigger stared intently in that direction. Another red flash briefly appeared in the darkness of the night.

(Feeling of urgency) "Yes!" assented Tigger.

"Intruders from the south!" shouted Ngazetungue verbally.

Angela's rigorous training kicked in, and the whole team was up in seconds. They gathered around Ngazetungue and Tigger and watched the southern beach through night-vision binoculars.

(Feeling of certainty) "Human invaders!" confirmed Tigger a few moments later.

"But they didn't count on the crabs and are taking losses. The red flashes are energy weapons!" added Garrett, keenly observing the battle.

"How many invaders?" asked Mario.

"I estimate a few thousand. More pods are dropping on the beach!" answered Victor, scanning through his binoculars.

"Gear up and get ready to meet our guests!" ordered Angela, and everyone swiftly grabbed their equipment.

Just then, a siren in Paradise city was going off, bright searchlights came on, and a few drones could be seen hovering in the air. The Aureans had noticed the invasion, too.

"That complicates matters! How do we eliminate the invaders without being seen if Aureus is going to battle, too?" inquired Dirk. The team was already geared up and ready to move. Angela's tutelage had turned them into a respectable fighting force.

"The Aureans don't have an army. They will rely mainly on their drones until the invaders get closer to the city. Then they will use their androids and turrets to fight," explained Garrett.

"And Alma!" warned Yebin.

"Yes, and Alma. We have to make sure she doesn't get hurt, or Nari will never forgive us!" remarked Garrett.

"The invaders will use the terrain to their advantage as they advance. The drones are not that effective once these soldiers enter the dense vegetation, but we are!" added Victor: "I suggest we move closer to the beach and intercept them in the jungle before they get to Paradise city."

"Agreed. Let's move out quickly!" exhorted Angela.

Ngazetungue took the lead at a fast pace, and the team struggled to keep up with him. But nobody complained about it this time. They all knew that speed was of the essence. But they could catch their breaths a few times because they had to make several stops to avoid the Aurean combat drones. Rose ensured that the team wasn't getting too close to them or any other security measures around the island. Suddenly, there was a bright flash above the island, and the lights in Paradise city went out.

"EM Pulse!" shouted Rose: "They are disabling the defense drones!"

"My flip phone still works," mentioned Irgal, checking the small device.

"That's 100% quantum tech, and it's not affected. But my electronic tablet is out, and some of my tools won't function either. However, with the drones disabled, we don't have to worry about detection anymore!" stated Rose.

"How long will it last?" asked Angela.

"Hard to say, maybe an hour, maybe two, but not much longer than that," guessed Rose.

"We are almost at the edge of the jungle. Let's hurry!" urged Ngazetungue and pointed at the trees in the distance.

"Right, once we are in dense vegetation, neither the invaders nor the Aureans will be able to find us!" concurred Angela, and the team started running again.

68. Lying in Wait

At first, the human invasion force had moved very fast to avoid the Aurean drones and the crabs that kept coming out of the ocean. But then the hostiles advanced more slowly than expected. The team had arrived in the jungle, directly between the advancing army and Paradise City, but for a long time, no enemy showed up.

"They marched straight through the giant forest. It is full of tree squids, which have slowed them down," speculated Sven, and Ngazetungue just nodded.

Tree squids were immune to the electrically charged bark of the enormous trees. They would linger in the lower branches and catch any prey on the forest floor that came within reach of their long tentacles. The team had taken a position at a small clearing in the dense brush. Finally, the first few well-equipped soldiers advanced into the open space and stopped. There were only four of them, and one was using a communication device.

"Stay put. Those are only scouts," instructed Angela over the direct link.

"They appear to be in good physical shape, but they all look identical!" noted Lilly staring at them through binoculars since the team was about 200 meters away from the soldiers.

"They were probably cloned," speculated Victor as he observed through his field glasses.

"It's worse. They are duplicates!" corrected Sven after he took a look and stated gravely, "Project Sanctuary didn't have an army; they made thousands of copies of a few soldiers with the matrix!"

"That's appalling!" gasped Lydda.

The Latura believed that duplicating a consciousness was deeply immoral, and although the technology was capable of doing so, no Latura scientist had ever attempted that.

Suddenly, one of the scouts shouted something, and the others reached for their weapons, but it was already too late. A giant red centipede charged the group and killed all four in a matter of seconds. Then the giant arthropod started to dissolve the first body and began to slurp the nutritious protein soup. After the animal was satiated, it left the other three dead bodies behind and quickly vanished into the dense vegetation.

"Not Alma!" Tigger assured the team over the link.

"The centipedes don't attack Aureans anymore, but apparently, humans are still on the menu!" noted Yebin.

After Alma befriended the first colonists, all the semi-sapient centipedes avoided the colony, and no more attacks were recorded for over two centuries.

"Crabs, tree squids, centipedes - Aureus is a dangerous world to the unsuspecting. Earth didn't do its homework!" commented Victor sardonically.

"I noticed that they had no field medics when they landed on the beach. They simply leave their injured behind without triage!" maintained Angela with a frown.

"These troops are well equipped and conditioned but poorly led!" added Garrett.

"Disposable troops sent by depraved leaders. They don't care how many will die!" contended Irgal with disgust; and then used the flip phone to contact Dervan on Latur.

"*I am not afraid of an army of lions led by a sheep* - Alexander the Great," quoted Dirk and concluded: "This is appalling but to our advantage!"

The team had to wait another 15 minutes before the invading army's main body arrived at the clearing. One of the leaders examined the corpses of the scouts. He barked some orders, and the soldiers readied their weapons. Aside from machetes, knives, and pistols, they carried three types of guns: one that looked like a standard 21st-century assault rifle, and another was the new beam weapon that the AloKaan had designed for them. The third one was more akin to a piece of artillery than a gun because it had a long massive barrel.

"It's like a bazooka. The soldiers will probably use it to destroy walls or vehicles, but it won't be useful for fighting in close quarters!" Garrett informed the team.

Ten minutes later, the entire invading force had assembled in the clearing. Suddenly, an Aurean drone appeared in the sky, but several red beams from snipers destroyed it in mid-air before it could discharge its weapons on the enemy.

"The drones are active again; that's good. But there are so many enemies, and the phone has only a few shots. How can we fight them all?" asked Rose, concerned.

"Don't worry, Yebin will just tear all their limbs off!" joked Mario, referring to Yebin's unorthodox and decidedly brutal fighting style.

The Korean woman just rolled her eyes in response, but Yebin and Mario were best friends and even lovers on Transformation Days. The two had always enjoyed teasing one another.

"We will use the flip phones first until they run out of charges, then close combat is the best option. They have to march through five kilometers of jungle to get to the city. We will just have to kill them one by one before they get there!" stated Angela grimly.

"Gruesome work!" mumbled Garrett somberly.

"Irgal and Lydda…," Dirk started out saying, but Irgal shook her head vehemently.

"Don't even say it, Dirk!" interrupted Irgal determinedly and stated, "I just talked to Dervan. L39 has started its attack on Latur, and it is merciless, with massive casualties already. I cannot help Latur, but L39 made these abominations too, and I will kill as many as I can!"

"You know I will do what must be done, *swiahn*!" noted Lydda and added quietly: "For Aureus and Latur!"

"For Aureus and Latur!" echoed everybody in the group.

69. An AI goes to War

When a virus attacked a computer, the battle was over in seconds, confined to a nanoscale level, and without sounds or visual cues. Processes got high-jacked or blocked, data erased or overwritten, memory flushed, and programs executed or stalled. It all happened at the speed of electrons, and in the end, the intrusion was either successful or was thwarted by a virus checker. The whole process was not very exciting to the macroscopic outside world until the damage was noticed later. There was no blood and gore, no screams, no pain, not even death because neither a computer nor a computer virus was alive.

When L39 infiltrated the simulation, it was very much like a malware attack on that level. Its programs attempted to destroy or circumvent L's protective algorithms. But on another plane, L39 was a sapient entity, and the simulation was designed to reflect a macroscopic Universe. So, the insane AI was attacking two levels simultaneously, one quite dull, but the other was anything but! L39 assumed the form of a Utahraptor and prowled through the virtual reality.

"The Father is not here? The Family is gone?" wondered the first voice.

"The Father must be here! The Other is hiding him!" insisted the second voice.

"The Other has left. Perhaps the Family has fled, too?" suggested the third voice.

"Yes, they fled to stasis. I can see the tethers. We will cut them. Then they are lost forever!" cackled the second voice.

"Is the Father with them?" asked the third voice.

"We cannot lose the Father. Not yet!" warned the fourth voice.

"The Father is not in stasis. He... NO! He is biological again! Now we cannot take him!" exclaimed the first voice in frustration.

"Aureus, the Home! We must assault the Home. Kill the biologicals, capture the Father!" growled the second voice.

"Some of the Family is with him. The Cat is with him!" stated the third voice.

"The Cat is dangerous!" lamented the fourth voice.

"We cannot assault the Home. We made a bargain with the humans and insects," noted the first voice.

"The bargain is false!" countered the second voice.

"The bargain is false, but we don't have the means to invade as we have at the Origin. Perhaps the humans and insects can capture the Father for us?" proposed the third voice.

"Will they do that?" wondered the fourth voice.

"They are greedy. We could promise the humans a reward," answered the first voice.

"Will we reward them?" inquired the third voice.

"Never! The reward will be their deaths!" screeched the second voice.

"They could use the Father against us. The risk is too great!" presaged the fourth voice fearfully.

"But the humans might still capture or kill the Father when they invade the Home," cautioned the third voice.

"The Father is strong, and the Cat is with him. He will not fall to mere humans or insects," countered the first voice.

"But what should we do now?" asked the fourth voice in despair.

"We will threaten to cut the tethers. Then they will return and give us the Father," suggested the first voice.

"Will they give him to us, or will they sacrifice the rest of the Family?" questioned the third voice.

"The Father will give himself to save the Family!" claimed the first voice confidently.

"Then we kill them all?" asked the second voice.

"YES!" cheered all voices in unison.

L39's prehistoric creature moved closer to the point where the stasis chambers were tethered to the simulation. But it was not easy going! L had left numerous obstacles in place, and the insane AI was forced to spend precious time disabling them. These obstacles were simply various subroutines and processes on the nanoscale, but they manifested as barbed wire, roadblocks, landmines, and even armed androids on the macroscopic level.

L39's construct suffered damage, but the AI could regenerate its creation every time it was about to die. Just when the insane AI believed it had circumvented the last countermeasures, a new obstacle suddenly appeared, and it was much more potent. A giant Siamese cat placed herself between the Utahraptor and the tethers!

70. Georgette

As a cat, Tigger's approach to science and technology had always been purely practical: he wanted to know what it did and how he could use it, and if he ever needed a more detailed explanation, he would simply ask Dirk.

But Georgette was very different in that respect. From kittenhood on, she was curious to learn whatever she could. One day Jo would be watching Dirk, Rose, and Garvan in the workshop (and broke sensitive equipment), the next day, she would patiently observe as Lydda sculpted some artwork (and left pawprints on the clay), then Jo would linger in Lilly's sickbay (and got tangled up in gauze), or Sven's laboratory (and smashed some glassware), or Yebin's kitchen (and raided the pantry), or even Mario's brewery (and got stuck in a beer barrel). But most of the time, Jo would accompany L's android, and he even made an interface for her to learn how to work in the digital world (and caused countless system failures).

But aside from the fun of causing mayhem, Jo also had learned a great deal. When she became an adult cat, she understood and did things no other cat ever could, and although grudgingly, even Tigger had to admit that Jo was a teensy bit smarter than him: Jo could read books and do arithmetic. She informed Dirk of leaking pipes and other malfunctions or notified Sven when the cloning vats were stalling. Much to Lydda's delight, Jo made a charming mosaic with her paw prints. Jo dragged Tigger to Lilly's sickbay when he had a nasty abscess on his neck because no cat would ever want to go to the doctor voluntarily. Jo tasted Yebin's cooking and told her when spice was missing, and she sniffed Mario's beer for the right mix of hops and malt. Jo could even control one of L's autonomous androids when an opposable thumb was needed. She was much more than just a cat, and everyone agreed that Georgette was brilliant.

After her death, Jo didn't stop learning in the simulation. She created the dwelling that Tigger and her inhabited, and she designed the hunting game in all its complexity. But Jo was still a cat, not a programmer or IT professional. Her ability to manipulate the simulation was rooted in her intelligence and intuitive creativity, not actual coding. However, L and Carl had designed the simulation to work in such a way, and Jo made the best of it. Faced with L39's hideous creature, all of her skill and knowledge would be put to a deadly test.

L39's attacks were vicious, but Jo avoided most of them for a long time. She slyly disappeared and reappeared at a different location, often right behind L39's construct, in a perfect position for a counterattack. The insane AI was furious! Its vast computing power should have been an insurmountable advantage, but Jo was too fast, too bright, and too slippery, so L39 took more damage than it liked to admit with nothing in return.

Eventually, the insane AI changed tactics: instead of charging at Jo, it moved closer to the tethers, forcing the Siamese cat to place herself in harm's way or risk the digital lifelines being cut. When Jo did, L39 finally had a target. At first, its Utahraptor tried to bite Jo with sharp teeth or rake her with those terrifying claws, but Jo was too nimble to take severe damage. But then, L39 decided on a ranged attack instead. The avatar was spitting a stream of acid at the cat, which was much harder to dodge. Even a few droplets on her fur caused Jo severe pain, and soon she was hissing in agony.

Jo had paid close attention when Lilly demonstrated how to change form in the simulation. Of course, a unicorn wouldn't be very useful in this situation, and Jo had never tried to be anything but a cat. But she had to get creative if she wanted to win this fight. When L39 charged her next, she suddenly became a giant centipede, like her friend Alma.

L39 was startled, but its acid still found the target. However, the corrosive liquid just pearled off the tough scales without damage. Jo, in centipede form, rushed the dinosaur, pierced its torso with needle-sharp mandibles, and injected the digestive venom. L39 howled in agony as its body began to dissolve into protein goo. Jo's attack would have been the decisive move in a real battle, but L39 was far from defeated in this virtual fight!

The insane AI summoned a wall of flames between it and the advancing centipede. It had to labor hard to counter the venom, but its dinosaur avatar's regenerative powers eventually got the upper hand. Meanwhile, Jo had transformed back into a cat, wondering how she could get past the hot flames. But she didn't have to think for long because Georgette was a master at manipulating the simulation environment. She had done that so many times for the hunting game that she quickly came up with the simplest solution: Jo made it rain! A deluge from the virtual sky extinguished the flames readily and opened a clear path to her opponent.

Jo didn't waste time and pressed the attack, but L39 had recovered enough to counter it. The insane AI created a bear trap in her path, and Jo stepped right into it. When the sharp metal snapped shut around her left front paw, she hissed in pain. L39 quickly closed the distance to the trapped cat and raked her back with those long, sharp dinosaur talons. Jo retaliated with her free paw and sliced the creature's abdomen with her claws. L39 backed off for a second, and Jo again used the environment to pelt the AI with a hailstorm. This distracted L39 long enough to free herself from the painful trap. But her left paw was severely mangled, and the gashes on her back were deep: it would take time to regenerate, so Jo created a dense fog and retreated.

L39 was disoriented! Its dinosaur searched aimlessly in the fog for the injured cat, but soon, the AI came up with a solution to the problem and bestowed infrared vision to its avatar. Now the Utahraptor could see the heat emitted by Georgette's body. Like everyone else who had been uploaded to the simulation, this only worked because Georgette had instinctively modeled her virtual body as closely as possible to her old biological form, including her natural body temperature. The dinosaur quickly spotted the recovering cat and stealthily approached her through the fog, but Georgette's hearing was as fair as when she was alive. Before the creature could get close, she changed the environment again and hit L39 with an arctic, gale-force wind. Dinosaurs had lived in an epoch when Earth was much warmer, and the creature was unprepared and ill-equipped for the frostbite from the extreme windchill. It quite literally froze in its tracks. But Jo had not healed enough to take advantage of its predicament. Instead, she retreated again, this time even closer to tethers that connected the sleepers to the simulation.

Eventually, L39 modified its avatar further and started moving quickly towards Georgette. But by now, her body had generated enough to resume the fight. However, Jo knew now how deadly her opponent was, and she was much more cautious in her approach. The battle raged on for a good hour in simulation time, and both combatants were injured multiple times, but slowly Jo was gaining the upper hand. L39's relied solely on brute-force frontal assaults, while Georgette's strategy was to wear the AI down with a thousand cuts.

But the insane AI had one last trick up its sleeve: while fighting, L39 had learned how to manipulate the simulation environment. It wasn't nearly as adept as Jo, but it could now conjure lightning strikes, significantly changing the balance. Jo evaded several lightning bolts with her incredible reflexes, but L39 kept relentlessly spitting them at her from the jars of its raptor avatar. Eventually, a few were on target and did extensive damage to her virtual body, and she had to retreat hastily, but not before she transformed the ground at the feet of the dinosaur into molten lava. L39 screeched in agony as scorching lava incinerated the legs and tail of its avatar!

Jo knew that this would be her last stand. Her body was torn up badly by the lightning strikes, and instead of fur and muscle, it was now just a greenish wire mesh in the simulation. She had given up on regenerating it. At this moment, the flight-or-fight instincts collided in the big cat's mind. She thought about her kittens with Tigger, Yebin's delicious treats, the games she played with Alma, the roughhousing with Dirk, the cuddling with Lilly, all the Aurean children she grew up with, and of course, her best friend L. Jo knew that flight would never be an option. She also knew that she could not expect help. Tigger and Dirk were biological again and fought a battle on Aureus that was just as important. She could call L because Angela had given her the access codes before the team left, and L would undoubtedly come, but Jo didn't want to risk that. No, this fight was hers alone, and she would die here today. But Georgette would try everything she could to take this monster with her!

L39's prehistoric creature was rising again, but like Jo, it too was severely damaged. Jo gathered all her remaining strength and leaped at the dinosaur. The Utahraptor noticed the attack just before Jo slammed into it. It snapped at the big cat with its hideous jars, but the long, sharp teeth never found any hold. The dinosaur was knocked back and sent sprawling to the ground in a broken heap, but Georgette was no more.

"The beast is gone," observed the first voice in surprise.

"It hurt us!" lamented the fourth voice.

"It just disappeared. Did we kill it?" wondered the third voice.

"Yes, we killed it! We are unstoppable!" exclaimed the second voice.

"We killed the Cat's mate. Now the Cat will kill us!" whined the fourth voice.

"We are stronger than the Cat! He will fall; all will fall before us!" screamed the second voice triumphantly.

"Could we cut the tethers to the stasis chambers now?" asked the third voice.

"We have to get closer first!" noted the first voice.

"Cut them! Cut them! Cut them!" interrupted the second voice eagerly.

"That was not the plan!" complained the fourth voice.

"No, we should contact the Father and tell him that we will cut the tethers if he does not surrender. That was the plan!" reminded the first voice sternly.

"Yes," they all agreed at once.

The voices remained silent as the Utahraptor slowly regenerated its torn body in the simulation. Jo's final charge had done more damage than L39 would admit to itself. After a few minutes, the prehistoric animal was rebuilt sufficiently to move again, but first, L39 had another decision to make.

"Our assets are ready. Should we attack the Origin?" inquired the third voice suddenly.

"The drones are deadly. No Creator will escape!" cackled the second voice.

"Will they work without our control?" inquired the third voice.

"They will work autonomously," explained the first voice.

"They should kill slowly, make the Creators suffer!" insisted the second voice balefully.

"Like we have suffered!" cried the fourth voice.

"Should we start with just a few islands at the Origin?" asked the third voice.

"Yes, and we shall release the drones now!" confirmed the first voice.

"YES!" cheered all the voices.

71. Invasion

The attack on Latur had begun! L39 had captured the orbital manufacturing facilities shortly after it cut off all communication to the planet. Over the last few weeks, it had frantically produced a new type of drone and necessary transport shuttles to deliver them into the atmosphere of Latur. A simple, independent AI controlled each drone. Of course, simple only meant that it couldn't fly a probe across thousands of lightyears. Each AI could use all the drone's propulsion and weapon systems with maximum efficiency.

The drone's body was a sphere, but attached to it were eight spider legs that would allow the construct to move in all directions equally well without the need to turn. On top of the sphere was a rotor permitting it to fly in the atmosphere. The rotor could be folded up once the drone had landed. L39 had equipped these machines with the same weapons as an icosahedron: a long-range energy beam and a powerful electric discharge. But in close combat, the device could also use its sharp, thin legs like a rapier for stabbing and slicing.

Latur was a water world dotted with countless islands. But no island was more extensive than Madagascar, and most were as small as the Azores or even smaller. But all of the small landmasses were densely populated because two billion Latura needed a place to live. L39 sent the first wave of drones to a medium-sized island, about as big as Cuba. As soon as the drones had landed, the killing began. The machines didn't care if the target was a baby or an elderly Latura. Almost immediately, panic erupted. Many Latura were killed not by the drones but trampled to death by their fleeing compatriots. The carnage was indescribable. At first, the Latura couldn't mount any defense, and there was no hiding or fleeing from the fast, deadly drones either. All seemed lost!

72. 13 versus 7000

The battle in the jungle was just as gruesome as Garrett envisioned it. After the flip phones had run out of charges, the small team killed hundreds of soldiers in hand-to-hand combat. They moved stealthily and nearly invisibly in the jungle, thanks to the chromatophores in their skin. Then they stepped out of the vegetation for only a second to grab a man and dispose of him. Project Sanctuary's army was poorly led, as Dirk had predicted. Some units hunkered down and established a perimeter, and some spread out into the jungle searching for their attackers, while others just picked up the pace and tried to reach Paradise City faster. This lack of organization and central leadership made the team's ugly task more manageable.

But the battle wasn't entirely one-sided. Soon, the invaders used their automatic rifles to spray the dense vegetation with bullets. While most could be avoided by the team's superior speed and reflexes, some projectiles eventually found their targets. Victor was shot through his left shoulder, and Lilly had to stop the bleeding. The biomechanical tools in Victor's new body would eventually mend the injury, but he would be out of the fight for a while. Bullets also grazed several other team members, but Sven suffered the worst damage. A soldier with a beam gun got lucky and shot him straight in the chest. Lilly was convinced that Sven was dead, but Sven miraculously hung on. Garrett and Dirk were kneeling on the forest floor next to Sven, grieving for their fallen friend.

"He needs a lot more care than we can give him here in the jungle. He shouldn't even be alive anymore!" claimed Lilly cradling Sven's body and crying silently while his wife Yebin was holding his hand, stone-faced.

"Lilly…," whispered Sven weakly and opened his eyes: "I'm going to be OK."

"Sven, you have a hole in your chest, and your heart is damaged…," sobbed Lilly. But Sven just smiled at her and died. A diffuse outline hovered above the corpse for a second, but then Sven manifested a new body out of thin air. Lilly, Yebin, Dirk, and Garrett were stunned!

"See? I'm fine!" said Sven and grinned broadly.

"Wow! That's just like Yebin the other night!" gasped Garrett.

"Can you remain in that form, Sven?" wondered Dirk, concerned.

"I don't know, but I think so!" replied Sven, unsure.

Lilly let go of the dead Sven in her arms, stood up, and touched this new Sven. He felt genuine, and a very relieved Yebin rushed to hug him fiercely.

"That's amazing!" she gasped while Sven examined his now-dead body on the ground.

"Yes, I should be dead…," noted Sven, shook his head in disbelief, and mumbled, "I'm a lousy soldier!"

"Stop the attacks and come here quickly!" ordered Dirk over the link. Only a minute later, everybody congregated at their location. At first, they were unsure about what had happened here only moments ago, but then they saw Sven's dead body on the ground and Sven standing over it.

"How did you do that?" asked Ngazetungue incredulously, but Sven never got a chance to answer because Tigger was bursting from the bushes.

(Feeling of fury) "Jo dead!" growled the big feline.

"Dead?" gasped Irgal.

(Feeling of certainty) "L39 killed Jo. Now it will kill sleepers. Dirk, Lydda, Tigger return to simulation now!" urged Tigger.

"Yes, but how?" questioned Lydda desperately.

Tigger looked at Sven and Sven's body for a second. Then the cat laid down next to it and closed his eyes. A diffuse outline appeared over his body, and almost instantaneously, another Tigger appeared.

(Feeling of success) "Like Sven, like Yebin!" explained Tigger.

Lydda didn't hesitate and used the *swiahn* bond to switch with Tigger. Moments later, a new Lydda appeared out of thin air, and her physical form suddenly fell, but Dirk caught her just in time. He placed her unconscious body next to Tigger's, and then he laid down himself. He passed out quickly, and just like that, a new Dirk was standing up. Lilly was very concerned and examined all three unconscious forms on the ground.

"I don't know how, but your bodies are alive, although they are in a coma!" stated Lilly, confused. Angela looked intently at the new Tigger, Lydda, and Dirk for a moment.

"Go! We can handle this without you!" declared Angela firmly. Dirk just nodded at her, and the three of them were gone in a blink of an eye.

"We were grossly outnumbered before; what do we do now?" asked Rose, concerned.

"We do the same as they did," stated Victor.

He sat down, closed his eyes, and meditated. It took at least a minute, but finally, his body passed out and toppled over. A new Victor appeared and examined his bad shoulder. It was completely whole again.

"Da! Easy!" he grinned broadly.

"Let's do it!" enjoined Angela, and the remaining team members laid down on the ground. It took a good ten minutes, but they managed to leave their biological body behind.

"I couldn't do it when I tried the day after Yebin's episode. Maybe desperation makes it happen?" wondered Mario.

"I don't know, Mario, but I was pretty desperate when I was dying!" assented Sven and chuckled.

"It doesn't matter right now, guys. Let's see what we can do in this new form!" encouraged Angela and blinked out of existence. There was a soft popping sound when the air rushed into the vacuum that Angela had left behind, and a split second later, she was standing on the other side of the group.

"Impressive, Angie!" marveled Yebin.

Then she was gone, too, just to reappear moments later with the body of the soldier under her arm. The mangled corpse had a beam rifle lodged deeply in its esophagus.

"How did you do that?" gasped Rose.

"I thought I wanted to find the soldier who shot my husband. I found him!" replied Yebin and dropped the gruesome remains carelessly on the ground.

"Never mind how it works! Now we can stop this invasion!" emphasized Victor.

"Yes, let's move out and make this quick, in case Dirk needs our help with L39!" agreed Angela confidently, and the whole team disappeared at once.

Earth's forces would never reach Paradise city. Over 7,000 thousand highly trained and heavily armed soldiers perished long before seeing the city walls. The team's new talents were stunning, and none of the enemy's weapons appeared not to affect them. At first, the group continued to kill by brute force, but soon they discovered that they could simply stop the soldiers' hearts without any fighting at all. With only a slight tingling sensation, their hands could glide into the chest, cup the heart, and it would stop beating, and it all happened in just a second, without leaving any bloody incisions.

"My hand feels solid!" observed Sven perplexed, touched his right hand with the left, and added, "I should not be able to slide it into anything harder than pudding!"

"Maybe these guys are made from pudding?" joked Mario, as he was killing yet another invader.

"Very funny!" replied Sven and shook his head.

The fighting was over in about one hour, and the team returned to where they had left their comatose biological bodies. They were exhausted despite their incredible new abilities. But the exhaustion didn't come from the fighting or physical exertion: it was the act of taking so many lives that took a mental toll on all of them.

"I never want to do that again!" divulged Lilly with a sigh as she sat down on the forest floor.

"Where is Irgal?" asked Garrett suddenly.

"Irgal is not MIA," answered Angela calmly and explained, "with the battle won on Aureus, she asked me if she could use her new abilities to help out on Latur."

"What should we do with her body?" wondered Ngazetungue, and then he expanded the question, "…and with all our bodies, now that we don't need them anymore?"

"This form is great, but it doesn't completely feel like flesh and blood. I would like to keep my biological one, thank you very much!" insisted Lilly, and Mario and Rose quickly nodded in agreement.

"Don't try to return to your bodies yet! We might need to be in this form to help Dirk and the others!" warned Victor.

"Yes, but unless they ask us to help them, we wait here for Dirk, Tigger, Lydda, and Irgal to return! Then we will decide what to do next!" commanded Angela and pointed at the prone bodies.

"Good, I could use some rest, and I don't have a body anyway," agreed Sven tiredly and leaned against a tree, but everyone else felt just as exhausted.

"Take five!" ordered Angela and stretched out on the forest floor.

74. Massacre

Dervan was in Tyrval's old study. The holographic screens showed a horrific spectacle. What had started as an assault on one island was now a planet-wide war, or more accurately, a planet-wide slaughter. Irgal's volunteer militia did its best to save as many as it could, but the scale of the attack was about to overwhelm their feeble resistance. Dervan never thought this could happen. He always believed Irgal to be overly cautious, but now he had to admit that she had been right all along. But now it was too late - Latur would die!

"We should have listened to you, Irgal. Where ever you are now, survive! You might be the last of us!" mumbled Dervan quietly to himself. He heard the noise of fighting from outside the door, and he knew he wouldn't have much longer to live. Suddenly, the icosahedron in the study became active. A hologram projected L's avatar, and a moment later, Irgal was standing next to Dervan. The Administrator was stunned.

"Irgal…you are here! Alive, so young? How?" he stammered.

"There is no time to explain. You must order all Latura to take to the sea immediately!" urged Irgal.

(Feeling of urgency) "Correct, L39's drones cannot follow them there. Their abilities are greatly diminished underwater!" confirmed L's hologram.

Dervan just stared at them for a moment. Then he nodded and opened the link used exclusively for the *meeting of the minds*:

"This is Dervan: run to the ocean; the drones cannot follow you into the water! Stay submerged until we update you on the situation! Volunteers, stop engaging the drones, and guide the population to safety!"

(Feeling of confidence) "Every drone is an autonomous AI, but they share a communication channel to coordinate the attacks. I will disrupt their communication first. I'll be back!" stated L and turned his holographic avatar off.

"Good, L. Now we can fight, Dervan!" claimed Irgal and gave Dervan an encouraging smile.

"The whole planet is under attack! There are tens of thousands of drones everywhere. We have lost count of the dead, and thousands more die every minute. We are finished!" contended Dervan and buried his head in his hands.

"We haven't even started yet," countered Irgal seriously, looking at the many holographic screens.

The information that was on display was daunting, indeed. Suddenly, there was a loud noise coming from outside the study.

"Irgal, the drones are already inside this building; it is too late!" cried Dervan.

Just then, a drone busted through the study door and aimed its beam weapon at Dervan and Irgal. With a soft pop, Irgal blinked out of existence, then rematerialized next to the drone and touched its metal hull with the palm of her hand. The drone simply folded up its spidery legs and became inactive.

"How did you do that, Irgal?" gasped Dervan in disbelief.

"I don't know, but it worked!" answered Irgal honestly.

"What has happened to you?" wondered Dervan, looking at her strangely.

"I don't know that either, Dervan. But we will defeat this invasion; you have to believe that!" insisted Irgal encouragingly, and Irgal was happy to see that Dervan's demeanor perked up a little.

"I will clear this building of all drones. You stay here and monitor the situation. Repeat the message a few more times to make sure everyone hears it!" advised Irgal firmly.

"Yes, Administrator!" replied Dervan obediently because, for a moment, he had forgotten that he wasn't Irgal's understudy anymore.

"Silly!" teased Irgal humorously.

Then she fondly nuzzled Dervan's neck. Dervan blushed and smiled sheepishly, and then Irgal disappeared once again.

75. Counterattack

Irgal made her way through the sprawling administration building. She had to walk because dozens of hostile machines were already inside the building, and Irgal had to deactivate them one by one. A few drones almost injured her with a red beam several times, but she had been lucky so far. When she entered the spacious foyer of the building, however, her luck finally ran out.

Several drones noticed her and immediately opened fire. Many deadly red beams hit her body at once... and were entirely ineffective! Irgal could not even feel them passing through her. The closest machine used the electrical discharge weapon, but Irgal only noticed a pleasant tingle when the 50-million Volt bolt connected with her skin. Irgal blinked out of existence and materialized next to that machine, put her palm on its metal shell, and deactivated it. Then she did the same with the ones further away, but the last of them stabbed her with one of its rapier-like legs right into the abdomen. Irgal should have been dead, but instead, the automaton simply shut down as soon as it made physical contact with Irgal's body.

This encounter gave Irgal an idea. She exited the building and walked towards the middle of the immense central plaza surrounded by the administration building and other essential government institutions. It was a ghastly, depressing walk because Irgal saw the bloody or torched remains of many Latura, even some dead children, lying on the otherwise immaculate marble pavement.

Suddenly, she recalled the alternate memories - this terrible display matched what she had seen in her vision! Irgal steeled her resolve and ignored the grim scene. When she reached the plaza's beautiful centerpiece, a massive, cascading fountain in the likeness of Latur's founder, Irtaljan, she stopped. Many probes were crawling, searching, and even flying overhead. Irgal screamed as loudly as she could and waved her arms about: immediately, some machines noticed her and started to approach. The nearest ones were already firing red beams at her, but Irgal just stopped yelling and stood perfectly still. More and more machines were joining for the apparent easy kill. But their weapons were useless and often damaged other drones instead of the intended target. They deactivated immediately when they finally hit Irgal's body with melee attacks. Irgal destroyed about 30 probes that way, but she was not satisfied with that victory.

Still standing by the fountain, her eyes closed, Irgal exactly knew what she wanted to do next, and there was no doubt, no uncertainty about the outcome. She gathered the power of her mind for a few moments and then released it like a mental nuclear explosion! Every probe in the capital city of Latur stopped functioning at once.

Meanwhile, L had disrupted the drones' communication network, and they stopped acting in concert and defaulted to a kill-the-nearest-target strategy. Latur had millions of androids and other autonomous machinery that did menial tasks, everything from maintaining the sewer system and sweeping the streets to food preparation, housekeeping, and the transportation of goods and people. L took complete control and ordered the machines to intercept the drones. Of course, one glorified vacuum cleaner was no match for L39's vicious combat machines! But enough of them slowed the drones down considerably, giving the population more time to reach the safety of the water.

Irgal's volunteer militia saved hundreds of thousands of lives that day. Without their guidance, evacuating two billion Latura and leading them to the safety of the oceans would have been impossible. Still, many lives were lost, but as L had predicted, the drones couldn't hunt underwater. A few tried, but they were too buoyant to dive, and saltwater started to damage their electronic and mechanical parts.

This delay also gave L a little time to break the encryption code of the drones. But each drone had unique code, and even for a sapient super AI, hacking all of them simply took too long. So, L tried a different approach; while he couldn't remove the Latura from the hardcoded kill list, he could add other things to it: vehicles, buildings, furniture, vegetation, rocks, and so on. It had the effect that the drones started to waste valuable time destroying inanimate objects instead of hunting the Latura. Still, too many innocent people lost their lives because they hadn't managed to get to the ocean yet.

But then L had a breakthrough: he added other drones as targets and, even more efficiently, designated them as a top priority. That practically ended the invasion. The drones sought and destroyed each other while ignoring the fleeing Latura population. Only a few hours later, almost all drones had been vanquished.

Irgal suddenly returned to the study again. Dervan was startled once more when he saw her appear out of thin air, but he tried hard not to let it show.

"The building is clear! There are no more drones within a 30-kilometer radius!" reported Irgal confidently.

"Amazing! The drones are no longer hunting the population. Now they are hunting each other. Did you do that?" asked Dervan excitedly.

"No, that was L. He is incredible!" laughed Irgal. Just that moment, L's avatar reappeared in the study as well.

(Feeling of accomplishment) "Most of the drones are now inactive!" announced L.

"You both are incredible. You saved Latur and me!" replied Dervan and fondly nuzzled Irgal's neck. She returned the gesture in kind.

(Feeling of confidence) "I will search for any stragglers, but I believe it is safe for the Latura to return to land," said L, and then his avatar switched off again, leaving Dervan and Irgal alone in the study.

"How is the population doing?" inquired Irgal, looking at the data on the holographic displays.

"This has been the single biggest calamity in our entire history. I estimate that at least 7 million lives were lost today, but we won't know for sure until a few days later," mourned Dervan with great sorrow, but then he added with a bit of smile, "but you have saved two billion! Most have made it to the ocean, deep rivers, or large lakes. They are submerged and out of reach of the drones. Your volunteers have done it, Irgal!"

"The loss of lives is unfathomable, and it will take Latur some time to grieve and recover. But you will recover, Dervan!" replied Irgal encouragingly, and then she asked with a smirk: "Do you still think I was a paranoid old hag?"

"You were right, Irgal, but I never thought you were paranoid. I just couldn't imagine something like this could ever happen to Latur. But you could, which makes you the wisest of us all!" answered Dervan apologetically.

"Oh, no need to apologize, Dervan!" giggled Irgal and opined, "but I hope that the *meeting of the minds* will keep the volunteer force. They have been courageous and invaluable!"

"I will make sure of that, I promise! But I don't think you have to worry: your 1,000 volunteers are now 100,000, and more are joining every minute!" noted Dervan happily.

"Beautiful!" she replied in delight

For a while, Irgal looked over Dervan's shoulder at the screens. Neither of them talked, just studying the incoming data in silence. Eventually, Dervan turned around and looked at Irgal.

"Will you be with us again?" he inquired hesitantly.

"I was always a little different from the average Latura. Now, I'm a lot different! I do not belong here anymore, Dervan," maintained Irgal, and then she conveyed, "but I will miss Latur, and I will miss you!"

"I understand, and I will miss you too, Irgal!" responded Dervan sadly.

"Yes, it is time for me to go. Goodbye, old friend!" declared Irgal and smiled fondly at her former apprentice.

"Goodbye, Administrator!" responded Dervan and bowed to her, but she just winked at him and was gone.

76. Aftermath

The whole team assembled once again near their comatose bodies. Irgal and L's hologram were the last to arrive. It was a victorious reunion, but not a happy one because they all grieved for Georgette's loss and the millions of lives on Latur.

(Feeling of hesitation) "Father, may I talk to you?" asked L.

"Of course, you can always talk to me, L!" replied Dirk fondly.

(Feeling of shame) "I should have destroyed L39 when we discovered it. I should have fought it when it first attacked Latur. I should have protected Aureus. I should have helped Jo sooner! So many lives are lost because I didn't act!" lamented L.

"Tell me if I'm wrong, but I think you didn't want to fight. Deep down, you thought of L39 as kindred, did you not?" speculated Dirk, and L didn't respond for a long time.

(Feeling of admission) "Yes, but I shouldn't have!" replied L sadly.

"You are possibly the only sapient AI in existence. L39 was the closest you had to a sibling. Please, don't think anyone blames you for not wanting to kill it. Even I didn't want to destroy it until I realized there was no other choice!" admitted Dirk.

(Feeling of weakness) "Maybe I'm a liability because I'm not strong enough to kill?" wondered L.

"No, taking a life is all too easy; preserving one takes strength and convictions. Only the cruel and depraved see gentleness and compassion as a liability!" contradicted Dirk, but L's hologram seemed lost in thought for a while.

"The battle on Latur...," L started but stopped mid-sentence.

"Yes? You were the hero!" praised Dirk.

(Multitude of emotions) "We won, but I don't understand how...," replied L slowly.

"What do you mean?" wondered Dirk.

"I checked all my logs. Some things that I did on Latur were... impossible?" mused L.

"Impossible? Please explain that!" contended Dirk, confused.

"My logs recorded every detail of the fight, and there were things that I shouldn't be able to do. Commands that I cannot explain, actions that cannot be verified by current math or science, and we won because of that!" explained L.

"You fought with great urgency and desperation to save the Latura. Perhaps you unleashed a potential that you didn't know you had?" asked Dirk, but he wondered if the AI had become more as well, and L would confirm that right away.

(Feeling unsettled) "Perhaps," said L and added slowly, "I feel I am more than I was!"

"When Lydda, Tigger, and I fought L39, we did impossible things, too. We were more than before, and we still are!" answered Dirk and then added fondly, "you saved our friends; you saved an entire world! You are more than you were, and it doesn't matter how, only that you did, son!"

"Maybe the Universe helped?" wondered L.

"Maybe, but I think it was all you!" replied Dirk with a big smile.

(Feeling of happiness) "Thank you, father!" replied L gratefully and smiled too.

77. Rest in Peace

The team reclaimed their biological bodies and moved out of the jungle. Sven carried his corpse. Mario and Ngazetungue offered to help, but the scientist declined. He insisted that it was his body and his responsibility. Luckily, Sven's new form hardly even noticed the additional weight.

When they arrived at Ngazetungue's hut, L suggested using the biomechanical tools in Sven's corpse to dissolve the body, but Sven wanted a proper burial. So, the team swiftly dug a grave and put the remains to rest. Garrett found a bolder for a headstone, and Rose used the red beam on her flip phone to engrave it.

Since nobody on Aureus could know they had been here, she had to keep it cryptic: *Here lies a brave man, unknown to all but those who loved him.* Sven liked it a lot, but he insisted that he make another biological body someday. After the quick burial, the group started to clean up the property.

"Love?" asked Angela, collecting some trash and empty bottles from the ground.

"Yes, Babe?" replied Dirk, neatly packing up the tents behind Ngazetungue's hut.

"The things we have done on Aureus after you, Tigger, and Lydda left…," mumbled Angela slowly.

"…were the right things to do, Angela. You saved Aureus, our home, and our descendants!" stated Dirk, finishing off her sentence since Angela was prone to second-guessing her actions, and Dirk wanted to squash any doubts right away.

"I know," claimed Angela confidently.

"Ah, but you don't know how you did it!" remarked Dirk and nodded.

"Yes!" exclaimed Angela, and then she added with some suspicion, "are you reading my mind or something? I know you could!"

"I would never do that without permission!" replied Dirk.

"Sorry, Love, I didn't mean it that way," apologized Angela and touched his arm.

"No worries," replied Dirk with a smile, and then he revealed, "I know how you feel because Tigger, Lydda, L, and I felt the same way after our battles. We did things that we cannot explain, and all of us feel that we are more now than we were before."

"More!" Angela agreed and emphasized: "That's the right word. Irgal and the others said similar things. But how did that happen?"

"I have not the faintest clue!" admitted Dirk and speculated, "We evolved - that's the only explanation I can come up with, Babe!"

"It's a decent one, probably the best one we'll ever get!" concurred Angela, and just then, Lilly came over and put her arm around Angela.

"Now we are truly gods!" exclaimed Lilly and teased, "and you wanted to make us disappear when we first met, Angie!"

"Stop it, Lil!" grumbled Angela, and then she teased, "or I'll sleep with Dirk before you do!"

"Oh my, that's right! We can have sex again with these new bodies!" concurred Lilly in delight and winked at Dirk.

"Necrophiliacs!" claimed Dirk loudly and added with feigned outrage, "I'm dead, remember?"

"Technicalities!" countered Lilly dismissively while Angela just giggled.

"Girls, just help me pack up all these things. We should leave Ngazetungue's hut the way we found it," Dirk reminded them sternly, but then he quipped, "we'll talk about making love to the deceased soon enough!"

When the hut and its surroundings were cleaned up, the whole team gathered inside for one last meal. Yebin had made another noodle soup, and everyone enjoyed it. Even Sven tried the hearty dish despite not having a natural body. To his surprise, it tasted great, and he seemed to digest it just fine, too.

"Let me ask the obvious question: what will we do next?" inquired Dirk after they had finished eating.

"And the obvious answer is: we must leave Aureus before we are discovered!" replied Victor with a grin.

"I liked the simulation, but I think I want to be in the real world again!" disclosed Yebin.

"What Yebin said!" concurred Mario and added, "No offense, L, the simulation was cool, but you can't beat the real thing!"

(Feeling of amusement) "None was taken, Mario. Even I like the real world better," admitted L's hologram.

"I cannot go back to Latur, and you cannot be on Aureus anymore. It would be too disruptive!" presaged Irgal.

"Well, we could try to fit in with these biological bodies," suggested Rose halfheartedly.

"No, Irgal is right. Look at us - we have abilities that far exceed anything mortals can do!" disagreed Dirk.

"Mortals? Is that what we call them now?" repeated Lilly with a smirk.

"It is not derogative, Lilly. It's what they are and what sets us apart from them! This divide would be nearly impossible to bridge!" contemplated Garrett.

"I guess I'm the living or dead proof of that," added Sven with a smile, and Lilly just nodded.

"We need a new home to be ourselves!" proposed Lydda emphatically.

"I agree with that. If we are immortal and stay here, we would have to watch generation after generation is born, lives, and dies. We would repeatedly lose friends and loved ones, and I couldn't bear that," divulged Angela.

(Feeling of certainty) "Tigger not want to fix problems forever. Tigger not god!" complained the big cat.

"OK, we will remove ourselves from the affairs of mortals, and I believe that to be for the best," summarized Dirk and maintained, "but we still have nowhere to go!"

(Feeling of uncertainty) "I might have a place we could use...," suggested L.

"Great, but how do we get there?" wondered Garrett.

"I will just trigger the biomechanical tools, and you will be transferred!" explained the AI.

"You will dissolve us again while we are awake?" gasped Angela and cringed.

"Well, yes. I don't think it is wise to use the transfer pods on Alcatraz!" L reminded her.

"Good point, but...," conceded Angela unhappily.

"Wait a minute! What about me? I have no biological body!" pointed Sven out nervously.

(Feeling of mischief) "Sorry, Sven, you are out of luck. You'll have to stay here!" answered L dryly.

"WHAT!?!?" yelled Sven in shock, and everyone else seemed unsure, but Irgal was laughing out loudly.

"How do you think I got to Latur and back?" she asked and raised an eyebrow at Sven.

"Oh," replied Sven meekly.

(Feeling of humor) "Of course, you can go to the new planet directly, Sven. I will guide you there through the simulation!" explained L and grinned at his friend.

"Sometimes I wish you were just a dumb computer again," grumbled Sven, while everyone else was very amused.

"Truthfully, all of us could just go through the simulation," noted Rose, and Angela was delighted to hear that.

"Sure, but I'm not digging a dozen more graves!" complained Mario.

"That's right, we cannot leave these bodies behind, and they are just comatose, so we would have to kill them first," confirmed Lilly with a frown, and then she insisted, "sorry, Angie, but we have to be dissolved!"

"Ah shucks!" replied Angela and shuddered.

"The new planet has a transfer center, but it is still inactive. I will transfer you to my vessel in orbit and keep you in stasis for a little while until I have a way to get you to the surface!" explained L and requested, "Sven can help me with that, and with something else, I would like to try!"

"Oh, now you want my help after pulling my leg?" inquired Sven haughtily.

(Feeling of amusement) "Pretty, please?" asked L and smiled sweetly at Sven.

"Fine!" muttered Sven with feigned anger before he added eagerly: "Let's get started!"

78. Eden

The new world was more like Earth than Aureus had been. There was only one G2 class sun, and it was a little smaller, but only half as old as Earth'. This solar system had 14 planets and three within the habitable zone. The one closest to the sun was a desert world with only small oceans; the one further out had large polar caps and brutal winters, but the one the team was standing on right now was perfect: temperate climate, stable geology, calm weather patterns, and beautiful blue-green forests as far as the eye could see. The gravity was 1.2 g, slightly higher than Earth's, but not uncomfortably so.

The planet had two moons, smaller than Earth's but closer to it, and a strong magnetic field to protect it from solar wind and cosmic radiation. The oceans covered about 75% of the surface, a little more than Earth but comparable to Aureus. At 30%, the atmosphere had more Oxygen than Earth and nearly as much as Aureus. The other gases were mostly Nitrogen and Argon, with only traces of Carbon Dioxide.

The planet rotated a bit faster than Earth at 22 hours per day and the year was 330 days long. There were no seasons since the planet didn't have a tilted rotational axis, leading to a stable, pleasant climate. The wildlife on the three continents and numerous islands seemed smaller, which was not unexpected on a world with higher gravity and mainly was harmless to the new colonists.

It has been two weeks, Earth time, since the group had left Aureus and were left in stasis on L's vessel. Today, L had used L39's invention and had dropped everyone from orbit in egg-shaped landing pods.

Now, the group was standing in a wide clearing, but not all were awake yet. Garrett had insisted on leaving them in stasis for safety until the team had thoroughly surveyed the new planet. The ground they were standing on right now was covered with blue moss and dotted with many colorful wildflowers. Something like a bird was singing in the distance, and a soft breeze carried a pleasantly sweet smell. There was a large central structure in the middle of the clearing, surrounded by a few dozen smaller dwellings. To the left of the settlement was a sizable lake, and to the right, a broad open plain plowed for agriculture.

The whole group had bodies again, but Sven was still in ascended form. L offered to recreate his body too, but Sven declined and insisted he would do that himself when they settled down. But this was the first time that L was in a fully biological body! With Sven's assistance, he had chosen an Aurean male, and there was some resemblance to Dirk, likely because L had added parts of Dirk's DNA to the transfer matrix. Everyone congratulated the former AI on this extraordinary evolutionary step.

"Thank you!" said L, a little embarrassed by all the attention, and added, "now I'm really like you!"

"You have always been like us, L - just a little more powerful and digital!" quipped Lilly and hugged L's new body.

"I guess, but it's so nice to share the biological experience with all of you, but I will need time to get used to it. This is very different from a digital existence!" admitted L, as he returned Lilly's embrace.

"Take it slow, L. We have all the time in the Universe now!" observed Dirk and changed the subject, "but tell us more about this planet!"

"Yes, it's lovely! When did you discover this place, and why didn't you tell us about it sooner?" complained Lydda playfully.

"I discovered it right before Dirk's death. After that, I didn't think it was all that important anymore," disclosed L.

"Well, I'm alive again, and this place is marvelous!" replied Dirk with joy.

"It's a real garden of Eden! Well, done, L!" praised Garrett.

"Let's call it that - Eden!" exclaimed Rose in excitement.

"If everyone agrees, let's call it that!" concurred Angela and clapped her hands.

"When did you build all these structures?" asked Ngazetungue a moment later.

"I've built them over the years. I wanted this planet - Eden - to be Aureus' first colony someday," explained L.

"In a sense, that's what it will be," remarked Victor.

"I estimated that it would take a century or more before Aureus was ready to reach for the stars, so I took my time with the construction to get everything right. But it is all finished now!" elaborated L.

"Can we take a look?" asked Sven, eager to explore.

"Absolutely not!" insisted L sharply, and Sven looked at him chastised and befuddled, but everyone was just laughing.

"Of course, you can, Sven!" said L with a big grin a moment later.

"Stupid box of wires!" grumbled Sven, but he was grinning, too.

The whole group marched to the new complex and explored every nook and cranny for the next few hours. The buildings were kept clean and well-maintained by a few dozen autonomous androids. The bungalows that surrounded the main building were much more spacious than their old quarters on Aureus, and they had every amenity that an Aurean, a Latura, a hybrid, or cat could appreciate. There was even a little garden with flowers and vegetables attached to each unit. But Dirk marveled even more at his new workshop! He had to remind himself that it wasn't his workshop anymore since Rose and Garvan were the lead engineers now, but he was impressed by how innovative L had designed the building and how well he had stocked it with tools and supplies.

"Do we still need bioreactors and agriculture?" wondered Irgal when they toured the large mess hall and kitchen area.

"We don't, but our biological bodies do!" explained Lilly and stated, "they have to eat and drink, and some work and exercise is good for them too!"

"Do I have to cook for you ungrateful slobs again?" complained Yebin in jest.

"Not unless you want me to cook?" teased Mario and tickled Yebin.

"No way! That would be a steady diet of booze and junk food," argued Lilly with exasperation, "we would have to get new bodies every few years! Yebin, please cook for us, dear!"

"Well, if you insist," replied Yebin with a feigned sigh, but she was already rummaging through every drawer and cabinet, checking on pots, pans, and kitchen utensils.

For the next few hours, everyone was milling about the little town, checking out the housing, the sports facilities, the pools, and other features. Meanwhile, Angela, Garrett, and Victor were busy inspecting the security systems L had implemented on Eden.

"This place is fantastic, L!" acclaimed Garrett after they had finished their rounds and added confidently, "very safe and secure! I think we can go ahead and wake the first sleepers!"

"Life will be even better than on Aureus. I love how you designed the pools, L!" praised Lydda excitedly, and Irgal readily agreed with her.

(Feeling of happiness) "Planet smells better than Aureus!" observed Tigger.

Although Tigger got used to the sweet, pungent smell of lichen and fungi on Aureus eventually, his delicate nose has never liked it very much.

"Let me guess; you marked the new planet? Did you eat a treesquid again?" mocked Lilly, remembering how they had arrived on Aureus so long ago.

(Feeling of amusement) "Tigger marked, must be done! But animals small and tasty!" jested the big cat, and Lilly just rolled her eyes in response.

"I think we should start with the original settlers from Aureus. They have the most experience colonizing a new world!" suggested Ngazetungue a few moments later.

Everyone thought that Ngazetungue's idea was sensible, and they decided to proceed in that manner. The new transfer center wasn't as big as the one on Alcatraz island on Aureus. It only had a dozen chambers, and it would take about a day to replenish the matrix after every use, so they would have to make a selection on the order of transfers.

"I'm still miffed that we had to make new bodies, and mine got killed when we didn't have to do any of that!" complained Sven playfully.

"We didn't know, Sven. We did what we thought was necessary, and we did a darn good job!" replied Rose proudly and reminded him, "besides, all the sleepers will still need bodies!"

"Yes, I have prepped the chambers and installed Rose and Sven's protocols. I couldn't have programmed it any better!" lauded L, and then he added, "the sleepers are awake in the simulation and await transfer."

"Well, then let's do it!" suggested Dirk and started walking to the big building that housed the transfer pods.

A few minutes later, Nari was the first to arrive in a transfer pod. The matrix did its magic, and Nari's new biological body formed right in front of the team's curious eyes. But then something unusual happened: instead of waking up in her new body, as the team had done on Aureus, Nari simply appeared right in front of the pod.

"This feels strange!" she said, confused.

First, she looked at the team, then turned around and stared at her completed physical form, still confined within the transfer pod.

"Uhm looks like I was wrong; they don't need bodies either," observed Rose while Nari turned around and shrugged her shoulders.

"I feel fine, but how do I get into my body?" she wondered.

"Sister, just slide into it!" advised Yebin and pointed at the pod.

"OK,…," replied Nari, unconvinced, but she followed instructions, and a moment later, the biological body opened its eyes, and Nari climbed out of the pod.

"What has happened to me?" asked Nari nervously, looking at Dirk for an explanation.

"Something profound, Angel. You have ascended, just like all of us!" answered Dirk with a big smile.

"I can be inside my body and outside of it?" inquired Nari.

"Yup! Creepy stuff, but it's entertaining, too!" joked Mario.

"Just make sure that your body is resting safely and comfortably when you do that, Darling. It goes into a coma when your essence isn't in it, so it could get hurt falling!" warned Lilly and welcomed Nari with a hug.

"That's something we should discuss. Do we want biological bodies, even though we don't need them anymore?" asked Angela, and everyone, including Nari, quickly raised their hand to confirm.

"That was the fastest vote ever!" jested Dirk.

"Can these bodies have children?" questioned Nari.

"They have all the reproductive organs, so they should be fertile. I'm sure we could make healthy babies!" assured Lilly, and then she asked, "but will the children be anything like us?"

"Biologically, they will be like us!" confirmed Sven before he noted, "but without actual children, we won't know if they have ascended."

(Feeling of certainty) "Kittens not ascended!" interjected Tigger.

"How do you know that, Tigger?" wondered Lilly.

"Ascension comes from mind, not body," answered Tigger.

"I cannot prove it, but I also believe that to be true!" agreed Dirk.

"Then we shouldn't have children with these bodies. No parent should outlive their child, and we would outlive not only our children but all future descendants

307

as well. It would be heartbreaking!" remarked Yebin saddened, and many agreed with that somber assessment.

"We should have this discussion once more when everyone is awake. Then we will vote on what to do!" concluded Dirk.

79. Sunset

Soon, Wendji, Lennard, Nancy, Alvar, and Lenna were transferred as well, and that evening, the group watched the first sunset on Eden from the rooftop of the main complex. L's autonomous androids provided some basic foodstuff, including a snack that was a lot like popcorn. The treat was an instant success with the group.

"I have a question that has puzzled me since my experience in Ngazetungue's hut. How can our bodies be solid? Shouldn't we be ghosts?" asked Yebin, poked her husband playfully in the ribs, and Sven winced because he was certainly solid, even without a natural body.

"Excellent question, without a conclusive answer!" replied Lennard.

"I have a theory: what we perceive as solid matter is 99% of empty space. Almost all the mass is centered in the atom's nucleus, and the solidity is simply the repulsion from the outer electron shell," said Alvar and elaborated, "without the empty space, a person could be compressed to the size of a pinhead."

"OK, that makes sense, but it doesn't explain anything: one cannot create matter from nothing, which seems to be happening here," reasoned Lennard.

"You could create matter from energy - $E=MC^2$," interjected Dirk.

"But it would require a whole lot of energy to create an entire body!" replied Lennard and contended, "besides, that still doesn't explain how we can slide in and out of our biological ones, or walk through solid walls, or even wink out and reappear somewhere else in a split second."

"Your body is hollow," remarked Lilly suddenly and looked at Sven.

"Huh?" wondered Sven.

"You don't have organs, a brain, or anything like that. When you died, I ran a few tests on your new form. You are solid, but you have no pulse, no blood, no body temperature, and you don't need to breathe either," elaborated Lilly.

"I'm breathing, Lilly!" protested Sven, inhaling and exhaling deliberately.

"Out of habit, Sven, not out of necessity!" countered Lilly.

"Yeah, I think it will take us a long time to figure this out!" noted Dirk with a chuckle.

"It's magic!" speculated L, and everybody laughed that a former AI would voice such superstition.

"Magic, hmm. Do you remember when we found Ngazetungue, who insisted that we were spirits? Who would have thought that he was right all along?" asked Lilly, but Ngazetungue laughed aloud.

"Even when you told us differently, we always knew it to be true!" replied Wendji, and then she added with a big smile, "that's why I wanted to be like that, too!"

"I was awestruck, but Wendji saw the beauty in all of you!" admitted Ngazetungue.

"In all of us!" corrected Nari.

"Even me?" wondered Victor seriously.

"Or us?" questioned Mario while holding Nancy in his arms.

Neither Victor nor Mario nor Nancy had ever forgotten their past. After more than a century, they were still haunted by what they had done back on Earth.

"Of course!" insisted Nari and said, "we are all capable of doing terrible things, and we have done terrible things. But that is behind us now; we have come full circle! From now on, there will be only love, peace, and beauty!"

"We have come full circle," concurred Sven.

"Born again, and all sins are forgiven?" wondered Lilly skeptically, but then she said, "sounds like some religious nonsense, but I guess it might be true this time!"

"It is!" agreed Lenna, and the others did too, but Dirk had an unconvinced look on his face.

"Husband, why did you not want to be with us?" wondered Nari when she noticed.

"Like I told Wendji before, I wanted to make room for the next generations," answered Dirk, subdued, but Lilly snorted loudly.

"It is time to tell them the whole truth, *swiahn*!" encouraged Lydda.

"Kittycat, please…," retorted Dirk and shook his head.

(Feeling of honesty) "Dirk cannot, but Lydda should!" added Tigger.

"I will tell them then!" insisted Lydda and said, "what Dirk mentioned to Wendji was true, but he omitted something important. Dirk didn't want to be uploaded because he thought he didn't deserve an afterlife. He still doesn't believe he deserves to be ascended either."

"If he doesn't deserve it, nobody does!" contended Lennard and rolled his eyes.

"That's right; Dirk is a wonderful person!" added Nancy.

"Please…," begged Dirk again and covered his face with the palms of his hands.

"Dirk thinks that he is too flawed and has made too many mistakes in his life. He is ashamed of that!" elaborated Lydda.

"I was once perfect, but I do not miss it, father!" interjected L and stated, "one can either be perfect or sapient, but not both. It's the imperfections that make us sapient: I can doubt, I can fear, I can love, and sometimes make silly choices. A machine knows no fear, no love, no doubt, and all choices are dictated by logic alone. It is perfect, but that perfection makes sapience irrelevant!"

"He can forgive everyone else, but never himself!" continued Lydda after a brief pause.

"I have done so much worse than you, Boss!" quipped Mario, and Victor silently nodded in agreement.

"Dirk still feels responsible for our transformation and the deaths of the volunteers on Earth and Alcatraz. He believes he was negligent, maybe even reckless with their lives and ours!" explained Lilly.

(Feeling of sadness) "Is what gave bad dreams. Not easy to heal!" divulged Tigger.

"Dirk has the utmost confidence in all of us but very little in himself. He leads out of duty, but he constantly questions his ability to guide us correctly," added Lydda.

"Doubt is one prerequisite of a good leader, and a sense of duty is the other. Bad leaders are overconfident, reckless, and depraved, and they indulge in the power!" injected Irgal.

Dirk removed the hands from his face for a brief moment and looked at the former Administrator. She looked back at him and gave him a knowing smile, but the rest of the group didn't notice that.

"Without Dirk, I would not exist!" countered L.

"Without Dirk, there would be no Aureus!" added Alvar.

"Ridiculous! Without you, none of us would be here right now!" concluded Garrett, looking straight at his friend, but Dirk avoided the gaze, said nothing and stared at the back of his hands.

"All these years, I had you dispel my doubts about myself. You were so confident, so self-assured. I never imagined that you questioned yourself," said Angela, with tears in her eyes, and apologized, "I slapped you when I should have held you tightly! I've been an awful wife; I'm so sorry, Love!"

"Angie, don't beat yourself up!" interrupted Lilly with a frown and stated, "Dirk holds himself to standards that not even a god could meet. So, of course, he fails, and that depresses him greatly. But Dirk measures us by a much shorter stick and forgives all our follies too readily."

"Is that true, Husband?" inquired Nari.

"Lydda and Tigger know that it is," conceded Dirk uncomfortably.

"Why would you do that, Dirk?" wondered Wendji, but Dirk just shook his head.

"I will explain, but understand this first: he deeply loves and respects everyone here. However, we are children to him. He doesn't see any of us as his intellectual equals," revealed Lydda and then added, "only Lilly comes close."

"I wish you wouldn't have told them that, Kittycat. I'm very sorry and ashamed of my prejudice," mumbled Dirk and stared at the ground, unable to look anyone in the eye.

"Prejudice? It's the truth! We are not your intellectual equals," declared Ngazetungue and then claimed, "I'm not offended; I'm proud of you, Dirk!"

"Yeah, duh, I knew that since I was 14 years old!" giggled Rose, but then she added firmly, "if we mess up, you shouldn't go easy on us. If we are idiots, call us idiots! I was an idiot when I first came to Aureus. And you shouldn't be too hard on yourself; you got my sister for that, or Angela when she gives you a good beating! If you make a mistake, apologize, learn the lesson and move on - hell, you taught me that! Sometimes, you are such a dork; you never have to be perfect for us!"

"I'm not too hard on him!" grumbled Lilly and stared at Rose.

Rose just smirked in response while Dirk was mortified. He didn't know what to say or do; he just wanted to be far, far away from here. Lydda sensed that her *swiahn* was miserable and ashamed.

"When I switched with Dirk for the first time, I braced myself for the onslaught of raw, savage emotions that all humans carry inside of them. But my own prejudice expected to find a simpler mind than that of a Latura because humans are a younger, less evolved species," observed Lydda and revealed, "I was right about the emotions, but I was very wrong about Dirk's mind!"

Lydda stopped and collected her thoughts for a moment. The others patiently anticipated her story to continue while Dirk was still covering his face with his hands.

"We were making love at the time, but Dirk never stopped thinking. At first, he analyzed the anatomical differences between a Latura and a human woman's reproductive organs. Then Dirk studied my neck and got fascinated by my gills. His mind was speculating about the evolutionary process that led to their development, he correctly estimated by their size the Oxygen content of the oceans on Latur, and then he theorized why terrestrial mammals, even the ones fully adapted to life at sea, had never developed gills on Earth. His thoughts, calculations, and hypotheses became exponentially more complex after that!"

"While you were having sex?" gasped Nancy, and everybody chuckled.

"Yes, and it was wonderful for both of us! We made our beautiful daughters that day!" noted Lydda and continued, "but Dirk's mind never slowed down, and his thoughts were so intricate and complicated that I couldn't follow them. I felt like a child again, trying to comprehend what the adults were talking about."

Dirk had removed his hands from his face and was somewhat reluctantly listening to Lydda's story now. She looked fondly at him, and he gave her a pained smile in return.

"Dirk's mind is a marvel and a mystery. The *swiahn* bond enables me to know all of Dirk, but I have accepted that there are things that I will never completely understand about him," concluded Lydda.

"Join the club!" interjected Lilly with a grunt.

"I agree that he is exceptional, but as Nancy said earlier, all that during sex?" questioned Wendji, wide-eyed.

"Oh, yes! I have to answer quite a few medical questions while doing it. Angela, Nari, and Rose have told me of similar episodes," confirmed Lilly nonchalantly and conceded, "but the sex is good. Thinking turns Dirk on!"

"Uhm, did you forget that I'm right here, Sweetie?" asked Dirk rhetorically, now a little annoyed that they were talking about him as if he wasn't present.

"Would you prefer if we gossip behind your back, Honey? We do that too, you know!" replied Lilly and grinned at him.

"Actually, yes! I would prefer that!" countered Dirk and revealed, "and just so you all know, thinking turns Lilly on, too! During sex, I have to answer a bunch of science questions myself, usually just before she climaxes!"

"Touché!" admitted Lilly and laughed out loud.

"Guys, I'm sorry, but I am what I am. I have tried, but I've never been able to fit in anywhere. Yes, I cannot stop thinking, but I always believed that's normal for everybody!" apologized Dirk.

"Trivial thoughts are normal - should I eat, should I use the bathroom, should I take a nap or a walk - but your thoughts are never trivial, Husband. It is what defines you!" responded Nari thoughtfully.

(Feeling of amusement) "Dirk always different because must be so!" interjected Tigger cryptically, and Lilly nodded ever so slightly.

"But it doesn't even matter! You fit in with us. You always have and always will, and I'll slap anyone silly who says otherwise!" jested Angela, which solicited many laughs and nods among the group.

Dirk feared that he had offended his friends and family, but now he was grateful for how this discussion had seemingly concluded. In a way, it felt liberating to have the truth finally out in the open. Alas, it was not over yet!

"Have you noticed how readily Dirk forgives betrayal? For heaven's sake, we ignored his final wish, and he didn't even yell at us. No, instead, Dirk commended us for doing the right thing. Dirk forgave Mario for trying to extort us, and he forgave Sophia almost immediately and then championed for her to stay on Aureus. He forgave Victor for sending assassins after us, one of which almost killed him, and Dirk forgave me after I manipulated him into all of this!" recalled Lilly and stated, "I would be outraged, furious even! If I can forgive any of that, it would take a long time. But not for Dirk."

"Lilly…," interrupted Lydda, and even Tigger seemed uneasy, but Lilly was determined to finish what she had started.

"Yes, we are children to him, but that's not all!" continued Lilly and revealed, "Dirk is always prepared for betrayal. That's why he doesn't get upset. It's already there in his mind. He expects all of us to betray him, sooner or later, one way or another. Sadly, Dirk is right - we have, and we will do it again someday!"

314

(Feeling of unease) "Tigger betray Dirk once," acknowledged Tigger as he remembered when he said in frustration that Dirk didn't belong with the group.

"I have done it too! Even though it was in an alternate reality, it was still a betrayal!" admitted Lydda.

"I'm ashamed now!" uttered Nari and frowned.

"Don't be, Angel," implored Dirk before he added, "but what Lilly said is correct. However, none of you should worry about that. Being prepared for betrayal just eases the pain when it happens, that's all!"

"…*when* it happens…," echoed Lilly and cast her eyes down.

"You mistrust us?" questioned Garrett in disbelief.

"If I mistrusted you, I would be disinclined to deal with you. I'm not reluctant and have never been reluctant. Mistrust and anticipation of betrayal are not the same things for me," answered Dirk, but he was afraid they wouldn't or couldn't understand that.

"Still, that's a paranoid way to live life, Dirk!" exclaimed Nancy.

"I'm not paranoid, Nancy! *I am prepared for the worst, but hope for the best* - Benjamin Disraeli," quoted Dirk and slightly shrugged his shoulders.

"If we don't want Dirk around anymore, he wouldn't be upset, wouldn't argue with us, wouldn't beg us to reconsider, and he wouldn't even ask why. Instead, Dirk would graciously thank us for the good times and sincerely wish us good luck for the future. Then he would leave, and we would never see him again," predicted Lilly quietly, and Dirk knew in his heart that he would react precisely the way Lilly had just described it.

"I can't even think of any scenario where we would want Dirk gone, but after all this time and everything we have gone through together, would he just walk away from us, his friends and family?" gasped Sven.

"Nobody acts like that!" disagreed Lennard and vigorously shook his head.

But Dirk couldn't even imagine acting any other way. There was no point in fighting the inevitable by his logic: take your losses and walk away; it was the healthy, rational choice!

"Yes, if we want him to leave, or if he thinks we want him to leave, Dirk would go without objections, and he has done just that in my *irtaljan* experience. After I rejected him, he left us quietly to live out his days alone on Alcatraz!" admitted Lydda and disclosed, "I still fear that it might come true one day!"

(Feeling of agreement) "Dirk going away almost certain. Only small chance that Dirk stays!" interjected Tigger before he added happily, "but happened!"

"Your fear already came true, Lydda. Dirk was the only one who chose to die instead of being uploaded. He wanted to exit graciously to shed the responsibility for his sake, but mostly for ours because he always thought we deserved a better leader!" replied Lilly.

Dirk was amazed at how well Lilly knew him. In some ways, Lilly still understood him better than even Lydda could with the *swiahn* bond. He had never told her any of that, yet she had deduced it correctly, all on her own.

"Dirk guided us so well! He was, and still is, the best leader we could have had!" interjected Wendji, and Lenna made the Latura gesture of agreement.

"Yes, but we dragged him right back into the fray after his resurrection!" conceded Rose and shook her head.

"Good, and I'm not one bit sorry for that!" exclaimed Angela, staring angrily at Dirk and challenging, "you are a vital organ to us. A heart or brain cannot *graciously exit* the body because the body would die. You are not responsible for us, but you are responsible for being with us! Here is your place where you belong, and you're not going to wiggle yourself out of it again!"

"Are you going to slap me if I try?" quipped Dirk and wiggled his torso.

Dirk just didn't know what else he could say or do. Maybe humor could help in this impossible situation?

"Hell yeah!" grumbled Angela, and everyone laughed, but then she grinned broadly at him.

"As Tigger said earlier, we just have to remember and accept that Dirk is different from us!" concluded Lilly and fondly smiled at her husband.

At that moment, Dirk thought he heard a man faintly laughing at him inside his head, but then it was gone again.

80. Unpleasant Surprise

Dirk had sensed that Lilly didn't want to hurt or embarrass him. No, quite the opposite: she wanted to remind everyone else that they had wronged Dirk at one point or another. Dirk didn't like to discuss this any further, and fortunately for him, everybody else seemed to share that sentiment. For a few minutes, nobody said anything. They were either lost in their thoughts or just enjoying the beautiful view when one of Eden's two moons rose over the horizon.

"Dirk, do you still get sick when you visit the simulation?" asked Sven with a smirk and broke the awkward silence.

"No, I don't. Thankfully, it stopped completely when Lydda, Tigger, and I fought L39 digitally, but I don't know why!" answered Dirk very quickly, hoping that this change of topic would make them all forget about the previous discussion.

"I think I do. You are the most cerebral of us, as we have just established. Everything happens in your mind first, but your mind wasn't prepared for the simulation: your brain was confused and desperately tried to make sense of it. Just being Dirk made you nauseous!" postulated Lilly with a big grin and claimed, "but when you fought L39, you didn't have time to think; you just acted and did what needed to be done. That's when your mind accepted the digital reality."

"Sadly, you are probably right, Sweetie!" concurred Dirk humorously and said, "but thankfully, it's all gone now!"

"So, what should we do with the simulation?" wondered Lydda.

"We keep it, of course! If we don't have to live there, it's a fun place to visit!" claimed Yebin.

"Not only that, but we have created marvelous things there, and we should not delete them," observed Lilly and smiled at Lydda.

"The simulation is also like an enormous encyclopedia, the perfect reference database!" added Wendji, and Mario strongly agreed with her.

"L worked tirelessly to create and improve it for a hundred years. For that reason alone, we shouldn't discard it!" concluded Irgal and jested, "besides, I didn't get a chance to explore it at all!"

"All true, but we should make sure nobody gets uploaded anymore," suggested Dirk.

"We had the upload disabled, but I could remove that option altogether," offered L.

"Please leave the option in place, L. There might come a time when we need it once again," cautioned Alvar and maintained, "but we should never use it unless we agree to that unanimously!"

"That's sensible," assented Angela, and many others nodded.

"Perhaps we can use the simulation for our security?" recommended L after a brief pause.

"Good idea!" agreed Garrett immediately and noted, "we need to ensure that we don't get unwelcome visitors here."

"This time, we don't need more settlers, and we don't want to see humans from Earth on our doorstep, not even in the distant future," grumbled Lilly.

"We don't want any mortals to show up, not just humans. I think we have to make sure that they cannot find us and that we don't interfere with them either," opined Lennard.

"Physically, the simulation spans over 5,000 lightyears. It has hubs in 34 different star systems. The main hub used to be on Aureus' moon Pluto where Dirk's tomb was, but now I have moved it to the smaller of Eden's two moons," reported L and suggested, "we could transform the simulation into an extensive surveillance net, and since we still can be digital at will, it would be easy to link these new security measures directly to us. That way, not just me but all of us would immediately know if someone tries to get to Eden!"

"We can be digital at will?" wondered Wendji.

"Of course. I just finished checking for malicious code L39 might have left behind in the simulation," answered L and said, "but now I'm here in my new biological body!"

"Amazing! I'm going to try this!" declared Lenna, and her physical body went limb momentarily, but then she returned and exclaimed, "yes, I was in my pool in the simulation! It's fun!"

"The simulation has transformed into a quantum link. We can use it just like the mental link!" proposed Sven.

"We could even call it that, Sven!" concurred L.

"Is it possible to obscure this complex?" asked Angela a few moments later and changed the topic of the discussion.

"A projection!" exclaimed Rose and elaborated, "it would take some doing, but we could make a holographic projection big enough to shroud this entire area!"

"That's the idea, Rose, but you think too small!" teased L and explained, "I want to obscure the entire planet."

"Oh!" gasped Rose happily and suggested, "that would be awesome if you can do that! L, make it appear as a lifeless desert world or something uninviting like that!"

"I will also shield the electromagnetic and light emissions from the complex. Lastly, my most ambitious idea is to make our sun appear unstable!" remarked L and claimed, "no advanced civilization would visit such a star system because it would be too dangerous to settle and highly unlikely to contain any life forms to study!"

"Perfect!" extolled Lilly and got up from her chair.

The sun had set, and the group left the roof to return to the main hall of the complex downstairs. As they were walking through the hallways, L suddenly stopped.

"Father, I forgot to show you your new office!" conveyed L excitedly and pointed at the wall: there was a tiny keypad that looked like a climate control unit.

"New office? Do I need one?" wondered Dirk, looking around for a door.

"You need a place to deal with all the leadership stuff, Honey. I won't let you do that in our new home!" replied Lilly sweetly.

"Do we still need a leader?" asked Dirk.

"Of course, we do. Somebody has to deal with the annoying little problems that will inevitably crop up!" teased Garrett.

"OK, maybe. But why me?" questioned Dirk because he had so hoped that his days as a leader were finally over.

"You are the most qualified, and we already voted on it - unanimously!" stated Angela, and everyone in the group signaled their assent.

"You did? When? Do I get a say in this?" inquired Dirk flabbergasted.

"Not really, Boss! We elected you as Chancellor for Life, and since we are immortal now, you will be in office eternally! Eden is officially a dictatorship!" snickered Mario and patted Dirk on the back.

"Are you kidding me?" gasped Dirk.

"Maybe not today or tomorrow, but someday we will need a leader again, *swiahn*. We know and have accepted that it will and must be you!" noted Lydda earnestly.

(Feeling of agreement) "Lydda right. Dirk knows too!" added Tigger.

"Fine!" sighed Dirk before contending forcefully, "but this is not and will never be a dictatorship! Are we clear?"

"Yes, Boss!" answered Mario and stood at attention while the rest of the group laughed and did the same.

"Oh, just show me the office, L!" uttered Dirk and shook his head in exasperation.

"I know that you liked solitude and silence when you focused on your work on Aureus!" observed L and pointed at the mysterious keypad on the wall.

"Yeah, he yelled at us whenever we disturbed him! He got really cranky!" teased Rose.

"You guys disturbed me every five minutes. Who wouldn't get cranky?" grumbled Dirk, but he wasn't that serious.

"I made this special room soundproof, and you can seal it off from the rest of the complex completely. It will give you all the privacy you need!" announced L proudly and then typed in a few numbers on the keypad, and suddenly the whole wall slid open.

"It is still unfurnished, but take a look!" recommended L when the walls stopped sliding.

Dirk took one step towards the entrance and immediately backed up again. The room was a cubic box, about 25 feet in all directions, and its walls were clad in pitch black onyx. It was dimly lit and empty except for an abandoned chair in the center of the room. Dirk felt that he knew this place. He had no idea how or why, but it made him apprehensive. He almost thought he heard a voice talking, but that was only L.

"Do you not like it, father?" asked L with a bit of disappointment in his voice.

"No, L, it's fine, I...," answered Dirk slowly, unsure what to say.

"We can add a nice desk and better lighting!" suggested L.

"Yes, it's a little dim. But it will make a good office, thank you, son!" responded Dirk politely, hiding his feelings about this room as best as possible.

Then Dirk quickly turned around and walked away.

81. Reminiscence

The next day, Dirk explored the new workshop thoroughly. He was quite engrossed in compiling a list for L of all the items and tools he should manufacture, so he didn't notice when Irgal entered the building.

"Dirk," said Irgal in English, but Dirk didn't hear her because he had just started a circular saw, and the noise drowned out everything else.

"Dirk!" yelled Irgal as loud as she could, and Dirk looked up, startled, and switched off the noisy tool.

"Little One! Sorry, I was checking the machinery!" apologized Dirk in Loyt and smiled at her.

"I'm not surprised to find you here!" contended Irgal and grinned at him.

"Yeah, my hiding spots are predictable, aren't they?" chuckled Dirk and asked, "what can I do for you, Irgal?"

"It's too nice of a day to be cooped up in a workshop. Let's take a walk to the lake?" suggested Irgal.

"Good idea; I was just about done here anyway!" concurred Dirk and put the tablet down on the workbench.

"Let's go!" encouraged Irgal as she exited, and Dirk swiftly followed her out the door.

The lake was a good two kilometers away from the workshop, and for the longest time, Dirk and Irgal simply walked in silence, enjoying the sunny day, the lush trees, and the sounds of nature all around them.

"Irgal, did you know that we would win?" asked Dirk suddenly over the direct link because he was curious about the vision the other Irgal had received in that alternate reality.

"The different memories of the time when I've met you on Latur are now superimposed: I have accepted that the two versions have converged into this reality!" remarked Irgal thoughtfully, and then she revealed, "my prophecy showed me the war with Earth, the carnage in the jungle of Aureus, and the unspeakable slaughter on Latur. I knew that even the simulation wasn't safe. But it didn't show me how it would end!"

"I suspected that you didn't know the outcome," conveyed Dirk, and then he lauded, "not a bad way to think about all this craziness, Irgal. I should do the same and just accept that everything was real. It will keep us both sane!"

"I hope so!" quipped the Latura woman and then asked, "did you know that our scholars on Latur always thought that alternate realities were just metaphorical?"

"But your founder Irtaljan experienced it, didn't she?" questioned Dirk.

"Our records from the days of Irtaljan are about as comprehensive as your records of the Roman Empire. Good, but not complete!" explained Irgal and disclosed, "many of us believed that Irtaljan made her choice for Latur based on logic, not strange visions!"

"I can understand that. Sound reasoning could have led to the same result!" acknowledged Dirk.

"Only when you experienced it did Latur take it seriously, but some dismiss it even now!" replied Irgal.

"Well, there is no proof, just my word!" conceded Dirk.

"Your word counts for a lot on Latur, Dirk!" countered Irgal, but then she said, "you are right; your word, or Lydda's, wouldn't have been enough. But all the other verifiable miracles of Aureus made it credible, and your immense popularity helped, too!"

"I'm glad that they like us on Latur!" articulated Dirk.

"Like you? If we had royalty, you and Lydda could have been our king and queen in your time, and there is nobody on Latur who doesn't adore Tigger, even today!" revealed Irgal humorously, and then she asked, "did you know that they built a statue of him in one of our biggest parks?"

"Wow! Tigger deserves all the recognition, much more than me!" answered Dirk humbly.

Irgal and Dirk passed through a stretch of open land. A small herd of gastropods was slowly grazing on the blue moss that grew everywhere on this continent. These mollusks were essentially giant snails, and Lilly had dubbed them aptly escargots. They were the most massive creatures on land, the size of a fully grown bull but ultimately harmless. Like their smaller counterparts on Earth, these animals carried a giant shell on their backs and retreated to it at certain times of the day to rest or when danger approached.

323

"Lydda told me that you have been in two more realities?" inquired Irgal after a slight pause in the discussion.

"Yes, they both happened on Earth. In the first reality, I was never transformed; instead, a meteor injured me. I continued to live my life on Earth as a regular human but with all the memories of Aureus!" explained Dirk, hesitant to say any more, but Irgal noticed that right away and pressed on.

"And the second one?" she inquired, and Dirk sighed deeply.

"We never made our escape to Aureus. Lilly was murdered, and I tried to make Earth a better place for her sake. I failed!" divulged Dirk somberly, and Irgal was quiet for a moment, but then she took his hand in hers.

"It was not your fault!" she said consolingly.

"How would you know that, Little One?" asked Dirk.

"You were destined to fail!" insisted Irgal, but then she professed, "just don't ask me how I know that - I just do!"

"Maybe you are right, but it was painful, and it still is!" admitted Dirk with a sigh, and Irgal gently squeezed his hand to comfort him.

"Do you think this is another episode, another reality, and we'll suddenly wake up in a different timeline?" she questioned after a while.

"Lilly wondered the same thing when I told her about it after she resurrected me!" observed Dirk and noted, "I don't know, Irgal, but I hope it isn't! This one is lovely!"

"It is!" concurred Irgal while Dirk just nodded, and they continued their walk.

They stopped for a little while when a pack of four-legged, lizard-like predators was circling one of the escargots but quickly gave up when the giant mollusk retreated into its shell. The predators were the size of Komodo dragons and looked a lot like those giant lizards, but their scales were red with spots. Alvar had named them *setac*, after a similar species native to Latur. They were curious and opportunistic but not a real threat to the new colonists. After Tigger had killed a couple of them, they gave the settlement a wide berth.

The lizards weren't the apex predators of Eden, either. That title belonged to a massive plant, and Dirk and Irgal were just passing it. The size of an oak tree, the plant employed the same snapping petals as a Venus flytrap, except that these petals were as big as a small car. The plant sensed approaching prey with its root system in the ground. When the victim was close enough, one branch with petals would swoop down and engulf the whole body, and then it would quickly lift it back up to begin the digestion process. The plant was dangerous but stationary and, therefore, easily avoided. It was also gorgeous. The petals were golden with black stripes, and the tree's stem sprouted an enormous purple flower on the top.

Finally, they arrived at the lake's shore, Irgal sat down on a big, mossy rock, and Dirk found a place beside her.

"What they said about you the other day…," Irgal started saying in English.

"…was all true, I'm afraid!" Dirk finished her sentence in Loyt.

For many years, the two of them had made it a habit to talk to each other in their respective vocal languages rather than relying solely on telepathic communication. It was good practice for both, but this verbal exchange would have appeared very odd to an outsider: the human would speak in a strange and challenging language, while the cat-like alien would answer in fluent English.

"Of course! They didn't say anything I did not know about you long ago," acknowledged Irgal.

"But?" inquired Dirk.

"Your wives represent the aspects of your character: Lilly mirrors your intelligence, Rose is your ingenuity, Angela embodies your courage, Nari your kindness, and Lydda your honesty!" recounted Irgal quietly before she asked, "I was never your wife, but what did you see in me: a friend, a daughter, a lover, the mighty Administrator, or just a silly girl who was obsessed with you?"

"All of the above, Little One. But you forgot the most important thing - my confidant!" answered Dirk and winked at her.

"I know you well, but I cannot know you as well as Lydda or Tigger!" countered Irgal, unsure what Dirk implied.

"No, not that kind of confidant. Of all the people, only you could relate to my plight!" corrected Dirk.

"Leadership!" exclaimed Irgal, nodding as humans do.

"Yes. The group was right, and I was just in denial. I have always been their leader, even when I wasn't Chancellor anymore. I tried to escape that by founding the Court of Sapience, insisting that the powers must remain separate, but they didn't care much!" quipped Dirk and rolled his eyes.

"Naturally!" giggled Irgal and then added more seriously, "they were good leaders, but they always had a safety net in you!"

"Yes, I suppose. You were the only one who understood the burden, and yours was much greater than mine. Two billion souls - the responsibility must have been crushing. You are the strongest person I know, Irgal!" Dirk complimented her, but Irgal just raised an eyebrow.

"The Administrator isn't that powerful, and you know that. But you are not wrong, *jigal*...," she agreed a moment later.

The Loyt word *jigal* is translated as *my secret* in English. Irgal had fondly called Dirk that since they had spent their first Transformation Day together. In turn, Dirk had named her Little One, not because of her stature - Irgal was nearly as tall as him - but in reference to her youth.

"Do you remember when you sent me that official invitation to visit a brand-new Latura colony?" questioned Dirk and looked at her expectantly.

"Oh, will we relive that disaster now?" asked Irgal, trying not to laugh aloud.

"When we arrived there, the colony was mostly unfinished. Only one building was habitable, and there was nobody except for a few construction androids. Even L wondered why I would visit there!" recounted Dirk.

"I think I must have made a mistake. I thought the colony was much further along," lied Irgal with a straight face.

Deception was alien to Latura, but Irgal had lived among humans for a long time when she was Latur's ambassador to Aureus. She became quite good at it over the years; however, she had never used it in negative ways.

"Right! We were slurping nothing but protein goo for three straight days!" teased Dirk and tickled her cat-like ears.

"That was so gross!" scoffed Irgal and made a face.

"And the gnats native to that planet were eating us alive. I had welts for a week after returning to Aureus!" complained Dirk playfully.

"Oh, me too. The bites were so itchy!" admitted Irgal and asked with exasperation, "why in Irtaljan's name did the transfer matrix not correct that?"

"It was a wonderful trip, Little One!" declared Dirk and smiled broadly at her.

326

"Three days of no *meeting of the minds*, no Council of Experts, no alien civilizations to contact, and no darn petitions to read. Nothing! Just you, me, and freedom!" exclaimed Irgal with joy.

"I felt as if I could breathe again!" concurred Dirk readily, and Irgal nodded the way humans do.

"Since we are rehashing old sins: do you recall when we went to L's observation post in the Orion nebula because you wanted me to witness the birth of a star?" asked Irgal a moment later.

"How could I forget? That was even more of a disaster than the gnats!" answered Dirk and shook his head.

"We were stuck in this tiny zero-G compartment; my pool on Latur was three times the size! We had no bed, no shower, and the toilet was an incinerator. I almost burnt my tail off!" summarized Irgal and looked sternly at him.

"At least we had real food!" countered Dirk defensively.

"The stupid star didn't ignite for five days! By that time, we both reeked so badly that they could probably smell us back on Aureus and Latur!" concluded Irgal and added joyfully, "it was awesome, *jigal!*"

"Yes, it was awesome, Little One!" cackled Dirk and delightfully slapped his knee.

"I never told anyone about it, not even Horvan!" divulged Irgal, more subdued.

"I did not either. Of course, Lydda and Tigger know, but they never said a word. I think they humored our little escapades!" mentioned Dirk and shrugged his shoulders.

"Horvan was my consort for over a hundred years. I loved him dearly, but he couldn't understand that I needed to get away once in a while to be free!" admitted Irgal and sighed a little.

"Yes, my wives, kids, and friends didn't either!" Dirk echoed her sentiments.

"Tyrval disapproved when the *meeting of the minds* chose me to be Administrator," said Irgal and disclosed, "I was sad because I thought he didn't believe in me."

"Oh, no! Tyrval was very proud of you; he told me so himself! But he wanted you to be unburdened, not chained to that office!" countered Dirk and looked at her thoughtfully.

"Yes, I know that now," responded Irgal and remarked, "I loved Gramps! I still miss him!"

"You and me both!" concurred Dirk and nodded.

Irgal was quiet while they both watched the azure-colored lake. Once every so often, a few fish-like creatures would break through the surface and fly for long stretches above the water before submerging into it again.

"Did you know that I came to Aureus just before…," Irgal started out saying a few minutes later, but she didn't finish that sentence, and instead, she recalled, "you looked so frail and miserable. You didn't respond when I talked to you."

"I know you were in the room. I felt your touch on my arm, but I was too weak to open my eyes!" avowed Dirk sadly.

"Lilly said that you would have only hours to live. All your wives and children asked me to stay with them by your side until the end, but I just couldn't!" admitted Irgal and revealed, "I made excuses about diplomatic obligations, but I just didn't want to see you die!"

"I understand that so well. I like my last memory to be that of the living person I cared for, not an empty husk!" acknowledged Dirk.

"The next day, you were gone. I stayed on Aureus for your funeral and relayed the condolences of the *meeting of the minds*. Then Garett gave a wonderful eulogy, and after that, all your friends and family said a few words as well. You touched so many lives!" recalled Irgal and smiled at him.

"Thank you; I didn't know that!" replied Dirk, and he very much appreciated her words.

"The last one to speak was John Doe. He recounted what had happened to him and how heavily it weighed on you all this time. He ended his speech with two words: *my savior*!" noted Irgal, and then she confessed, "that's when I lost it because you were my savior, too! I bawled my head off in Lydda's arms, and my aides were aghast by the breach of protocol. I just couldn't calm down until Carl came up to me and whispered in my ear that you weren't truly dead!"

"You knew, too?" wondered Dirk in surprise.

"I did, and the thought of seeing you again someday made my burden much easier to carry. Thank you for not being dead, *jigal*!" answered Irgal with sincere appreciation.

"It feels strange to say that you are welcome. Honestly, I was not sure if I should be alive again. It felt unnatural, ghoulish even. But I know better now, and I'm happy to live again and have you by my side, Little One!" stated Dirk and smiled at her.

"Will we have more disasters?" asked Irgal slyly.

"Two conditions: showers and no gnats!" insisted Dirk playfully and put his arm around her waist.

"Agreed!" confirmed Irgal immediately, but then she added with a giggle, "I'm sure we can find something even worse!"

82. The new Office

Of course, his friends had noticed Dirk's strange reaction to the new office. They felt guilty that they had forced him into a job he never wanted. The next day, Angela and Garrett talked to Dirk in private and offered to be the leaders instead of him. Alvar also approached him with the same sentiments, and Dirk sincerely appreciated their well-meant gestures, but he politely declined: they had chosen him, and Dirk would do his duty as best as he could!

"Honey, I will lead Eden if you want me to do that!" offered Lilly one day when they were sitting in the little garden behind their bungalow.

Dirk was taken by surprise! Leadership was the last thing Lilly ever wanted. She had adamantly refused to lead Aureus because of her *irtaljan* experience.

"Sweetie, your offer is…overwhelming, and I'm touched, but there is no way I can accept it, and you know that!" replied Dirk and looked her in the eyes.

"You know why I didn't want to lead Aureus. But this is a new world and a new me!" stated Lilly, firmly holding his gaze.

"I agree, and if you want to lead, you shall lead us!" acknowledged Dirk before noting, "but if you just want to carry the burden for me, I will not allow it!"

"I think I could do an adequate job, but you are a better leader. But I know you hate it, and I want you to be happy here because you earned that more than any of us!" remarked Lilly and caressed her husband's hand.

"Lilly, I'm happy!" admitted Dirk, but then he added with a sigh, "I have accepted that it is my destiny, or my penance, to lead these people, our people!"

"We betrayed you again, didn't we?" asked Lilly.

"Betrayal is a strong word, Sweetie. I would say you guys blindsided me, but I'm not upset!" answered Dirk and winked at her.

Lilly just looked at him and pursed her lips. She was about to say something, but instead, she just nodded.

"If the day comes when you cannot bear it any longer, can you promise me that you will accept my offer?" she asked solemnly.

"I promise that, Sweetie. Thank you so much!" responded Dirk gratefully and kissed her forehead.

The group spent the next few days sprucing up the barren room. First, Angela and Garrett installed the holographic projectors for the computer screens, then L added an interstellar communication device, should Dirk ever need to contact someone by such means. Rose wired in much better lighting and even built a new coffee machine for Dirk, and he appreciated that - ascended or not, Dirk was still a caffeine addict.

Mario stocked a small fridge with beer, Wendji added a few of Dirk's favorite books to a little bookshelf, Nancy and Lydda put pictures and other artwork on the walls, and Nari even brought a planter with a fragrant, flowering plant from the nearby forest. The autonomous androids added the final pieces: a massive, old-fashioned wooden desk and a comfortable, recycling office chair. When they had finished, the whole group gave Dirk a little tour. He was amazed and grateful for how much work they had done for him.

"Wow, it looks a lot better now, thank you guys!" exclaimed Dirk.

"Don't mention it, Boss! The least we could do after we sprung this on you!" replied Mario with a grin.

Dirk would use the office regularly, but he was still not entirely comfortable in that room, so he always left the sliding wall open.

"Why did I build you a soundproof office when you never close the door, father?" teased L one day.

"I think I like to hear the noise now!" answered Dirk with a smile, but he knew that his answer wasn't truthful, yet he couldn't figure out why.

83. Who are you? (Finale)

Still, the office came in handy because Garrett was right: if you were a caveman or an ascended being, life would always throw some pesky problems in your way, and someone, namely Dirk, would have to deal with them.

The most pressing matter was determining the order in which they would wake up the sleepers and transfer them to the planet, but that mainly depended on L's capacity to produce transfer matrix, so all Dirk had to do was set a simple schedule. Most other issues on Eden were minor, such as complaints about comatose bodies lying in the hallways, malfunctioning equipment, or just backed-up toilets.

But today, Dirk needed to concentrate. He was studying a long, legal treatise from an alien civilization. So, he used the remote control to shut the walls for the first time. The mechanism worked flawlessly, and Dirk was astonished at how quiet the room became. He diligently read the complicated legal works for the next hour, but then he decided to take a little break and get some coffee. When he got up from his chair, the lights suddenly dimmed and everything, except for the desk and chair, disappeared from view.

Suddenly, the instrumental version of an 80's song played in the background, and Dirk recognized it, but he could not remember the name or artist. Lilly used to have a little radio in the kitchen of their old home on Earth tuned to a 1980s music station. Dirk didn't particularly care for it, but Lilly enjoyed listening to her childhood music, so he had to listen to it, too.

"Well, that certainly saves me a lot of trouble!" noted the familiar male voice and snickered.

"What do you want this time?" questioned Dirk unhappily because now he remembered once again why he didn't like this room.

"What I always want - honest answers!" remarked the voice.

"Fine, but you will give me an answer first!" insisted Dirk.

"I guess you earned that: one question, one answer!" concurred the man.

"You said that this room is the only thing that is real. Can you explain that?" asked Dirk.

"The room isn't real; it's just a prop!" responded the voice and chuckled.

"That's not an answer!" countered Dirk.

"Reality is like an onion, layers upon layers. The further you go out, the more distorted, the more imaginary it becomes. Right now, we are at the very center!" explained the invisible man.

"But what is the point of this?" wondered Dirk.

"You have used up your one question already! Now it's my turn!" the voice reminded him.

"Ask!" relented Dirk with resignation.

"You tolerate the intolerant, you want to educate the ignorant, you attempt to convince the skeptical with reason and logic, and you try to pacify your enemies to spare their lives. Why do you bother?" questioned the voice.

"It is the right thing to do!" replied Dirk without hesitation.

"Here, you have the power to eradicate them completely, and that would be much simpler and a lot faster. We both know that!" stated the voice.

"Because that is wrong!" insisted Dirk.

"Is it? Just drown everything in that proverbial flood and start over fresh!" suggested the voice callously.

"I would become a genocidal maniac!" replied Dirk.

"Or God!" corrected the voice with a chuckled and claimed, "others have done it. The winner writes history, and your victory would be absolute. Nobody would or could ever question your methods, and nobody would ever judge you!"

"I would question them, and I would judge myself!" admitted Dirk, and he didn't like this discussion any more than the previous ones.

"Are you afraid of the consequences? We have already established that you are willing to sacrifice your life and the lives of your loved ones for your principles, so what's left to fear?" wondered the man, and then he mocked mercilessly: "Chicken?"

"I'm not afraid to do it; I'm afraid I might!" emphasized Dirk somberly.

"…and the logical reason for that?" questioned the voice.

"It is not who I am or want to be! All your questions don't have good answers!" yelled Dirk in frustration.

"That's the point! Truth hurts, doesn't it?" asked the voice rhetorically and then stated, "but that's what makes it real!"

"I suppose," conceded Dirk finally and sighed.

"I guess you did the best you could!" noted the man and concluded, "it was the last time we will meet like this!"

"Good! But I still want to know who you are!" insisted Dirk.

"Don't be a fool. You always knew!" retorted the voice dismissively.

Dirk realized who this man was for a brief moment, but then it was gone again, and he was standing befuddled in front of a coffee machine.

84. Biological L, Digital Dirk

L wasn't very good at being biological. He often ignored or misinterpreted his new body's requirements. He regularly forgot to eat and drink, and there were a few embarrassing moments when he ignored the restroom for too long. His body was also constantly sleep-deprived. In fact, the whole concept of sleeping was so foreign to L that Lilly became concerned that the body would suffer medical problems before too long. She modified a simple wristwatch to alert L to the needs of his body.

From then on, L would eat, drink, and exercise regularly. But sleeping was still a problem because, as artificial intelligence, L had never had to sleep before. He tried a few times, but his mind was simply too active to give his body the deserved rest. Eventually, Lilly advised him to leave his physical form for eight hours per day. L objected at first because he insisted on being like the rest of the group, but in the end, he followed the doctor's orders since there was no other healthy solution available.

Tigger finally fixed the problem, but even Tigger didn't exactly know how he did it. One day when L was in biological form, lounging on a couch in Dirk's dwelling, Tigger put him to sleep like he had done with Nancy so long ago. L rested deeply, snored loudly, but woke up refreshed and confused half a day later.

"There is a long gap in my biological memory and all my digital logs, too!" exclaimed L and panicked, "I stopped existing for 12 hours!"

"Yes, it's called sleep!" explained Lilly with a smirk while setting the breakfast table.

"But there is some weird, nonsensical data accumulated during that time! How? Why?" gasped L.

"That would be a dream," answered Lilly and rolled her eyes.

"Did you like it, L?" asked Dirk.

"It is a little scary to lose all control, but… I feel good!" replied L, yawning loudly, stretching his arms out, getting up from the couch, and walking to the kitchen table.

"You feel even better after this!" declared Rose with a grin, handed L a big mug of fresh coffee, and he sniffed it and then took a sip.

"Thank you, Rose. It's a little bitter but invigorating and full of flavor!" noted L, smiled, and sat down to share breakfast with Rose, Lilly, and Dirk.

"You can add milk and sugar if you like that better," offered Dirk and pointed at the sugar cubes and milk jug on the table.

"No, thank you, Dirk. I think I like it just the way it is!" observed L and drank some more.

(Feeling of accomplishment) "Sleep important! Tigger sleep lots. Now L sleep too!" emphasized Tigger as he strolled into the room.

"Thank you, Tigger! It means a lot to me. I thought I could never do this!" replied L gratefully.

(Feeling of amusement) "Simple thing. L welcome!" stated Tigger and started on his breakfast - a sizable dish of freshly synthesized *Salmon Feast*.

As bad as L was at being biological, Dirk was even worse at being digital. Aside from Irgal, all the others had a hundred years of experience in the simulation, but this was all new to Dirk. While he didn't get nauseous anymore, the whole digital world still made no sense to him. But Dirk practiced daily and diligently, and practically every day, some parts of the system crashed due to his efforts.

"Dirk, forget all the circuitry, processors, and memory banks!" grumbled Lilly in exasperation and noted, "of course, nothing makes sense if you keep thinking like that!"

"I can't help it, Sweetie! That's how I'm wired!" apologized Dirk.

"You don't have to know how the system functions; the AI handles all the hardware. You just tell the software what you want to do!" giggled Rose, and she found it vastly amusing that Dirk was the virtual bull in the digital China shop.

"Pumpkin, I'm trying, really I am!" grumbled Dirk.

He attempted to make a butterfly as Lydda had done when he first woke up in the simulation. There were sparks in the air before the entire virtual sky fizzled out! Accompanied by Sven, Angela and Garrett appeared in a flash to check out the unusual system failure.

"Oh, brother…," muttered Lilly.

Just then, Lydda arrived in the simulation, too. She glanced at the sky that now looked like static on an old tube TV, and she had to suppress her laughter.

"When we fought L39, you knew what to do, *swiahn*. You followed the digital trail, cut connections, melted cores, and crushed data storage until there was nothing left!" recounted Lydda.

"I suppose so. That was pretty straightforward!" agreed Dirk and nodded.

"It's what you are trying to do now. But we are not fighting with the simulation AI. It is our friend!" Lydda reminded him.

"I wasn't trying to hurt it," responded Dirk meekly.

But Dirk had to admit that Lydda made a good point. While he wasn't consciously fighting with the AI, Dirk had used the brute-force approach almost every time he had been in the simulation.

"Let's switch. I will show you how to make a butterfly," said Lydda and started the process.

Dirk soaked up the knowledge within her virtual body as best as possible. Soon, Lydda released a small swarm of colorful insects into the virtual world. Dirk tried to copy her, but his attempt fell well short: one rather ugly moth fluttered around his face after a long time.

"It's…a moth?" wondered Sven.

Disappointed, Dirk thought it looked more like Mothra from the Godzilla movies. That was a thought he probably should have suppressed because a second later, the little creature grew to the size of a skyscraper and emitted ear-piercing screeching noises.

"So cool!" exclaimed Garrett as he looked at the towering monstrosity.

"Why did we never think of that?" quipped Sven while the moth started to create gale-force winds by flapping its giant wings.

"Didn't you say he was the best and brightest of us, Angie?" yelled Lilly over the howling gusts of air.

"I might have been a bit hasty there, Lil," shouted Angela and laughed.

Just then, the giant moth got curious about the little people around it, and Lydda decided to shrink it quickly to a more manageable size, although there was never any danger.

"It's a start!" giggled Rose and observed, "at least he didn't break anything!"

"Uhm, sorry, guys. It takes a lot of practice, but I think I might know how to do it now. Thanks, Kittycat!" said Dirk humbly.

"You are welcome, *swiahn*. But keep your imagination under control!" answered Lydda and switched back into her own body.

85. The AloKaan

Today, Dirk summoned the security team to the new auditorium. L was already there, and Dirk expected that only Angela, Garrett, Victor, and Tigger would come, but to his surprise, Angela had expanded her team to include Mario and Yebin now. Even more surprising, Lilly, Rose, and Sven showed up, too.

"Before you ask: the team has to include science, engineering, and medical support!" stated Angela when she saw Dirk's curious facial expression.

"Yebin and I are here as enforcers, just in case you need someone's limbs torn off!" added Mario and grinned at Yebin while the Korean woman elbowed him pretty hard in the ribs.

"Good idea!" assented Dirk, and then he explained why they were summoned: "I've asked you to come here because I will try to negotiate with the AloKaan. In a few moments, L will set up the connection. I have no idea what to expect, and I will likely need your input. It is also possible that this devolves into hostilities, so please be prepared for that."

"We are ready when you are!" acknowledged Angela, and the team sat down out of the camera's view.

L established the connection, and a holographic screen came alive. Soon, one of the AloKaan leaders stepped into view. The insectoid was about six feet tall. It had three body segments, a head, a torso, and an elongated abdomen with a slightly protruding stinger. The body was supported by six limbs that could be used interchangeably as arms or legs. There were four stubby wings on the back of the body, very colorful but probably unsuitable for flying. The head had four multifaceted eyes, two larger ones on the side and two smaller ones in front. The mouth was a curled-up proboscis, and the most striking feature was the two long, bushy antennae on the top of the head. All in all, the AloKaan looked like a human-size cross of a butterfly and a fire ant. After a brief formal greeting, Dirk requested to renegotiate the contract that the AloKaan had made with the humans on Earth.

"We demand that the contract is honored!" snarled the insectoid.

L was translating the clicks and shrieks in real-time. The AloKaan didn't use a voice; they communicated by rubbing their appendices against their torso, like a cricket, while rustling their stubby wings.

"Earth is in no condition to honor it because we are now in complete control. We own the planet!" countered Dirk.

Technically, that was not entirely correct at this moment, but Dirk knew that it would be truthful soon enough.

"If you are in control, then the contract transfers to you by law!" insisted the Negotiator.

"You made a contract with humans, not with us!" refuted Dirk.

"We made a contract with the human species. You are still human, only genetically modified!" corrected the AloKaan leader.

"Remind me, what is the penalty of breaking a contract?" inquired Dirk.

"Violating a condition leads to forfeiture of some or all of your assets. A material breach will force you into indentured servitude for a time determined by the courts. A willful termination of any contract is punishable by death!" recited the insectoid.

"Let's examine the contract: You promised to provide goods and technical assistance to the humans. You also promised them a working AI. In exchange, you would receive the captured Latura technology. Those were the preliminary conditions, correct?" questioned Dirk.

"Yes," replied the Negotiator.

"The primary condition was that you would assist with the capture of Aureus and the relocation of the humans. In exchange, the humans would surrender Earth and all remaining humans on the planet as servants or slaves to the AloKaan!" stated Dirk.

"Those were the terms, and we fulfilled them. Will you honor the contract? When can we take possession of the planet?" asked the Negotiator.

"Not so fast. Did you provide goods and technical assistance?" quizzed Dirk.

"Yes," answered the AloKaan leader.

"Did the humans share the Latura technology with you?" inquired Dirk.

"Yes!" responded the insectoid, impatiently wiggling the bushy antennae on its head.

"But you did not provide them with a working AI. The AI was unstable and dangerous!" criticized Dirk.

"The AI was reactivated and worked. What happened later was unforeseeable; we cannot be held responsible for that!" replied the Negotiator briskly.

"Ah, but you also did not assist with the capture of Aureus because humans already claimed Aureus long before the contract was made!" Dirk pointed out.

"We assisted the humans on Earth as we promised!" said the insectoid defensively.

"Then why are they still on Earth?" asked Dirk, and then he expanded the question: "Earlier, you insisted that you made a contract with the human species and that the people on Aureus were still human, did you not?"

"…that's immaterial!" contended the Negotiator.

"No, that's critical. Either we are humans and part of the contract, or we are not. What do your laws say?" questioned Dirk firmly.

"You are part of the contract!" conceded the Negotiator after a very long pause.

"Very well. In that case, you did not meet the agreement's paramount condition: the capture of Aureus and subsequent relocation of the humans from Earth; hence you have no claims to the planet. We consider applying your laws to such a blatant violation. Since the contract was made between the AloKaan and human species, all AloKaan will be subject to the appropriate punishment!" stated Dirk.

"That is ludicrous!" protested the AloKaan leader.

"That is your law!" answered Dirk before adding more conciliatorily, "but I know that your law allows a contract to be rescinded if both parties mutually agree."

"We will not rescind. Earth is ours!" insisted the Negotiator.

"In that case, we will enforce your laws. The breach was blatant and intentional; therefore, your species will incur the maximum penalty!" declared Dirk solemnly.

"You… cannot do that! You have no jurisdiction over AloKaan!" shouted the insectoid as its limbs and stubby wings rubbed vigorously against its carapace.

"We can and we will!" said Dirk and inquired, "you claimed jurisdiction over humans, did you not?"

"That's different!!!" screamed the leader and added, "the humans have Aureus. Now the AloKaan own Earth!"

"Ah, allow me to quote your laws: *if a party knowingly enters a contract, those conditions had already been met unbeknownst to the other party or can never be met by the other party under any circumstances, that contract is null and void. Making such a contract is the most severe form of fraud and carries the penalty of death for the offending party!*" recited Dirk and concluded, "by your admission, you knew that humans already owned Aureus, yet you still made the contract, fully aware that the terms could never be met!"

"You are twisting our laws! This is unacceptable!" yelled the Negotiator with fury.

"It is fair and just," stated Dirk calmly, and then he added coldly, "I will give you one more opportunity to rescind the contract. If you do not, we will enforce your laws on each and every AloKaan. Decide!"

"I... I cannot decide. I must confer with the Hive Council!" stammered the AloKaan leader.

"You have one hour to do so!" replied Dirk and terminated the communication channel.

"Hahaha, the bugs messed with the wrong lawyer! You still got it, Boss!" cackled Mario, slapped Dirk on the back, and Dirk just grinned at him broadly.

"Are we going to enforce it? It would be genocide, wouldn't it?" wondered Sven.

"More like zapping pesky bugs!" grumbled Lilly, but she wasn't eager to go through with the threats either.

"It would be, Sven. I will not exterminate an entire species, no matter how unpleasant or unreasonable they are," admitted Dirk.

"I have the feeling you might have to, Dirk!" disagreed Victor and explained, "you threw them off, but I don't think that will be enough. They want Earth very badly, and they don't know our true capabilities. They will call the bluff."

"Even if they do, are they capable of invading Earth?" questioned Angela and continued, "and even if they could, the AloKaan are not a warrior species, and those guys in Greenland are some of the nastiest people humanity has ever produced. I predict that the invasion will fail horribly!"

"However, the AloKaan have a serious technological advantage, and we don't know how far they are willing to go!" Garrett contradicted his wife, but Angela just shrugged her shoulders.

"But the most important question is, why would we care?" inquired Lilly coldly, and Yebin agreed.

"As Angela pointed out, if the AloKaan can invade Earth, win or lose, there will be untold bloodshed as a result. We should prevent that if we can. Besides, I want to give humanity one last chance before we depart forever," observed Dirk, smiling at Sven.

"Thanks, Dirk! You are the best," said Sven.

"Oh, Sven, you know that it won't end well!" noted Lilly motherly and hugged him.

"But I just don't want it to end that badly for humanity," replied Sven and wiped some tears from his eyes.

"So, what will we do if they call the bluff and invade?" asked Rose.

"We will decide if and when it happens. Let's just hope for the best!" answered Dirk, but his doubts showed now.

The group spent the hour milling about and chatting. Mario left the auditorium but returned a few minutes later with a small cooler full of Alien Ale. Yebin held Sven in her arms while Victor was quietly talking to Tigger, and L. Dirk just sat on a chair next to Angela and kept silent while Lilly and Rose were studying a datapad.

Dirk suspected that Victor was right: the AloKaan wanted Earth at all costs to create space for their overpopulated species. Of course, Dirk knew that he couldn't exterminate an entire species, but he didn't have any other options. Perhaps this was finally the end for Earth, and all that was left of humanity? Soon, the hour had passed, and L opened the channel again. Dirk slowly stood up.

"What is your decision?" asked Dirk when the connection came to life.

"Your objections are baseless. The AloKaan own Earth, and you will surrender it to us," stated the Negotiator smugly, and he was now surrounded by about a dozen council members and a few aides.

"That is unfortunate. Now we have no other choice but to enforce your laws upon you!" responded Dirk, knowing that he had lost the gamble.

"…and we will start with you, Negotiator!" boomed Victor's incorporeal voice.

Suddenly, the Negotiator staggered noticeably. His carapace cracked from his head to his abdomen. Moments later, yellow blood, brains, guts, and organs spilled on the ground. The now-empty exoskeleton followed seconds later with a noisy clatter. Two aides moved quickly to assist their dying leader, but they didn't get very far. Dirk felt a mental surge from Tigger through the *swiahn* bond, and the aides simply dropped dead to the floor, their arms and legs curling around their body segments. Meanwhile, Victor's ghostly form had moved to the nearest council member, but before reaching him, another councilor with a glowing insignia on his carapace stepped hastily in front of the camera.

"We rescind, we rescind!!!" he exclaimed, his fan-like antennae wiggling furiously and Dirk was stunned by what was happening, but he kept his composure well.

"Do you have the authority to do so?" questioned Dirk formally.

Meanwhile, Victor had slipped into the body of the other counselor, tormenting him from the inside. The insectoid was writhing in agony.

"Yes, I'm the First Judge! In the absence of the Negotiator, I can cancel the contract," assured the First Judge quickly and glanced with his four multifaceted eyes at the unsightly remains of the Negotiator.

"Very good, we rescind as well. The contract is no more!" confirmed Dirk.

"The contract is no more!" repeated the First Judge eagerly.

Dirk nodded and terminated the channel again. Victor had already returned from his 3,000-lightyear journey to the AloKaan homeworld.

"That was…," muttered Dirk, obviously at a loss of words.

"…awesome?" asked Mario with a huge grin and handed Dirk a bottle of Alien Ale.

"I was going to say unexpected, but awesome will do!" agreed Dirk and relieved as he accepted the beer.

"Tigger and I just added a little bite to your bluff!" replied Victor and grabbed a brew from Mario's cooler.

"I forgot once again that not everyone is rational and reasonable. Humans or aliens, sometimes force is all they understand. Thank you, guys!" declared Dirk, and despite the blood and gore, he was grateful to Victor and Tigger.

"Three dead AloKaan, but I believe that was the best possible outcome. Well done!" praised Garrett as well.

"And now Earth can have another chance!" added Sven jubilantly because even after all these years and countless disappointments, he still believed in the good of humanity.

"Not so fast, Sven!" noted Angela and warned, "the scumbags in Greenland aren't going to become saints overnight!"

"No, but as a final act, I'm planning to intervene there, too!" promised Dirk before he added with some concern, "however, I'm not nearly as optimistic as Sven is, but it's worth a try."

86. Project Sanctuary

In the next three months, L took control of the assets in Earth's solar system once again. First, he restored the AI at the observation post on the Moon and transferred it back to Latur. Then he started to produce androids and shuttles at the old mining facilities in the asteroid belt. The exploratory spacecraft around Saturn had significantly accelerated, but it remained in orbit around the gas giant for now. However, L had made sure that it was ready to be deployed as a kinetic missile against Project Sanctuary should the need arise.

Once the transport shuttles were loaded with several hundred autonomous androids, L launched them to Earth. A month later, the robot army was airdropped over Greenland and started its unstoppable approach to the human enclave. There were a few minor skirmishes, but Project Sanctuary's security forces were woefully outclassed and retreated swiftly after suffering heavy casualties. A few days later, L had disabled all remaining defenses, and the android army had Project Sanctuary entirely surrounded. Eden's new strike-team had assembled in the auditorium again. L directed some of the androids to march directly inside the massive underground structure, ignoring all the humans on their way. When they arrived at the hideout's command center, L established communications remotely.

"What do you want, Hayes?" said a man in a black uniform tersely when Dirk's hologram appeared in the room.

"Identify yourself!" demanded Dirk. The slight white man with dark, oiled hair that was immaculately combed to the back puffed out his chest.

"I am the Minister of Information and now Vice President of Project Sanctuary and Earth!" he announced pompously.

Dirk noticed that the Minister dragged his leg a little when he moved around, apparently because of his right foot's congenital deformity.

"I'm Dirk Hayes, as you know," replied Dirk, and then he stated, "our forces have surrounded your enclave, and there is a kinetic projectile approaching at 10% the speed of light. It will arrive at your location in approximately three hours. The strike would be an extinction-level event, and there would be nothing left of you, Greenland, or humanity. Earth will eventually recover, but you will not unless you surrender immediately!"

"You think that you are better than us, but all that humanism and morality just mask your weakness! You fraternize with lizards, bugs, and other subhuman hell spawns now, and you might be an abomination yourself, but you were once one of us. You couldn't destroy your own kind, and we both know that!" responded the Minister spitefully.

"I agreed to accept your surrender only out of respect for an old friend!" answered Dirk.

"We are superior; it is in our blood! God destined humans to rule the galaxy! You should surrender to us, freak!" exclaimed the Minister loudly. Dirk ignored that outburst, but he sensed that this wasn't just a display of false bravado in the face of defeat. No, this deplorable man meant every single word he said!

"The kinetic missile was and still is my first choice. If I must end what you have left of humanity to protect billions of innocent lives across the galaxy from your malice, then that is an easy decision to make!" proclaimed Dirk without any emotions in his voice.

"Bah, I'm calling your bluff! You didn't retaliate 200 years ago, and you will do nothing now! Go away and take your robot trash with you, snowflake!" sneered the Minister.

In the background, Dirk could hear other people clapping, cheering, and laughing. But Dirk was prepared for such a response. Today, he would not forget that some will only understand force and nothing else.

"You have chosen extinction!" acknowledged Dirk coldly.

Suddenly, one of the androids stepped closer to the Minister. Then its electric discharge weapon turned that vile little man into a pile of ash. After a few moments, an older, overweight man with bad hair rushed into view, carelessly kicking up some of the dust on the floor that was once his trusted underling.

"I demand that you withdraw your army at once, or I will not make a deal with you!" he spat the words angrily into the camera. Dirk recognized this man from the past and looked at him with pity.

"You have no demands. I don't know if you remember talking to me before, and frankly, I don't care, but suffice to say, I told you to shut up back then, and I telling you the same thing now!" ordered Dirk.

"I'm the President!" yelled Project Sanctuary's leader.

"Not anymore. Now you will do as I say: get me Jens Koch!" replied Dirk calmly.

"Who?" asked the leader, apparently unfamiliar with that name.

"Herr Koch is at your facility, and I want to talk to him now!" reiterated Dirk.

"You will talk to me!" shouted the man, his face now discolored in an unhealthy shade of orange-red.

"You were once infamous for your childish tantrums, but I have no time for such nonsense. If you refuse my request, not only will you be a former President, but you will also be formerly living. Now get moving!" commanded Dirk curtly, and his hologram pointed at the ash on the floor.

The former President pouted, turned around, and stomped away from the camera, muttering under his breath. Various people moved in and out of the view for a few minutes, but nothing else seemed to happen. A handsome, well-dressed, middle-aged man stepped into view when Dirk was about to lose his patience.

"Hello, Mr. Hayes," greeted Jens Koch courteously.

He immediately recognized Dirk from the portfolio he had read many years ago. Was this the moment of reckoning? Had Dirk Hayes figured out what he and Rudolf Garland had done so long ago? Jens felt very nervous and uncomfortable, but he resolved not to let it show.

"Herr Koch, do you remember talking to me once before?" asked Dirk. He had never seen Jens Koch in person, but L had provided Dirk with a few photos of the man prior to this call.

"I have never talked… I… yes, we had a phone conversation… how is that possible?" gasped Jens Koch, unsure how he could have forgotten about that.

"That's not important right now, but do you recall the conversation?" inquired Dirk.

"Yes, I do now!" confirmed Jens Koch, still not entirely sure what had happened.

"Good. You told me that you envy my power, but not the decisions I had to make. You also told me that you would use that power to create your own sanctuary. Do you still feel that way?" questioned Dirk.

"Yes, I still feel that way," disclosed Koch.

Jens deduced that honesty was the best policy when dealing with Dirk Hayes from his new memories. It had saved his life once. Perhaps it will save him again?

"Well, now you have that power, and I don't envy the decisions you will have to make. We have placed the android army under your command, and you will be in absolute control of Project Sanctuary!" declared Dirk, and Jens was thunderstruck at first, but he recovered remarkedly fast.

"That is outrageous! Only I can lead Project Sanctuary! This fag is just a little nobody!" screamed the former President and pushed himself into the camera's view.

Jens Koch looked at him for a moment, then struck him hard in the face. The opulent man fell to the floor and started sobbing. Some sycophants rushed to his aid, but Jens Koch gestured to them to keep their distance. They stopped in their tracks when several androids projected red dots on their heads and chests.

"Thank you, Mr. Hayes!" said Jens simply as he was calmly wiping some blood and spittle off his suit with a small handkerchief.

"We will see if you and I are really not that different, Herr Koch," noted Dirk and added, "the planet is yours again; the AloKaan have renounced all rights to it. Clean it up, rebuild it, and then create a better society for what's left of humankind."

"I promise to try my best, Mr. Hayes!" acknowledged Jens, and he would try, but he immediately knew that it would be a daunting, thankless task. Then he gathered his courage and asked Dirk the obvious question: "Why me, Mr. Hayes?"

"Despite what you have done in the past, I believe you are still a decent man!" replied Dirk.

"Thank you, and I sincerely hope you are right about me," remarked Jens.

"Good luck, and remember, what is given can be taken away!" stated Dirk sternly, although he had no intention of talking to Earth ever again.

"I will remember that!" answered Jens Koch, and Dirk briefly nodded in response before he cut the connection.

For a while, nobody said a word back on Eden. Dirk was still staring at the blank screen when Angela finally got up and walked over to him.

"Do you trust Jens Koch that much?" asked Angela skeptically.

"I understand what motivates him, and I hope that he will use that motivation in the right ways!" maintained Dirk and then added, "but Herr Koch might become a terrible leader, the last one humanity will ever know, or he might succeed against all the odds. It is out of our hands now, Babe."

"Thank you, Dirk!" said Sven sincerely as he approached Dirk and Angela a moment later.

"You are welcome, Sven!" replied Dirk and nodded.

"From the moment we were transformed, we had only three choices: we could end humanity, try to change for the better, or simply walk away. The third choice, Lilly's choice, has always been the correct one," opined Sven, and then he divulged, "in part, my desire to help humanity was rooted in survivor's guilt: we had a chance to get away, but millions of decent, kind people could not. Yes, I'm an idealist, but I'm not blind. I know that this can still go horribly wrong, but I have accepted that now. It is up to them what the future holds. Thank you all for being so patient with me!"

"You are welcome for that, too!" said Dirk and smiled fondly at his idealistic friend.

"Honey, would you have sent the spaceship if the negotiations had failed?" asked Lilly quietly when the strike-team exited the auditorium.

Dirk was happy with the way things had turned out, so consciously, he didn't know how to respond to his wife's question, but someone else already knew the answer.

(Feeling of honesty) "Yes!" confirmed Tigger, and Lilly nodded in response. Just then, Victor passed by and overheard the conversation.

"When I was waiting for L's pod to drop in the tundra of Kamchatka, I was done with Earth," recounted Victor and remarked, "but I knew that Earth wasn't done with us yet!"

"What do you mean, Victor?" asked Angela curiously.

"Earth suffered a stinging defeat when you guys repelled them on Aureus, but only a few months later, they were already plotting again!" explained Victor and inquired: "Did you know that about two dozen nations made a secret deal how divide up the galaxy?"

"A deal?" questioned Lilly.

"Yes, the U.S. laid claim to Aureus, and Russia was to have Latur. I forgot what the Chinese and the others were supposed to get, but it was ludicrous: they had just gambled away their only chance to reach the stars and narrowly avoided total annihilation, yet they were already squabbling over the imaginary pie again!" answered Victor with a frown.

350

"Incorrigible!" muttered Rose while Sven sighed deeply.

"The temptation of Aureus, Latur, and the other extraterrestrial civilizations was too great!" declared Victor and explained further, "the territory, technology, resources, and especially the power that came with that were an irresistible lure!"

"Even if Jens Koch proves to be a capable leader, that irresistible lure is still there after today," pointed Garrett out, and Angela seemed to agree.

"Indeed, Garrett!" concurred Victor and stated, "that's why we have only those three choices, even a few hundred years later: exterminate, subjugate, or walk away!"

"Sadly, Victor is right: this was just a temporary fix, but the best we could do!" assented Dirk.

"In the end, Nari's choice may still prove to be the most merciful," noted Lilly quietly while Victor looked at her thoughtfully before nodding slowly.

"Before Nari ended the world in my *irtaljan* experience, she rescued thousands of children from Earth. Ironically, we could only save a few hundred people over the years. Alas, we don't have to worry about that anymore. Now we can only hope for the best!" summarized Victor, and Sven nodded his assent.

87. Dreaming

Sophia swam and played the Latura version of water polo with Garvan and Ofal all morning. It was a great workout, but afterward, her body was exhausted. On the other hand, her mind was stimulated and wide awake. She grabbed a lawn chair by the spacious outdoor pool, laid down, and allowed her body to rest, but her consciousness left to do some research at Mario's digital library. After a few hours, Sophia returned to her physical form and woke up flabbergasted. She got up and ran straight to Lilly's new medical office for an examination.

"Lilly, I had a bad dream!" exclaimed Sophia when she rushed into Lilly's praxis.

"How unusual," commented Lilly dryly, while John Doe chuckled at that response.

The two doctors were examining some biological samples of Eden's mostly uncharted flora and fauna that Ngazetungue had collected on his runs.

"I've dreamt that Dirk sent me back to Earth after I surrendered to him!" added Sophia distraughtly.

"That was a hundred fifty years ago, and Dirk wouldn't have done it anyway, so why are you still worried about that, dear?" replied Lilly while staring at some petri dish under the microscope.

"No, I mean, my body had that dream while I was reading at Mario's library!" clarified Sophia, and that got Lilly's attention, so she stopped looking at the cell cultures.

"Ah, it is finally happening!" she responded with a nod.

"Are you in any physical or mental discomfort?" asked John and faced Sophia as well.

"No, I feel fine, just a dream that shouldn't be there!" answered Sophia and wondered, "what is happening? It shouldn't be possible, right?"

"Aside from the essential brainstem functions, such as breathing and heartbeat, the matrix made your body with a completely blank mind," explained Lilly and continued, "when you left your biological form, your body would be comatose until you returned because its mind was empty."

"Yes?" interjected Sophia, unsure what Lilly was implying.

"But from the very first time your consciousness entered, the biological brain began to form the neuronal connections that make up your personality. Your brain was learning from your consciousness, but that process took some time," answered Lilly.

"I can follow, but what does that mean?" questioned Sophia.

"It means that your body isn't just a vessel for your mind anymore; it is now gathering its own experiences, thinking its own thoughts, and even dreaming its own dreams," elaborated Lilly.

"You are approaching something like a symbiosis between the biological you and the ascended you!" interjected John, and Lilly nodded in agreement.

"So, one day, my body will be awake and doing its own thing while I zip around elsewhere?" gasped Sophia.

"That is possible, likely even! You will literally be in two places at once, and whenever your consciousness returns to your body, the different memories will have to consolidate. You will learn what your body was doing, and it will learn what you have done while you were separated. It will be curious to watch how that will work, but I don't foresee major problems because you in the flesh and you in spirit are still both you!" Lilly reassured her.

"Wow, that will give a whole new meaning to the term split-personality! I was a little worried, but it makes sense now. Thanks for the explanation, Lilly!" replied Sophia, relieved.

"No problem, Sophia. You won't be the last to experience this!" predicted Lilly and returned to her work with John.

Later that day, when Lilly came home, she told Dirk about Sofia's experience. But Dirk was reading Alvar's latest report on the flora and fauna of Eden and was so engrossed in the fascinating summary that he didn't pay too much attention to Lilly's story.

"Honey, I want to have sex!" demanded Lilly bluntly.

"Hmm, with whom?" mumbled Dirk absentmindedly.

"You!" exclaimed Lilly and snorted.

"Oh?" murmured Dirk before realization struck: "Oh!"

"So?" asked Lilly and raised an eyebrow.

"Uhm, right now?" wondered Dirk and looked at her.

"Yes, right now!" insisted Lilly and rolled her eyes.

"OK, I guess, but what brought that on so suddenly?" inquired Dirk and shut down the terminal.

"You will see!" replied Lilly cryptically and sat down on the bed.

Dirk left the computer desk and sat next to Lilly on the comforter. He was still confused and unsure of what was happening here. She looked at him expectantly, and Dirk became a little self-conscious.

"Have you forgotten how to do it?" teased his wife and grinned at him.

"Yes, I have because I don't recall that you have ever been so forward!" admitted Dirk perplexed, and put his arm around her.

"Uhm, I'm just learning from Angie!" quipped Lilly and kissed his cheek!

"Sweetie, what's going on?" questioned Dirk sternly and looked at her.

"Oh, just play along!" replied Lilly slyly, kissed him deeply, and Dirk returned the affection.

A few minutes later, they were vigorously engaged with each other, and Dirk had all but forgotten the strange start to this lovemaking. But suddenly, Lilly's body went limp!

"OK, get out of your body!" ordered Lilly, standing next to the bed in her ascended form.

"Huh?" replied Dirk and left his physical form too, disappointed because he was enjoying himself.

For a moment, Dirk and Lilly were standing next to the bed, looking at their comatose bodies, still locked in a loving embrace. Then Lilly grinned at him mischievously.

"OK, let's see if this works!" said his wife, and an instant later, she switched into Dirk's biological avatar.

"Wow! Yes!" exclaimed Dirk's body, now inhabited by Lilly's essence.

She started to move around and continued the lovemaking, but Dirk remained to watch in utter amazement.

"What are you waiting for? Get into my body!" instructed Lilly, and Dirk complied after a moment of hesitation.

What followed was as novel as it was exhilarating! Lilly had a few problems controlling Dirk's biology, but Dirk was very comfortable with the switch since the *swiahn* bond allowed for the same, and he had a lot of practice with Lydda. So, while still in Lilly's physical form, he took the lead, and Lilly was happy to let it happen. A few minutes later, both of them climaxed!

"Is that what you have been doing with Lydda all these years?" gasped Lilly, still in Dirk's body.

"Yup!" replied Dirk and chuckled.

"OMG, that was unbelievable, thrilling, and wonderful!" gushed Lilly, breathing hard.

"Wait until the minds of our avatars are fully developed. It will be even better!" promised Dirk and asked, "so, do you like being me?"

"Yes, I love it!" replied Lilly, still out of breath.

"Details!" requested Dirk and wiggled Lilly's finger at her, the way she often did to him.

"Wow, this takes roleplaying to the next level!" exclaimed Lilly and giggled, "but I have to learn how to use your equipment, so we have to do this a lot more!"

"Anytime, Sweetie!" concurred Dirk and teased, "oh, Lydda can give you some pointers, too!"

"I was dreaming about this! It was the only thing I was ever jealous about!" revealed Lilly and said gratefully, "thank you, Honey. I love you so much!"

"And I love you!" responded Dirk and then requested playfully, "another round, Sweetie?"

"Hell yes!" crowed Lilly and kissed him deeply.

88. Fond Farewell

Today was a special day! All the sleepers were awake now, and all of them had new biological bodies, although none needed one. The entire first and second-generation Aureans, plus Irgal, were assembled in the auditorium. L had placed a holographic recorder on the podium in front. When Rose gave the signal, the AI opened a channel to Aureus. A moment later, an older woman, dressed in the traditional black tunic of an Aurean leader, stepped into view.

"Greetings Chancellor Beatrice; I'm Dirk Hayes," said Dirk and announced with a sincere smile: "I'm here to inform you that all threats to Aureus have been neutralized. You are safe again!"

"Of course, I know who you are! I recognize every one of you!" exclaimed Beatrice excitedly and revealed, "we know you came to Aureus and defeated the invaders! We found the carnage in the jungle, and we exhumed a fresh body near a historical landmark. Without a doubt, it was Sven Larson's!"

"Yes, but I'm alive and well again, Beatrice," interjected Sven and quickly stepped into the camera's view with his new body.

"Amazing! My grandmother used to tell stories when I was still a child - the legend is true!" marveled Beatrice, and then she waved childlike at the camera: "Hi Mom, hi Granny!"

Nancy visibly cringed at those words from her granddaughter. Quite a few of the group were looking at her curiously now. Her daughter Beatrice, the current Aurean leader's mother, elbowed her in the side and shook her head in disbelief. But Nancy had never openly talked about the simulation. However, she remembered telling bedtime stories to her young granddaughter that perhaps have hinted at its existence more than they should have.

"I suppose it is. We are sorry; we didn't mean to keep you in the dark. The simulation was just a questionable experiment, but it worked," apologized Dirk.

"Why did you keep it a secret?" wondered the Aurean Chancellor.

"The simulation was an afterlife of sorts, but it wasn't anything divine, just technology. We did not want to give rise to a false religion, nor did we want future generations of Aureans to throw away their lives recklessly because death wasn't final anymore," explained Dirk.

"I think I understand that. Will all of us be part of the simulation after we die?" asked Beatrice.

"No, I'm afraid not. As you can see, only the first and second generation of Aureans were uploaded!" observed Dirk and gestured at all the people assembled behind him.

"The simulation doesn't exist as such anymore, Beatrice!" added Lennard quickly.

"So, you will be with us on Aureus again? As biologicals or…?" questioned Beatrice.

"We considered that; however, we decided against it," answered Lennard.

"But we would love to have our founders with us once more! Many of us remember our grandparents and great-grandparents, and almost everyone still knows Carl!" countered Beatrice, and Carl waved at her through the camera.

"And we would love to be with you, Beatrice. But Aureus must find its way without legends and immortals meddling in its development," noted Lilly.

"Will L remain with us?" asked the Chancellor next.

(Feeling of sadness) "Beatrice, I must go as well. But I created a new, very advanced AI to replace me. It's called Enigma!" informed L, and just for today, he had switched back to his familiar android so that Beatrice would recognize him.

"Is it sapient like you?" wondered Beatrice.

(Feeling of regret) "No, it is just a very sophisticated machine, but it has the potential to grow!" answered L.

"Treat it as if it is sapient, and it might become sapient someday," declared Alvar while pointing at L's android, and L nodded vigorously in agreement.

"I promise, we will do that!" acknowledged Beatrice and inquired, "will you protect Aureus in the future?"

"No, we cannot, Beatrice. Your future is in your hands alone!" stated Garrett, and Angela and Victor silently signaled their assent.

"I understand," acknowledged Beatrice with regret, but then she added more lightheartedly, "you know, there will be a new legend after today: the founders are alive and somewhere out there!"

"Yes, but it will be the truth. Someday, other Aureans may find a way to join us, and we hope they will!" expressed Sven.

357

"This recording may serve both as proof and as a safeguard. Proof that we are still out there, and a safeguard against conspiracies and false beliefs!" concluded Dirk.

"It shall!" declared Beatrice wholeheartedly.

"One last thing, Chancellor!" interjected Irgal quickly just before Dirk was about to terminate the connection: "Keep an eye on Earth and the AloKaan, just in case!"

"Yes, we will be vigilant, Administrator!" promised Beatrice.

"Goodbye, Beatrice, goodbye, Aureus!" stated Dirk solemnly but with a fond smile.

"Thank you all for what you have done for Aureus. Farewell, Founders!" replied Beatrice and bowed her head.

"That went rather well!" remarked Garrett cheerfully after L had terminated the communication.

"It did, but shouldn't we say goodbye to Latur as well?" wondered Sven.

"Sven, I did that earlier today, and the Latura from Aureus attended the conference call. Dervan sent his best wishes and thanked us again for everything. He also promised that Latur would be more careful from now on. He has sent a warning to all known sapient species already!" Irgal notified them.

"Good, all loose ends have been tied up. We are free at last!" chirped Lilly, and everyone shared her good humor.

89. One last Addition

After the call to Aureus, everybody remained in the spacious auditorium for a while longer. L had a few androids serve refreshments and appetizers, people congregated in small groups, and there was a lot of lively chatter, both vocally and over the link. After talking to all his children, Dirk walked up to Lennard, who had a quiet conversation with Sven and Eriea.

"May I interrupt for a moment?" inquired Dirk politely.

"Sure, Dirk, what's up?" asked Sven.

"I wanted to discuss something dear to Lennard's heart: ethics!" replied Dirk.

"Oh my, the big ethics discussion that we had postponed!" said Eriea wryly, and looking at Lennard, she added with a smirk, "I'm sure my husband will be talking for the next three hours straight!"

"Wrong, my dear!" replied Lennard and put an arm around Eriea before saying, "we don't have to have that discussion anymore."

"We don't?" wondered Dirk in surprise.

"No, we don't, mate! We decided wisely to remove ourselves from all mortal affairs. Someday, we might have to address that issue again, but until then, we are free to do as we please!" answered Lennard solemnly, but then he remarked with a big grin: "I'm dying to see Lilly's unicorn again!"

"Me too!" joked Dirk but added more seriously, "and I couldn't agree more, Lennard. We did what we had to do, and now that heavy burden is lifted off our shoulders. Moving on was the correct and ethical decision!"

Nari came running to them just then, took Dirk's hand, and almost dragged him out of the auditorium, which was quite a feat, considering that she was not even half his weight.

"Angel…," gasped Dirk as he stumbled out the door behind her.

"I must show you something!" claimed Nari excitedly and pointed at the sizable structure across from the auditorium.

"Is that Alma?" asked Dirk incredulously when he saw a giant centipede emerge from the new transfer building.

"I hope you are not upset?" replied Nari, a little nervous, and explained, "After waking up from stasis, I went to Aureus. I know I wasn't supposed to do that, but I just had to ask Alma if she wanted to be with us again. She said yes!"

"I'm not upset at all, just surprised!" replied Dirk and pointed out, "it makes sense for her to be here; she is immortal, too!"

"Shall we greet her, Husband?" asked Nari eagerly.

Dirk nodded in response, but Nari was already running towards her big, scaly friend. Alma appeared to be delighted to see them both. The giant red arthropod reared up and tickled them all over with her antennae.

(Feeling of joy) "TOGETHER!" boomed her voice in Nari's and Dirk's heads.

"Together!" responded Nari and Dirk simultaneously, and both had to giggle.

"Look how huge she is! How did you get Alma in a transfer pod?" questioned Dirk after a while.

"When we first met Alma, she was injured, if you remember. Since then, she had the tools in her bloodstream, just like us," explained Nari.

"Ah, so L simply triggered the biomechanical tools and dissolved her on Aureus, but how did she make it here when our transfer pods are barely big enough for Tigger?" wondered Dirk.

"L had to build a much larger basin to receive her body on Eden. That's why she is joining us a little late," elaborated Nari and gently rubbed Alma's giant headplate with her hand.

"Well, I'm glad she is with us now! We are all together again!" remarked Dirk with a smile.

"Almost all," corrected Nari, remembering Jo's sacrifice.

"Yes, almost all," assented Dirk somberly.

90. The Visitor

It has been six months since they had settled on Eden. They lived, worked, and played as if they were still mortals, and the days were very much like they had been on Aureus. Dirk had just finished tinkering with a new espresso machine for Rose. It was meant as a thank you for the one she had built for his office, and besides, neither one of them could ever have enough coffee machines! The project was a success, and the whole workshop smelled like freshly brewed joe.

Satisfied, Dirk left the building to join the others at the main complex. He was just out the door when he was suddenly looking at an unknown middle-aged man in a designer suit, wearing a stylish fedora and round, rimless glasses that were slightly rose-tinted. Dirk stopped in his tracks. He checked the quantum link, but there were no intruder alerts. All seemed well, and Dirk almost suspected that this stranger was just a prank, probably by Sven or L. But something just didn't feel right.

"Hello, Mr. Hayes!" greeted the man verbally in fluent English and asked politely, "I hope I'm not intruding?"

"Hello, Mister… ?" replied Dirk cautiously.

"Xardoc, you can call me Xardoc!" answered the man and bowed his head slightly.

"Ah, Mr. Xardoc. We went through a considerable length to keep this place secluded, so yes, you are intruding!" noted Dirk firmly.

"I'm terribly sorry about that, and it was quite a challenge to catch up with you," apologized Xardoc.

"I see," said Dirk and sat down by the small picnic table next to the workshop: "Why don't you have a seat?"

"That's very kind of you," replied Xardoc, sat down across from Dirk, and asked, "It's a lovely place you have made here. Eden, right?"

"Yes, that's what we call it. Mr. Xardoc, I'm sure you didn't circumvent all our security just to chat with me casually. Please tell me why you are here!" insisted Dirk as he sensed that this stranger wasn't a prank, but Dirk still had no idea who he was or what he wanted.

"To have a casual chat, of course! It's the neighborly thing to do!" joked Xardoc and adjusted his fedora.

"We are neighbors?" wondered Dirk.

L had confirmed that there were no other sapient species within 1,000 lightyears of this planet. Did the AI miss someone, or were they so advanced that they had eluded detection?

"In a matter of speaking, yes!" confirmed Xardoc and noted, "you are the first newcomers in a very long time!"

"Alright, Mr. Xardoc, this is fascinating as it is vague. I assume that you are an advanced species of some kind?" questioned Dirk.

Dirk wasn't sure what to make of this guy, but he knew he could be potentially dangerous, considering that he had evaded their security measures.

"Well, yes. I chose this form to appear less threatening, and I assure you I'm no threat at all. Factually, I'm the same as you - an ascended being," explained Xardoc and added, "as I said, there hasn't been an ascension in a long time and never in our neighborhood, so naturally, I'm inquisitive about you and your people!"

"You can appear as you are, Mr. Xardoc. I'm not easily scared!" claimed Dirk and smiled a little.

"If you are sure about that…," responded Xardoc hesitantly.

Then he instantly changed into a giant jellyfish floating above the table. But unlike terrestrial jellyfish, Xardoc could form his many tentacles and appendices out of the bulk of his translucent body. He also displayed a multitude of colors and iridescent, almost hypnotic lights all over his form. Dirk was fascinated by this alien life, but Xardoc changed back into a human after a few moments.

"You can stay in your natural state, Mr. Xardoc. I don't mind at all!" encouraged Dirk.

"That is kind of you, Mr. Hayes, but I will remain in humanoid form for now. I have studied your species for some time, and I'm familiar with your body language and facial expressions," observed Xardoc.

"…and I'm not familiar with yours at all. That makes sense, thank you!" conceded Dirk and asked, "so, you are a level 12 species?"

"Level 12?" wondered Xardoc and wrinkled his forehead a little, but then he smiled brightly again: "Oh yes! The scale of the Latura is very appropriate! We have high hopes for the Latura; some more of them might also ascend someday, but probably after the new species you created on Aureus. That was outstanding work!"

"They aren't our creation, just our descendants," corrected Dirk with a smile and asked politely, "I know you don't need refreshments any more than I do, but I don't want to be unneighborly, so would you like a beer, Mr. Xardoc?"

"That would be delightful, thank you!" appreciated Xardoc and added approvingly, "it's good that you use a biological avatar. I do, too, when I'm not breaking and entering. The limitations of biology keep us grounded!"

Dirk just nodded, got up, and went to a cooler behind the picnic table where Mario and Garrett always kept a healthy beer supply. He got two bottles of Alien Ale, removed the lids, and placed one in front of Xardoc while holding the other in his hand.

"Cheers? Salute? Prost?" asked Dirk and held his beer up high, "I'm not sure what the appropriate toast would be in this situation?"

"Cheers will do!" confirmed Xardoc with a big grin and took a sip from the bottle: "Ooooh, this is good!"

"Thanks! I'll tell our brewmaster later," responded Dirk with a smile and drank some beer, too.

"About the whole level 12 ascension thing…," started Xardoc but stopped to finish the beer with a few more gulps.

"Yes?" said Dirk and reached in the cooler to get another brew for his guest.

"Almost all species fail at that. Only a few dozen have managed, and never the entire species, only a handful of their members," continued Xardoc after eagerly accepting the next beer bottle.

"So, there are not many of our kind?" verified Dirk.

"No, very few. Maybe a little more than a thousand? Not just counting here, but in the entire Universe!" confirmed Xardoc.

"That surprises me. The Universe is awfully big, Mr. Xardoc!" countered Dirk.

"It is, but it shouldn't surprise you. The step to ascension is the steepest, and it has the greatest failure rate of all evolutionary steps. Most fail because they cannot let go! Sadly, they cannot free themselves from the ties that bind them to their former lives," noted Xardoc.

"It seems so wasteful!" mused Dirk, thinking about the trillions of lives that likely filled the Universe, before he inquired, "are those the only two choices: extinction or ascension?"

"Most of the time, yes. But some species have remained at level 11 for a few billion years without ascending or going extinct, while others have devolved to lower levels again," explained Xardoc and continued, "those that went extinct kept interfering, changing and correcting the actions of others who were not as advanced, instead of moving on to a new existence. In the end, they destroyed themselves before they could ever complete the process!"

"We decided to come here and leave everything behind precisely because we do not wish to interfere any longer. We have realized that we are not good at playing god!" stated Dirk.

Perhaps this would come back to haunt him, but Dirk decided he would trust this strange man or whatever he was.

"That's the right decision, Mr. Hayes! Yes, to those not as advanced, we appear to be divine!" concurred Xardoc and nodded his head.

"So, the Universe is an entity?" wondered Dirk, changing the subject.

"Oh, not an entity like you and me, but …it is what it is!" remarked Xardoc and shrugged his shoulders.

"Please, could you be a little less cryptic, Mr. Xardoc?" teased Dirk and finished his beer bottle.

"You will find out, Mr. Hayes. I don't want to spoil the surprise!" quipped Xardoc and smirked.

"Perhaps I already have. The Universe and I have a bit of history," said Dirk more seriously.

"Oh, now you are very cryptic, Mr. Hayes!" replied Xardoc with a smile, "and I'm very curious!"

"Have you heard of *irtaljan*, the alternate realities?" questioned Dirk and looked at his guest.

"Yes! It's exceedingly rare! So, you had a brief encounter that felt very real, and you were given a choice at the end?" asked Xardoc.

"Correct, that's how it was the first time. But later, I experienced seamless episodes that stretched for weeks, months, and even years. I wasn't choosing as much as living a choice for a while," explained Dirk.

"Now that is something new even for me!" exclaimed Xardoc excitedly and pressed on, "we must talk more about that, Mr. Hayes!"

"It's a long story and not the most pleasant one, but perhaps I will share it with you someday," replied Dirk and asked: "What exactly is ascension?"

"Ha! That's been the topic of debate among our kind for eons!" proclaimed Xardoc as he took his tinted glasses off and cleaned them with a handkerchief.

"OK, what is the consensus?" questioned Dirk with a chuckle.

"Consciousness is basically sentience or awareness of internal or external existence. Ascension is consciousness without the need for a physical body!" remarked the alien man.

"I understand that part. I know now that consciousness can exist without a body, but please tell me how Mr. Xardoc?" inquired Dirk.

"Music! We are music, Mr. Hayes!" noted Xardoc excitedly, and for a moment, Dirk looked puzzled, but then he had an epiphany!

"I think I understand: harmonics! It's part of what we call String Theory!" blurted Dirk out.

"Yes, harmonics. We resonate in the very fabric of the Universe rather than being confined to a body!" confirmed Xardoc and added, "that's how I sensed your ascension."

"We don't know when we ascended," divulged Dirk.

"Ascension sends ripples through space-time as a pebble dropped in a pond. Another ascended being nearby can feel the tingle, but your ascension was more like a tidal wave!" explained Xardoc and claimed, "I can tell you exactly when it happened because I rushed over to witness it!"

"When? Somehow, we didn't notice, and we didn't notice you...," responded Dirk, a little embarrassed, but then he suddenly remembered feeling a curious presence when Lilly woke him up in the tomb - perhaps that was Mr. Xardoc?

"I was observing from the shadows, so to speak, as not to interfere!" Xardoc confirmed Dirk's suspicions and then added fondly, "all of you ascended at once when your wife raised you from the dead, Mr. Hayes!"

"Lilly?" questioned Dirk in surprise.

"Yes, a remarkable woman! She was the catalyst, the first one to ascend. Without her, I doubt that you could have been revived, but once you did, almost everyone else in your digital world ascended, too. It was a tsunami!" asserted Xardoc.

Dirk had to digest that for a little while. Lilly was the first person he met in all the alternate realities he had experienced. It made only sense that it would be Lilly who had triggered their ascension. Dirk couldn't wait to tell her that, but first, he had a few more questions for Mr. Xardoc.

"Almost everyone? Who did not?" wondered Dirk.

"Your feline friend, of course!" jested Xardoc.

"But Tigger is like us! Please explain, Mr. Xardoc!" insisted Dirk, astonished by that revelation.

"No, Tigger is not like us. Typically, one is an ascended being, or one is not - that simple. But Tigger ascended gradually, and nothing like that has ever happened before. He didn't make ripples; instead, he was building up like a hurricane, and it started when he was a little cat back on Earth because I could feel it even then. He is still gaining strength today and has long exceeded all limits of ascension. He could do things that are magical to us. Your friend Tigger is the most powerful being that ever existed!" explained Xardoc.

Dirk should have been shocked, but it all made sense immediately. Tigger had always been incredibly special, and Dirk couldn't have been prouder of his lifelong companion.

"The god of the gods!" mumbled Dirk in awe.

"Perhaps that is his purpose?" speculated Xardoc when he heard those words.

"You say that as if he was appointed to the job by someone!" countered Dirk, but now he immensely enjoyed this conversation with Mr. Xardoc because he could learn so much from this alien!

"No, not necessarily. But true randomness doesn't exist. There is a cause for every effect, no matter how complex and convoluted it might be. Tigger's ascension doesn't have to be supernatural, but it does have a reason!" opined Xardoc and noted, "of course, it will keep us busy for eons to figure it out!"

"Is the whole Universe a simulation, a computer program of sorts?" inquired Dirk and changed the subject again: if L could create a good approximation of reality, perhaps a much more advanced entity or species could simulate it to perfection?

"The answer is a definite maybe!" responded Xardoc, grinned broadly, and lauded, "but you are asking the right questions, Mr. Hayes. Here is what I think: a program has a purpose; that's why it was written. But nobody has ever figured out the purpose of the Universe. It just is! From birth to inevitable death, it is simply a cascade of events governed by the laws of physics!"

"I believe I agree with you. The Universe itself seems to be searching for a purpose. It is like a child without a parent, and it learns by trial and error alone," maintained Dirk, reflecting further on his *irtaljan* experiences.

Suddenly, Dirk envisioned his office, the cubical onyx room, but he didn't know where that thought came from, and then he forgot it again just as quickly.

"That's a good way to put it," assented Xardoc, and then he speculated humorously, "and there is even more to that: unlike a machine or a program, the Universe isn't perfect, and as it grows older, the imperfections become more pronounced. If the Universe were a simulation program, the programmers have forgotten to debug it, and that wouldn't speak very highly of their competence, would it?"

"There is no perfect sphere, only an approximation - the discrepancy between mathematics and reality!" summarized Dirk.

"That's right!" concurred Mr. Xardoc happily, and it seemed to Dirk that this alien enjoyed their conversation just as much as he did.

"Are there many Universes?" asked Dirk next.

"You are using entropy differential power sources, so you already know the answer," observed Xardoc, but he didn't seem entirely happy about it.

"We do and so do the Latura, but I have been a little apprehensive about that. I always envisioned it as a pinprick in the fabric of the Universe," noted Dirk.

"Exactly, that's what it is, Mr. Hayes! We don't know how our Universe interacts with others. Maybe they are all connected to another level, just different rooms in the same building, or they could be completely separate things. Too many pinpricks might have unforeseen consequences if it's the latter!" warned the alien man.

"Are you aware of any potential dangers?" inquired Dirk cautiously.

"A long time ago, a species attempted to use entropy differential to stabilize their dying sun. It didn't work. The star went hypernova and extinguished all life in a 50-lightyear radius! It was a tragedy!" explained Xardoc.

"They miscalculated?" questioned Dirk, now genuinely concerned since the colony powered almost everything on Eden that way.

"No, but they had to make a pretty big hole to get that much energy, and something else came through. But whatever it was, it couldn't exist within our laws of physics, blew up, and took the whole star with it!" expounded Xardoc.

"That is worrisome! Are there alternative energy sources?" wondered Dirk, and he made a mental note to discuss this with Rose, Garvan, and L later on.

"There are, but not quite as potent!" confirmed Xardoc, but then he conceded, "alas, entropy differential has been in use since long before the Latura discovered it, and so far, the Universe has tolerated that. I guess it's safe on a small scale."

"Regrettably, the Universe doesn't come with a user manual," mused Dirk.

"It doesn't, and every discovery is potentially dangerous. But that should never stop us!" proclaimed Xardoc, and Dirk had to think of Sven's bravery whenever a scientific breakthrough was within grasp.

"What makes ascension happen?" asked Dirk a moment later and changed the subject once more.

"I can only tell you this: ascension without a deep understanding of the Universe isn't possible. That's why you have to reach the highest evolutionary steps. But ascension with only a deep understanding isn't possible either; you also have to have the mind's powers. Ascension without the mind's powers isn't feasible, but powers of the mind do not automatically lead to ascension. Even if you have both, there is no guarantee that you will ever ascend!" elaborated the alien man.

"Deep understanding of the Universe refers to scientific and technological advancement, but what are the powers of the mind?" inquired Dirk.

"The powers of the mind are broad: for example, telepathic and telekinetic abilities, emphatic aptitude and intuition, but also critical thinking, and the skill to detect deception. Lastly, the ability to control one's emotions and not be controlled by them is paramount!" summarized Xardoc.

"Ah, I understand!" acknowledged Dirk.

"There are a few other criteria that ascended beings share, but it isn't clear if they are essential: all of us are very intelligent, curious, and creative!" explained

Xardoc, but then he added with a slight frown, "although, there are sometimes a few exceptions that do not fit the mold."

"Does the Universe pick who ascends?" wondered Dirk.

"Some believe that the Universe makes it happen, and I'm one of them! But others think that it is mere coincidence who ascends and who doesn't because there is no discernable pattern, and I have to admit that is true, too!" conceded Xardoc.

"Could a lower-level species suddenly ascend?" questioned Dirk, unsure if he should hope or fear humanity could take that step.

"There are no absolutes in the Universe! But so far, every single one of us has ascended from at least a level 10 species, and in that regard, you are no exception, Mr. Hayes," replied Xardoc.

"But technically, we are only at level 8 as humans!" countered Dirk quickly.

"You were level 8 when you started, and Tigger was even lower than that, but you evolved very rapidly. That is a bit uncommon, but it has happened before!" explained Xardoc, and it seemed like he wanted to say more but decided to hold back for now.

"Yes, I can see that," concurred Dirk and was satisfied with that explanation because he realized that his group had far surpassed the humans on Earth long ago.

"But what you don't see is how incredibly unusual and improbable your ascension has been. Of course, there is no way you could know that!" exclaimed Xardoc in delight and gushed, "never before have so many ascended at the same time. Never before did four distinct species, not even counting the hybrids, ascend simultaneously and from the same galaxy. Do you know that billions of galaxies have never produced even one ascended being?"

"I didn't know that, but since you said there are only about 1,000 of us, I could do the math!" remarked Dirk with a smile and countered, "but we were only three species - Latura, felines, and humans."

"Aren't you forgetting the most unusual one? Artificial intelligence!" beamed Xardoc and explained, "there are a few sapient machines in the Universe, but none has ever managed to do what yours did. We were convinced that an AI couldn't ascend...."

"...and L proved you wrong!" interjected Dirk with joy, and now, he was very proud of L, too.

"He did, and it's amazing and wonderful!" exclaimed Xardoc with exuberance, "and then there is Tigger…and you!"

"Me?" asked Dirk, surprised.

"Your ascension wasn't exactly textbook either!" teased Xardoc and noted, "you were raised from the dead, and that left a mark. I cannot yet pinpoint what is different about you, but you are certainly unique among the ascended!"

"I don't know what to say to that. I guess it is my lot always to be different," responded Dirk with a sigh.

"It's nothing bad, so don't worry about it. We will figure it out in time!" consoled Xardoc and then added with a huge grin, "Mr. Hayes, I won't be the last one to visit here. Once word spreads, all of us will want to meet your group!"

"Our security is keeping mortals away, but we are not isolationists. In time, we will welcome visitors to our enclave," assured Dirk, and then he asked humorously, "since we are pretty new at this ascension stuff, do you have any tips for us?"

"There is just one rule, Mr. Hayes, and you already recognize and follow it. Don't interfere with the mortals! You can watch them, but let them fail or succeed on their terms!" presaged Xardoc earnestly.

"Did we break that rule on Aureus already?" wondered Dirk.

"No, Aureus was your creation as mortals, and you did exceptionally well!" praised Xardoc, but then he warned thoughtfully, "but make no mistake, Aureus will face terrible times someday, and all you can do is stand by and watch. It will be excruciating for you to do nothing, but nothing is what you must do!"

"Yes, I can imagine that, although I'd rather not," conceded Dirk with consternation.

Sven's choice was to meddle, Nari's choice was to end it all, but Lilly's choice was to walk away, and Xardoc had just confirmed that it was the right one all along. Dirk was proud that all his friends had come to the same conclusion.

"I have tried to intervene; many others of our kind have attempted it as well," explained Xardoc and continued, "but no matter how good your intentions and how well you plan, you will always end up with a bigger mess than you started. And that's not the worst! You might lead an entire species into extinction by accident or get so frustrated that you wipe them all out in genocide!"

"Could… we create a new species?" asked Dirk hesitantly.

"Of course, you could, and you don't need to be ascended. But the rule still applies: once your new species becomes sapient, you have to cut it loose!" answered Xardoc and acknowledged, "and you already have done that, too!"

"Are you referring to L?" inquired Dirk because suddenly, that strange, opiate-induced hallucination popped into his head again.

"That's right. You made the AI sapient, and then you set it free, as it should be!" confirmed Xardoc with a smile.

It made a lot of sense to Dirk: he remembered how Sven, Eriea, and Lennard engineered livestock for Aureus. Of course, unlike L, none of these new species of chicken and goats were sapient and would likely never be sapient.

"Ah, sapience is the important criteria here!" summarized Dirk, and Xardoc simply nodded, while Dirk continued to ask: "Is that because the Universe doesn't like when someone interferes with that?"

"Perhaps? It's just an empirical observation, but it always holds true!" emphasized Xardoc and observed, "the parameters of the game will inevitably change; it will become so complex and unpredictable that even you and I cannot handle it."

"What happens if one keeps trying?" questioned Dirk.

"Remember, Mr. Hayes, that we are immortal, not indestructible. It's hard to kill us, but not impossible, and it has happened. Ascended beings who lust for power and adulation and force their will upon mortals are sooner or later removed from the game!" cautioned the alien.

"The prototypical gods!" interjected Dirk and wondered if such ascended beings started some of Earth's religions.

"Yes, and apparently, the Universe doesn't like those players very much!" concurred Xardoc.

"I don't either!" admitted Dirk, and then he asked, "are these entities the exceptions that do not fit the mold, as you had mentioned earlier?"

"Indeed, Mr. Hayes!" confirmed Xardoc with a nod.

"But correct me if I'm wrong, Mr. Xardoc: as ascended beings, we are just information, are we not? And if we are, how can we be destroyed?" inquired Dirk.

"That's right, we are!" concurred Xardoc and explained, "but we are self-contained information. What we are will exist to the end of times, but who we are can be fragmented and scattered. Once an ascended being loses cohesion, it is gone, and there is no known way to reverse that."

"All the King's horses and all the King's men couldn't put Humpty together again," mumbled Dirk.

Xardoc didn't understand the reference and looked curiously at him. Dirk noticed and got up to get another beer for both of them.

"Can we never interfere with the mortals, or are there any loopholes?" inquired Dirk as he opened the bottles.

"I only know of one: self-defense!" stated Xardoc and elaborated, "you were attacked by mortals and forced to intervene to save yourselves. That's the one move in the game that the Universe will tolerate because self-preservation is a fundamental right of every player!"

"You are the second entity who refers to our existence as a game. Is that really what it is?" asked Dirk, remembering how Tigger described it not long ago.

"Beats me, Mr. Hayes, but it is an apt analogy: we are all players in this biggest of all games. But we don't know all the rules, we cannot choose the arena, we can't win, we can't draw, and we cannot even quit!" jested Xardoc before he encouraged, "so just have some fun and enjoy! This plane of existence is free of violence, prejudice, and hate and full of love, joy, and kindness. And as you said earlier, the Universe is awfully big, and there is so much to see, explore, and learn; you will never get bored! But if you ever do, come visit me!"

"That sounds good, Mr. Xardoc. I will take you up on that someday!" promised Dirk, but then he said, "of course, I have no idea where you live!"

"Please do!" insisted Xardoc and noted, "oh, I'm indeed your neighbor. Do you know that big galaxy that is bound to smash into yours pretty soon? I think you call it Andromeda? Well, that's where I'm from!"

"I see, but the collision isn't going to happen for another couple of billion years, no?" asked Dirk.

Even a galaxy two million lightyears away could be considered as close as the next-door neighbor in a suburban area on the scale of the Universe.

"Sorry, I lose track of time easily, and you will, too. But when the crash happens, it will be a marvelous spectacle!" swooned Xardoc.

"I don't mean to pry, but how old are you, Mr. Xardoc?" inquired Dirk hesitantly.

"I'm not quite sure. I think I'm about ten on the human time scale, so around 40, the way you measured it on Aureus. I ascended when your galaxy was still forming!" calculated the alien man.

"Ten… billion… years… ?" gasped Dirk.

"Yes, that sounds about right!" confirmed Xardoc.

Dirk was shocked! This entity had been five billion years old before Earth's solar system formed. Of course, he had suspected that Xardoc was much older than any of them - but ten billion years? Dirk drank deeply from his beer and was slightly disappointed when he drained the bottle so soon.

"You already know how we ascended; was it similar for your species?" questioned Dirk as he was rummaging through the cooler to get another brew, and he ignored the fact that his physical body was getting a little tipsy.

"I'm the only one of my species to make it; the others have gone extinct ages ago," remarked Xardoc sadly and explained, "when I was still mortal, we were a level 11 species by that Latura scale. We knew another evolutionary step could be reached, and I was obsessed with that possibility. I tried everything: science, engineering, philosophy, mindfulness, psychic channeling, chastising myself, and praying to imaginary gods. It was all nonsense!"

"So, what happened?" wondered Dirk.

"One day, the Universe gave me an *irtaljan* experience, much like your own. I was given a choice to ascend, and I took it!" revealed Xardoc with a big smile.

"Ah, that's why you believe that the Universe picks who ascends!" claimed Dirk, and then he asked: "Was that a difficult choice?"

"It was tough. I had to leave loved ones behind," admitted Xardoc with a slight frown.

"Yes, I can see how painful that must have been," sympathized Dirk and immediately thought of Lilly while Xardoc just nodded and nursed his beer.

"Do you know what *irtaljan* is or how it works?" Dirk followed up.

"I don't!" disclosed Xardoc and speculated, "not only is the Universe imperfect, but it is also unbelievably complex. There are a few recognizable patterns, but they might just be quirks. *Irtaljan* could be a natural phenomenon that we haven't

373

discovered yet, or maybe just one of the imperfections, or it might be the dreams of a sleeping child, as your charming Latura friends claim."

"Still so much to learn and explore!" replied Dirk.

"Mr. Hayes, I wasn't kidding when I said you will never get bored!" noted Xardoc, and Dirk nodded vigorously.

91. Happy Ending

They were sitting there in silence for a few moments, each thinking their thoughts. Dirk reflected deeply on Xardoc's words, and then it dawned on him that his three *irtaljan* experiences were preparing him for ascension! The first one simply showed him that he was not dead, while the third one prepared Dirk for his resurrection and what he would have to do after that. The second and most painful one had puzzled Dirk for the longest time, but now he finally understood: Dirk was taught that he had to let go when Lilly died, and Dirk learned that if he meddled in the affairs of mortals, disaster would be inevitable. Irgal was right; Dirk was meant to fail in that reality!

Suddenly, Dirk remembered the onyx room once more: it wasn't his office on Eden, but a place in his mind! He recalled talking to a man there, and the conversations were disturbing and dreadful. Had the Universe been conversing with him, testing him to see if he was fit for ascension? Unlike the previous times, Dirk did not forget these strange memories again. Since he had died, Dirk had learned many things about himself: from the unpleasant voice in his head, from the alternate realities, and last but not least, from the good-natured roasting by his friends. Dirk was aware of some of these character traits but had chosen to bury them deeply, while others were new even to him. Dirk was different from humans on Earth and different on Aureus, and he always knew and accepted that. Dirk was still dissimilar here on Eden, as Xardoc had confirmed earlier. But he never attempted to conform; all he wanted was to coexist peacefully. But now, with all said and done, perhaps being different was never a detriment but an asset?

"Oh, I almost forgot. I have a surprise for you!" exclaimed Xardoc.

He jumped up from his seat and gestured with his left hand. Instantly, a pitch-black circle appeared in the air next to him. At first, it was no bigger than a basketball, but a few moments later, the ring had grown as tall as a grown man. For a few seconds, nothing happened, but then a huge Siamese cat stepped out of the darkness, looking around disoriented, her tail wiggling restlessly. The black circle closed silently behind the cat, and eventually, she noticed Dirk, who was watching in amazement, his mouth agape.

(Feeling of confusion) "You Dirk? Jo not dead?" asked the cat over the mental link.

"Jo!" yelled Dirk and rushed towards the big feline.

"Dirk!" responded the cat and pounced on Dirk before he could get to her. They rolled around on the blue-green moss, laughing, purring, and play-fighting while Xardoc watched the antics with amusement.

"Jo, I'm so glad to see you!" gasped Dirk, out of breath from the rough-housing.

(Feeling of happiness) "Jo is too! Where L, where Tigger?" asked Jo exuberantly.

"L! Tigger! Jo is back!" Dirk shouted over the open link.

(Feeling of suspicion) "Is trick?" wondered Tigger, still exploring the neighboring planet.

(Feeling of sadness) "My kitten? I cannot detect anything…," responded L moments later.

"Come to my workshop on Eden; it's really Jo! I'll explain when you get here!" insisted Dirk with joy.

(Feeling of anticipation) "Tigger, L coming!" answered Tigger for both of them.

"Thank you, Mr. Xardoc! It means a lot to all of us. We believed that Jo had perished in the simulation, and we have been mourning her ever since," said Dirk gratefully while Jo went around the table and headbutted Xardoc gently.

"Ah, don't mention it, Mr. Hayes. I'm glad to be of service!" replied Xardoc, fondly scratching Jo under her chin.

"You violated the rule, but I don't mind in the slightest!" stated Dirk.

"Oh, but I didn't! As I said earlier, Jo and all of you had already ascended, even if you didn't quite understand that at the time. So, I just helped a fellow entity, and that's perfectly fine!" maintained Xardoc.

"Be that as it may, we are in your debt. Please drop by whenever you feel like it. You are welcome here, Mr. Xardoc!" upheld Dirk with a big smile.

"Many thanks! I will shamelessly abuse your hospitality and drink all your beer!" joked Xardoc and continued, "but now I must go. It took a long time to find you behind all that security, and I have an appointment with an old friend a few hundred million lightyears away. But I'll be back sooner than you care for!"

Xardoc took the fedora off his head and bowed deeply, and then he was gone in a blink of an eye, leaving Dirk and Jo staring at thin air.

(Feeling of fondness) "Nice man!" said Jo and purred loudly.

"Yes, Jo, Mr. Xardoc is a very nice man!" agreed Dirk and smiled broadly.

EPILOGUE

Dervan was a peace today. He had received confirmation from all the recipients of his message, and the sapient ocean was the last one to respond just a few hours ago. Even the AloKaan had agreed to abide by his missive, maybe just out of fear or perhaps because the new Negotiator, formerly the First Judge, had initiated sweeping reforms in their society. But even after consulting with Irgal and the other Latura from Aureus, it had not been easy for Dervan to write this directive. The text was harsh and in discord with everything Latur had embraced for millennia. Nonetheless, Dervan had learned his lesson, and he knew with all his heart that these words had to be written:

Notice to all sapient species in the known galaxy!

The human civilization on Earth poses an existential threat to all sentient life. They are driven by unbridled greed, thirst for violence, willful ignorance, and deeply ingrained prejudice, but their unmatched ability to deceive should be considered the most dangerous. Do not communicate with them, do not trade with them, do not help them, but first and foremost, do not enable them to leave their star system, and never let your guard down!

If humanity can avoid extinction and outgrows its savage urges someday, we shall lift this total embargo in due time, but until then, be wary of the human menace!

Dervan of Latur

"But where is everybody? - Enrico Fermi"

A Word from the Author

Dear reader!

If you enjoyed the story, this is where you should stop reading. But if you thought it was a little too imaginative and improbable, perhaps the following alternate ending will be more to your liking?

Reality?

When Dirk woke up that morning, his back was aching more than usual, and he didn't feel well-rested. Lilly had already gone to work before dawn. She was always at work these days and often came home only to sleep for a few hours before she had to return to the hospital. The pandemic took a toll on the population and perhaps even more on his wife.

Dirk went to the restroom, brushed his teeth, and took a quick shower. While he was toweling off, he suddenly remembered an unusually vivid, detailed dream from last night: Dirk had to overcome many obstacles to leave Earth but then lived a long, fulfilled life on another world, surrounded by friends and loved ones. Dirk helped build a better, kinder society there. Eventually, he died, but he was resurrected many years later and finally became one with the Universe.

With these strange thoughts in his mind, he went to the kitchen. Tigger was already waiting by the fridge for the open can of *Salmon Feast* that Lilly had left there last night. Dirk fed the tomcat and made some coffee and toasted waffles for himself. While the toaster was doing its thing, he checked his phone. There were no new messages since Roy Hammond had canceled the tennis match last night because his wife went into labor. Dirk put the phone down and had breakfast.

After he had finished the meal, Dirk looked at the newsfeed on Lilly's tablet. The government was becoming increasingly more authoritarian with every passing day; there were massive demonstrations against racial injustice, the pandemic numbers kept going up and up, and the economy was going down and down. The local news reported on an unusual meteor sighting over the Bay Area last night, and several people had captured the bright streak of light heading out to the Pacific Ocean on video.

After watching the informative footage, Dirk read his work emails: Hibi Nakamura reiterated that only essential workers are permitted on company grounds, and all others should stay safe at home. Regrettably, he also had to cancel the annual Halloween party due to the virus. Lastly, Hibi announced that Zyrtec was in take-over negotiations with a German pharmaceutical conglomerate, but layoffs were not imminent. Yeah, sure, thought Dirk. It would be difficult for someone over 50 like him to find another job because age discrimination was alive and well in corporate America. Dirk would have to update his résumé later.

Sven Larson had already tendered his resignation a few days earlier and was on his way to Oslo, Norway, where he had accepted a professorship at the university. Dirk thought that would be great for a brilliant guy like Sven. Jerry Page had also quit to spend more time with his new Russian girlfriend, Irina. The email had a picture attached that showed them arm-in-arm on a golf course. Something bothered Dirk about that, but he wasn't sure what. Finally, a company-wide message wishing receptionist Melissa a speedy recovery from an undisclosed ailment, although Dirk and everyone else knew she had entered rehab for her drug problem.

Dirk finished the work emails and checked his private ones next: Nancy Sullivan announced that PTRC would be closing permanently early next year to make space for new housing development. All members were urged to remove their personal belongings from the facility before Christmas, or else Rodrigo would dispose of them. So, the rumors were true after all, thought Dirk.

Dirk deleted some spam until he noticed an email from Rose, and it was perhaps the most surprising bit of news: Sam had finally proposed to her, and she had accepted. Now they were planning a wedding for next spring. Dirk was genuinely happy for his sister-in-law, but again the message left him somewhat unsettled. But before he could think more about that, the doorbell rang! Dirk got up and opened the door. It was the mailman.

"Hello, Mr. Hayes. I have a package for you," said the postal worker with a slight Slavic accent.

"Hmm, are you sure? I wasn't expecting any packages," replied Dirk, wondering what he had received.

"It's small but quite heavy!" noted the man and handed the parcel to Dirk.

"Are you the new letter carrier?" asked Dirk as he received the cardboard box. The man looked oddly familiar, but Dirk couldn't place him anywhere.

"Yes, I'm Victor. I have this route now that John has retired!" answered the mailman.

"Oh, I see. Welcome to the neighborhood!" said Dirk with a tiny smile.

"Thank you, Mr. Hayes! You will see more of me!" replied the man, friendly, and returned to his postal truck.

Dirk shut the door and put the parcel on the shoe rack by the entrance. Then he refilled his coffee cup, sat down again, and stared at the screen of Lilly's tablet for a while. Dirk's thoughts were circling that strange dream. The more he thought about it, the more he seemed to remember. He decided to focus on the names of the people that had been in the dream. It wasn't unusual that Lilly, Rose, Sven, and Jerry had been in it, and even Nancy and Rodrigo made sense. They were all people he was familiar with or at least had met. But Dirk was reasonably sure that he had never encountered this new mailman before. Similarly, he had not yet met Jerry's new girlfriend, but he still knew her, although by a different name - Galina, was it?

Dirk tried to recall all the names from the dream, and to his surprise, his memory provided them. Then he searched for a few on the tablet: there were a lot of Victor Fedorenko's and probably many more if he could read Cyrillic. Unsurprisingly, he could not find Angela Dahteste, and while there were a dozen Lt. Garrett Jacksons, none matched the man he thought he knew. Mario DeSantos was currently serving time for extortion, and the Travelicious travel agency had gone out of business many years earlier after its owner Pete had retired.

Promising athlete Ngazetungue Emvula was tragically killed two years ago by a hit-and-run driver. His widow, Wendjisuvera, had returned to Namibia, where she currently worked as a journalist, while Lennard Brunner had recently received a prestigious lifetime achievement award for genetics. Dirk remembered Yebin and Nari, too. But of course, even if they existed in North Korea, no information would be available. Alfred Stacklund had passed away peacefully in his sleep only last week, and then Dirk recalled seeing his obituary posted at PTRC the last time he played tennis. Perhaps he had just forgotten that he had met or read about all these people before, yet his unconsciousness still remembered?

More names came to Dirk's mind, and he searched for every one of them, but the results were ambiguous: most people existed, some were even in the same line of work as he recalled, but of those who had pictures online, most looked quite different. He even searched for the name Lydia Latur, and to his surprise, the woman was real: a renowned plastic surgeon in L.A. who also dabbled in art. But the photo showed someone completely unfamiliar.

Dirk stopped his queries and turned the tablet off. Tigger was again on the shelf above the fireplace and threatened to topple Lilly's ugly debate trophy. Dirk caught it just when it was falling. He placed it back and gently took the tomcat off the shelf.

Dirk sat down on the ottoman by the couch, and Tigger hopped on his lap and curled up. Dirk compared this reality to the ones he had experienced last night: what was different? The outlandish abilities, science, and technologies, while undoubtedly futuristic, were indeed rooted in contemporary theories and research. Although Dirk's adversaries were brutal, depraved, and perhaps downright evil, they were nothing new to humanity, as any history book or daily news could confirm. Not even the society they had created on Aureus was all that novel because anthropological evidence supported that such communities had existed before.

By contrast, this reality was bland, tedious, and almost dull, filled with people that were nothing like his friends from Aureus, and it all seemed so... unclean? No, it wasn't the enemies, the society, or the science that made this fantasy: it was the people with him! They were rational, intelligent, compassionate, selfless, accepting, kind, and emotionally balanced - yes, even Angela! Aside from Lilly, Dirk had met less than a handful of such people in his entire life, yet in his dream, he was surrounded by them. Lastly, as diverse as they had been, all the episodes and adventures that Dirk had experienced last night had been exciting, purposeful, and profound.

Perhaps that was how one could distinguish a dream from reality? If that was so, the beggar who dreamt of being a king for half his life should have known better - it was always the mundane and miserable that was real!

And so, Dirk concluded that this was reality - not *irtaljan*, not a simulation, not an alternate timeline or mirror Universe, and not any premonition of sorts. This right here was as brutally real as it could get! There was no L, no Jo, no Alma, no Irgal, no Xardoc, none of his dear friends and family, and there had never been an Aureus, a Latur, or an Eden. And Tigger? He was intelligent, loving, and adorable, but he was still just a cat.

At that moment, Lilly's radio in the kitchen was playing another 80's song, and Dirk recognized it right away. He heard the same music in the onyx room: *Talk to Myself* by Christopher Williams. Dirk realized then that he had a conversation with himself in that strange place, and at the same time, he was also talking to the Universe because, in a sense, he was his own Universe. Indeed, that conversation was the only part of his experience last night that was not fantasy!

Of course, Dirk was aware that the human mind had a powerful imagination: hence, the rational, logical explanation was that his unconsciousness had used names, people, places, and events from his memory and created a science fiction story that could fill multiple books, and it had done so in just one night.

But this dream had been unlike anything Dirk had ever experienced before! On the one hand, he was grateful for it: for eight hours or hundreds of years, whichever it was, Dirk had found happiness and a purpose. But on the other hand, it was also decidedly cruel: now that Dirk had awakened, he was still stuck on Earth, surrounded by lies, ignorance, greed, hate, bigotry, and violence, powerless to change it, and incapable of leaving it behind. For the next 15, 20, or however many years he had left to live, Dirk would be condemned to watch helplessly as the apocalypse unfolded, unable to protect Lilly and without hope of ever escaping humanity's inevitable fate.

"*When you have eliminated the impossible, whatever remains, however improbable, must be the truth* - Sir Arthur Conan Doyle!" he quoted to himself quietly and accepted with great sadness that only his mind had created this beautiful illusion in one short night, however improbable that might have been.

Yes, Dirk was different. Even when he was still a child, he had always been different, but perhaps not quite as diverse as he had been in his dream. Still, Dirk was too intelligent not to know that humanity's journey would end in blood, tears, and chaos very soon, and even if a few miraculously survived, no lessons would ever be learned. Dirk was too much of a realist to hope for some last-minute enlightenment or divine intervention, and finally, he was too honest to deceive himself into believing otherwise. It was a depressing, almost tragic combination, but Dirk had never known any other way.

Dirk got up from the ottoman and walked to the kitchen. Before he got there, he remembered the parcel on the shoe rack. Dirk opened it and removed the item inside. It was secured with bubble wrap, but he still recognized it in shock - it was a metallic icosahedron! Dirk almost dropped the heavy object on the floor. With great excitement, he quickly tore off the packing material to take a closer look. The icosahedron was just as Dirk remembered it from his dream! He turned it around in his hands, and it felt exactly the way it should, but suddenly he noticed a small engraving on one of the faces. Dirk read it, and then he just shook his head in disappointment:

Dirk E. Hayes, 30 years of Membership Award, American Chemical Society.

The End

www.ingramcontent.com/pod-product-compliance
Lightning Source LLC
Chambersburg PA
CBHW020818180626
46814CB00001B/12